The
Sinkhole Chronicles

The

Sinkhole Chronicles

Gary's Inferno

By M.J. Todd

Dedicated to

Caroline and Kris

Thanks to

my coffee machine that has been by my side

through thick and thin

Contents

"Perfect! But could you add just one little thing?"

GJG

Introduction

Ashburn-on-Sinkhole, formerly known as 'Ashburn-on-Collick', is a little-known village somewhere between 'erm' and 'oh never mind'. It is pretty much as significant as dust on a cowpat. Even Google and Yahoo! never acknowledged its existence, but only because they themselves never knew about it. The only people to care about Ashburn-on-Sinkhole are the villagers who live there, both living and dead.

Recently, a smartly dressed, elderly looking gent visited Ashburn and luckily for the residents of the village, no one knew that this eloquent gentleman was a vampire. Sometimes ignorance is bliss… and doesn't cause a village wide panic.

The vampire, one Uriah Tomkins, had broken out of Hell and had tried to return to his beloved home. Reluctantly, Death had agreed to bring Uriah back to Hell on the behest of Lucifer, who, for reasons, had changed his name to Gary. Death himself had had a change of name and was now called Steve. A bit of a long story, but worth a read.

And so, the story continues…

Dear Eddie, or Jeremiah (whichever you prefer)

I am a collector of fine arts and I am aware that you can... acquire pieces of art that ordinarily cannot be acquired. Let's be honest here. Can you steal me some art that I've wanted for hundreds of years?

Please don't think I'm exaggerating when I say hundreds of years and yes, you'd be right. However, locations are not important right now. The piece I'm wanting is important and now locations become important too. The piece is called 'Mappa dell'Inferno' or as you may know it. Please stop interrupting my letter with your thoughts. It's very rude.

It is located in the Vatican Library in Rome, and before you think, yes, it is in the Vatican City. Belvedere Courtyard, to be exact. If you would be so kind as to obtain this for me, I'm sure we could come to some arrangement financially... and if you only wanted that amount, then I'd be happy to pay that as money isn't an issue.

Please make any arrangements necessary to obtain the required article and include any fees within your final invoice. I shall be in touch.

Kind regards

Gary

Gary

3

Prologue to the Prologue

Life in Heaven had been a little different since God had made some changes to his appearance. At first, everyone is gobsmacked when he appeared, walking down the pathways in a tuxedo, checking his cufflinks, with his entrance music changing from harps to a guitar. Even the one man who at first sight and sound of God approaching had changed tact from shouting something about copyright to not even caring.

However, having said all that, Heaven was still a little different... and so was God. He was always known for shying away from vanity, but for the last few weeks, he had taken to befriending Sandro Botticelli, an Italian painter, whose works had been commissioned for the famous Dante's Inferno in the book called The Divine Comedy. Both God and Sandro had disappeared into God's office with Sandro carrying his precious brushes and palette for the last week, coming out several hours later with God patting Sandro on the shoulder and saying 'Same time tomorrow?'

It was definitely fair to say that since God had chatted with Gary, whose previous name was Lucifer, the change of which no one quite knew the reason, things had changed in Heaven. Not for the better and not for the worse, just... changed.

"A tell thi, that crafty old bugger's up to summet," said one cherub to his opponent, whilst sitting on a cloud playing dominoes.

"Sandro?"

"Nah y'daft apeth. God."

"Not 'ny more. It's Godjustgod," corrected the other cherub as he placed a double six down on the chain of dominoes.

"Ooh y'little bugger! Any road up, a still think he's up to summet."

"D'ya reckon?"

"Aye. Since when does he want a selfie? Notice he din't ask Salvador?"

The other cherub just shrugged his shoulders and placed his last domino down with a smile and an *'In Your Face!'* aimed at his friend.

***

Travis had just entered Heaven and was scanning the area to see where he could place his surfboard so he could have a good look around.

He was a young surfing fanatic who would be called by many as a 'surf-dude'. With his long, straggly, sun-bleached hair and his mid-20's slender, yet muscular body clad only in a pair of board shorts and thong sandals, he stood there holding his precious surfboard. Travis wasn't into the 'sitting around and playing a harp' sort of thing, or even dominoes, as he had seen two chubby little kid like beings doing. He was more into surfing, chatting to shapely bikini-clad surf girls, barbeques by firelight, and smoking 'weed'. None of which he could see the makings of in his current position.

6

"They gotta be here somewhere's," he muttered to himself.

So with a nonchalant shrug of his shoulders, he wandered off to find a safe place for his board and to find a party.

Travis had just passed the two cherubs, who were setting up for another game of dominoes, when he saw Godjustgod walking down the path, waving goodbye to some old dude in a smock with some painting stuff in his hands. Travis came to a sudden halt.

"Whoa, dude! Who's died?" exclaimed Travis, seeing Godjustgod in his tuxedo.

Godjustgod stopped, looked around, and smiled.

"Well... Pretty much everyone. You must be Travis. The newbie."

"True dat," came the reply.

Not knowing exactly what the young man's response meant, Godjustgod figured it was surf speak for 'yes'.

"Would you like a little guided tour? I've got a little time to spare," said God, placing one hand on the surfer's shoulder as if to help guide the young man.

"Epic dude."

And the two began their whistle-stop tour of Heaven.

"So dude. You the G-man?" asked Travis, looking up and down God.

"G-man. I like that. Yes. I'm God... Justgod," God said with a smile.

"Awesome dude! The G-man himself!... So what's with the Armani?" said Travis, looking at his host's attire. "I thought you'd be..."

Travis didn't really know what to expect, but whatever it was, it surely wasn't the supreme being in a tuxedo.

"Do you like?"

God puffed up his chest and was about to check his cufflinks when Travis hit the deflate button.

"Dude! Not cool... You're the G-man, not some Bond-esque fake-azoid."

God was halted in his tracks. 'Bond-esque' and 'Fake-azoid' didn't sound good at all.

"Bra'. Board shorts and ink, now that's the bomb."

Travis continued to wander, leaving God a few paces behind and needing to catch up.

God was stunned.

"Not cool?! What about the sharp suit and fast car? Not cool?!" he thought to himself.

As the surfer wandered ahead of his guide, God caught sight of the young man's tattoo across his shoulders. As impressive as it was, God had no idea what it meant, if anything.

God jogged a little to catch up with his new resident.

"So! Remind me. How did you come to be here?" he said as he drew alongside Travis.

"Dude! What a bummer. Was so stoked. It was gnarly, and the tubes were just sooo righteous. I got da' bomb and was a sweet ride until some kook face-timed my personal space."

God had not a clue what Travis was saying, but by the actions of his narrator, he guessed it was a surfing accident.

"Well, my board took a dive and wiped out a Great White that was wanting me for human sushi. BANG! Side of its head and Shark Heaven. I took a roll, but Jaws had other plans and took me down with it. I was pinned under him as he hit the bed. It was rad!... But a major bummer, dude!"

God was getting the gist of what he had been told and tried his best surf-dude expression to convey how impressed he was.

"So bra'. I'm scoping somewhere to put my board so I can spark and chill before we hit the party and chicks."

"I'm sorry," God admitted defeat. "I have not a clue what you're on about."

"Some of my own homegrown dude. Never go anywhere without it."

God looked blankly at Travis.

"My own very Tom Jones, dude!... My green green grass of home."

The lightbulb shone brightly.

9

"Oh, cannabis!"

"Shh! You just never know who's listening bra'," said Travis shiftily, looking around the place.

This puzzled Godjustgod. Who'd be listening?

"This is my crib," thought God, and wondered why he had called Heaven a crib.

Because of a recent excessive delegating phase that God had gone through (and was now regretting passing on too much work), he had plenty of free time. So, God carried on with the tour of his 'crib' with his new, but strange talking, friend.

***

Mario Panini closed the door of his small apartment, ensuring he locked it before removing his clip-on tie and hanging it up on a coat hook next to his security jacket. He wandered into the kitchen, hitching up his trousers as he did, and lit the gas on the hob under his stovetop espresso maker.

For some reason, it had been especially boring at work today. The corridors of the basement of the Vatican library in Belvedere Court were quiet at the best of times, but today's shift had hit an all-time low. As he waited for the coffeemaker to bubble, and dragged his hand over his stubbled face, reckoning he could go another day without a shave, there was a knock on the door.

To say that Mario kept himself to himself would be a diplomatic way of saying that no one really wanted to entertain the gargantuan man whose personal hygiene resembled that of a village tramp, one who would always sit, propped up next to a bus stop and hurl abuse incoherently at passers-by. With his head poking out of the kitchen like a curious puppy, Mario peered at his front door, attempting to use his x-ray vision to look through and see who was there, to no avail. A second set of knocks on his door set his cogs in motion and with a hitch of his trousers and combing his chubby fingers through the black curly mop on his head, Mario ventured to see who was knocking on his door.

With the security chain in place and opening the door, Mario attempted to peer through the door jamb. Unfortunately, being the size that he was and the architects of the apartment block not taking into consideration the more voluminous tenants, Mario couldn't see through the tiny gap, so with an apologetic 'scusi' closed the door to release the chain. As he opened the door on the stranger, Mario filled the doorway, taking aback his unexpected visitor.

"Mio Dio! Signore Panini?"

"Si,"

"Signore Mario Panini?"

"Si,"

"Bloody hell! Your mother didn't scrimp on the servings, did she?" said the well-suited visitor as he adjusted his tie. "May I come in?"

Mario, even though having never seen this person before, and working as a security officer for the Vatican, felt a sudden calm drift over him and allowed the visitor to enter. As he moved out of the way, the smartly dressed man, carrying a briefcase, entered and made his way to Mario's lounge. Not even thinking of how the stranger knew where his lounge was, Mario followed and invited him to sit in his favourite armchair. As the stranger brushed off the biscuit crumbs from the seat, Mario offered him a coffee.

"No thank you, but I'll wait until you get one," said the softly spoken stranger.

"Grazie," said Mario with a nod of his head.

With the grace of a walrus on a unicycle, Mario scurried into the kitchen to return moments later with a tiny espresso cup, pinched between his thumb and index finger and the cup's saucer in his other hand, waiting to catch any coffee drops that may escape the cup.

As Mario's visitor sat down, he placed his briefcase, upright, on his lap.

"I know you don't know me, but I have a very important job for you which my boss believes *you* are just the man for it," said the visitor with a smile that conveyed 'screw this up and you're in for it,' in a nice way.

Mario lowered his body onto the sofa, keeping his eyes fixed on his visitor.

"OK..."

Mario listened, as he took a sip from his cup, to what his guest had to say in the minutest detail, nodding, interspersed with the occasional 'Si' throughout the entire briefing.

A short while later, Mario's front door opened and his guest left the apartment, turning and giving a courteous bow of the head. A huge chubby hand appeared in the hallway requesting the visitor's hand, and after a brief

12

shake of hands the door was closed and the visitor
walked off towards the main apartment block door,
wiping his sweaty, soiled hand on his trousers as he did
so, minus the briefcase.

***

On the Viale Della Ombreggiato, opposite to number 17;
Edoardo's Belle Arti, and underneath one of the avenue's
trees, sat Lorenzo and Nicolo, two stray mongrels.

"Woof!"

[Translation]

"So she called me a son of a bitch," said Lorenzo.

"She never! So what did you say?" replied Nicolo.

*"What could I say? She was my mother and I'm a dog.
Sometimes you just cannot win an argument."*

"I would not have stood for that. I'd have left right away,"
Nicolo replied defiantly.

*"Why do you think I'm out here now? It's surely not for
your company. It gets a little tiresome with you sniffing
my arse."*

"Lorenzo, we are dogs, that's what we do."

"Not when I'm 'entertaining' Loretta, dammit!"

"OK. I'll admit, I went a little too far there."

"D'you think?!"

Just then, the two dogs noticed a black Mercedes limousine pull up outside Edoardo's shop and a huge burly man in a black suit alighted from the front driver's side and quickly opened the rear door, whilst keeping his other hand close to the buttons of his double-breasted jacket.

"Who is this at this time of the evening?" said Lorenzo, looking over at the parked car.

"Cannot be anyone important or they would have a Ferrari," replied Nicolo.

"Fair point well made my friend."

Michele D'Ley *was* a member of the Italian Special Forces Unit until they required him to leave because of a misunderstanding between himself and his Commanding Officer. It transpired that evacuating his bowels on his C.O.'s desk after being reprimanded for calling his Drill Sergeant 'a lightweight nancy-boy' was not the expected response. When this was pointed out to Michele, in a heightened fashion by his C.O., Michele apologised by seizing the framed photo of the C.O.'s wife, that had been located on the desk, and placed it against his groin in a suggestive way. That day had not been a good day for either Michele, the C.O., or the C.O.'s cleaner.

Michele now worked for the Caster family organisation as a bodyguard for their Don, Giovanni Caster. Michele was a giant of a man and would go everywhere that Don Caster did, never leaving his side unless instructed by the man himself. Michele opened the rear door of the Mercedes and stood to attention as his boss got out and smoothed off his suit jacket, giving a nod and a slight wink to his bodyguard by way of saying thank you.

14

"Wait here Michele," growled his boss, in an 'I've got this' kind of way.

"No *problem,* boss."

Michele didn't know why his boss would visit an art forger with the money and connections that he had, and if he was truthful, neither did he care.

Don Caster sauntered over to the door of Edoardo's shop, with his overpowering cologne following, and placed a finely manicured finger on the doorbell and kept it there.

Edoardo was a small chap of only 5 feet tall and average build, and like so many Italian men of his maturing age, was eclipsed by his own charisma and style. His overly black slicked-back hair complimented his choice of cologne, as did his Visconti Roma watch with his Luigi & Son suit. He was pouring the last of his wine into his glass when the piercing rattle of his doorbell broke the ambience. Pavarotti's CD was midway through and he was singing for all he was worth, filling every room in the apartment with a heartfelt rendition of something that only opera fans would know.

"Bugger!" complained Edoardo. "Whoever you are, you can wait until I've poured my wine."

The doorbell continued to scream at Edoardo, informing him that someone was there and demanded an audience.

As the last drop had hit the inside of the glass, Edoardo made his way to his flat main door and pressed the button on his intercom.

"Take your finger off my doorbell or I'll break said finger," came the scratchy voice over the speaker to his unwanted guest.

"I doubt that very much Edoardo, now open your door or I'll get Michele to open it for you."

"Oh, merda! On my way, Mr Caster," came the reply, closely followed by a sound that resembled a sack of potatoes rolling down the stairs.

Seconds later, Edoardo stood in front of the open doorway, combing his hair back into place and smiling as he gasped for air after his little sprint.

"Mr Caster, so nice to see you. How can I?..."

"It's Don Caster and you can start by moving aside so I can enter," replied his guest, who made his way in before Edoardo had a chance to move.

Similar to his host, Don Caster stood at a height of 5 foot 2 inches, but that is where the similarity ended. He was a hugely girthed man whose taste in Hawaiian shirts repulsed most, but no one dared to comment because of his lofty position within the organisation.

Two minutes later, the breathless Don had traversed the short stairway to Edoardo's flat and stood, heavily breathing, in the lounge's doorway.

"Why do low life scum like you have to live on the top floor?" panted the aging, unfit man.

The reply of 'Drop dead, you overweight unstylish slob. You have a similar taste in colognes as you do in shirts. You sicken me,' stuck in Edoardo's throat, as a more 'Please take a seat,' was delivered instead.

16

The heavyset frame of Don Caster slumped into Edoardo's favourite seat, making the floorboards and chair creak under the weight. A sweaty hand reached for the glass of wine and it was downed in seconds.

"Dammit!" thought Edoardo through a gritted smile as he sat on the less comfortable sofa, "How can I help you, Don?"

Don Caster shuffled forward into a more upright sitting position, which put an inordinate amount of stress on the zipper and stitching of his trousers.

"I'm going to make you an offer you *can* refuse... I would highly advise against it, but you can if you wish."

Edoardo smiled and relaxed back into his seat.

"It's ok, I don't do death. It's bad for my health. How can I help you, Don?"

Edoardo knew that a job was coming his way and having Don Caster on his books gave him a higher status in his field.

***

"It sickens me that such cars are even made," said Nicolo, glowering at the parked Mercedes and the giant of a human standing next to it.

"It's not that bad, I've seen worse," replied Lorenzo.

"And look at him! Stood in front of the abomination like he's a hard man."

"He probably is, you daft mutt," replied Lorenzo.

"I'll show him," said Nicolo, who wandered over to the stationary vehicle in a way that only stray dogs can.

"Nicolo! You're not going to do what I think you are!"

Lorenzo went from a sitting position to standing, just in case there was a need to run, of which he was pretty sure there would be, imminently.

As Michele stood and watched the skinny mongrel saunter over, he glared at the dog as he passed by close to the Mercedes. Just as he thought that the coast was clear, Michele caught out of the corner of his eye the mongrel's hind leg lift, and a stream of liquid cascaded onto the rear tyre.

"Why you little..."

It was too late. The dog had already finished and was running away before the bodyguard had time to make it to the rear of the car, intending to deliver a hefty kick to the back end of the dog.

"Nicolo! You crazy son of a bitch!"

Lorenzo trotted after his friend, ensuring he gave a wide berth to the car and the angry human.

***

"So how long will it take to make a copy of Botticelli's Mappa dell'Inferno?" enquired Don Caster, with his eyebrows raised, suggesting the time should be relatively short.

"Just a couple of weeks," replied Edoardo. "I'll start the preparations tomorrow."

"Excellent. I'll have my man pick it up from you then he can swap it for the original and the original brought back here for you to keep, just in case. I'll come and pick it up in about a month."

At that, Don Caster heaved his body out of the recliner chair and smoothed his suit jacket down, leaving an indentation in the leather cushion similar to that of an asteroid leaving a crater on the moon.

"We'll not talk until this is over, then payment will be forthcoming."

"Sure, no *pro*blem. I'll look forward to seeing you then," replied Edoardo, stifling the urge to express his thoughts of his latest client and his morbidly obese, Hawaiian shirt clad carcass.

Edoardo escorted his latest and probably biggest (in more ways than one) client to his main door leading onto the avenue.

As the door opened onto the pavement, Michele decided that it may be a prudent move if he were to open the rear passenger door on the opposite side to the damp tyre, in case his boss took umbrage to the moistened tyre.

Don Caster shuffled across the pavement and turned to Edoardo and with a nod of his head at the forger, got back into the car. Moments later the black Mercedes drove off, leaving the forger stood in the open doorway watching as the car disappeared around the corner.

Prologue

In the rear of an art shop, situated on the square of a no-mark village, Ashburn-on-Sinkhole, sat a conman and painting forger, Fast Eddie, or better known to the villagers as Jeremiah Brown, behind his desk. He had been in the process of closing his fine arts shop, or so the villagers thought, when he had stumbled across a letter which had somehow lodged itself under his shopfront doormat. It was only when he bent down to fasten the lower bolt of the door that he noticed the missive peeking out from under the mat. Whilst the address was somewhat vague;

'FAO Eddie

Jeremiah Brown Fine Arts

(Yeah whatever!)

Ashburn-on-Sinkhole'

It had still been delivered, and without a stamp or postmark. Believing that they must have hand-delivered it by 'persons' unknown', it couldn't have been anyone from the village as he had made sure that his true identity had been kept a secret.

The reason for his anonymity had been because of a miscalculation in a previous caper, whereby a person who shouldn't have been conned, had been, and they had found out. Eddie had to make a choice, either have his legs broken, or worse, or as they say 'do a runner'.

21

Eddie chose the latter and became Jeremiah Brown, a fine arts dealer in a sleepy village called Ashburn-on-Sinkhole.

The wax seal on the back of the envelope was broken and the lemon-scented letter removed.

"Mmm citronella. Nice touch," thought Jeremiah.

As he started to read, he was surprised to see that they had written the letter as if the author had known that the intended recipient would pause and make comment whilst reading. Normally this would unnerve anyone who would receive a letter like this, and Jeremiah, being like any other normal person, was equally unnerved. The difference between normal people and Jeremiah was that normal folk could resist the possibility of a con. He, on the other hand? The cogs began to whir.

As Jeremiah's mind raced into action, he turned on his banker's desk lamp and reached for a bottle of scotch and glass from the bottom right desk drawer. As he poured the whisky into his glass, it shone with a wonderful, mottled golden glow over the very fine paper, dancing over every line of the letter. The thought of 'money not being an issue' made Jeremiah's eyes light up.

As Jeremiah raised the glass to his lips, he paused to inhale the aroma of his favourite Speyside dram, before letting the liquid touch his welcoming lips.

"This could be quite a profitable little job," he said and smiled as the warming sensation flooded his chest.

Jeremiah replaced the glass on the desk, next to the resting letter, and re-read the correspondence from Gary, whoever he was.

He was always up for a con job or slightly adrift of the straight and narrow path of legality. There was something about this request that he couldn't quite put his finger on. Should he try to con his unknown new client or should he do as asked and get the painting? Money was not an issue at the end of the day.

[Jeremiah's brain]

"There's something very fishy 'ere," said Caution.

"Rubbish! What we're looking at is a perfect way to get back into the painting forgery business in a big way," replied Greed.

"True, but I'm going to side with Caution on this one. We do not know who this Gary is or why he would scent his letter with lemons? I mean! Who does that?! It's almost the work of the Devil!" added Logic.

"Who cares?! We're looking at mucho deniro dans la skyrocket!" argued Greed.

"I care if we get caught out!" added Pain, *"You don't have to deal with the aftermath. I do and I can tell you it'll not be pleasant!"*

"I agree with Pain..."

"Oh, shut up Logic. If money isn't an issue, then we could be sitting pretty, but instead, you just want to live out the rest of your synapses in this boring little place selling booze to greedy landlords who haven't got two brain cells to rub together!"

Greed was getting annoyed as he suspected he was losing the battle.

"Back me up 'ere Argument."

Argument, who had not bothered listening in the first place to what was going on, decided to do what he did best. Unfortunately for Greed, Argument started arguing with the first thing he picked up on... Greed's comment.

"Back you up?! Did we have another bang on the head without me noticing? The only way I'd happily back you up is if you were a toilet and I had had several pints of stout and a curry!"

"??" Greed was lost for words.

"So do we agree that this 'Gary' is a bit dodgy?" queried Caution.

"We're all a bit bloody dodgy! That's who we are! Oh, for crying out loud."

Greed had had enough and decided that it wasn't worth the effort.

Parts of Jeremiah's brain, who were involved in the debate, had been joined by Experience, who had decided to call Greed a 'cock' and sided with the majority.

"Sod the lot of ya! This could've been the BIG ONE, but oh no! Let's side with Caution. You bunch o' Jessies!"

Argument pondered over what had just happened and wasn't too sure if he'd picked the right side, but to save face, decided to stay put.

"I think we ought to go with finding a way to get the original and then whatever it costs just double it and add

another nought on the end. If money isn't an issue, then why not?" said Logic.

"Oi! I'm Greed, not you!" came a distant shout.

"I think we know someone in Italy who could assist with the task," said Memory, *"In fact, I'm sure we do."*

"Then it's agreed," butted in Decisiveness, *"We're going for the easy route with minimal risk."*

"Y'bunch o' Jessies!"

"Can't we just ignore him?" said Caution.

"Unfortunately not," replied Auditory.

"Dammit!"

"Bloody heard that!"

Greed then wandered over to Sympathy but got nowhere as Sympathy had joined forces with the majority.

Indecisiveness didn't know what to do, so he informed the rest of the brain that he had to go as he thought he'd left the oven on, rather than join any side.

Jeremiah took another sip of whisky and listened to the tiny screaming voice in the back of his head. It was an unusual voice as it had instructed him to play it safe, rather than do what he normally did and rush headlong into what they commonly knew as a 'shitstorm'.

The rhythmic drumming his fingers on the desk didn't help Jeremiah as he pondered over how this could be possible. Nothing appeared to be coming to mind. Even another sip of the golden fire water resulted in a negative result.

"Bloody hell, Memory! Hurry up with the details of this contact in Italy before he changes his mind!" shouted Urgency.

"I'm on with it! Give us a second. I've loads of stuff in my banks... Well, I never! I'd forgotten all about that! Hey guys, you'll never guess what this dirty pervert did with Alice Scoggins behind the bike shed at middle school!"

"GET ON WITH IT!!"

"OK! OK!... I'll tell you later."

"Hurry up please!" added Fear, *"I'm nearly cacking myself!"*

"Cacking?!" butted in Swearing, *"Don't you mean shi..."*

"I know what I mean, Swearing. God, can someone teach him some manners?"

"Don't bother. Politeness tried and failed," said Swearing with a smile.

Jeremiah got up from his desk and paced around the room with his hands on his hips, trying to magic from nowhere an idea on how to get the painting. Neither staring at the ceiling or floor seemed to help. That was until he passed a half-finished copy of Da Vinci's Mona Lisa. Suddenly, the conman's face lit up and a smile quickly formed.

"About bloody time!" said Swearing with Fear giving a slight nod in agreement.

Jeremiah darted back to his desk and pulled open the shallow centre drawer, retrieving a wallet of business cards. As he shuffled through the cards, he sat back in his chair, searching for the card that had the details of the one person who could help him. Just then, Jeremiah raised a card out of the pack, angling it for more light from his desk lamp. With the grin that formed on Jeremiah's face that continued growing, the card could well have been a lottery scratch card with a big prize on it.

Like placing a sacred cloth over the Ark of the Covenant, Jeremiah placed the business card on top of the finely written letter. After taking another sip of his whisky and replacing the glass, he reached for his mobile phone from inside his jacket pocket. After several beeps of him tapping the phone number onto the screen, the phone chirped into life with a continuous ringtone that only occurs when making a call abroad.

***

Luciano Pavarotti was singing his heart out on a small CD player on a dresser in the lounge of Edoardo da Veloce's compact flat. Edoardo had finished for the day in his art gallery underneath his flat at 17 Viale Della Ombreggiato on the outskirts of Vatican City. He wandered into his lounge with a wineglass half full of Barolo Riserva and an unlit cigarette, balanced precariously between his lips, loosening his tie as he did with his free hand.

After closing his shop for the day, he had then gone to the rear of the business premises and finished off a painting for a rather important client, changed into his suit, and was settling down for the evening. He eased himself into his fine leather recliner chair, placing his wine on a nearby side table, and produced a gold lighter from his trouser pocket. The flame dance around the tip of his cigarette as Edoardo lit it, inhaled, and relaxed.

A painting complete for a client, a fine wine, a cigarette, and Pavarotti on the player. The perfect way to end the day. Suddenly, Edoardo's mobile phone shattered the serenity.

"Sodomita!"

[Translation]

"Bugger!"

Edoardo's phone danced as it vibrated on the table, nudging up to his glass of wine causing tiny ripples on the blood-red liquid. Taking a long steady drag on his cigarette before reaching over and picking up his phone to see who was calling.

"Si,"

"Edoardo, my old friend!..." chirped Jeremiah.

Click!

Jeremiah looked at his phone.

"The poncy git has hung up on me!"

Edoardo placed his phone on his lap and reclined his seat. As he was conducting the orchestra that accompanied Luciano with his cigarette, he closed his eyes and waited for his phone to sound again. He didn't have to wait long before he tapped the screen again.

"Si,"

"Edoardo. It's Jerem... I mean Eddie from..."

Click!

"Dammit! The pompous tw..."

Edoardo took another drag on his cigarette and stood by for his phone to spring to life. Moments later, as expected, the mobile phone sprung into life.

"Si,"

"I've a job for..."

Click!

"Oh, for crying out loud!"

Edoardo sipped his wine and this time, when his phone eventually sang out, he let it sing and dance a little longer.

"Si,"

"MONEY! LOTS OF MONEY!... Edoardo?... You still there?"

"Si,"

The Italian's low and overconfident voice subtly changed to be slightly more interested.

"Don't hang up. I've a job for you that could net you some serious money."

"Si?"

Jeremiah, or as Edoardo knew him as Fast Eddie, was unsure as to what Edoardo's last 'Si' meant. Was he agreeing to not hang up or was he interested in making money?

"Si?"

Eddie relaxed and sat back in his office chair.

"I have a client who wants a particular piece of art that you are in a perfect position to obtain. He's willing to pay handsomely for it, BUT, it has to be the original."

"Si?"

"It's in quite a difficult place and it will need a professional outfit to get it, so just name your price and it's yours."

Eddie was feeling quietly confident that the last part of what he had said would hook his Italian colleague.

"And ze piece is?" queried Edoardo as he took a drag on his cigarette.

"Ah well, here comes the difficult part. It's a painting by Botticelli... and it is located in quite a secure place within the Vatican City..."

Edoardo's left eyebrow lifted, which for people in the know meant only one thing. A scam was forming in his head.

"...The Mappa dell'Inferno."

"Si... Mappa dell'Inferno. No *problem*. Give-a me a month and it will be yours. You still in that squalid little place?"

"Ashburn? Yes, but it's actually quite..."

30

Click!

Edoardo settled back into his chair, replacing his glass of wine for his phone on the table whilst Luciano blasted out Nessun Dorma from the speakers. A smile formed on the Italian's face, as the piece of art he had just finished forging was the exact piece required by his English acquaintance. A month would give him time to create another copy that would be sent over to his shabby styled friend in the rat-infested cesspit he called home.

"Bloody self-absorbed Italian git," muttered Eddie, but still smiled as the game was now on.

Only a month to wait and he would be sitting pretty.

"Oh, be still my beating heart," Eddie said and drained his glass, ending it with a smile.

Chapter 1

Night shift had started at 9.00 pm sharp for Mario Panini. As usual, he got ready for work and made his way there on foot. Even the warm Italian evening had an ultra-cool and suave air about it, the type only an Italian evening could have. The moon hung in the air and was surrounded by clouds like an Italian superstar swamped by young female fans vying for his attention.

Mario, on the other hand, was far from cool, or suave, as he made his way to the Vatican Library. As usual, he had arrived half an hour before work started to get the final things ready, like a fully charged radio and his museum authorised hasp. That was where 'usual' stopped and 'what on earth?!' started.

Mario strolled through the main security door with a relaxed attitude similar to that of a cat wandering through a stray dog compound in the afternoon just before feeding time.

There were a few raised eyebrows from his colleagues as he entered, seeing their large colleague who had had a shave and showered. Even the use of deodorant and a not so expensive aftershave! However, no one really noticed that the bumbling, sweaty security guard was carrying a rather out-of-place briefcase. Neither did anyone see Mario act extremely nervous or sweat profusely. To be fair to his colleagues, they usually saw Mario sweat. A man of his stature and fitness, they expected nothing less.

"Sera Mario. Bene?" mumbled Luca Presley, Mario's colleague and friend at the desk where the signing-in book lay.

Luca's surname was originally Russo, but because of his fascination with rock-and-roll music and one artist, in particular, he decided to change his name by deed poll. However, Luca's fascination did not stop at name changing. The raven black hair and sideburns coupled with 1970s gold-painted Las Vegas-style sunglasses were also a must.

The Security Chiefs of the Vatican Library did not welcome the guard's whole appearance. An overweight male in his early sixties with receding hair and looking as he did wasn't the image they really wanted to portray. However, not breaching any regulations, they had no other option but to allow their employee's eccentric ways. By way of punishment, Luca had been permanently posted at the Security Office, which oversaw the signing-in book, a boring job that suited Luca perfectly.

"I'm fine, thanks. Why d'you ask?"

Mario was overtly defensive, which was not his usual manner, but because of Luca's relaxed and not caring attitude, it went unnoticed.

"Do not forget to sign in... Th'nk yo', Th'nk yo' v'ry much."

The last part of Luca's gratitude was said in an Italian slant on an American accent.

The security guard's signature was written on the appropriate line and smudged by the sweaty hand of the nervous man.

Mario had always been a law-abiding man and to be approached by someone and asked to do an act which, if found out, could land him in prison, weighed heavily on his mind. Not to mention tax his already overworked deodorant.

With the briefcase below desk height, Mario nervously smiled and nodded at Luca, and hurried to the male locker room. The destination was a short distance from the security desk and Mario left his friend mumbling something about what wise men say and why fools rush in.

As Mario overtly sneaked into the men's locker room, he quickly made his way to his private locker. The air in the room was pungent with several types of deodorant and aftershaves that Mario knew to be very expensive, and probably not worth their price. After unlocking the padlock on his locker, Mario deposited the briefcase that contained a copy of a masterpiece. A masterpiece he wished he'd never agree to swap over. It was too late now, and he knew the deed had to be done.

Every inch of the Vatican building was covered with CCTV cameras and patrols were made on a frequent basis, which made parts of Mario's body sweat even more. It didn't matter that he had been assured that upon making the swap, the cameras wouldn't show him doing it or that it was 'allegedly' for a good cause. All Mario could think of was what he was doing could land him in prison with a cellmate called Giovanni whose predilection was for large ex-security guards.

As the shift wore on, Mario's heart started to beat faster, knowing the time would be close to when he was instructed to make the switch. No amount of returning to the locker room for a blast of deodorant would help Mario or the ambience of the entire building.

2.15 am had arrived, and the time was upon him, like a man trapped under a lorry load of watches, for the scary swapping of the art. The nervous rotund guard entered the locker room and hitching up his trousers, he leaned into his locker and retrieved the briefcase.

"Heyyy Maario! New lunchbox, I see!"

Antonio Cazzo had left one of the toilet cubicles and was in the process of washing his hands when he noticed his colleague.

"Joost a snack, eh?" he continued the taunt.

Mario nervously laughed at the unfunny joke and watched, wide-eyed, as the young slender guard exited the locker room, leaving behind him an unholy stench emanating from the toilet cubicle.

"OK. Come on, you can do this," came the encouraging voice within Mario.

With a wipe of his brow and a deep breath, Mario left the locker room.

Carlos Humperdinck, another fan of 1960s music, was sat in the control room with his feet resting on the control panel. He was halfway through eating a pastry, expertly catching all the pastry flakes on his shirt, whilst watching over a wall of CCTV monitors, when Luca wandered in, explaining that it was coffee time.

Nothing ever really happened in the library, apart from that one time when Antonio's girlfriend visited to wish Antonio a happy birthday in a most amorous way on one of the desks in the public area. Luckily for Antonio, this had occurred on a night shift. However, unbeknownst to

36

the guard, the rest of his team, which became more than apparent, had watched him when upon escorting his girlfriend out of the premises they were met with a round of applause.

"OK, but only if we have a coffee *and* smoke break," Carlos' deal was accepted and the two men retired for their hard-earned break.

The Italian air was still warm and a blanket of stars had appeared to watch over the two officers as the usual boring night shift rapidly turned into anything but.

***

In the vacant control room, all twenty-four monitors relayed what they usually did - nothing, apart from the odd security guard strolling down a corridor with his hands in his pockets or removing the contents of their nostrils with their index fingers and wiping the same on the seat of their trousers.

At exactly 2.15 am, the videotape that covered the doorway of the securely vaulted room, located in the basement, had ended, and had been ejected by the machine. A few moments later, the monitor that covered the same area showed a large sweaty security guard, looking as guilty as a court judge in a whorehouse, step into view.

Mario's heart was beating so loud and fast, he thought that at any moment it would burst out of his chest. The air-conditioned corridor did nothing for the guard, who was sweating more than a pig at a butcher's convention.

"OK! In, swap, and out. That's it. That's all I have to do," he told himself, eyeing the corridor's both ends.

Mario reached for his I.D. badge that was clipped to his left breast pocket, unclipped it, and after punching in the key-code on the numbered pad, swiped the card reader. The red light next to the keypad quickly changed to green, the door-lock clicked, and the room was now insecure. Not that it made any difference, but Mario opened the door as little as possible and squeezed his rotund frame into a gap that would barely allow him entry.

Mario breathed an enormous sigh of relief as he entered and placed the briefcase on an island table top in the centre of the room. His thick thumbs clicked open both latches on the case and lifting the lid, he revealed what he thought was an exact copy of Sandro Botticelli's Mappa dell'Inferno.

It was almost an exact copy... almost... apart from the very tiny addition of another person on the lowest circle of Hell. A person so tiny that you could easily miss if you didn't know was there. A person who surprisingly looked like, as daft as it sounded, God in a tuxedo, waving and smiling.

Mario composed himself by taking another huge intake of breath, and making his way over to the metal shelving, removed a large square shallow metal box, returning to the island and his open briefcase.

"Oh dear God, forgive me," said Mario under his breath, as he unlocked the box and removed a similar cardboard box from within.

Mario very carefully placed the box on the island and reaching down, obtained a pair of white cotton gloves from a drawer and put them on. Opening the box revealed a large leather-bound folder containing the original piece of priceless art.

Mario wiped his beaded brow with the sleeve of his shirt and returned to the shelving. He quickly scanned the labels on the metal boxes until he found the one he wanted.

'First Edition: Signed Copies
Author: Mary Berry'

Deftly placing the box on the tabletop next to Botticelli's and opening it up to reveal pristine copies of several cookbooks, Mario transferred the artwork into Mrs Berry's secure container. After closing it, he returned it to its exact position.

The hardest part was now over, nevertheless, the security guard was in a world of panic he had never ventured into before. Nervously replacing the original with the copy from his briefcase, Mario returned Botticelli's metal container onto the shelf.

Upon removing the gloves and placing them back into the drawer, he quickly left the room, with his briefcase tight under his arm. Quietly closing the security door behind himself, Mario decided it was time to get some fresh air, and maybe another spray of deodorant.
As he turned the corner, leaving the corridor and thinking he had made it, Mario's heart stopped.

"Heyyy Maario!... You had your leetle snack?"

The smug and well-maintained face of Antonio smiled at Mario.

"Err yeah," he replied, wondering if Antonio had caught him out at the last second.

"Maan, you need to lose some weight and work out like I do, then you may get the ladeez."

To emphasise his point, Antonio started to dry hump fresh air.

Mario had always been a little jealous of Antonio's good looks, but his attitude stank more than Mario's underwear at that very moment.

"I'll give it some thought," smiled Mario in return and bid him farewell.

Watching the heavy framed security guard scurry off into the distance, Antonio's smile disappeared and a focussed look descended. Turning quickly down the corridor, Antonio swiftly walked to the same doorway his colleague had just come from. With the numbers punched in and a swipe of an I.D. card, Antonio entered the secure room.

Quickly heading for the metal box that had recently been open, Antonio removed Botticelli's metal container from the shelving and placed it on the island table top. Opening the metal and cardboard boxes in quick succession, and lifting his shirt, Antonio revealed a large tinfoil covered paper envelope taped to his torso. Painfully ripping it from his chest, he placed it on the table next to the open box and dug deep into his trouser pocket to produce a pair of cotton gloves.

He quickly placed the gloves on his manicured hands, opened the leather folder and revealed the Mappa dell'Inferno. A swift exchange of paintings, replacing the metal box on the shelf and Antonio was out of the room with Mario's copy taped to his chest inside the tinfoil covered envelope.

Carlos and Luca had returned from their coffee and smoke break and had entered the control room when they saw Antonio sat in Carlos' seat. Antonio had just finished wiping the entry log records for a certain secure room in the basement and had sat down, satisfied that he had completed the task set by a certain high-profile member of the Caster Organisation.

"You want my job, eh?" Carlos asked the young upstart.

With a confident smile, Antonio replied.

"Well, I thought about it, but if I needed to look like you to do the job, then I'll pass. Grazie."

The young security guard slowly got out of the guard's seat and passed the two larger officers deliberately close enough for them to notice his aftershave.

"Antonio, just a suggestion, but maybe a little less aftershave? You couldn't sneak up on a dead skunk, let alone anyone wanting to break in."

Antonio's reply was given by way of his middle finger waving in the air as he left the room.

For the rest of the shift, Mario was as nervous as a long-tailed cat in a room full of rocking chairs, waiting to be called back to the control room. He'd walk in and see his supervisor and Carlos looking at him with his face on the monitor entering 'the' room.

This would be subsequently followed by him being escorted out of the building and into a prison cell where a large chap called Giovanni, who had a penchant for ex-security guards, would be waiting. Luckily for Mario, the visitor he had had only recently, was true to his word, and so far, things were going to plan.

7.00 am had arrived and the night shift at the Vatican Library had come to an end. The early turn officers had arrived and again the locker rooms were overpowered by the aroma of numerous aftershaves all vying for pole position. The night shift had all wandered into the now vacant locker rooms and were preparing for their journeys back home. The guards were removing their radios and hasps, where soon it would be like a Le Mans start for the car park.

Mario, not being one for rapidity, brought up the rear. He could see the exit in sight as he hurried along the corridor and past the security office. He was almost free. He could almost smell the warming Italian air. His heart raced at the thought of making it out without being stopped and introduced to his cellmate, Giovanni. As he passed the security office, Mario didn't bother looking at Luca's early turn counterpart but gave a relieved "goodnight" to the officer. Suddenly;

"Oh, Mario! Stop!"

Mario stopped dead in his tracks. Deep within his brain, a very loud Klaxon siren exploded, and just like in the war films, normal lighting quickly went to a panicky red light.

"Mio Dio! We've had it!" screamed Fear.

The part of Mario's brain that controlled his bowels was ready for action and simply waiting for the signal.

"Oh crap!" shouted Swearing.

"No! Not literally!" interjected Logic, who was aware that the bowels were being held on a hair-trigger.

"Now hang on! It may not be as bad as what we think," continued Logic. *"Something just isn't right."*

"D'ya think?!" screamed Fear, who if given the opportunity would race around the rest of Mario's brain in a blind panic.

"No, honestly. Something isn't right. What have we not done?" continued Logic.

"Kept on the right side of the bloody law for a start," replied Swearing.

"Excuse me! I have Sweat on the line. Can we make a decision about what to do? Apparently, he's working his arse off at the moment and would like to know when he can rest?" called out a junior synapse in the Control Centre.

"Tell him he'll have to wait. I've got Bowel Control awaiting instructions and the trigger-happy morons will take matters into their own hands if we're not careful and believe me, none of us want that to happen!" bellowed Logic. *"And will someone turn off the bloody siren!"*

"Sorry," apologised Drama. *"Shall I return to normal lighting too?"*

"YES!!" Logic was struggling to maintain control.

"Easy tiger," butted in Facetious.

"Piss off!" replied Logic.

"Excuse me. I now have Bladder Control on the line... Was that a signal for go?" enquired the junior synapse.

"No, it bloody wasn't!"

"Oh, OK. Thanks. I still have Sweat demanding to know what's happening. What shall I?..."

The junior synapse felt Logic's anger ripple through the entire brain.

"I'll just tell him to hold his horses!"

The junior synapse then left the scene muttering something about not getting paid enough for this 'shitshow'.

"Right! Muscles? Turn him around and make him smile... Oral? You ask if anything's wrong! Sweat? Bloody calm down. Bowels? Don't you bloody dare!"

Logic had managed to keep it together, even though Fear and Drama had hindered the situation.

Mario, not knowing what was going on in his head, turned around and felt a smile appear on his sweat streaming face.

"Anything wrong, Stefano?"

"I would say there is," replied the stern security guard at the desk.

"I'm warning you, Bowels! Don't!" Logic screamed.

"Since when do you not sign out?" and a hairy muscular hand appeared from the security office opening and pointed at the signing book.

"Oh, sorry. It's been a long night."

Mario's entire body sagged with relief and returned to the desk, picking up the well-used biro and signed out.

A sweaty right hand was raised by way of giving an apology and a simultaneous 'goodnight' offered. Mario then turned to leave.

"No excuse, Mario. Rules are rules," rebuked Stefano.

"Asshole," muttered Mario as he passed the threshold and inhaled the fresh air, filling his lungs with freedom.

Morning was up and awake and had kicked nighttime back where it belonged, behind morning. The air had that freshness about it, with a hint of fresh deodorant, aftershave, and perfume as the city began to wake and get ready for work.

The traffic had realised that it had been quiet for way too long and had started to get busy. This meant several fists from driver's windows being waved along with insults questioning other driver's visual acuity and parentage followed by responses involving middle fingers. Another normal day in the beautiful city.

Chapter 2

Nicolo and Lorenzo were taking their morning walk around the city. It was breakfast time for the two strays and they were making their way, slowly, to their favourite eatery.

Francesca had opened her boss' café and had already served several office workers with their obligatory espressos before they rushed off to start work waving goodbye and each leaving a tip. At 25 years old, she was the personification of Italian beauty with a heart to match. She was wiping down the stylish outdoor metal tables when she was greeted by her two favourite males.

"Good morning, you two, and how are we today?" she said with a smile as big as her brown eyes.

Nicolo and Lorenzo sat looking up at the waitress, both with their tails wagging.

"Let me guess. Breakfast time, is it? Just a second," and she finished wiping down the table and disappeared inside.

"I really like this human. There's just something about her," said Nicolo, with his eyes fixed on the open café door.

"Might it have something to do with the fact that she feeds you and scratches your ear?"

47

Before Nicolo could answer, the pretty human appeared from inside the café with two pastries, loosely wrapped in a paper serviette.

"There you go, my handsome men. Don't tell anyone where you got these from, OK?"

As Francesca bent down to give the dogs their morning treat, the two met her halfway and stood up with tails wagging and tongues out. The exchange was made and the two strays trotted off, holding their breakfast in their mouths and tails, still wagging. Today was going to be a good day.

Francesca strolled back into the café, washed her hands, and continued with her morning routine.

"Morning Francesca," Mario called out as he took his usual seat outside the café.

"Hey, Mario. The usual?" came the reply from inside.

"Mine too," called out Michele as he also took his typical seat, "Hey Mario, how's it going?"

"So glad to be out of work right now," said Mario overtly sounding relieved, placing his hands palm down on the table, sitting upright and inhaling.

"Tough night?"

"You just don't know how much!" came the reply as Francesca brought out a pastry for Mario and an espresso for Michele.

"There you go, gentlemen."

"Grazie," replied to two men in unison.

The two men sat in silence. One had recently finished work and relieved, and the other about to start.

***

7.20 am on the Viale Della Ombreggiato, strode the lithesome figure of Antonio Cazzo, leaving a trail of expensive aftershave in his wake. As he reached number 17, Antonio scanned the area for anyone looking similar to that of the local police. Apart from the odd office worker briskly walking by, checking their watches, and a street worker hosing down the pavements, Antonio was in the clear.

Two sharp stabs at the intercom doorbell should have received some form of greeting, but instead, Antonio was left waiting. Edoardo did not rush for anyone he did not have to. Another two sharp stabs, and a third longer ring brought a crackly 'Si?' from the intercom.

"It's me, Antonio."

"Si?"

"Antonio Cazzo?"

"Si?"

"!!! Antonio Cazzo from the Vatican Library!"

"Si?"

"Mio Dio! Open the damn door!"

Click!

"Did he just hang up on me?" thought Antonio, who again pressed the buzzer and kept his finger on it this time.

It took about a minute before the exasperated officer heard the padding of footsteps coming down the stairs and the door being unlocked.

"Si. I heard you," said the unshaven face that appeared from the doorjamb.

Antonio was taken aback at the sight of Edoardo, whose hair resembled that of a monochromatic peacock that had been caught unawares in a wind tunnel. The white vest and blue stripe boxer shorts finished the ensemble.

Antonio was then allowed entry, but only far enough so the door could be closed after him.

"Give it to me," demanded Edoardo, with his hand held out.

"Oh! Yes! Sorry," Antonio said as he lifted his shirt to reveal the taped envelope.

Before he could gently peel off the tape from his torso, Edoardo swiftly ripped it off, resulting in an involuntary squeal from Antonio.

The young man had barely taken a lungful of air to remonstrate over the barbaric act when the door was opened and he was pushed out onto the street. Unfortunately for Antonio, the street worker had started to wash the exact spot of pavement with his hosepipe where he was. An icy chill hit the back of his legs before the reprimand from the street cleaner hit his ears.

Nicolo and Lorenzo had finished their breakfast and were taking their morning constitutional when they came upon two humans being verbally aggressive with each other. One in a security uniform and the other in high-visibility trousers and shirt. The younger human stood shouting and appeared to dance whilst the other shouted back, waving his free hand in the air as his other had a running hosepipe aimed at the dancer's crotch. Both dogs stopped and looked at each other as if to say, 'Oh well! Stupid humans' and continued on their way.

Edoardo ignored the dispute coming from the other side of his apartment door and made his way back upstairs with the envelope in his hand. In his kitchen, Edoardo opened up the envelope and placed the piece of art on top of a brand-new towel laid on his kitchen table. Next to this was another piece of art, exactly the same as the one he had just laid down and again on another new towel.

Edoardo had figured out the best way to send forgeries through the normal mailing system was to create a bogus company called 'Towel in a Tube'. A fake company that would sell towels online and post them to customers. The art would be rolled up with the towel and placed in the tube for posting. No one ever suspected that such an innocuous item would contain Edoardo's primary source of income.

With two empty cardboard tubes, one for each towel and painting, Edoardo placed the items, rolled up, in the containers. Not yet having his morning coffee and unknowingly to the dishevelled forger, the parcels had been mixed up. The piece that should go to his huge, grotesque Italian client had been placed inside the tube marked with a British address.

Securely sealing the tubes, Edoardo placed the package for the rat-infested hovel of a village on his coffee table and the one for Don Caster in his cupboard, for safekeeping.

"I'll post that later," he muttered to himself. "First, I need a coffee."

Combing back his stuck up hair with his hand, the forger ventured back into the kitchen to make a fresh pot of coffee. Moments later, Luciano Pavarotti was singing for all he was worth from the small tinny CD player in the kitchen, accompanied by a much less talented, scruffy male, wearing only a white vest and boxer shorts.

Chapter 3

It had been a shade over a month since the residents of Ashburn-on-Sinkhole had accidentally slain a vampire, and life was steadily getting back to normal. Well, the people of the village were not aware that the fellow had been a vampire, nor that he had escaped from Hell. Neither did they slay him as much as he had fallen on a garden dibber after being shocked at the sight of a mature lady of rotund stature who was an avid gardener and naturist. The vision was like that of a Basset Hound's ears resting on a football.

Not only were the residents of the village not aware that the poor chap who lay with a dibber sticking out of his chest was a vampire, but they were blissfully unaware that Death had been following this fellow on behest from the Devil himself. Death, however, had decided to have a name change, and no longer wanted to be called 'Death' or 'The Grim Reaper'. The response that you would receive if you ever called him 'The Ferryman' was;

"Do I look like I own a bloody boat?!"

Steve was Death's new name, as given by Gary, whose previous name was Lucifer, Satan, or just plain Devil.

The only residents who were aware of 'Steve's' presence in the village were a young lad by the name of 'Shifty' Miller and two ghosts; Bernie Aberline, recently deceased and Clarabelle Windleson, not so recently deceased... and once the village harlot.

The incident, which resulted in the vampire's demise, occurred in the garden of Charles and Edith St.John-Fox. After a brief chase from an irate vegan health food shop owner, who's partner had not long before been attacked by said vampire; Uriah Tomkins, the vampire, had evaded capture by hiding behind the hedge of the said garden. One thing led to another, and Steve removed Uriah and escorted him back to Hell.

As the naturists' garden had been the scene of a fatal accident, the local police officer, PC Rick Higgins, had taped off the garden with strict instructions for it not to be touched, to prevent any contamination of forensic evidence.

It had been some time, and nothing had been done, regarding forensics, or weeding of the garden, the St.John-Fox couple had been champing at the bit to get back into their pride and joy.

It was Rick's immediate superior who had reprimanded him and demanded that all tape should be removed and the St.John-Fox's be allowed to tend to their precious garden once again. Rick's superior was not his Sergeant or Inspector, but his wife Felicity, a local schoolteacher whose temper was the complete opposite of her normally gentle attitude. Due to the severity of the reprimand which was initiated by Edith, who had had a brief chat with the officer's wife, pleading that she have a word with her husband and allow them back in their garden, Rick had removed all tape.

The constable was on his daily patrol along the lanes of the village when he came upon the recently re-opened garden of Charles and Edith. The couple had been eager to tend to their precious greenery, and intended to do just that, baring all to anyone who cared to see. Edith had disappeared to the potting shed at the rear of their home and was retrieving the necessary tools to de-weed, whilst Charles exited the house by the front door in search of her.

"Excuse me, Richard. Have you seen my wife?" called out Charles.

Charles stood proud of the threshold like a guard on sentry duty, displaying his manhood, which resembled a grey nest containing two shrivelled eggs and an acorn.

"I have Charles and you're a braver man than me," came the reply.

"I'm sorry?"

"She's just nipped round the back. Something about getting a tool. My first thought was you, but apparently, I was wrong."

Charles's hearing wasn't as good as it could have been and just picked up on the necessary. With a smile and a casual salute, he thanked the officer and strolled around to the side of the house. Before calling for his wife, Charles turned and beckoned the officer.

"Oh Richard, when can I have my dibber back?"

"When the temperature warms up. It looks like an acorn in a crow's nest," muttered Rick.

"Sorry?"

"I'll get it from the evidence store and bring it back here this afternoon if that's ok," replied the constable in a louder voice.

"Thank you so much, Richard, really appreciate it," said Charles with a smile and continued on his search for his darling Edith.

Rick watched as the elderly naturist disappeared down the side of the cottage and gave a shudder as the wrinkly body disappeared from sight.

"More wrinkles than screwed up tin foil," he muttered, and continued his patrol back into the village.

Life down in the village was ticking over quite nicely. It was a sunny afternoon with only a couple of white fluffy clouds keeping the radiant sun company. The wind had decided to wait until a little later in the evening to cool the cobbles in the square with a cool breeze after being baked by the sun. People went about their business as usual, and the staking of a rather natty dressed man in the naturist weirdo's garden was all but a memory and becoming more distant by the day.

A few miles away, in the nearby village of Lower Fitterton, life was not ticking over as nicely. In fact, life was not there at all. Prior to the slaying of the vampire, the residents of Lower Fitterton should have been collected by Steve, who at that point still went by the name of Death. A UFO crash should have seen to that, however, because of a minor miscalculation by the aliens, they crash-landed on a nearby asteroid and an alien human trafficker group had taken the residents instead.

This was not welcomed by the village folk, in particular the landlord of the village pub, The Hammer and Tong, Big Frank. This was also becoming an unwelcome abduction by the aliens themselves, as they had also taken the residents of the local nursing home and had been inundated by requests for bedpans; prior to demands for mops and buckets. The stench of stale urine and butterscotch sweets was quite overpowering.

In the control room of the craft sat the commander-in-chief, Dissel, and his second, Pitrol. The engineer, Forsta, had disappeared, once again, to the alien version of a toilet. Dissel was becoming more annoyed with the requests for mops and buckets and the stench that emanated from the holding area that contained the entire village folk.

"For crying out loud! What the hell is a 'mopandbucket'?! And why does it smell so bad?!" demanded Dissel, "And where the hell is Forsta?"

"Don't know, don't know, and don't know," replied Pitrol with a tired 'I've told you before,' tone to his voice.

"Dammit!"

Dissel reached over and pressed the intercom button.

"Forsta! Where in Quintok's good name are you?!" came the broadcast, which to the captives just came across as a series of clicks.

Forsta had just finished in one of the cubicles and had decided that that was the last time he would steal from the captives something called 'kebab meat with chilli sauce'. On hearing his commander over the intercom sounding quite irate, Forsta decided to finish and make his presence known.

After a quick wash of his hands, he darted out of the toilet area and ran down the corridor, only to stop and return to switch off the light. Not looking at what he was doing, Forsta had *not* switched off the toilet light, which was situated next to their holding room, but had inadvertently unlocked the holding room door that held the captive villagers.

Big Frank was pacing like a caged tiger behind the cell door. At 4 foot 2 inch, whilst not huge in stature, he *definitely* made up in rage.

Prior to being the landlord of The Hammer and Tong, Frank had been a doorman for a local club but had been sacked for causing more fights than the drunken patrons had. His slicked back, thinning black hair gave him the appearance of a vintage Count Dracula, if Dracula had been scarcely over 4 feet.

Big Frank was muttering to himself as to what he would do, given the opportunity, if he was ever let out of his prison, when he heard a slight click. Suddenly stopping, he looked over at the door and noticed it was ajar. Fire and brimstone flashed in Frank's eyes, and regardless of the little grey bastards being far more technologically advanced than he was, he was going to show them his method of communication.

Similar to the firing up of a jet engine, Big Frank welled up with blind fury and the cracking of his knuckles let his nearby friends know that something nasty was about to take place. Just then, a gentle hand took hold of the crook of Frank's elbow and held him back. Frank's daughter, Janine, who was the brains in the family, stopped her father from going nuclear and suggested that they overpower their captors en masse. On doing so, they could get 'Enzo' to fly the UFO back to earth.

Alvin Blatherwick was Lower Fitterton's one and only car thief and could pretty much drive anything. Alvin went by the nickname of 'Enzo' due to his claim to fame of stealing the celebrity, Nick Guest's, Ferrari. Nick Guest was the host of a village makeover programme and had visited Lower Fitterton in an attempt to make the place 'ultra-contemporary'. Alvin had other plans for the celebrity, or more so his car.

Within minutes, Big Frank had led the charge on the bridge and had sacked the aliens. With only shoelaces and bra straps, all three aliens were trussed up and thrown into the holding cell where the acrid odour or urine and butterscotch was unbearable.

"Right, Enzo. Do your thing." Big Frank commanded.

"OK, bruv," replied the car thief, not quite knowing how, but knew he'd figure it out.

Every single button and lever was pressed or pulled within a matter of seconds and shortly afterwards, the UFO was being piloted by a 22-year-old car thief wearing white nylon tracksuit bottoms and a crew neck Christmas jumper.

It didn't matter if it was possible or not, Enzo attempted a handbrake turn in space and headed back to Earth, red-lining the thrusters all the way. The fact that locating his home planet didn't bother Enzo, and neither did entering the Earth's atmosphere.

The problem came when it was time to stop. As a car thief, Enzo hadn't really felt the need for brakes as crashing seemed the better option, so why should a UFO be any different?

This, however, did not go down well with his passengers, who watched, wide-eyed and open-mouthed, as terra firma approached at a great rate of knots, hearing 'Yippee ki-yay mother f...' just prior to the silver disc-shaped craft skimming across a field like a stone on the water.

59

The UFO eventually came to a halt in a field near to an old ramshackle garage and just on the village boundary of Ashburn-on-Sinkhole. With the craft's angle when stopping, and the force with which it had hit the earth, the inside of the windscreen was showered with a tidal wave of urine, generously donated by the elderly from the nursing home who had witnessed the landing, from the comfort of their wheelchairs.

"You stupid bastard! Why didn't you stop?!" demanded Frank.

"Err, I fink you'll find we did stop, bruv," replied Enzo smiling as he sat back in his chair.

"You... Pillock!" Frank was not happy but relieved that he was back on his favourite planet.

Chapter 4

Rick Higgins was wandering down the lane, and heading towards the police station, after his patrol, and a request for the 'dibber' from the St.John-Fox residence. He was struggling with the image of Charles' naked body when he saw something flash across the sky.

From where he was standing, he witnessed something, whatever it was, disappear over the wooded area on the other side of the village, and a split second later a small plume of dried earth appeared. Rick stood looking toward whatever had just crash-landed. For a moment, the officer thought that he should drop everything and see what had just happened and if he could help. Then, the real Rick Higgins came back to life.

"Oh well. Not my patch. That's Fitterton's problem, not mine."

With a shrug of the shoulders, the officer carried on his way to the station.

***

In a barren field, recently ploughed by its owner, and close to Kenneth Turnkey's Garage, lay a somewhat knackered unidentified flying object. With smoke coming from the overworked thruster ports and dust settling all around, a small metallic door opened.

Not quite making the ground, the door was left swinging in the air, when the villagers of Lower Fitterton emerged from the opening and congregated around the crippled craft. Not knowing where to look, whether they should stare at the UFO or where they had landed, folk looked at both.

The drop from the open doorway was quite a distance for Big Frank and his 4 foot 2 inch stature. Vehemently refusing help from one of the carers from the nursing home, he jumped down and land like a paratrooper with a militaristic roll at the end.

With a brief dusting off and looking around to see if anyone had even the slightest of smiles at the way he had alighted from the craft, for which a fight would start, Frank then marched to the roadside. Muttering something about 'bloody aliens' and 'kicking their arses again if they try that crap once more', Frank left the field through a farm gate which was close to the driveway for Kenneth's garage workshop.

The entire village followed suit, like a shepherd and a flock of bewildered sheep. Enzo was the last to leave the craft and held back when everyone else was leaving. He waited until all had left the field, then quickly jogged a short distance away from the crippled UFO and retrieved his mobile phone from his zipped tracksuit bottoms. At arm's length and with an enormous smile and a 'thumbs up', Enzo took a selfie with his latest conquest in the background. Quickly checking to make sure it was suitable, the young car... and UFO thief smiled and rushed after the rest of the village folk.

***

Perched on the gable-end of Kenneth Turnkey's Garage were two Peregrine Falcons, Hugo, and Clifford.

"Arrrk!"

[Translation]

"What the bloody hell was that!" screeched Hugo.

"I'm assuming that was a rhetorical question, dear friend," replied Clifford.

"To be frank, I'm not too sure it was rhetorical. I mean. Really! What the bloody hell was that? I've never seen anything that shape before. OK, many a time we see those human chappies leaving those flying things, but they usually have some primitive basic wings. Plus, they usually land on those long roads with lots of flashing lights. This, however! Really, what the bloody hell is that thing?"

The two falcons looked at each other, then returned their gaze to the dented craft.

"It is a bit of a doozy of a question, I must admit," said Clifford staring at the UFO.

"Whatever it is, it needs practice at landing as it doesn't look too healthy."

"Hugo, you're not wrong." Clifford agreed.

With their eyes fixed on the craft as the steam from the thrusters subsided, Hugo piped up.

"Should we take a look and see what it is?"

"We could... If you want?" replied his friend.

"Any chance I could have a look?" came the small voice of a field mouse pinned under Hugo's talon.

63

Both birds looked down at the trapped mouse, then at each other.

"Where's my manners? Of course," and Hugo released his grip.

Cedric, the field-mouse had been intending to make a run for it as soon as he was free of the falcon's grip. However, seeing the craft and knowing it was not the usual thing, decided that there was safety in numbers and cowered behind Hugo's leg.

"What the bloody hell's that?"

"My question exactly," replied Hugo with his gaze on the craft.

"And you want to take a closer look! Are you mad?!" shivered Cedric.

"I mean, you can if you want, but I'm stopping here," he continued.

"You know I think you may be right, little man. It may be a prudent move not to do a fly-by," replied Clifford.

"Yes, you may well be right. OK, let's just go."

The two falcons took flight in the opposite direction, leaving the field mouse stranded on the roof. In a flash, Cedric realised that he was free, and no longer was he going to be falcon tea. The realisation lasted seconds, closely followed by a swoop and a slight gust of wind as Hugo had returned for his afternoon snack and took flight with the field mouse clutched tightly in his talons.

"Oh, bollocks!"

"You steaming great blagsnaf!" said Dissel as he glared at Forsta.

Forsta wasn't listening, as he was trying his best to keep whatever contents he had left in his stomach in situ and not projectile vomit them into the puddles of urine with a flotilla of butterscotch sweet wrappers dancing on the surface.

"Well, in a round-a-bout sort of way, at least we don't have to deal with their constant whining over 'mopandbuckets' and that foul-smelling stench," added Pitrol, who always tried to see the positive in things.

"D'you reckon? Well, if my nasal cavity deceives me, I can still smell it and now I see where it's come from!"

A minor positive comment was not going to change Dissel's mind.

"And how do you think, Mr Positive, sriff hugging, crag eating shifler, do you think we can escape here?!"

Pitrol's tiny shoulders sank as he looked around the holding room and saw the only exit, that was shut tight.

"Well... I'm sure something will happen so we can get out of here. Maybe a secret trapdoor or something."

"You really are deluded, aren't you."

"You say that but, you just never know."

"Oh, give me strength!"

Dissel struggled to stand up and wandered around the secure room.

Forsta, who had been keeping quiet and trying to keep down the contents of his stomach, suddenly lit up.

"Of course!" he exclaimed and jumped up.

Running over to the door, dodging the puddles of urine and sweet wrappers, he headed for the sign by the side of the door that read.

'ESCAPE IS FUTILE'

Expertly sticking out his tongue and using it as a lever, Forsta lifted a flap, disguised as an 'escape is futile' sign, revealing a small white button.

Dissel and Pitrol stared at each other in amazement.

"Can th'none elth thee?" said Forsta, requesting assistance.

The two alien traffickers ran over and assisted their colleague in pressing the button.

With a 'click' the door opened and with a free toe, Dissel managed to open the door enough for freedom to be theirs.

The three tied up aliens made their way to the kitchen and locating a knife from the drawer, they released themselves from the shoelaces and bra straps.

Freed from his shackles, Pitrol smiled at Dissel, with a smugness that under normal circumstances would have resulted in a slap. Dissel knew, however, that no amount of chastisement would work. A slap was still given, just in case it did.

"So at what point were you going to tell us about the door button?" said Dissel, glaring at Forsta.

"Well, this isn't the first time the wrong folk had been locked in, so as the engineer, I decided to hide a 'get out' just in case," replied Forsta looking sheepish and kicking away some dust that wasn't there.

"Give me strength!"

***

Evening time had descended, and every resident of Lower Fitterton had managed to make it back home. This was a great comfort for everyone who didn't live at the 'Golden Years Nursing Home', as they were getting fed up hearing about how their 'bunions hurt' and that their gout was 'playing up something rotten'. The amount of 'Are we there yet?' followed by the crinkly unwrapping of butterscotch sweets had got unbearable from the elderly residents, so much so that even the young children of the village threatened that they would turn around and take them back to the spaceship. Under normal circumstances, the children's parents would chastise their children for such disrespectful words, but on this occasion, they felt it was warranted.

Big Frank and his daughter, Janine had walked into the pub carpark when Frank noticed that the pub doors were open. Janine felt a disturbance and looked down at her father, who was silently but visibly raging and had braced himself for a punch-up.

He swiftly marched up to the open doorway and burst in, shouting something about someone getting an 'ass-kicking' if he found them. Janine slowed down and waited to either hear that the coast was clear or the clattering of tables and chairs, closely followed by men running out holding either badly broken arms or cradling swollen eyes.

"What the bloody hell?!" rang out and Janine ran inside to see what had happened.

Janine dashed through the pub's front door and turning towards the main lounge, she saw her father standing in the doorway where there once were the lounge doors. Right behind her father, Janine stopped and noticed that the doors had been placed on the other side of the room and were propped up against the wall.

"I'll bloody have whoever did this!" Frank said with clenched fists.

Janine rested a comforting hand on her father's shoulder and worried for the poor soul if her father ever found the culprit.

Chapter 5

"So, let me get this right. Stoked is excited and 'the bomb' could be good or bad," God confirmed with his new friend, Travis.

Both the tuxedo-wearing Deity and board short wearing surf-dude were sitting under a rather large olive tree, somewhere in a quiet and leafy area of Heaven.

"True dat," said Travis as he inhaled the smoke from his lit spliff.

Never in his wildest dreams did the young surfer think he'd be sitting with the G-Man under an olive tree smoking cannabis, yet here he was.

"And gnarly tubes are quite aggressive waves when they break."

"Dude, you're getting the vibe maan... You sure you don't wanna try?" Travis held out the lit, rolled-up cigarette in God's direction.

"I'm good thanks, I'm feeling quite dizzy just with smelling the smoke... and a bit peckish too, I don't know why?"

God crossed his legs and rested his head on the tree trunk, closing his eyes as he did.

"So is life always like this for you?" God enquired.

"No dude," Travis took another drag on the cigarette. "Sometimes I just chill."

A plume of sweet smoke rolled into the air.

"But most of the time I'm on my broad catching a..."

"A gnarly tube?"

"Dude. You are the beezneez!" Travis smiled.

God wasn't too sure as to why being right meant he resembled parts of a pollinators' legs, but figured it was more surf-speak. Education was a good thing and change necessary, so today was a good day.

"Dude! Rad Plan!" a look of revelation came over Travis. "Beach party!"

Travis nipped the end of the reefer to extinguish it and turned to God.

"We need a beach party, dude!"

This raised the divine eyebrows.

"A beach party?... Err yes, sure, why not... What does it involve?"

Travis jumped to a kneeling position and faced his new best buddy.

"Oh, maan! You're gonna think you've died and gone to Heaven. There's waves, boards, chicks, kegs, music, and chicks... Did I say chicks already?"

"Yes, you did."

"Well, more chicks then."

God could see that Travis was getting 'stoked'.

"D'you have a beach round here? You need a beach for a beach party and waves! You need plenty of waves... Oh, and a fire and tiki lanterns for when it gets dark."

"I'm not too sure about an actual fire, but how about if it's like a bio-ethanol fire? Would that work?"

"Your crib, G-man, your rules," Travis smiled at God.

It was party time.

"Awesome! Party at the G-man's," smiled God and high-fived Travis.

"Oh dude, one thing maan. You gotta lose the tux. Its board shorts and bikinis."

God could see that Travis was serious about the dress code and figured it would have to be board shorts for him as a bikini was out of the question.

"I can do board shorts... dude," God paused with a puzzled and concerned look on his face.

"However, I'm not too sure what Peter will think of this. He can be a bit tense."

"Dude, Pierre has to chill maan. I'll get him there."

Travis reached into his pocket and produced his stash bag.

"Diggin' the vibe?" he continued with a wink.

The penny dropped and God gave a smile that conveyed mischief and a 'should we really do this?... Sod it! Why not!'.

God was right about St. Peter being a bit of a stickler for rules, more so with his register and who should be allowed through the pearly gates. It was made more tense when Steve (Death) who acted like one of those annoying delivery men who would leave parcels on your doorstep and a card through your letterbox claiming they were sorry they missed you. Steve did this now, which messed up Peter's system completely, much to the annoyance of the saintly gatekeeper.

"To heck with it. Let's do it!" God was sold.

"Hell yeah!... Oh sorry G-man, no offence."

"None taken... dude."

Chapter 6

Morning had come early for the village of Ashburn-on-Sinkhole. The sun had decided that today was going to be a productive day, as it had a lot to do. The moon would have normally argued this and put up a fight, claiming that night was as important as day and 'how dare he ask for more time'. However, on this occasion, the moon had had a tough one and was happy for the sun to take over.

Mist, that had been rising from the nearby fields, had started to slowly evaporate in the warmth of the rising sun's rays. It was a little early for the cows and sheep in their fields who were reluctantly waking up but had figured that if the sun was up, then surely it must be breakfast time.

Beyond the fields, in the woodland, the diurnal wildlife had stirred, and wondered what on earth was happening and 'why was it so bright at this time?'. All the birds had been caught on the hop, including the night owl who refused to believe it was daytime and continued with its nightly hooting.

The first sound from nature that called out that daytime was present was a wood pigeon who cooed and enquired as to what was going on at this time? This was closely followed by a crow who was awoken by the pigeon and crowed at the pigeon to shut up at such an ungodly hour.

This, in turn, woke a gang of sparrows, whose immature ways decided that if they were awake, so should everyone else be. Within a few brief moments, the entire woodland was a cacophony of nature sounds, all squawking, squeaking, chirping and any other sound that the creatures felt necessary.

The cows in the nearby field, hearing the woodland come alive, figured it would only be fair if they joined in the chorus with their lowing. The sheep soon followed suit with their bleating.

Don't be fooled when people say 'You should go to the country. The peace and quiet is so calming'. The countryside surrounding Ashburn-on-Sinkhole was anything but peaceful or calming.

***

Walter Hollybank, the village's only millionaire and steampunk fanatic, lived across from the woodland in his newly constructed mansion, that was built to appear old and stately. The slight man, in his maturing years, who had made his fortune by patenting the 'yawn', was asleep in his emperor size four post bed. Some would say that a man of his stature didn't need a bed so large, but Walter had designs on a certain Ms Hilda Swindlebrook and was determined to share his life, wealth, and bed with her.

Walter was fast asleep with his steampunk design silk eye mask on and wearing his favourite cotton nightshirt. It was unclear if it was the sun who had found the slightest of gaps in the heavy, crushed velvet, blood-red curtains and had shone through with the ferocity of a nuclear blast, or the chattering beasts outside that awoke him, but it was clear one of them had.

After removing his eye mask, the first vision to hit Walter's eyes was a black wet shiny nose and a pink panting tongue. Bertrand, his faithful Jack Russell, was always happy to greet his human. The morning had started, and Walter had a feeling that today was going to be a good one.

A smile grew on Walter's face as he remembered that today he was going to pick up the love of his life and drop her off at the Women's Institute, so she and Elsie Bagshaw could get the rooms ready for the clairvoyant show. The entire world would see Hilda getting out of *his* car. Well, the entire village anyway. One step closer to having this gorgeous lady in his life forever.

Down in the village, things began to stir too. Reginald Golightly had opened his newsagents and was carrying into his shop the recently delivered newspapers that had been dumped on his doorstep.

Betty Grisslebush had just opened her café, and with no help from her fat ginger cat, Ziggy, had taken out her tables and chairs for the morning's regulars. Ziggy did his best to make this operation far more difficult by laying across the threshold of the café and ensuring that Betty had to step over him whilst carrying the chairs.

It was too early for her regular outside customers, but she knew they would turn up soon, so things had to be ready. The aroma and sounds of sizzling bacon emanated from the kitchen, and there was always one customer who came early whenever it was an early opening for Buttercup Moonchild's Health Food shop.

Buttercup's brother, Dogweed, was always teasing his sister by window shopping at her vegan-friendly shop whilst he munched on a freshly made bacon and brown sauce sandwich, just as she would arrive and open up.

The same conversation would always take place, which usually ended with Dogweed saying he was 'just window shopping' and Buttercup storming into her shop, closely followed by her partner, Jensen. Dogweed would saunter back to his mini supermarket at the other end of the square with a devilish smile, knowing he had wound up his sister to boiling point.

As expected, Dogweed shortly turned up and after a friendly chat with Betty about how wonderful the day was and with a glint in his eye, like a 60-watt bulb, Dogweed smiled and bid his farewell. Betty watched, with a shaking of her head, as her first customer of the day wandered over to peruse the wares in the shop window only to be admonished by the store's owner.

It was a pleasant village with not much out of the ordinary happening, Betty thought to herself. She then realised that she was performing her first clairvoyant show the next evening at the Women's Institute. That, in itself, wasn't 'out of the ordinary' but for the fact that she had been able to do this because she had made friends with Bernie Aberline, who until recently was the local school's drama teacher.

Whilst Bernie *had* been the drama teacher, he was now the village ghost, and accompanied by another ghost Clarabelle, the very ex-village harlot, they had hatched a plan to put on a show and make Betty some serious money. All for the price of getting high on cannabis, of which *she* had to smoke and the two ghosts wander through the sweet-smelling exhaled smoke. This was far from the ordinary!

It hadn't been long until Stephen and Stewart visited Betty's and took their rightful seats outside.

"Morning, you two. Where's Sylas? Is he not joining you today?"

Betty was taken aback a little as the three elderly men went everywhere together. She actually enjoyed the friction between Stephen and Sylas as the two men bickered whilst Stewart would bury his head in his newspaper.

"I do hope he's ok," she continued.

"Morning Betty. I'm sure he'll be here soon," assured Stephen. "Could we have our usual please?"

"Of course, sweety. Coming right up."

As two-thirds of the trio settled down into their usual seats, Betty waddled back into the café with the order, humming a happy indecipherable tune.

"She does have a point, you know," Stewart said, with an air of mild concern.

"Oh, I'm sure the little ragamuffin will be up to some mischief somewhere. I just hope he's not harassing Elsie from the W.I." replied Stephen.

Noticing that Reg's newsagents was open for business, Stephen rose from his seat.

"I'll get the papers, including Sylas', as I'm sure that he'll be here shortly with some epic mishap that has befallen him," Stephen said with a sigh of resignation.

"Much obliged and I'll get the brews," replied his friend.

As Stephen wandered across the cobbled square, searching for his coin purse located somewhere in his

77

tweed jacket, Stewart waited for Sylas, the pots of tea, and his newspaper.

The sun had burnt through the haze and the day was well on its way to being a glorious one. Stewart was enjoying the fresh morning air as he sat at the usual table, facing the open café door. A kindly voice from behind him called out.

"Good morning, Stewart, are you well?"

Dr Ulysses Fletcher was making his usual morning visit to Betty's. It was just as well his dear friend Sylas wasn't here yet, as no doubt he would make some lurid comment about the doctor and Betty. Stewart smiled, turning around to face the doctor, and replied.

"Oh good morning doctor, I'm very well thank you, and yourself?"

Ulysses stopped at the side of the table, making it easier for Stewart to chat with him.

"Good thanks. I'm just here for my morning cuppa. Here alone today?" he queried.

"No... no such luck. Stephen has just gone for the papers and I have no idea where Sylas is."

"Oh, I'm sure he'll turn up. He'd hate to miss seeing me walk into the cafe and make some accusation about Betty and me."

"Ah, you know about that?" Stewart sat back in his chair and felt a little awkward.

"I may be getting on a bit, but there's nothing wrong with my hearing. In fact, speak of the Devil," Ulysses looked up and smiled. "Morning Sylas."

Sylas had just entered the square looking like a novice horse rider that had just done 8 hours in the saddle.

"Morning, Doc. You're just the person I need to see. Any chance of a private chat?"

Sylas hobbled up to the table like he had an invisible roll of carpet between his legs.

Stewart and Ulysses looked at each other with raised eyebrows.

"Sure, young man. Would you like to step into my second office?" came the reply as a left-arm pointed toward the quiet café.

Dr Fletcher followed Sylas into the café, leaving Stewart outside wondering what was ailing his dear friend.

Sylas looked around the café, to make sure that the proprietor was nowhere to be seen, and leant on the back of the chair with both hands and breathed a sigh of relief.

Dr Ulysses Fletcher visited Betty on a daily basis as not only was she a lovely owner of a very pleasant café, she was also a bit of a witch, and could make up potions that worked quicker and cheaper than normal prescriptions. More often than not, he would cure his patients with Betty's help rather than some rich pharmaceutical company.

Betty was in the rear kitchen of her eatery and getting together the doctor's daily batch when she heard the doc and Sylas chatting in her café. Respecting the privacy of both doctor and patient, Betty stopped what she was doing and listened intently.

"What seems to be the problem, Sylas," Ulysses said, taking a quick glance at the lower half of his present patient.

"Doc, I'm in so much pain. You gotta help me!"

Ulysses mirrored his patient and leant on the rear of a chair, a trick he'd learnt from one of those magazines that were usually found in his waiting room. Apparently, mirroring had something to do with making the patient feel at ease.

"I'm sure I can, old friend. What seems to be the problem?"

"It's like this," Sylas started, "Last night I had pie and mushy peas for my tea, along with a pint or two of stout."

"Yes," Ulysses said with his usual understanding tone, which always eased his patients.

"And I get a little windy, if you know what I mean afterwards... I fart like a bas..."

"Yes, I know what you mean," interrupted the doctor.

"Anyway, there was nothing out 'a ordinary last night, but this morning I woke and my guts were aching like a bugger. I was all bloated so figured all I need was to fart."

"And?"

"And I did... Doc, I think I've dislocated my arsehole!"

Ulysses Fletcher thought he had heard everything over his many decades of being a G.P., but as is always the case, there always something around the corner, and coming around today's corner was Sylas.

Suddenly there was a shriek from the kitchen, closely followed by Betty calling out.

"It's OK. I just slipped on some flour!"

Betty had overheard Sylas's problem and was bent double trying not to laugh, with one hand on her jiggling stomach and the other over her mouth.

"A dislocated anus, you say?" Ulysses' poker face came into play, with only a raised eyebrow to express his surprise.

"Doc, it's bloody murder. I can't walk, can't sit down, I just don't know what to do!" pleaded Sylas.

With a smile and a reassuring hand on his patient's shoulder, Ulysses gave Sylas his answer.

"Come see me in my surgery in about an hour. I'm sure I'll have something for you."

A pained but grateful smile came over Sylas' face.

"Thanks, Doc. I'll be there."

An exuberant hand shaking of the doctor's hand, and Sylas left the café to be with his friend, who had now been joined by his other friend and three newspapers.

Watching as the elderly man hobbled out, Ulysses smiled, and turned to meet his supplier of medicines in her kitchen.

"Betty, my dear, are you in here?" he called out as he wandered into the kitchen.

Betty was unable to reply and was struggling to breathe, she was laughing so much.

"I gather you heard then."

With a nod of the head, Betty admitted that she had, still trying not to laugh out loud for fear of being heard by the poor chap. With a quick raise of his eyebrows and allowing himself the briefest of smiles, Ulysses shrugged his shoulders as if to say 'hey ho!'

"So do you have anything for... a dislocated anus?"

The blue touch paper had been lit and Betty exploded into fits of laughter.

"You OK, Sylas?" enquired Stewart as his friend appeared from the café.

Stephen was sitting in his usual place at the table and had already started on his newspaper, glancing up to see his compadre.

"Been better, but I'd rather not talk about it if you don't mind," came the reply.

"Oki doke, not a problem. So are you sitting down?" Stewart said, moving Sylas's chair out from under the table.

"I think I'll stand, just for now if that's OK," replied the pain addled friend, gripping the rear of the chair with both hands and leaning on it.

The daily requested medications had been handed over to the village G.P. along with the short notice prescription for 'fire and brimstone haemorrhoids'. With a nod of a head, by way of thanks, Ulysses left the café, bidding his farewell to the three elderly men outside, and made his way back to his surgery.

"Y'know what. Bugger this. He said an hour but sod it, I'm off now," exclaimed the defiant Sylas and off he hobbled in hot pursuit.

Stephen looked up from his newspaper at his remaining friend and exchanged puzzled looks.

"Here we go, gents... Oh! Where's Sylas?" Betty had brought out the teas.

"Think he has a little problem. I'm sure he'll be back before his tea goes cold," replied Stewart.

The refreshments were placed on the metal café table and with a 'Thank you very much' from the two remaining men, Betty waddled back inside.

Chapter 7

The village square was reasonably quiet with just the birds singing, the rustling of newspapers, and Betty singing along to some tune on the radio.

"Morning gentlemen, and how are we today?"

Jeremiah Brown, aka Fast Eddie, had appeared from around the corner and approached his 'fine art' shop. Stephen was always glad to see Jeremiah as he had an affinity for the chap and the 'high class' that he portrayed.

"Jeremiah! We're good thanks, and how are you?"

Stephen always spoke to Jeremiah with a tone similar to that of a mother seeing her son's girlfriend for the first time. Overly posh.

Jeremiah smiled back whilst unlocking the shop door and replied,

"Tickety-boo Stephen. Absolutely, tickety-boo."

As the conman cum paint forger entered his shop, thoughts of Big Frank and why he hadn't heard from him in such a long time flashed across his mind. This ended with Jeremiah intending to contact the landlord soon to see if he wanted any more stock.

It was then he noticed a letter on the doormat. The same type of letter that had requested a certain piece of art from Italy... at any cost! Immediately, swooping down and retrieving the letter, Jeremiah quickly turned on the shop lights and, not breaking his gaze on the letter, made his way to his counter.

The aroma of lemons was thick in the air due to the well handwritten missive, and Jeremiah carefully opened the letter, breaking the wax seal. Behind the shop's counter and sitting on his shop stool, Jeremiah read the letter.

Gary, his mysterious client, had enquired as to an update on his soon to be acquisition. He had also anticipated the amount that was to be requested and had agreed to it. Even when Jeremiah had wondered how 'Gary' could have known the fee for getting the piece, the letter went on to say about not interrupting the letter. It was at that point the man's eyes widened and his jaw drop.

"Tomorrow?!" exclaimed Jeremiah. "He's coming tomorrow? It's not here yet! Oh, bloody hell!"

Jeremiah scrabbled for his mobile phone and quickly put in a call to a certain Edoardo. After several rings, the call was answered.

"Si?"

"Edoardo! It's..."

Click!

"Goddammit!! Not now, you Italian git!"

Several rings later.

"Si?"

"MONEY!!"

"...Si?"

"Have you sent the, you know what? The client is coming today and if you want paying, then it best be on its way!" Jeremiah was in no mood to play Edoardo's games.

"Si."

Jeremiah waited for an expansion to the last reply, but none came.

"When?! When did you send it?" nerves were getting frayed by the second.

"Last week. The usual way so, expect a tube any day now."

"Good God! That wasn't difficult now, was it? Why couldn't you just have said?"

"You didn't ask," came the calm reply.

Click!

Jeremiah glared at his mobile phone with an incredulous look.

'Piss off, you pompous git!' would have been heard from just outside J. Brown's Fine Arts shop if any passer-by happened to... pass by.

Jeremiah slammed his phone down on the countertop and wondered what he could do to avert a potential crisis. A client coming and no art to give him! No art meant no payment and with the figure he had come up with, which somehow was agreeable with his client, even though it hadn't been mentioned, could well be lost. If the piece wasn't here today, he would then have to put his client up somewhere nice until it did arrive.

His place was out of the question. Suddenly the idea came to him. The Blind Cobbler's Thumb! The rooms there weren't that bad, and they even had a really nice one. Yes, that'd do. Jeremiah jumped up from his seat and quickly made his way out of his shop, jogging down the square, slowing down when passing Stephen and smile calmly, just to maintain his lofty exterior with the silly old duffer. As he passed the elderly gent, Jeremiah resumed his jog.

Terry, the landlord of the village pub, was restocking the clean pint glasses on the shelf when a panicky knock came at the door. Shadow, Terry's German Shepherd, who was really a lazy wolf who couldn't be bothered hunting for food, was in the kitchen finishing off his breakfast, detected the knock, and came to investigate.

"'od y'orses! I'm coming!" shouted Terry to the panic-stricken knocking.

Over the noise of his knocking, Jeremiah heard the unmistakable sound of doors being unbolted so stopped trying to break the door down.

"Bloody hell mate, are you that desperate for a drink?" said Terry with a puzzled but friendly smile.

Jeremiah breathed a sigh of relief.

"No, nothing like that, but I do need your help, Terence. Is your best room available? Only for a day or two?"

Terry, being one for making his position seem bigger and better than it actually was, had a puzzled look on his face.

"Ah! I'm not sure, mate. I'll have to check my booking-in book."

Jeremiah rolled his eyes as he followed Terry into the pub.

"Yeah, that's right! Cause you're so busy here in this sleepy tiny village!" Jeremiah thought.

Terry went behind the bar and reached down for the ledger and opened up the book, flicking through a couple of pages. With a look of 'hmm not sure,' and sucking of his teeth, Terry asked.

"Soo... When are we looking as it seems quite busy?"

"Well... I have a very important client coming and he needs your best room for a day or two... Starting tomorrow."

"Mmm. I'll have a look but as I say..."

"Oh, come on, Terry. This is Ashburn, not London. No one comes here!" interrupted Jeremiah with an air of exasperation.

Feeling somewhat attacked by the comment, Terry fired back.

"No one, eh? Well, your 'client' is, isn't he?"

A little wink and a 'touché' smile from the landlord put Jeremiah in a position where tongue biting was necessary. With a resigned intake of breath, he replied in a calming way.

"Yes, OK, you're right. However, is the room free?"

Briefly flicking through the book, and thumbing down one page, Terry looked up with a smile.

"You're in luck, Jeremiah. It just so happens we have a cancellation so, yes, the room is available."

"Excellent!" Jeremiah smiled, "Book it for me and I'll pay the bill when my client goes. Just make sure he doesn't run up too much of a bar tab."

Jeremiah could feel the stress ebb from his body and a calm 'nailed it!' feeling washed over him.

Retrieving a pencil from the side of the cash register, Terry touched the nib of the pencil with his tongue and wrote in the empty book.

"And what name shall I write down as coming?"

Jeremiah realised he had no other name but 'Gary' for his client's identity.

"It's Gary. Just Gary. Y'know like Madonna and Prince? Just a single name."

Terry looked up with his eyebrows leading the way.

"Just Gary...oohhhkaaay. Gary, it is, mate."

"That's fantastic, thank you so much," Jeremiah replied with a broad smile.

"No problem. Anything for you, my old friend. I mean, that's what friends do for each other, isn't it? I scratch your back and... you scratch mine."

Jeremiah knew there would be a request for a discount on the stock that he sold to the landlord.

Jeremiah had managed to convince Terry that he could get very good quality counterfeit beer for cheaper than Terry sold it for. Terry, simply hearing the words 'cheaper' and 'counterfeit', and not the other words, had jumped at the chance of making a quick buck.

However, if he had listened, and if he had known where Jeremiah had got his stock from, which was the local 'cash and carry' he would soon realise that he could get the pub's stock cheaper by not having to pay for Jeremiah's cut and the delivery charge paid to Big Jake.

"How about five percent off your next order?"

"How about ten?" Terry bartered.

Jeremiah knew what he was willing to lose on Terry's order, and had just halved it, expecting Terry to double his offer to exactly what he wanted to lose, and no more. Jeremiah 'hmm'd' and 'ahh'd' making out that he was actually thinking of the offer, and with a pained grimace, purely to make Terry think he'd got a good deal, agreed.

"So, when are we looking at another order?" continued Jeremiah.

"By next Thursday if that's ok?"

"Let me just jot that down," Jeremiah replied, pulling a notepad out of his pocket, "The usual is it?"

"Fantacka!" said Terry with a smile, thinking he had got one over on his supplier.

"Lovely. Right, I'll get Big Jake to drop it off... and you'll look after my guest, won't you?" Jeremiah asked with an expression on his face that demanded, 'You *WILL* look after my guest,'.

"Oh most definitely," replied Terry with a look on *his* face that uttered, 'Yeah! Whatever!'

"So glad we got that sorted," Jeremiah nodded his head to say 'thank you' and turned to leave the pub.

"Oh, one more thing. Could you make sure my guest doesn't bump into your dog, Shadow? I think everyone is aware of the hound's flatulence and I'd rather that secret be kept to the villagers and not my guest."

"Dog fart. Got it!" said Terry with a nod and a wink.

As Jeremiah left the pub and returned into the brilliant sunshine that bathed the square, he saw Fergus Hamilton, the local postman, crossing the square behind the fountain. With a wave, Jeremiah called out to the visually impaired postman and jogged over to him.

"Fergus!... Fergus just one second of your time, if I may."

Fergus Hamilton and his wife Morag ran the local post office, Fergus delivering the mail whilst Morag sat behind the counter, dealing out stamps and taking in larger parcels. Both past retirement age, with Morag being very hard of hearing and Fergus not being able to see a Sherman Tank in a field full of sheep, may not have been the best people to run the post office but no one else wanted the job, so there they stayed.

Through his thick-lensed glasses, Fergus squinted in the caller's direction, and noticed a blurry brownish, pinkish blob approaching him.

"Can I help you?" he replied, not really knowing who he was talking to.

Jeremiah caught up with Fergus, slightly out of breath.

"I do hope so... Fergus, it's Jeremiah... from the art shop?"

Recognition spread across Fergus' face.

"Oh good morning, sir," Fergus was always polite.

"Oh! Yes, good morning. I was wondering if you had delivered a letter this morning that didn't have a stamp on it... With lovely handwriting."

Fergus pondered this for a second or two.

"Nope, sorry. I don't recall that one."

"A cardboard tube hasn't landed by any chance, has it?"

"Not that I'm aware of, but I'll ask the missus when I've finished my rounds."

"No, it's OK, I'll go see your lovely lady myself. Don't bother yourself, but thank you anyway."

Jeremiah bid Fergus a good day and walked across to the post office, passing a very bouncy Sylas who was heading back to the café and his friends.

"Good morning, gentlemen!" said Sylas as he reached the café table and his pot of tea that was still quite warm.

Both men turned to look at the chap with one of them smiling, Stewart, Stephen only smiled at well-to-do people as he considered anyone else below his own deluded lofty height.

"Is everything alright old lad?" Stewart enquired.

Sylas plonked his scruffy little body on the seat like someone dropping a sack of coal, having just stubbed their toe on a kerbstone.

"Bloody marvellous now. Tell y', that is one bloody good doctor," Sylas picked up his newspaper and thumbed to the crossword page.

**

Walter Hollybank's day had not gone according to plan. He had had every intention of picking up the love of his life, Hilda Swindlebrook, and dropping her off at the W. I. so she could work on the hall for tomorrow evening's clairvoyant show. Whilst this was happening, he didn't envisage having to pick up Elsie Bagshaw, Hilda's second in command as well. Bang went the wooing on the journey into the village.

**

The village square had had its morning rush hour, and things were settling down. The three men were busy with their crosswords and all the shops were now open for business. All residents of the village were hard at it, whatever they did, and the sun was in full swing.

Sylas started to chew the end of his pencil as his underactive brain red-lined on one of the clues.

"Here's a doozy," he said, looking at his friends for help and guidance. "Three letters and the clue is 'Feline'."

Stewart looked at Stephen and watched as his educated friend put his paper down and condescendingly raised his eyebrows in despair. Stephen always had an unwanted air of superiority, just waiting to be used for such occasions.

"OK. Here's a clue. Dogs hate them," he said.

Sylas looked at his clever friend and, upon receiving the extra clue, looked up to the sky for some divine guidance.

"Aha! Of course! Stephen, you're a gem! Three letters, feline, and dogs hate them," Sylas put pencil to paper. "V... E... T!"

"I give up!" said Stephen in despair and continued with his own paper.

Chapter 8

Hell had gone through some chaotic changes of late. Some may say that Hell was chaotic anyway, but up until recently even the demons who lived there were finding it hard. Lucifer had changed his name to Gary and had demanded that all his demons change their names to evildoers, the higher-ranking demon, the eviler the person's name.

He had gone from smart to slob and back to smart again, and this was all because of a plan that had gone slightly awry. Gary had tried to trick God into losing his white robe and long beard and adopt a more top secret agent tuxedo get-up. Whilst this worked, it worked a little too well and God was now rocking the new look. Envy then stepped in and Gary, who had been the smartest dressed of the two, had decided that the slob look was easier.

He had dressed down to a point where a pair of, not-so, white Y-fronts were his complete ensemble. On seeing and hearing the rave reviews God was getting with his new appearance, Gary decided that he would show God how to do it properly, and resumed his stylish ways.

Hell kept its citronella aroma as bio-ethanol was still replacing the normal sulphurous fuel which lit Gary's kingdom. It appeared that the 'eggy fart' smell had been too much even for the Prince of Darkness.

Deep within the bowels of Hell was Gary's throne room, come office, where he was holding court with De Sade, who was giving the daily KPI reports. Genghis was standing to attention at the door, whilst Adolf stood proudly to the left of Gary, who was sitting in a casual but regal way on his throne.

"... So whilst the 'snowflakes' appeared to be making their mark on the world, it would seem the population has now started to ignore them and even mock them. I suggest we create something whereby said 'snowflakes' can be seen to be right and the rest of the world bow down to their deluded superiority," concluded De Sade.

Gary had his chin resting on one hand whilst he tapped his lip whilst deep in thought, not about the snowflake issue, but his own matters.

"Forget the whiny little toads," he replied. "They're a bunch of useless idiots that seemed a good idea at the time, but when push comes to shove they just can't cut the mustard. The global population knows that and so do we... Let's move on... Let's revisit the 'goatee beard'... but this time let's give it to the women!"

De Sade simply looked at Adolf with a gaze that conveyed 'is he mad?', Adolf gave a slight shrug that luckily for him had gone unnoticed by Gary.

"OK... I'll see what I can do."

With a bow of his demonic head, De Sade left the room, wondering how on earth would women accept the 'goatee' look, let alone have the ability to grow one?!

As Genghis closed the door behind the bewildered demon, Gary got up from his throne and addressed the two remaining demons.

"I've decided to take a little road trip, only for a day or two, so the place will be left in your hands for that time.

I'm assuming that you two dunderheads can cope without too much disruption?" Gary turned to the two demons with a glare that said 'DO NOT screw up!'

Adolf and Genghis looked at each other in surprise. Gary had never left Hell before! Where was he going? And who would be in overall charge whilst he was gone?

"Big Bill will be delivering my car very soon,"

Hell's doorbell rang, only the once, as the sign on the gate had demanded.

"Well, speak of the Devil!"

Gary smiled and made his way out of the room, leaving two very puzzled demons behind.

As he reached the long, flame flanked, 'Walk of Shame' path that led to Hell's gates, Gary saw several souls waiting to come in and a little white postcard size item propped within the bars of the gate. Gary smiled as he knew who had dropped these souls off... Steve.

Another one of Gary's masterstrokes was making Death change his name to the one that most delivery men have. 'Y'see? By doing that, you can do what other delivery men do and not bother seeing the recipients but simply leaving a note stating that you were sorry you missed them and leaving the items on the doorstep.'

Steve soon came to the conclusion that he no longer had to see or speak to either Gary or St. Peter, and very quickly, was sold on the idea. Behind the small group of souls was a rather large man wearing a baseball cap and a clipboard in his hand.

The foreboding gates creaked open as Gary smiled at the waiting souls.

"Someone will be with you shortly, in the meantime, if you could get out of my way so I can see to this man," indicating to Big Bill.

"Ta very much. Just sign 'ere, pal."

The clipboard was handed over and signed. With a tug on the peak of the baseball cap, Bill removed the trade plates from the very expensive-looking hypercar and disappeared into the darkness.

Gary stood in awe of the four-wheeled black Italian beast that presented itself to him.

"The Demone Infoucato! Now, you *are* a little beaut!" smiled Gary, eyeing the car and all its splendour.

"Gary!"

Adolf and Genghis came running up the path, slightly breathless, having argued as to who would be in charge of who.

"Just sort it between yourselves, I'll be back soon. And don't do anything stupid."

Gary got into the car but before closing the door he smiled at the group of souls, who were wondering what the hell was going on.

"These two will look after you, now be good damned souls and do what they say or I'll deal with you myself when I get back. Oi! You two. Don't ever let the flames go out... or else!"

With a solid thud, the car door was closed and the roar of the engine came to life, thrusting the car into the darkness, its tyres screaming whilst they tried to grip whatever road was available.

Adolf and Genghis looked at each other and then at the group of bewildered souls.

"Right, you 'orrible lot. Get your arses in 'ere NOW!" shouted Genghis, with a fire in his eyes that even spooked Adolf.

Chapter 9

Morning in Ashburn had been in full swing for some time when afternoon decided to come and join in. The sun didn't care less as to who was in charge, whether it be morning or afternoon as it was still enjoying itself, beaming down at the village who were happy to be warmed by it.

Stewart, Sylas, and Stephen had left Betty's establishment and Betty herself was busy keeping all the tables and chairs dust free with a white tea towel.

With her back to the front door, Betty didn't see Bernie Aberline enter the café. In fact, nobody did. Only Betty could see him... if she was facing him.

"Morning Betty, or is it afternoon?" Bernie called out with no warning.

Betty jumped up and pirouetted with her hand planted firmly on her voluminous bosom to face her visitor.

"Jesus Mary, Mother of God! You nearly scared me to death!"

"Oh, I'm so sorry!" replied the sheepish spirit.

Bernie hadn't quite mastered this ghost malarkey yet and was still quite a novice at it, even though he did have a little help from the ex-village harlot, and now his ghostly friend, Clarabelle.

"Look! Just announce yourself and *not* in a grand way. Just a little cough will do. Especially, if you creep up behind me," Betty explained, calming down and realising she had upset her new 'cash-cow'.

Since Bernie had died, and it was only Betty who could see or speak to him, he decided that since she made such wonderful cream cakes, he would stay rather than go 'up' or 'down'. Anyway, he was having fun with his newfound status, plus helping his friend in her new venture meant getting high, which he found out was down to the secret element in the cakes.

Bernie was pretty sure that would never happen in Heaven. The secret ingredient, being a certain illegal herb which due to Bernie's exuberant nature whilst alive, was baked solely for him in the hope of calming him down. Now being a ghost, the only way to get the sensation that Bernie enjoyed was for Betty to smoke a 'herbal' cigarette and blow the smoke in Bernie's direction. A small price to pay for Betty if Bernie was going to help her with her new line of business.

"OK, promise. Anyway, I thought I'd just pop and see you just to let you know that Clarabelle has been chatting to some of the guys in the graveyard and they were more than happy to come to tomorrow evening and help out. They even said that it would be nice to chat with someone else other than themselves, as it had been getting boring lately. This kind of ended in a tussle between a few of them who hadn't liked the fact that others thought they were boring. I, myself, enjoy all this ghosting thingy, but I suppose it's still new to me."

Bernie was a bit of a chatterbox, which was the reason why the cream cakes were suggested in the first place... by the entire village.

Betty was a kindly soul, but even with her patience, Bernie did push her boundaries.

"OK, OK, Bernie. So long as there's going to be no fisty-cuffs tomorrow. Not that anyone would see, but I'd find it difficult to explain why the show had to end so quickly."

"Oh, Clarabelle said she'd sort it out in her own way. I'm not too sure what she meant, but it's in her hands now."

"I'm sure it would be, Bernie," replied Betty with a knowing smile.

"Anyway, I just thought I'd pop in and say that. I'll be going now as Clarabelle said she'd be done within the hour and she would then give me another lesson in ghosting. You'd think it was easy, being a ghost, but I gotta tell you, there's loads which they never tell you about!" and with a smile and a little wave, Bernie left the café.

"God, he's hard work at times," muttered Betty and carried on with her cleaning.

***

Jeremiah had just finished an email regarding a Mondrian piece of art when his 'other' business mobile phone buzzed on the shop's counter. Big Frank's name flashed onto the phone's screen, which pleased Jeremiah as that could only mean one thing, business.

"Morning Frank. I thought you'd disappeared off the face of the Earth," said Jeremiah with a chuckle.

"How d'you know?" replied Frank.

105

"Sorry? Oh well, never mind, how can I help you?"

"It's order time fella, but this time can I have double?" came the voice from the phone's earpiece. "But because I'm ordering double, I'd expect a bit of discount."

"Everyone wants something for nothing these days!" thought Jeremiah, realising that he was actually conning him in the first place.

"I'm sure I could sort something out for you. Is there a party going on?"

Big Frank leaned on the bar of his beloved pub and surveyed the damage.

"Nope, but expect large orders from now on. We're going to be England's own Roswell."

Thinking that Frank had misplaced his marbles, Jeremiah ignored the last bit and primarily focused on the bit about 'large orders,'.

"OK Frank. Sounds very interesting. I've got your previous order so I'll just double it and get it to you soon. You know the score, just pay Big Jake when you see him."

"Yeah, yeah, I know the score. Oh, by the way. You haven't heard of anyone going around trashing pubs, have you?"

Puzzled by this, Jeremiah replied,

"No, sorry I don't... but if I do, I'll be sure to let you know."

"Good lad. It seems I need to have a chat with someone about visiting my pub whilst I was out of town. Right, I'm off, let's know when you'll be dropping it off. Make it soon though, alright?"

Click!

Jeremiah looked at his phone with disdain.

"Why, oh why, does everyone have to hang up on me?!"

Chapter 10

Kenneth Turnkey was Ashburn's star mechanic. Well, their only mechanic, but could fix anything... literally anything. Such was his prowess that a rumour had slowly and silently spread, like a raging bull with Deep Heat sprayed on his nether regions, that he had been 'asked' by American secret agents to visit Nevada and in particular a 'certain' hanger and fix something that 'wasn't there'.

Kenneth disappeared for two weeks, having been escorted from 'Turnkey's Garage' by two suited men wearing dark glasses and some curly wired earpiece protruding from their ears. They were definitely American by the sound of their voices when one muttered into the cuff of his dark suit, 'Foxtrot, Romeo, Oscar,' and the other muttering, 'Lima, Oscar, Bravo'.

Kenneth, as good as he was with anything mechanical, was ridiculously bad with directions and even though he had run his garage for thirty years, he still needed young Shifty Miller to escort him there. Shifty was the eyes and ears of the village, but nobody knew this as all Shifty would say was "Nuffin" and "Shifty. Shifty Miller". That was until the day that the two dark-suited American men arrived and took Kenneth on a two weeks paid vacation. Shifty at that point decided to break his silence, purely for this one occasion.

When asked where he had been, Kenneth suddenly appeared a little nervous and simply replied, stating that they were his nephews and had come to pick him up so he could fix their mother's car. He ended with a definite confirmation that it had *nothing* to do with a UFO, Roswell, and something to do with 51 acres!

It had just turned afternoon when Kenneth thanked Shifty for getting him to his garage once again. It was a little late in the day, but as Kenneth still couldn't find his way there, he knew he would have been much later without young Shifty. As he turned to thank his escort, his usual attire made the ruffling sound that only blue oily boiler suits can make. With his right hand outstretched and his magnified eyes peering through his thick-lensed spectacles, Kenneth smiled.

"Thanks, young Shifty. Where would I be without you?"

"God knows," thought Shifty, but gave a shrug as his reply.

In Kenneth's right hand was an even oilier folded five-pound note which would have been given to Shifty if he had shaken the young man's hand, but Shifty having eyes like an out-house rat simply raised his hands and said 'Nuffin'.

"Are y' sure lad? You help me out so often, it's the least I could do."

Shifty smiled, shook his head, and waved as he turned to head towards Ashburn.

"He's a good'n," muttered Kenneth with his back toward his garage, "Now where's mi shop?"

A raised hand from the leaving youth pointed to the ram-shackled building behind Kenneth.

"Thanks, lad," shouted the mechanic, and he turned to make his way to the double doors of his beloved workshop.

The garage doors were secured with a hefty padlock, and reaching into his trouser pocket to retrieve the padlock key, something shiny caught Kenneth's eye in the adjacent farmer's field. With a look similar to that of a mole sniffing the air, having just come from underground, Kenneth peered at the crash-landed UFO.

"And what the bloody hell are you doin' 'ere, my little beauty?" he muttered, looking at the craft with its nose buried in the ground.

Kenneth gave a wry smile as he figured a job was on the cards. He put the padlock key back in his pocket, pulling out an oily rag, and wiping his hands on it before clambering over the small wooden fence separating his gravelly forecourt from the adjacent field. With his eyes firmly fixed on the silver disc, he casually approached the craft.

"I know this model," he said to himself through squinting eyes, "Oh yes, I'll have you sorted in next to no time."

Kenneth finished wiping his hands and approached the side of the craft and with a wave of his hand in the exact location, a seal appeared and the door opened. Poking his head inside, looking to see if there was anyone there who he could chat with.

"'Ello? Anyone in? Want 'and fixing this? Seems someone d'unt know where 'brake pedal is."

The old mechanic climbed on board the craft and headed towards the bridge.

"Oi! Captain Kirk! You 'ere? Bloody hell! It smells like a toilet in here and b' looks of it, it was used as one too!" he said, trying to waft the odorous stench away from his nose whilst eyeing the puddles of urine close to the screen.

Secretly having worked on the same model of craft in a place that 'didn't exist' before, Kenneth knew the craft inside out and started to explore the rest of the vessel, in search of its occupants.

"C'mon y'little buggers, where are ya?" he called out.

The three aliens who were in the kitchen having a cup of something alien, warm and brown, were trying to figure out how they were going to get their damaged craft working again. Suddenly, Dissel's eyes lit up.

"Did you hear that?"

"I did!" replied Forsta.

"I wasn't talking to you," fired back Dissel with a glare.

"'Ello? You lot having a synchronised dump? Ooh bugger, That's the wrong door switch. Bloody hell! That's rank!"

Quickly slamming the holding cell door shut as the smell of urine and butterscotch hit Kenneth's nose like a perfectly landed punch from a prizefighter and burying his nose in the palm of his hand, the earthling protested.

"Jesus and saints preserve us! Don't these guys know that the toilet is next door?"

"We're fully aware, thank you!" came the terse reply from the nearby kitchen.

Dissel was both relieved and annoyed that such a lower life form would ask such a question. Turning to see the kitchen door open and three dejected aliens sat around a table, Kenneth approached the trio.

"Alright then, fellas. Had a little accident have we?"

All three aliens stared at the earthling with a look that conveyed a desire to punch the man. Luckily for Kenneth, and the aliens, these looks were wasted on him as he couldn't see any difference in their little grey faces.

"Oki doke you three," Kenneth said eyeing up the three aliens, "If you come with me, I'll get mi truck and tow you t' mi garage, and get this sorted for you. I'll have it as right as rain before y'know it." Kenneth smiled and started to make his way towards the exit.

"Do you know this man, Dissel?" queried the nervous Forsta.

"Oh yes! Of course I do. I go round to his home for a chat every time I'm passing this planet."

"Really?!" Forsta's eyes widened in surprise.

"No! Not really! You federschit! How in Quintok's name would I know this earthling?!"

This was quickly followed by a slap round the back of Forsta's head.

"I did wonder," replied the alien, rubbing the freshly struck part.

The three aliens jogged after Kenneth, who had now disappeared around the corridor whistling a non-distinct tune.

113

After half an hour of trying to find the mechanic's garage, retrieving the tow-truck, and dragging the craft back to the workshop, with directions from the head alien, Kenneth managed to get the dented craft safely in the garage, behind closed doors.

"Right you three, 'afore a start on this little beaut, it's cuppa time. Want a brew?" questioned the man as he wandered toward the rear of the workshop.

The three aliens looked at each other in puzzlement, wondering how this earthman could even think he could fix their disabled craft, and what the hell was a cuppa or a brew? Dissel thought it was his place to take charge, and that this was the only 'earthman' he had come across who wasn't the slightest bit scared of the aliens. He wasn't pleading not to be anally probed! With a smile and a nod, Dissel thanked the human for his kindness.

Turnkey's Garage was a typical ramshackle place with the main working area taking up most of the space, apart from a lean-to wooden office just to the left of the double door entrance. Unlike most independent garages of this sort, Kenneth did not have a calendar with some semi-clad young lady posing provocatively on it and covered in oily thumbprints.

Kenneth was more interested in the calendar and posters he had on display; old petrol engines with close-up shots of spark plugs and, as he considered, very sexy carburettors.

Along the rear wall, underneath a mezzanine, was a full-length workbench with hardly an empty spot, as it was covered in oil cans and numerous tools dating back from the late 1960s to gleaming modern ratchets. Behind the office and leading up to his sparsely occupied parts storage area was a rickety wooden stairway that even field mice thought twice about going up, just in case it collapsed.

The whole garage was decorated in a fine layer of heavily used oil and had a smell about it you could only get after years of passionate vehicle fixing. The place was the antithesis of its latest customer's vehicle, which was now positioned carefully over the garage's inspection pit.

Kenneth made his way over to the far left corner under the stairs, where a once-white kettle stood to attention, along with a platoon of chipped mugs huddled around it and flanked by another once white microwave oven.

"Only have tea, I'm afraid," said Kenneth, looking back at his latest guests, "Strong and milky. You alright with that?"

The three aliens looked dumbfounded at each other and with all three shrugging, agreed it was the only way to have it. Four mugs were cleaned with an oily rag, produced from Kenneth's pocket, and a teabag popped into each mug. Kenneth's tea bags were like everything else in the garage and had seen better days. They appeared to resemble something that had been in a fight with a psychotic otter and badly lost. Kenneth opened and reached into the microwave, and pulled out a carton of milk, which after sniffing and wincing a little, placed it by the awaiting mugs.

"Is that what I think it is?" asked Forsta, pointing at the microwave oven.

"This old thing? A microwave oven? Aye, but I only use it for putting mi milk in," replied Kenneth.

Forsta chuckled and was swiftly rebuked by Dissel with a swift flick of the back of his hand in his groin area. Forsta stopped chuckling and leant forward in some discomfort, whilst muttering something that sounded like "ooh you b"

"A microwave oven... Do you know that we gave you that technology a long time ago?" started Dissel.

"But it wasn't for warming up whatever 'cold pizza' is," continued Pitrol.

Dissel and Pitrol waited for Forsta to continue, but the backhander that had been issued had taken the wind out of the alien, so after a pregnant pause, Dissel continued.

"It is actually a form of propulsion. One we used aeons ago."

Kenneth's eyes lit up.

"We gave you this so you could transport yourselves to our planetary system. We figured that if we gave you it and you could work it out, then you would be ready to explore the rest of the universe. However, here we are, several decades later, storing your white liquid in a metal box, along with the technology you have to traverse the cosmos."

Dissel's last comment came across disappointingly, which Kenneth quickly picked up on.

"Propulsion, you say? An engine?"

The cogs in Kenneth's head started to whir.

"If I fix your craft, will you show me how it works?"

Dissel and Pitrol looked at each other, and with a nod of agreement, accepted the offer. Kenneth's face beamed. A new form of an engine with intergalactic power? Oh, boy, was he going to be happy tinkering with that.

"So, how's it work?" Kenneth asked as he passed the steaming mugs around.

Dissel looked inside his mug to see the tiniest of oil slicks floating on his hot dark brown liquid. Pleasantly surprised by the pretty colours dancing on the surface of his brew, he smiled and looked at Kenneth.

"There is a long way and a quick way to inform you but I think..."

"Quick way, fella... please. Hurry up and dun't spare 'orses," Kenneth was as eager as a child outside an 'all you can eat' sweet shop.

Kenneth passed his mug to Forsta, who had now recovered from his testicular discomfort, Dissel approached the smiling wide-eyed mechanic. As he raised his hands to touch Kenneth's temples, Kenneth could no longer contain himself.

"Oh, bloody hell! I've got a fizz on."

Not quite sure what this meant, Dissel continued and place his index fingers on each of Kenneth's temples. An internal flash of light thundered across Kenneth's synapses, and suddenly it all made perfect sense.

"Well, crap in mi shoes and call me Barbara!" exclaimed the enlightened mechanic, looking upwards in awe.

None of Kenneth's guests knew what this meant and wondered if Dissel had gone too far and fried the human's brain.

"Right. Sup up and I'll crack on wi' it. If you lot want to stop upstairs until I've done, you're more than welcome to. I'm sure I've some sacking up there that you can use for bedding. Unfortunately, I reckon I'll need parts and I'll not be able to finish it today."

The three aliens examined the perilous ascent they'd have to make and decided that it may be easier to stop downstairs rather than face earth's gravity head-on mixed with a shower of wooden splinters.

"Suit y'selves."

Kenneth picked up his pencil and a scrap of paper and started scribbling down all the parts he'd require.

Fifteen minutes later, Kenneth was in his little office on his telephone chatting to someone called Lenny and asking that the parts be delivered as soon as possible, whilst the three intergalactic travellers settled back with their mugs of tea.

Chapter 11

For all external appearances, Hell seemed to be its usual chaotic and hellish place. However, in the throne room, tensions were rising and so was to volume of the debate going on in there.

"Look, I know what Gary said, but I do think that I should take overall command. I am number two when it comes down to it," pitched Adolf.

"Oh, you're a number two alright," replied Genghis, "This place has been managed in a precise and regimented way and it should remain that way, so it's me who should be in charge."

"Two points. One, it is 'I' not 'me' who should be in charge, and two, this is Hell and should be chaotic and hellish, not a regimented boot camp." Adolf had an air of superiority.

Genghis looked puzzled.

"So you're saying you shouldn't be in charge? And what's wrong with a boot camp? Gary had me make it like that so we got everyone in and in the right areas of torture."

"What?! I never said I shouldn't be in charge. Look, I have the tools to be in control and you don't."

Adolf's air of superiority was looking more like frustration.

"Yes, you did. You said, and I quote, 'not me who should be in charge'. Also, when it comes to tools, I have to admit you're right. You are a tool, that's for sure." Genghis displayed a confident smile.

Just then, there was a timid knock on the throne room door. Adolf, whose temper had passed simmering and was on full boil, stormed over to the door and opened it to see a cowering demon called Gacy.

"Not now, you little sh..." The door was slammed shut.

Gacy was a lesser demon who was in charge of procuring the fuel for Hell's flames and needed a signature on the order form before he could get any. He had the appearance of a red tennis ball with spindly arms and legs, and a nose that would look good on a snub nose pig. Gacy was not what you would class as a 'good looker'.

The disgruntled demon was staring at the door that had been slammed in his face and feeling thankful for his snub nose, for if he had had a normal one, it would have been broken by that point.

"Only wanted to get a signature for the fuel. You, silly arse," Gacy muttered.

Gacy turned to walk away and as he did, Gary's little joke was noticed all along the corridor. For the damned soul of his, Gacy could not understand why Gary would attach bicycle horns to his heels so as he walked anywhere, you could hear a squeaky honking sound with every step.

"Silly arse. Oh well, we'll just be a little cooler down here. Not my fault," muttered Gacy as he honked off down the corridor.

120

"Who's that?" demanded Genghis.

"Gacy, anyway, as I was about to say..."

"What d'he want?"

"How the home should I know?! That little toad is always wanting Gary to sign stuff. Bloody jobsworth! Anyway, I did not say *I* didn't want to be in charge. I was correcting your grammar."

"What she got to do with this?"

"Who?"

"My grandma."

"What the bloody home are you on about?!" Adolf's blood was boiling to a point of steam.

"Hey! You brought the daft old bat into this conversation, not me!" Genghis fired back.

Gacy had honked back to his demonic office and slumped down in his office chair. Berkowitz, his second in command, glanced up from his desk with a questioning look and ducked as a stapler came flying past, nearly hitting the side of his head.

"Don't ask," demanded Gacy.

"It's just that we're down to one d..." Berkowitz ducked again as a chair came whistling over his head.

"D'you think I don't know we've only one day's fuel left?! We can't do anything until we get the order form signed and as Gary is out for however long, I have to deal with bloody Laurel and Hardy up there. It's a bloody nightmare! Can we just see if we can stretch it out a little more? Gary'll be back soon and he can sort it out."

Berkowitz, picking up the chair and retrieving the now broken stapler, gave Gacy a sharp intake of breath, the type that only garage mechanics do when they're looking at a customer's car.

"We can try... I'll do what I can. I'll get Manson and one of his 'oppos' onto it."

Gacy gave a resigned sigh, not really listening to the subordinate.

"Whatever. It's just gotta last."

***

The sun had had a long hard day and decided that it was time to retire for the day and let nighttime have a go. Nighttime, however, wasn't quite ready, and asked dusk to cover only for an hour or two whilst it prepared itself. Dusk was overjoyed at the fact that it had been asked to cover as it felt that it was an under-used commodity, so agreed without hesitation. It was decided that dusk would be warm and balmy as it felt that if it could a good job then maybe it may be asked to cover again.

PC Rick Higgins was off duty that evening and decided that as it was such a lovely evening, he should take his lovely wife, Felicity, to the pub for a drink. Not wanting to go to The Blind Cobbler's Thumb, Felicity suggested they try The Hammer and Tong in the neighbouring village of Lower Fitterton. Desperate for a pint, Rick was happy with the suggestion, and shortly afterward both were ready and riding along in the rear of Irvine Collier's gold Ford Cortina estate taxi.

"Anyway, I said to Thatcher, I said, Maggie, listen, don't let your son go out there in that desert, he'll get lost, but did she listen? No, she bloody didn't, and look what happened. Anyway, next time she was in my taxi she tapped me on my shoulder and apologised then asked my thoughts on privatisation, well I..."

"Just drop us off here Irvine would you," Rick interrupted Irvine's monologue.

"Oh, you sure? The pub's on'y round t' corner," replied Irvine.

"Yes! Yes, I'm sure, thanks, Irvine. How much d'we owe you?"

Irvine smiled at the couple through his rearview mirror.

"For the local copper and his lovely wife? Give over, it's a pleasure. Oh, Mrs Higgins? I've been working on a subject that you could teach your kids in class."

Felicity was a kind woman and although she had heard enough from, as she said in her head and not out loud, this 'gobshite', she agreed to listen.

"Well, this Einstein bloke got it all wrong with his e=mc2..."

"Thanks, Irvine I'm sure that's an interesting theory. I'll give you a shout when we want picking up," butted in Rick, as he ushered his wife out of the back of the car.

"No problem, you two... See y'then."

The couple watched as the Ford Cortina trundled off up the street and made their way towards the pub. Moments later, their path was lit by the headlights of Big Jake's

Morris Traveller as it left the rear of the carpark, with the behemoth of the man behind the wheel. Big Jake recognised the couple as he left, gave a cursory wave and continued on his way.

"He's a nice man," Felicity smiled.

"Irvine?!"

"No dafty. Jake. He's always a gentleman with everyone. Sort of a gentle giant."

"He's bloody huge!"

"Mmm, I just get the feeling that there's more to him than meets the eye."

"I'm not too sure about that. The way that his jeans fail to hide the crack of his arse, I doubt there's much more you'd want to see."

Rick took hold of his wife's hand as they entered The Hammer and Tong.

***

Steve had annoyed St. Peter at the pearly gates of Heaven once again. Seventy demonstrators, who had decided to protest about the wrong dictator, were now complaining at being dumped there with a 'Sorry we missed you' calling card. Steve was on his merry way when he heard his mobile phone ring out. Every part of his cloaked skeleton sagged when he heard the ring tone.

"Ohhh, crap!" Steve tapped his phone, "What now, Gary?"

"Steve, my old mate, how's it hanging?"

"What d'you want now, Gary? What's that sound in the background?" Steve queried.

"Oh, that'll be the car's engine. I'm having a little road trip."

"What?! You on a road trip? What's goin' on there?"

Steve's eyebrows would've raised if he had any.

"Doesn't matter, mate. Anyway, I've just rung to let you know that the little incident in Lower Fitterton a while ago? Well, they're all back now if you want to pay 'em a visit."

Death, as he was called then, was supposed to have taken the entire village when an alien craft *should* have crash-landed there, wiping out the whole village, but because of a miscalculation, had collided with a passing asteroid instead. Annoyed that he had wasted his time looking for any soul, alive or dead, in the village, Steve thought that a stern talking to was going to take place. It was clear that Gary was only telling him this so that trouble would ensue, so Steve thought it better not to thank him as the 'Prince of Darkness' would consider it as a 'favour owed'.

"Right, I suppose I ought to have a chat with 'em," replied Steve in a non-committal way.

"Na! You're welcome. Anything for an old friend and they don't come much older than you. Anyway, how's the delivery service going?"

Click!

"Steve?... Steve?... You there?"

125

Gary tossed his phone onto the passenger seat and smiled. As he drove along, he figured he'd got time to pay North Korea a quick visit before he needed to be in Ashburn-on-Sinkhole.

***

Rick and Felicity had just sat down in The Hammer and Tong with their drinks and were settling in for a pleasant night. As the murmuring of patrons and the sound of Patsy Cline warbling from the jukebox filled the air, a tall dark cloaked figure entered the lounge. Just like the horror films of the 1970s, everyone stopped what they were doing and looked at the stranger. This unnerved Steve a little, but after what this bunch had done by wasting his time, he decided to continue with firmly rebuking the lot of them.

"Can I 'elp you fella?"

Big Frank was leaning on the bar from the other side and chatting to one of the regulars.

"Who's in charge here?" boomed Steve, removing his scythe from the inside of his cloak.

Big Frank stood up and puffed up his chest defiantly.

"I am. What's it to do with you?"

Frank then noticed the scythe.

"'ere! Did you do this?" pointing to the damaged pub lounge. "Well?... Did you?"

Steve recalled being in a rage when he entered the pub, damaging the doors when he was on the look-out for some souls.

"Err..."

Big Frank looked right into where Steve's eyes should have been. Steve watched as Frank stepped down from his little step ladder that he used, so he could lean on the bar, and walk into the public area.

"Well?... I'm talking to you... bony!" demanded Frank with piercing eyes.

Even though Steve was shocked at how far he had to look down at his aggressor, which under normal circumstances, he would have just laughed at, he felt a little trepidation. A prod in the sternum of the cloaked figure dislodged one of Steve's calling cards that floated down to the ground. As the name 'Death' clearly held more gravity than 'Steve', Steve reverted to his old name.

"Listen 'ere you little munchkin. I am Death! How dare you talk to me like that..."

"I'll talk to you however I feel, bony. Now, answer my bloody question! Did you cause this damage to my pub?"

"I am DEATH!" thundered Steve.

"No, you're not!" came the firm school mistress's voice of Felicity. "Your name is Steve and you're a delivery man!"

Felicity had seen the descending calling card, swiftly picked it up and waved it in his face.

"What?!" Steve was on the back foot. "Err... no really, I am Death!" he protested.

"Answer my bloody question! Did you cause the damage to... my... pub?"

Rick felt it was time that he intervened.

"Right, fella. You don't have to say anything..."

"Oh, don't you start!"

Suddenly Felicity shot up out of her seat,

"Hold it one-second, gobshite! You talk to my husband like that and I'll ram a pool cue so far up your arse you'll be sneezing chalk dust for a month!"

No one in the pub had ever seen Felicity fly off the handle like that before, and a few of the patrons would have been quite happy if they hadn't seen it this time. The fire in her eyes gave away the message that maybe this petite young lady may not be the one to tussle with. Even Big Frank was taken aback.

Steve was getting a little irked by this, and a little concerned for his own wellbeing, so with a wave of his skeletal hand, the entire pub suddenly came to a halt. Every person, even Patsy Cline, suddenly stopped. Steve noticed a gentle relief come over him.

"Right. Now I have your attention. I should have taken the bloody lot of you, but as it is, and I now see it wasn't your fault, I'll let you off this once. BUT! If this happens again, I'll not be so forgiving. D'you understand?" he said, pointing a bony finger at his opponent. "And you, you fiery tart!"

Steve threw up two bony fingers in defiance towards her.

Big Frank didn't reply, but only because he was unaware as to what was said. Steve had the ability to stop time completely, so as far as Frank and Felicity were aware, nothing had been said.

"Take this as your final warning. I'm leaving now, but I'll keep my eye on you and if ever you step out of line?... I'll have ya, you little shit!"

Big Frank's angry gaze stared into the abyss as Steve turned and walked out of the pub, with the speed of a child running upstairs having watched a scary film and had just turned the lights off. As Steve was leaving the pub and making sure he was clear of the establishment, he waved his hand and time started back on its usual momentum.

Big Frank took a step back in puzzlement as the prime suspect for his damaged, beloved pub had somehow simply disappeared without a trace.

"Where the bloody hell's 'e gone?!"

As Steve continued to walk away from the pub, he heard the bellowing voice of the landlord and fearing for his safety, quickly tore a hole in the fabric of space with his scythe, and disappeared.

***

Gary had just entered the demilitarised zone of Korea when his phone blasted out the Bohemian Rhapsody ringtone.

"Steve, my old bony friend. How can I..."

"Change your name to Steve you said. Make life easier, you said. Oh, what a great idea. Oh yes, absolutely bloody marvellous! You ARSE!"

Click!

Gary studied his phone and with raised eyebrows and with an 'Oh well', continued to drive past the armed guards at speed whilst they raised their weapons and shouted something in Korean.

Chapter 12

The Blind Cobbler's Thumb was having its usual steady night. The regulars were there, along with the semi-regular guest, a bearded man called Martin, who had written a book about 'Prodding a Vampire', according to Liam, the glass collector of the pub. Terry had decided to pluck up the courage and approach his patron and ask him about this book thing and why would anyone want to prod a vampire.

"Alright fella? Is it dead?" Terry said, pointing at the empty whisky glass on the table.

"It is matey, thanks. Oh, any chance of another?"

"Sure, no problem," Terry paused. "I see you've got your notebook. Liam, our glass collector, said you were writing a book about prodding a vampire or something."

"Yeah, something like that," Martin chuckled. "Anyway, it's out now and I'm onto my second book."

"So you're an author, eh?" Terry's eyes widened. "Any chance you could put me in your next book? I reckon I'd make an excellent character."

"I'm sure I could work you into my next one mate," came the reply with a wry smile.

Terry beamed and turned to walk to the bar.

"Nice one. This whisky is on me, mate. Thanks... Oh, how about if I play a spy or hard-man? Something like that?" he smiled, looking back at the writer.

"Like your thinking. Let me figure something out for you."

Terry had poured and delivered the whisky as Jeremiah entered the bar area.

"Good evening, Terence. Nice night, don't you think?"

Terry had just returned behind the bar and smiled.

"Not so bad, Jeremiah. How's it going? The usual?"

"Oh, go on then. Just a single this time... Oh, by the way. Is everything ready for my guest tomorrow?"

Terry placed a single malt whisky on the bar and gave a confident sigh.

"Yess! Don't worry, everything is alright. Spick and span, as they say. Whatever spick and span is."

"It's 16th century Dutch. It means..." replied Jeremiah, who didn't take kindly to Terry's sigh.

"OK, never mind. It's 16th century Dutch then," interrupted the landlord who wasn't keen on some toffee-nosed git who was trying to show him up.

Jeremiah swiftly downed the drink and smiled an insincere smile.

"Thank you, Terence. Put it on my tab, will you?"

"You don't have one mate. That'll be..."

"My guest has one and as I'm paying, you can put it on that. Thanks again."

Jeremiah nodded with a wink, turned, and nonchalantly waved goodbye, leaving Terry somewhat irked that he had been put in his place.

"Little shit!" muttered Jeremiah as he left the pub.

"Pompous cock!" muttered Terry as he watched the door close.

Jeremiah stood on the cobbles of the village square and inhaled the evening's balmy air. This was going to be an easy number for the con artist, and the best thing was that he didn't have to do anything but have a priceless piece of stolen art delivered to his door, for whoever this 'Gary' was? Jeremiah smiled and looked to the stars.

"Evening, Jeremiah."

Jensen Moonchild broke Jeremiah's 'happy moment'. With an unwanted crash back to reality from his dream, he gave a brief nod of his head as he came to and smiled at his passer-by.

"Jensen. How are you, young man?" Jeremiah smiled his professional smile.

Jensen was out, giving his beloved partner's dog, Sebastian, an evening walk.

"Oh, can't complain, y'know? Just out walking Seb whilst Buttercup sorts out the books for the shop. He needs a walk."

Jensen looked around to see if the coast was clear.

"To be honest, so do I. It's getting a little tense at home. It's always about this time when the books need doing, plus for some reason, I feel hungry, and going out for a walk makes me feel so much better."

A shrug of Jensen's shoulders confirmed that he had no idea why he would feel hungry at that time of evening or why a walk would stave off the cravings. Jensen, who had been bitten recently by the strange, smartly dressed, Uriah Tomkins, didn't realise that this man was a vampire who had escaped from Hell and had been taken back by Death himself. Due to the circumstances surrounding Uriah and the biting incident, Jensen had adopted some of Uriah's qualities but also kept some human ones too.

The reason for not knowing why a walk in the evening air would satisfy his hunger was due to his human side shutting down whilst the vampire side took over. When the blood lust subsided, the human side would return without a clue what had happened.

Jensen's vampire side had found rats as a bit of a delicacy. This was good for the people in the village, all but one, Dave the former rat catcher. Dave had found himself out of a job as the rat population had been on the decline so had to find work as a delivery driver for Buttercup Moonchild's health food shop.

"How curious. It must just be the cool fresh air that fills you," replied Jeremiah, who really didn't care but had to maintain his gentlemanly persona.

Jensen chuckled at his acquaintance's reply.

134

"I know you're full of it and that you're up to no good... Why can I see the vein in your neck pulsing?" thought Jensen.

"You could well be right, Jeremiah," replied Jensen, "Anyway, Seb won't walk himself so I'll be off. Have a good evening."

With a nod of the young man's head, he bid farewell to his acquaintance and continued across the village square and out past the Women's Institute hall.

Jeremiah watched the man leave with a puzzled look on his face.

"He's a strange one. I could've sworn he was looking at my neck just then. Wonder if he's a vampire!" Jeremiah chuckled to himself about the last part of his thought.

"Yeah, right! A vegan vampire. How's that working out for you, fella?" he muttered with a smile as Jensen disappeared down the side of the hall.

Jensen had left the square and when he knew that he was out of sight of the old man, looked back.

"There's something not right with you, old lad," he muttered to himself. "An art dealer? Bet most of your stuff is fake," Jensen chuckled. "Bet your name isn't even Jeremiah. It'd be something like Swift Nick or Fast Eddie." Jensen let out a little laugh.

The young man and his canine friend had left the street behind the W.I. hall when suddenly Seb stopped, sniffed, and growled at a nearby hedge.

"What is it, lad? Can you smell a rat?"

135

Before Jensen could move his gaze from the dog to the hedge, he felt a warm wave rush over himself for what was a brief moment, then sudden blindness. All Jensen could pick up on in that briefest of time was a shrill ratty squeal and the crunching of rodent bones followed by a syrupy slurping sound. It appeared Dave the rat catcher would never return to the job he once loved.

Chapter 13

The sunny morning haze had all but burned away from the centre of Ashburn-on-Sinkhole, and the village was steadily coming to life.

Betty Grisslebush had been open for her early regulars and had already placed her café tables and seating in the village square, outside her shop, in anticipation. Steven, Stewart, and Sylas hadn't arrived yet, which was just as well, as she was busy with a bacon sandwich order for Dogweed Moonchild.

"There you go, my lovely. By, you've the Devil in you, young Dogweed. Always teasing your sister like this."

Betty smiled as she handed over the warm bacon sandwich wrapped in a white paper bag, along with a flimsy white paper napkin, tucked between the bread roll and paper bag. Dogweed smiled as he reached over to take it from the nice old lady,

"Why Betty! I'm I don't know what you're on about. I just really fancy a bacon and brown sauce butty from the best place this side of Heaven."

"Is that so? Well, in that case then, you won't want to know that your sister has just entered the square," Betty said with her eyes looking in the direction of the trouble causer's sister.

The devilment from Dogweed's eyes was bright enough to light the inside of the café.

"Oh my! Is that the time? I best get going, Betty. I've a shop to open," and he turned and quickly left the café, unwrapping his fresh sandwich.

"Morning sis, how's it going?" Dogweed said as he took a huge bite from his butty.

From behind the café's counter, Betty chuckled as the Moonchild feud continued, fuelled by her bacon sandwiches.

"Oh well, she deserves it by the way she treats that young Jensen. What say you Ziggy?"

Betty looked at her cat as he sauntered out from behind the counter and into the square.

"Meow!"

[Translation]

"Like I give a crap 'ooman."

Briefly wiping the countertop with a tea-towel, Betty made her way to the café door and gave Ziggy a tiny nudge with her foot as he had decided to take up residence on the door's threshold. Betty smiled at the world whilst taking in the morning air with her hands on her voluminous hips. She felt that the evening's clairvoyance show would go down a storm, that's if Bernie and Clarabelle could get the spirits there on time. Just then, the murmurings of her regular customers came around the corner.

"No, you imbecile, JFK was shot by the book depository, not by the suppository," Stephen corrected his friend.

138

"What's the difference? He was still shot, wasn't he? I can't imagine that he'd care if it was by a depository or suppository," argued Sylas. "Mornin' Betty love. The usual please," he continued.

"What's the difference?!" Stephen looked annoyed and shocked at the same time.

"One's a storage for books and the other goes up your back-passage!"

"Well, as far as I'm concerned you can shove the difference up your arse," retorted Sylas as he pulled out his usual chair from the table to sit down.

"With what you said yesterday, I'm sure you *could* shove it up there."

"I'll 'ave less o' that fella or you can buy your own," warned Sylas, pointing an admonishing finger at his friend.

"It was kind of funny," Stewart interjected as he sat alongside his friend.

"Not from where I was sitting, it wasn't," returned Sylas.

"I think you'll find you weren't sitting at all yesterday," said Stephen with an air of superiority.

"Bugger off ya wazzock!"

Grandpa Cyril had just passed the bickering trio as he strolled to the newsagents and thought he'd stick his oar in.

"Couldn't agree more!" smiled Sylas.

"Ya wazzock!" replied Cyril.

"Hey! Thought you were on my side."

Sylas turned in his seat to see Cyril wander over to the shop, deftly waving two fingers in the air at the seated men.

"Ah, sod the daft old bugger. Anyway, who's turn is it for the papers?" smiled Sylas as he looked at Stephen in a way that said 'your turn,'.

Stephen begrudgingly rose from his seat and removed a small leather coin purse from his trouser pocket and followed Cyril towards Reginald Golightly's newsagents muttering something on the way.

"He's a good'n," smiled Stewart.

"No, he's not. He's a pillock!" replied Sylas, shuffling in his metal patio seat, which was a little uncomfortable with his recent anal issue.

"No, he's alright. It was my turn for the papers today. He bought them yesterday, but as he didn't say anything, I just figured he was doing me a huge favour," smiled Stewart slyly.

"Tha' crafty old goat!"

Sylas laughed, hunching his shoulders up like a mischievous child, Stewart just sat and smiled.

"Thank you, Reginald, have a good day," Stephen called as he left the newsagents.

"Bugger off ya wazzock!" Cyril replied for Reg, as he was still in the shop mulling over other items.

"You too, Cyril," smiled Stephen uncomfortably.

With up all three papers under his arm, Stephen made his way over to his friends, and welcomed with two smiles along with the recently placed refreshments on their table. He settled down into his usual seat and handing out the tabloids, the three elderly men began their customary morning ritual.

***

Bernie Aberline, the retired drama teacher, now recently deceased, and the village's newest ghost, tiptoed past the three old men who were ensconced with their crosswords and entered Betty's café.

Bernie hadn't quite got used to this 'death' malarkey, and whilst accepting his current state, he was still unsure about the fact that no one could actually see him. For some reason and for the life, or death, of him, he couldn't fathom out why Betty was the only one able to see him and everyone else couldn't.

Everyone else apart from Betty's cat, who would quickly disappear when he approached. This was fine for Bernie as when he was alive and visited Betty, Ziggy hated the man, and the feeling was definitely mutual.

"Morning Betty, I'm coming into the kitchen area of the café," called out Bernie, walking through the front door and into the main seating area.

Bernie had surprised Betty in the past by just quietly wandering in, and certainly didn't want her being scared to death, as there were enough ghosts in the village as it was.

141

As Bernie entered the kitchen, his gaze immediately, and involuntarily, dropped to the huge posterior that faced him, as Betty had bent down to retrieve something from a low cupboard. The dress that would normally cover, quite adequately, the lower half of the nice lady, was now struggling, and was unable to hide the back of the knees and the two white carrier bags of golf balls that were the back of Betty's thighs.

"Oh, my god!" Bernie tried to look away, but just like seeing roadkill, could not avert his gaze.

Betty stood up and turned to face her guest with a smile.

"Morning my lovely, how are you this fine day? Are we all set for tonight's show?"

Chapter 14

The three men were all engrossed with their individual crosswords when the rumbling sound of Walter Hollybank's Mercedes thundered into the square. In the front passenger seat with a flowing chiffon scarf was the love of Walter's life, Hilda Swindlebrook, and sitting right behind her was her second in command, Elsie Bagshaw. Bertrand, Walter's faithful canine friend, was sitting behind his master and enjoying the warming countryside air as they drove into the square.

"Eyup! Sterling Moss is 'ere," said Sylas, without looking up from his paper.

"And it appears that he's brought Hilda and Elsie," added Stewart.

Sylas immediately looked up when he heard the name, Elsie.

"By 'eck!" Sylas gave a lustful grunt. "I wouldn't mind seeing her knickers on my bedroom floor."

"Oh, for goodness' sake! Do you mind?"

Stephen put his newspaper down and looked away in disgust.

"Not in the slightest! She's hot stuff." Sylas licked his lips. "Morning Elsie love! So when's you and me gonna get it on?" he called out.

Elsie was getting out of Walter's car when she heard Sylas's lustful query. Her heart belonged to another, but being wanted by another man still made her feel like a giddy schoolgirl.

"Sylas, you dirty old man! You know I'm a lady. I don't do that sort of thing," Elsie called back with a devilish glint in her eye and a smile that said she *would* 'do that sort of thing'... with the right man.

Sylas gave a dirty, quiet laugh, only audible to his friends.

"By! She's like a roll of carpet in an empty room. Prime for laying!"

"Oh! I've just about heard enough of this uncouth language. For the love of God will you stop?!"

Stephen was genuinely embarrassed by the comments made by his friend, and this could clearly be seen by the reddening of his face. For Sylas, this was simply a green light to make more lurid comments, but by a tap on his foot by Stewart and a slight shake of his head, Sylas knew to stop.

"Some bloody fun you are," Sylas muttered, sarcastically.

The lecherous old man's comments were drowned out by the rumbling sound of Walter's car that had dropped the two ladies off at the Women's Institute hall and was now traversing the square and parking up outside Betty's café.

"Morning gentlemen. Nice day for it," smiled Walter at the trio.

"With Elsie, any day would be a nice day for it," replied Sylas, which resulted in a sharp kick to his ankle.

"Ah, good day Elizabeth."

Betty had appeared at the café's door.

"Walter, my lovely, and where's my little man?"

Walter alighted from the classic car and left the door open for his dog, who quickly bounded out, knowing what was to come.

"There he is!"

Betty beamed as Bertrand galloped over to her for an ear rub and his daily doggy slice of carrot cake.

"The usual is it, Walter?"

Walter lowered himself into his usual seat alongside the three men and removed his steampunk-themed leather driving helmet and goggles.

"Ooh yes please, Elizabeth."

"Right you are my lovely,"

Betty waddled back into the café, humming a tune and wiping her hands on a tea towel she had plucked from her apron.

"So gents, will you be attending tonight's clairvoyant show at the hall?" Walter asked the three men.

All three had known about the show and how Betty was to be chatting to the dead folk, but none of them really believed in such 'twaddle'.

"We might do," replied Stewart, diplomatically.

"I'm sure it'll go down a treat. The ladies are just setting up for it now."

Walter longingly looked over his shoulder at the hall's doors, and to where his love had recently entered. Hilda had just placed the evening's show poster in the glass cabinet next to the main doors and gone inside to ready the main hall.

Suddenly, a roar from a thunderous engine broke the tranquillity of the village, as a very expensive-looking car sped into the square, shooting past the hall, screeching around the square, and ended up behind Walter's car.

All four men looked in astonishment at the car that was imperceptibly vibrating as its hellish engine purred like an angry tiger. With wheels spinning, the car suddenly lurched forward and passed Walter's car, only to park in front of the classic Mercedes, leaving the steampunk clad millionaire irked that someone should even consider being ahead of him!

The tiger's purr stopped and the stereo from the car took over, invading the village tranquillity. The theme tune from the film The Exorcist bellowed out and stopped moments before the car door opened and a smartly dressed stranger hopped out, smoothing down the buttons on his jacket.

Gary smiled at the three astonished men, one very annoyed steampunked man, and a dog that was cowering behind its owner's legs.

"Guys! How's it hangin'?" Gary said with a smile that only the Devil could do.

146

Before anyone could answer, Gary nodded his head as if to bid his farewell, and made his way to Jeremiah Brown's Fine Arts shop. It was then Jeremiah walked around the corner into the square and was filling his lungs so he could greet the four regulars at Betty's.

"Eddie!" Gary said with open arms.

"Eddie?!" Sylas looked at his friends. "Who the hell is Eddie?"

A nervous looking shop keeper smiled as he fumbled for his door keys.

"Ah, you must be Mr?..."

"Gary. Just call me Gary," Gary turned to the café's patrons. "Who needs surnames, eh?"

Gary turned to Jeremiah, rubbing his hands together, and smiled.

"Shall we?" indicating at the shop's closed door.

"Of course! After you."

Jeremiah escorted his new client in, allowing Gary to go first. He looked at the men outside the café, mouthed,

"My middle name," and disappeared into the shop.

Jeremiah hopped into his shop, finding Gary wandering around, perusing the art on display.

"So. How's it going, Eddie? Oops! Jeremiah," said Gary playfully.

Jeremiah had no idea as to how this man knew his actual name, and the way he came across, made the cautious part of his brain scream out. However, the decision was made to play it cool and just go along with it, thinking of the money coming his way soon.

"Oh, y'know. Not bad. Yourself?" replied Jeremiah.

"Can't complain. Well, I could, but what would be the point?" smiled Gary, taking up position behind the counter.

"Very philosophical of you! Life can be hell sometimes, can't it?"

"Oh boy! You are so right," smiled Gary. "So... My picture?" he enquired, resting both hands on the glass countertop.

Jeremiah's face lit up as the pound signs flashed before his eyes.

"Oh yes. I'm hoping it'll be here tomorrow. I'm assured it was posted to me, and should be here then. In the meantime, I've got the 'executive room' at the pub, just a couple doors down from here. There's an open tab for you and I've insisted that the staff treat you like a prince."

Gary smiled.

"Funny that. I have been known by that name... Prince."

"Really? Prince?... Of where?"

Gary smiled and shook his head, indicating that that was the end of the conversation.

"Anyway. Would you like to show me to where I'll be stopping this evening?" Gary walked to the shop's door.

Jeremiah, jumping to attention, bounded over to the door and opened it for his wealthy client.

"Of course. Please. This way." Jeremiah smiled and waved his hand as if to beckon Gary through the door.

The two left the shop and as the couple passed the café's customers, Gary deliberately approached his car and whilst smiling at Walter, who was clearly seething, pretended to polish the wing of it. Wilfully winding up the old millionaire, the smug Gary announced.

"She's a beauty, isn't she? I reckon faster than that hunk of junk."

Gary left the old man boiling as he caught up to Jeremiah.

"Ooh, you're a devil," said Jeremiah from the corner of his mouth.

"Eddie? You don't know the half of it," replied Gary.

"Are you alright, Walter?" asked Stephen, who could see the back of the old man's neck turning crimson.

"YES! YES! I'M FINE!" snapped Walter, his gaze not faltering off the smarmy stranger.

"I'm glad you're fine, Walt, as to me you looked totally fu..."

"NO! Like I said, I'm fine!" Walter interrupted Sylas as at the same time a swift kick connected with Sylas' ankle.

Jeremiah knocked on the pub's door, and upon being opened moments later, he allowed his guest in first. Walter's brain shot into overdrive. How this young upstart could insult the village's only self-made millionaire and his beautiful car was beyond deplorable! Something must be done to put this man in his place.

The three other men at the café could easily sense the atmosphere, and even Sylas thought it better not to say anything. Whether it was because he didn't want another bruised ankle or his eye poked out with some steampunk apparel, it really didn't matter. Silence was the best tactic right now.

"Right then gentlemen," Walter suddenly burst into life, "I think it's time I bid you all farewell as I've an errand to run."

Walter, jumping up out of his chair like an exuberant jack-in-a-box, swiftly made his way back to his beloved Mercedes, opened the car door and whistled for his faithful friend to join him. Bertrand was suddenly in a bit of a dilemma, as just at that moment the nice lady in the shop had brought out a slice of cake for him. Like a spectator at a tennis match, looking back and forth, the Jack Russell was torn between his loyalty for his master, and his love of the cake that was presented to him.

"Come on, Bertrand! Hurry up, old lad. Oh sorry Elizabeth, I'll be back very shortly. I just have to do something. Just put a cosy over my cuppa and I'll be back in five minutes." Walter smiled as his dog reluctantly got into the car, looking back at the delicious morsel waiting for him.

"Oh! Oki doke. Right you are then." Betty was a little surprised, but only a little, as this was Walter at the end of the day.

The Mercedes engine fired up and Walter deliberately revved the engine loud enough so that anyone who may be in the local pub could hear. With a jolt, the classic car sped off out of the village square and towards a certain garage owned by a certain Mr Turnkey.

"Bugger me!" exclaimed Sylas.

"Well, I wouldn't have used those words myself," replied Betty "but you're right. What's been happening?"

Not wanting his two friends to steal his thunder, Stephen briefly and eloquently gave a synopsis of the recent events.

"I do think you're right, young Sylas, with such terminology. I sense trouble coming," said Betty.

She looked at where the car and the furious driver had exited the village square, and with a slight shake of her head, Betty carried the cake and hot drink back into her café, as requested.

Chapter 15

Kenneth was hard at it in his garage, working on the alien's craft, when the roaring sound of a classic Mercedes rumbled into the forecourt of his garage. A voice from outside, calling out his name, confirmed who it was.

"Right guys, you wait here and I'll just sort my customer out. You carry on playing."

Kenneth had taught the aliens how to play dominoes whilst they waited for him to repair their ship. All three were sitting in the craft's doorway with a snaking row of dominoes on the craft's floor, and each with a handful of other domino tiles in their hands.

"Two ticks, Walter!" called out Kenneth.

Walter had pulled up to the garage door and was standing with his hands on his hips, whilst Bertrand remained in the car. Kenneth opened up the garage door just enough to get out with no one seeing in, and squeezing out, greeted the steampunk clad gent.

"By 'eck Wally! Tha's dapper today," said Kenneth as he eyed up his friend. "What can I do for you?"

"It's Ingrid," Walter said, looking at the bonnet of his car. "Would you believe some blighter has just pulled up in front of me in the village and insulted her? He was in one of these fancy Italian looking cars," Walter sneered as he described Gary's car. "Wonder if you could put a bit more pep in her lungs, just so I can put this blaggard in his place."

Kenneth's face lit up like a pyromaniac's bonfire.

"D'you want her to go a little faster?... or a lot faster?"

Without hesitation, Walter plumped for the 'lot faster' option and smiled.

"So when can you do it? I'm in a bit of a rush, to be frank."

Kenneth looked at the car and back at his closed garage doors and 'hmm'd' and 'ahh'd' whilst scratching his chin.

"I couldn't possibly have it done before tomorrow morning. I could try for tomorrow afternoon? That OK for you?" Kenneth hoped that that would be alright for his friend, but on seeing a huge smile on the millionaire's face meant it was more than alright.

"Absolutely wonderful. Kenneth, if ever I buy a star, I'll name it after you. Did you know you can actually buy stars? Oh, any chance of a lift back down to Betty's? My cuppa is going cold there."

"Not a problem Wally, I'll go get mi keys. Oh, you didn't see young Shifty Miller in the village, did you?"

Walter thought of a second.

"Oh, I'm sure he'll be there somewhere. He's always skulking around somewhere. Not sure I fully trust the young chap. Don't get me wrong, he's done nothing wrong to me, but he is just a little... shifty."

"He's alright is lad," defended Kenneth, who also wanted Shifty to help him back to his garage.

Kenneth disappeared into his garage to return moments later, smiling and waving some keys.

"Right then, Walt. Let's get you back to your cuppa."

All three, including the dog, got into Kenneth's van that was parked alongside his workshop, next to a window.

"I say!... What in Heaven's name are you working on in there?" exclaimed Walter, looking at the visible craft inside the garage.

"Oh, it's nothing. Just some metal plating that I need for a job. Honestly, it's not a UFO," Kenneth replied nervously.

Kenneth fired up his van and quickly got his customer out of view of the ship he was working on.

"Let's get you to Betty's for your cuppa."

***

Bernie, having left Betty's, was now sauntering up the lane towards the churchyard to meet up with his friend, Clarabelle. It was a glorious morning and Bernie was in no rush at all. He liked his friend, but the sun shining down was Heavenly, so he wasn't in a rush, even to see her. Bernie chuckled at his thoughts,

"Heavenly! That's a good one, old chap."

"Morning Bernie."

Bernie's blissful thoughts were interrupted by Clarabelle, who was leant against the nearest Yew tree to the road in the churchyard.

"Good morning, Clarabelle. How are we on this absolutely fantastic day?" beamed Bernie.

Clarabelle hitched her bust up in an already snug fitted bodice and smiled at Bernie.

"All the better for seeing you, kind sir."

Bernie instantly blushed, which made his female friend burst into fits of laughter. The one thing that Clarabelle loved doing was embarrassing her new friend, and she was so good at it too.

"Oh, for goodness' sake!" Bernie shied away from the bulging sight presented to him.

"You love it," replied Clarabelle as she wandered from the tree and through the stone wall towards her friend.

"Anyway, I've not yet spoken to all of them here, but I'm sure they'd be up for a chinwag tonight, down at the hall," she said as she pointed towards the gravestones.

"Excellent!" beamed Bernie, "Shall we let them have a lie-in before we speak to them?"

Clarabelle's laughter was always on a hair-trigger, and it didn't take much to set her off. With her hands on her hips, bending over slightly and in full belly laugh mode, she shook her head.

"Oh Bernie, you're such a one! 'Let them have a lie-in'! Most of these have been doing just that for the last hundred years!"

Clarabelle found this most amusing and bending over in full laugh mode, just made it easier for her heaving bust to be more visible to the already embarrassed ghost. Not knowing where to look, even though his eyes knew exactly where to gaze upon, Bernie shielded his gaze, much to the disgust of the atrophic desire section within his ghostly brain.

"Seriously! Don't you have any turtleneck sweaters?"

"Bernie Aberline, you make me laugh so much. C'mon, let's take a walk in the sun. Escort me?"

Clarabelle took hold of Bernie's arm, regaining some form of composure, and the couple walked away from the churchyard wall and into the village.

Still bursting into ripples of laughter, Clarabelle clung on to her new friend. In ghostly terms, she had only known him for seconds, but it didn't matter. He was a true gent and easy to tease, and Clarabelle liked him.

The ghostly couple entered the village square just as Shifty Miller was getting into Kenneth Turnkey's van. Walter and Bertrand had taken their rightful place back at Betty's and Walter was waving goodbye to the mechanic and his guide.

"Is everything alright, Walter?" asked Stewart, wondering why Walter had arrived back at the café minus his beloved car.

"Oh, I'm sure it will be," replied the steampunk clad gent, with a vengeful glint in his eye.

"He's a bit weird is that man," said Clarabelle, pointing to Walter.

"He is a bit, but he's such a gentleman and has a sharp eye for business, that's for sure. Not sure what's going on with his apparel, but he's happy and he's not hurting anyone so all's good," replied her chaperone.

Bernie's pale ghostly skin went even paler and his eye's opened wider than a young boy staring at the top magazine shelf in a newsagent. His body suddenly tensed, as much as a ghost's body could, and started to tremble. Instantly noticing something was wrong with her friend, Clarabelle looked up at Bernie with a concerned look.

"Bernie! What's wrong?"

"Bugger me!"

"Now's not the time for requests, Bernie. What's wrong?"

Clarabelle followed Bernie's gaze to a figure who was dressed in a headmaster's black cape and had a purposeful gait to his walk. The tall, slender figure had stopped at the Women's Institute hall and was examining the poster for the evening's show.

"That's Mr Harper!"

"And who's he when he's at home?"

"Mr Harper! Bloody hell!" Bernie kept his gaze firmly on the man.

"You know him then? Shall we call him over and see if he wants to join tonight's show?"

Bernie very quickly turned to his friend and with fear in his eyes whispered in a loud voice.

"No! Good God No! He's an absolute ogre! He was my old Headmaster when I was a drama teacher. No one knew his first name when he was alive. We all called him Mr Harper, the pupils, and even the teachers. He had 'C. Harper-Headmaster' painted on his door when he was there. Everyone thought his name must be Charles or something. It was only when we all attended his funeral that we discovered his name to be Constantine."

Clarabelle looked confused.

"But you went to his funeral, he can't be all that bad. Bet his wife was grateful that you all turned up."

"That bad?! The entire school went, but only because we were too scared by what would happen if we didn't. Mr Harper was never married or to my knowledge never had any interest in anything of the sort!... If you don't mind, I think I'd prefer to walk the other way for now," Bernie turned and quickly ushered his friend back out of the square.

Constantine Harper peered at the poster with an air of disdain.

"Clairvoyant evening with Betty Grisslebush? How utterly ridiculous. Shoddy typeset and the margins are all over the place. I have never seen disgraceful work in my entire life! Whoever wrote this has the grammar skills of a baboon," he muttered to himself, "Commas in the wrong place! And why is a comma there?! It is not needed, and what on Earth is a semi-colon doing there?!"

The decision was made by the tyrannical headmaster to return later and properly scold the culprit for their slaughter of English grammar. The tall, slender, bony fingered ghost strode off with his hands clasped firmly behind him with his perpetual sneer glued to his thin ashen lips.

Chapter 16

Terry had shown Jeremiah and his important guest into the bar where Liam was clearing up the glasses from the night before.

"Come on through. This is the bar area, and this is Liam, our glass collector," Terry commentated like a presenter on a posh television show.

The trio were met with the back of a black T-shirt and the top section of a hairy bum crack peering over a pair of scruffy jeans.

"Liam!"

Terry looked back at Jeremiah and his guest and gave a nervous chuckle.

"Sorry about that. He's not usually like that... Liam!"

Liam stood up and hitched his jeans up as he turned to face his boss.

"Yes, Terry?"

Liam's T-shirt logo wasn't what Terry wanted his high paying customer to see.

'Constipation—Too cool for stool,'

Terry's heart sank, Jeremiah's eye's widened and Gary had all on trying not to laugh.

"Oh hi, Mr Brown. Is this your customer who's stopping here? 'ow do, my name's Liam."

The young glass collector approached Gary, whilst wiping his hands down his jeans and extended an open hand. Gary really hadn't shaken hands with anyone...ever. As to why would anybody want to do that with the Devil? Feeling delighted, Gary reached out and took hold of the wet, clammy hand of the young man.

"Nice to meet you fella. Call me Gary," smiled Gary with eyes that gleamed with mischief.

To shake hands with the Devil was a bit like petting a rabid jellyfish, something you simply wouldn't want to do. Liam, whose waistband was higher than his I.Q. didn't mind and just ran with it.

Sensing that some form of affinity had occurred between his member of staff and the cash cow customer, Terry relaxed a little and suggested that Liam take their guest to the 'executive suite', whilst he sorted out the paperwork with Jeremiah.

A puzzled look quickly developed on Liam's face, which turned into a relaxed smile when Terry informed him that the 'executive suite' was the 'posh' room. This very quickly morphed into panic as Liam realised that he had left a magazine in there that maybe shouldn't have been left in there.

"Oh, bloody hell! Yes, I'll show you the way Mr... Gary."

Liam shot off towards the stairs without waiting for Gary. As the thumping of heavy footsteps ascended the stairs, all three men looked at each other, and with a shrug of his shoulders, Gary followed the sounds of the footsteps.

"I'm really sorry about that, Jeremiah," Terry said, with a furrowed brow indicating not to sting him so much.

"Oh, it's OK, Terry. Obviously, though, this could affect the situation and maybe by way of compensation a discount on the final bill?"

"Bugger! Knew it was coming," thought Terry.

"I'm sure some sort of arrangement could be made," he replied, knowing that whatever the discount was, he would only add more to his bill to cover the loss.

Liam burst into the guest room and ran over to the bedside drawer. Gary, however, was a bit sprightlier than the overweight guide and catching up with him leapt over the bed. In a flash, Gary removed the magazine from the drawer before Liam could and devilishly smiling at the young man, opened the magazine. Liam's heart sank whilst the blush of embarrassment rose.

"I think this must be mine," said Gary whilst thumbing the pages, scanning over every page, "A nice complimentary gesture from the pub. I must thank the landlord for it."

Liam let out a little fart of anxiety and fear.

"It's OK I'll tell Terry that you're happy with the mag and we can leave it like that if that's ok," pleaded Liam.

Gary thumbed a few more pages, making Liam sweat a little bit more.

"Mmm, ok. You tell him how happy I am with his choice of magazine. Thank you."

Liam backed out of the room and nearly tripped over Shadow, Terry's pet dog cum wolf.

"Bloody hell, Shadow, I nearly fell on you. Come on, let's leave our guest to settle in."

Liam took hold of Shadow's collar and started to lead him away, however, not before the wolf's tail flicked, which was a sure-fire sign of something nasty was about to happen. Nothing was heard, but the overwhelming odour of rancid wolf fart hit the air like a rampaging bull, and it just happened to be pointing towards the 'executive' suite's open doorway. Gary sniffed the air for a few seconds as Liam dragged the reluctant canine away.

"That brings back so many memories of home, prior to Citronella," said Gary wistfully.

Chapter 17

St. Peter had scarcely managed to rid himself of another large group of incoming souls and had torn up another 'sorry we missed you' card, when a huge articulated truck pulled up. The driver's side window was already down and a chubby, unshaven face popped out and smiled.

"Delivery for a Mr G-man?"

Peter's look of surprise prevented him from replying, so the driver opened his door and jumped out of the cabin, turning his back on Peter as he retrieved a clipboard and pen. Turning to face the shocked gatekeeper, the driver smiled and held out the clipboard with the delivery note attached, and a well chewed pen.

"How do. I'm Stephen from H&H Supplies. Got a delivery of bio-ethanol citronella. You're lucky with the amount you've ordered."

Stephen gave a brief wave of the clipboard, suggesting that Peter should take it.

"Yeah, we expected an order from one of our regulars but never got it so as they say, first come first served."

St. Peter stood with his mouth open and eyes wide.

"Look, I'm really sorry but I have other deliveries and I'm on a tight schedule. This new-fangled GPS tracking and mapping system is a right royal pain in the derriere, so if you don't mind," said Stephen with a shake of the pen in the saint's direction.

Nonchalantly placing both clipboard and pen on Peter's lectern, Stephen shrugged and wandered to the curtain-sided trailer.

"Where d'you want it?"

***

God was in his office wondering what to wear for the evening's soiree. He had escorted Travis to an area he had just created, which was the perfect beach next to the perfect sea with perfect clouds in a perfect sky. Travis stood transfixed, staring out at the waves, before giving an almighty 'Whoop!' and picking up his board, ran towards his little personal piece of Heaven.

God was standing in front of his mirror, gazing over the image that presented itself of a very smartly dressed man in a tuxedo and wearing a very expensive watch. With a click of his fingers, the tuxedo vanished and a pair of Hawaiian board shorts appeared, accompanied by a pair of thong sandals and a thin leather string necklace with a shell pendant.

God appeared slightly puzzled at the unfamiliar apparel and wondered what else he needed. With an 'Aha!' God suddenly obtained a healthy beach tan and what was his perfectly groomed hairstyle was now a sun-bleached straggly cut. With a broad godly smile at his reflection, he made one more adjustment. A slender yet very muscular body appeared, and God knew he had got it just right.

God sat back in his chair and placing his sandal shod feet upon his desk, he picked up a canister and blowing a conversation into it, sent it 'thwooshing' to Gary via the pneumatic tube.

***

"What the hell do you know about keeping order!" yelled Adolph, standing toe-to-toe with Genghis, their noses touching.

"A damn sight more than you. You couldn't order a meal in a restaurant, let alone keep order in Hell!" shouted back Genghis.

'ThuB!'

Before Genghis could continue with his tirade, Adolph butted in.

"Get the bloody canister!"

Genghis knew where it had come from, so figuring he was more in charge than his lower colleague, broke off from the feud and see what 'HE' wanted from upstairs. As the demon turned to walk towards the waiting canister, Adolph smiled at his opponent.

"Can't order, eh? Just ordered you to get the canister."

Adolph laughed, then ducked as an unopened canister went whistling past his right ear and bounced off the throne room door, breaking open as it landed on the floor.

"Right, you little shit! I'll have you for that!"

Adolph launched himself at Genghis and the two demons rolled on the floor with punches flying and head-butts connecting.

God, who was on the other end of the canister, was suddenly surprised by the loud bang as the vessel hit the door, breaking open the canister.

"What in the name of me was that?!"

God listened to the two demons fighting and swearing at each other, informing the other what they would do with each other's rectum and what rather large article would be forcibly inserted into it. God quickly realised that this may not be the time for a call and that it was more than likely that Gary wasn't there, so hung up.

A smile formed on God's tanned face so leaning over, he opened his desk drawer and pulled out a mobile phone. Gently blowing the dust off it, God fired it up and hearing the small digital tune, notifying him that it was ready to use, he dialled a number.

***

Gary had been sitting on the bed thumbing the pages of his newly acquired magazine, much to the frustration of its previous owner, when an unusual ring tone came from his jacket pocket. He pondered as to who would have this number, and looked at the phone's screen, noticing it was an 'unknown number'. Gary answered the call.

"Hello, sir. Our records show that you have had an accident in the last year..."

Click!

Gary threw the phone on the bed by his side and continued perusing the magazine. Moments later the phone rang again and again 'unknown number' flashed onto the phone's screen.

"Persistent little bugger aren't ya," muttered Gary and picked up the phone.

"Listen, you little pumper! I did *not* have an accident in the last year and even if I did, I don't have insurance. Plus, I'd sort out the problem my own way. Oh, and before you start again, no I don't want life assurance or double glazing and no I wasn't mis-sold PPI. You do realise I invented your job. I know all your tricks and I'm sorry but whatever your computer screen has got you to say, I've heard it all before and probably worse, so why don't you piss off and bother someone else as I'm quite happy reading someone else's porn mag right now."

"Lucifer! Son! I just thought I'd give my least favourite angel a call. How are you?"

"Oh, for f…"

"Something tells me you're not at home at the moment," interrupted God whilst he twizzled the pendant on his necklace.

"Gary! It's Gary!"

"No, I'm sure the last time I looked in the mirror it was God… Justgod," smiled God.

"You know what I mean… Bond!"

Gary's blood was beginning to boil as he threw the magazine down and sat upright on the bed.

"Bond? Oh, of course! That's what you suggested, isn't it, BondJamesBond? Well, a slight change of plan now. Or should I say a slight change of name?"

Gary suddenly became intrigued. Who would have the persuasive power to overrule his suggestion?!

"Go on?" Gary said pensively.

"I've had enough of the Godjustgod thingy, or Bondjamesbond as you suggested. I no longer find being a divine villain busting spy who only tackles the most formidable foes, attractive. I am now leaning towards a more relaxed way of life," God said in his most chilled out voice. "Dude."

"DUDE?!... What in everything unholy are you on about? Dude?!" Gary's brain went into overdrive.

God could hear Gary's cogs whirring, and was enjoying the moment as the fallen angel's mind was in turmoil, wondering what on Earth could have made him do this.

"Yes... Dude," smiled God.

Gary was flummoxed. He searched his brain for any sort of comeback that he could think of... and failed.

"Anyway. If you're not in Hell, then where are you? And more to the point, why are you there? Didn't you say something about rules of Hell and not leaving there?"

Gary came crashing back down to Earth with the guile and grace of a stolen alien craft.

"Listen 'ere, whatever you want to call yourself now..."

"G-man."

"What?!... G-man?!"

Gary fell off the bed laughing on hearing God's latest name change.

"Are you serious? G-man? I thought BondJamesBond was pushing it a bit far and never thought you'd pick up on it, but G-man? Don't tell me. Bet you're learning how to skateboard," Gary continued his laughter whilst his ribs began to ache.

God knew better than to rise to Gary's taunts and continued with his relaxed attitude.

"So, you on a shopping trip? How *is* Ashburn these days? I mean, since your escaped vampire left the place."

Gary stopped laughing. How did God know he was on a shopping trip and how did he know he was in Ashburn?

"I suppose he's God and knows almost everything," Gary reassuringly thought to himself.

"Yeah, just a little shopping trip," Gary tried to sound not surprised that God knew.

"They've got a lovely little vegan health food shop here. Would you like me to get you something from there? G-man!"

God chuckled at Gary's response, whilst he looked at his tanned toes sticking out of the thong sandals, and wondered if they were suitably surfer-dude-ish enough.

"No, we're all good here thanks. Anyway, I've decided to hold a beach party here, so I've ordered everything necessary for it. Well nearly, just got to get some 'tuneage'."

"You have a beach?"

The thought that Heaven had a beach totally bewildered Gary.

"When did you get that? You sure as hell didn't have one before I decided to leave."

"Well, things change y'know Lucifer..."

"Gary!"

"Gary. Things change and now we have one, plus you may find that the decision to leave wasn't exactly yours but who's nit-picking. So beach party at my crib. Everyone who is anyone is going to be here, plus we have kegs, dogs, and chicks!"

God wasn't too sure if he had got his terminology right, but went with it anyway.

"And as I say, we just need a group to play for us. I'm sure we have a suitable band here somewhere. Oh, and not forgetting one of the fundamental things, a fire. Got to have a fire on the beach for when it gets dusk and chilly."

"You have dusk? And fire?! Actual fire? With flames and logs? Isn't fire my domain?"

"Well, like I say, some things change. Should be the bomb."

God remembered the 'bomb' word from his chat with Travis.

"Jesus!"

"Oh yes. He's coming. Anyway, I *was* going to say whilst you're there, don't do anything I wouldn't do, but that's in your nature, isn't it? Oh! Who's looking after Hell whilst you're there?"

"I have my finest demons on the case and I trust them implicitly."

Gary knew he had simply lied to God, as being a demon in Hell, and his top two demons, meant by virtue of their ranks, that they couldn't be trusted... at all.

"You're a braver man than me... OK, fallen angel and deity... Y'know what I mean."

"Hell is safe in their hands," replied Gary, and thought he'd just give them a quick call later to see if everything was alright.

"If you say so. Anyway, gotta go and get ready, so catch you on the flipside."

God hung up before Gary could make another exclamation.

Chapter 18

Hell was always known for its chaos, but since Gary had gone on his little jaunt upstairs, it had become somehow more chaotic. The demons, who should have been doing their respective jobs given to them by Gary, were just wandering about the place, claiming to not knowing what to do. They all knew exactly what they should be doing, but as the two demons who were in control had not kept them in check, then as the old saying goes, 'Whilst the cat's away'.

Murmurings were taking place among the lower end demons that Hell appeared to be going to... Hell. More and more demons were passing the portcullis and looking up the long paved, flame flanked path at all the lost souls waiting to come in.

Well, they weren't exactly champing at the bit to enter Hell, but as Steve had recently left them at the gate with a postcard saying that he was sorry that he'd missed them, they had all become restless. Comments were being shouted down the path to the main entrance to Hell like 'Half day closing is it?' 'Oi! Numbnuts! Are you letting us in or what?!' and 'If you don't let us in soon, we're going home!'

All the demons who had seen the angry crowd of souls had spoken to the others and informed them as to what they had seen. This, in turn, had made the others curious, and they came to visit the entrance to see for themselves. It was like a hellish zoo, but in reverse.

"D'you think we should inform Adolph and Genghis?" asked Wilkes-Booth.

"Not our job," replied Oswald, as he peered up the path to the angry mob.

Wilkes-Booth joined Oswald, peering up the path, and with a puzzled frown he turned to his friend.

"Well, actually it is. We are the welcoming committee."

Oswald paused and gave a brief sucking of his teeth and returned the look.

"We do as we're told, right?"

Wilkes-Booth nodded.

"And have we been told to let 'em in?"

Wilkes-Booth looked at the crowd and shook his head.

"Nope. I don't suppose we have."

The two demons then turned and left the mouth of the entrance, and the chanting crowd to fend for themselves. Oswald stopped and looked at his friend.

"Just one second mate. I've forgotten something."

Oswald jogged back to the portcullis, and in the centre of the opening, he taunted the crowd with a little dance whilst gesticulating with his index and middle fingers on both hands. A high kicking vaudevillian walk was Oswald's parting piece as he exited stage right, enraging the crowd more so and making his way back to his counterpart.

"What the home was that all about?"

"I just thought they'd appreciate it," smiled Oswald.

"I'm not sure calling you a ducking bat is a term of endearment, do you?"

"Think you need your ears cleaning out, mate. It wasn't a ducking bat they called me."

Wilkes-Booth and Oswald sauntered off, leaving the angry mob shouting at the gates of Hell.

***

Gacy and Berkowitz were sitting in their office with a heavy atmosphere brewing. Gacy had been shuffling papers and simmering, whilst Berkowitz scribbled figures on a pad and infrequently tutted to himself. Swiftly getting up and making his way over to a dial, Berkowitz tapped the glass on the dial to see if the needle had stuck.

"Seriously boss!" Berkowitz said, turning to see Gacy who had just launched his office chair at him.

"Don't you think I don't know?! I've already tried to tell Dick and Liddy and had the door slammed in my face!"

"But boss," pleaded Berkowitz, "If something isn't done now then we're going to be without flames. How the home is that going to look? Hell without hellfire?"

Gacy knew that Berkowitz had a point and that if Gary came back to an even darker Hell because the flames had gone out, then what?

"Right!" Gacy hung his head in resignation. "OK! I'll go and see Bodgit and Scarper."

Gacy left the office and trudged down the corridor with his feet honking as he did.

Even though Berkowitz was extremely concerned about the bio-ethanol levels, he couldn't help but smile at his boss. Gary had played a blinder with fixing clown's bicycle horns to Gacy's feet purely so he could hear him coming.

**

The fight was still in full swing between Genghis and Adolph, when Gacy honked up to the door. The sounds of crashing furniture and swearing told Gacy that right then was probably the worst time to interrupt the two demons. However, he had a choice; interrupt the fighting couple now or explain to Gary as to why he did nothing and left Hell in total darkness.

"Oh, crap!" Gacy inhaled deeply and knocked on the door.

Inside the throne room, Genghis had Adolph gripped tightly around the throat whilst Adolph tried to search for any splinter of wood that could be forced up Genghis' backside, when a thunderous knock came from the door.

"Answer that! It's your job!" squeaked Adolph.

Genghis' eyes went from anger and wanting to kill his cohort to 'I better answer the door. It is my job after all'. Genghis, releasing his grip and removing his knee from his opponent's chest, got up and staggered, slightly out of breath, to the door.

"See! I can order you too! Makes me the better demon to run Hell!" shouted Adolph as he located the perfect splinter of wood.

Genghis ignored the last comment and opened the door.

Gacy looked up as the door opened, and before anything was said from inside, he shouted out,

"We're low!"

"Of course we're low! We're in Hell! You can't get lower than that!" shouted Genghis and slammed the door in Gacy's face.

Narrowly missing the demon's nose by millimetres, Gacy glowered at the closed door.

"Pillock!"

As quickly as the door closed, it re-opened and a clenched fist came flying out, landing squarely on Gacy's left eye, knocking him back several feet and to the ground.

Genghis' head poked out from the door.

"I heard that!"

The door was slammed shut again.

As the swelling in to the eye started, Gacy picked himself up from the ground, dusted himself off and kicked at the door.

Genghis swiftly opened it and glared at the lower-ranked demon.

"WHAT?!"

Calmly, Gacy continued to dust himself off and defiantly looked at Genghis.

"If you don't sign this form, then I can't get any more fuel for the flames. So when I say we're low, I mean we're low on fuel for here."

"Why didn't you say that?" replied Genghis, even calmer and more menacing.

"Because you didn't give me chance!"

Gacy met Genghis, calm for calm and menace for menace.

Quickly, Genghis noticed that the corridor seemed to have gone a little cooler, and that the flames didn't seem to be as high as normal. For a split second, panic entered the demon's head, then left just as quickly as a plan formed.

"Give me the form now. I'll sign it. D'you think we'll get it in time?" Genghis asked quietly.

"I bloody hope so, or we're all gonna be in for it," said Gacy, handing the form over.

A quick scribble was done, and the form handed back, then Genghis disappeared back into the room, leaving Gacy to honk his way back to his office.

"Y'know what Adolph? I think you're right. You could well be the better demon to run this whilst Gary's away," said Genghis, walking over to his opponent who had hidden the splinter behind his back.

Taken aback a little by this resignatary comment, Adolph paused and smiled.

"At last. You've come to your senses."

"However, if you screw up, then I get to take over and tell Gary you've screwed the pooch," replied the demon, holding up one finger as if to stop Adolph's celebratory smile.

"Whatever! Like I'm going to screw up!" smiled the victor.

"Deal?" Genghis held out his hand.

"Deal," and the two shook on it.

Gacy had returned to the office and slammed the form on Berkowitz's desk.

"Do it. And pray to Gary that we've got it on time."

Berkowitz quickly picked up the phone and dialled the number.

"Oh hello, It's Berkowitz from Hell... I'm fine thank you, how are you?"

A quick slap around the ear told Berkowitz that pleasantries were not required.

"OW!.. Sorry, can we have our usual, but can you put it on express delivery? I know it'll cost more but it's kinda needed... Sure, I'll hold."

Berkowitz smiled at Gacy, gave a 'thumbs up' and mouthed,

"Just checking now."

A longer than normal pause, then a voice came back on the phone.

"No, not a problem, I thought you'd gone for your dinner," joked Berkowitz, "Oh!... none at all?... Can you look again? It's kind of important... No, I know you've just looked but can you look again... please?... Look, we need it and... I know we don't usually leave it this late but... What?... All of it? Who the hell needs that amount of bio-ethanol?... WHAT?! WHY?! Are you serious? Tell me you're joking! This is a joke, right?... Hang on one second."

Berkowitz turned to face his boss, who had heard the conversation and whose bum crack had already started to sweat profusely.

"You're not going to believe this boss."

"I can guess. They're out of the stuff aren't they?"

"Not just that, but it's who's bought it." Berkowitz pointed upwards.

"YOU ARE HAVING A BLOODY LAUGH!!"

"Nope. Apparently, he's having an eco-friendly beach party and bought the lot!"

Gacy slapped his hand to his forehead in disbelief. Then a voice on the other side of the phone chirped up.

"Yes, I'm still here... A week? I don't think we've enough to last the night let alone the week... Yes, I know, don't you think I know that?... What?... Won't it smell like a caravan?... Well, I suppose it *is* better than nothing. So how long would it be before you can deliver and how much is it?... How much?!... What d'you mean a deposit?... Look! We're wanting to buy enough for a week, not an eternity, and why do you need a deposit?... Of course, you're going to get the canisters back! Why would we want to keep the bloody canisters?... OK, OK, when?... The morning, eh? No later than that ok... You best bloody promise... Depending on the traffic? What traffic?!... No, I don't know. What traffic is your driver going to come into contact with? It isn't as though there's a motorway to here and rush-hour traffic twice a day! Look, just get it here as soon as you can. And no later than tomorrow... Yes, of course, I'll send over the order form now... Thank you, and you have a nice day too."

Berkowitz put the phone down and wiped the sweat from his brow.

"So rather than smell of lemons, Hell is going to smell like a caravan. One, massive, smelly, touring, caravan," Gacy wasn't pleased.

"Look! It's the best I could do! HE bought the bloody lot for his bloody beach party. What would you have me do?" Berkowitz replied.

"Dammit! We'll just have to make do. Something tells me though that Gary ain't going to be happy about this." Gacy honked over to his desk, "Pass me my chair."

***

A tear opened up at the crowded gates of Hell, as Steve brought another soul.

"Look, I really don't know where you get that idea from because believe me, there's none of them where you're

183

going fella," Steve pushed his latest delivery through the tear and followed him.

"I'll just get a card and... what the bloody hell?"

Steve eyed all the people he had dropped off recently and wondered why they hadn't been collected yet.

"'ere! How long have you guys been here?" asked Steve.

"Since you dropped us off," said a man wearing a black balaclava with a bullet hole neatly positioned in the middle of his forehead.

"What the hell is going on?" said Steve.

"You tell us! And whilst you're at it, you can explain to us as to why you think we deserve to be here? I was fighting for a cause and suddenly I'm here!"

"Look, it's not me. I only take you where my book says and you, you little toe-rag, belong here!"

Steve felt that he was being picked on, and under no circumstances was he going to be intimidated by some rancid little snot-bucket who didn't like the decision. With one of his bony fingers poking into the terrorist's hole in his head, Steve pushed the angry man away.

"Out of my way, you little toad. I'll sort this."

Steve parted the assembly like the biblical parting of the seas and headed for the doorbell. Where the sign clearly read that the bell ought to be, 'used only once', Steve hit the bell like a jackhammer, and continued for a short while until he felt that he may have got someone's attention.

"Right, you lot. That should do it. If you're still here when I return, then I'll..."

Steve didn't know what he would do, so left it there and quickly disappeared to collect more souls.

Chapter 19

Gary felt a little uneasy, having had the phone call cut short by God. He had broken his own rule of no one leaving Hell. OK, his clothing expert, Uriah, was allowed to, but definitely no demon, or fallen angel for that matter. However, as he *was* Gary, previously known as the Devil, and therefore he was all about breaking rules, it seemed to be OK.

Still, Gary was a little concerned about his cherished home, and leaving it to two demons didn't ease his troubled mind. Whilst sitting on the bed with his back against the headboard and a well-thumbed adult magazine on his lap, Gary found himself nibbling on his bottom lip. Minutes passed by and still Gary pondered over his realm and what state that it would be in when he returned, which hopefully would only be a day or two longer.

"Don't be so stupid," he rebuked himself, "I invented worry and OCD and this is exactly what all this is."

Gary was more than happy to take credit for things he didn't actually do. Both 'worry' and 'OCD' weren't of his doing but a lesser demon's, who he'd overheard in Hell's canteen, next to Hell's kitchen, one day, whilst he had popped in for a quick latte. When it was found that it wasn't his idea, Gary would present a contract that clearly stated that,

'Any, and all ideas, were the sole property of Gary, formally known as Satan, Devil, Lucifer, HIM, Prince of

Darkness and all other names, officially and unofficially belonging to said Gary.'

Gary gnawed on his bottom lip for a short while longer before 'worry' took over. Leaning over, he picked up his phone and tapping the screen, brought the phone to life. On the phone's lock screen was a photo of himself in a dramatic pose, all suited in his latest attire. Gary took one last nibble of his lip before he tapped the screen again.

Face recognition immediately opened up the phone and with one more tap, Gary was taken to the 'Contacts' page. One more tap and after a moment, he heard the call tone in the earpiece.

Adolph was sitting on the throne sat and gloating, whilst Genghis stood in his usual place near the door. Genghis would normally stand to attention there, to prevent anyone from entering before permission was granted. However, this time he definitely didn't want anyone entering, purely so Adolph wouldn't know about the ongoing crisis with the bio-ethanol.

From the lofty position on the throne, with 'smugness' oozing from every rancid pore, Adolph's face changed to fear in a flash as the mobile phone next to him suddenly sprang into life.

Anyone but Gary, sitting on the throne, was *not* allowed under any circumstances. Not even if Gary had left the room to use another... 'throne'. Nervously jumping off the hallowed seat, Adolph picked up the phone and answered it.

"Gary! How's it going? You enjoying yourself?"

Gary sensed the nervousness in the demon's voice.

"It was alright, up to the point that you sat in MY chair."

"I wasn't. Not at all. Anyone sitting on your throne would feel my wrath if I found them, you know that Gary."

Adolph quickly brushed the seat of the throne in an attempt to remove any trace of him sitting there. Genghis seized the opportunity with both hands.

"You're right, Adolph. No one could sit on Gary's throne as it had your fat arse on it."

"You lying sack of..."

"Adolph! Shut up. NOW!" Gary interrupted the demon with more pressing matters.

"I just rang up to make sure that everything was alright down there. Nothing untoward is there?"

"Untoward?"

Adolph seemed a little nervous as to why Gary would phone up asking such a question.

"No, nothing at all. Why d'you ask?"

Gary relaxed further back into the headboard and hearing the tone of the demon's voice, suggested that he wasn't hiding anything.

"Just curious, that's all. It's the first time I've left you two in charge and I just wanted to make sure."

Adolph saw the opportunity.

"Honestly Gary, it's fine. Genghis realised that I could do a much better job than he could so decided to stand down and let me run the place whilst you were gone." Adolph puffed up his chest.

"But I did say that if you screwed up, then I was to take control and make things right," interjected Genghis.

"I sincerely hope for your sake that Genghis doesn't have to take over or I can see someone working under Berkowitz in Procurement.

A gulp was audible on the other side of Gary's phone.

"You can rest assured that I will *still* be in charge when you return," Adolph looked at Genghis and sneered.

"Oh, no you won't," said Genghis under his breath with a slight grin.

"I knew I could count on you," lied Gary. "Right, put Genghis on. I want to make sure he does what you say."

Adolph smiled and held out the phone for Genghis. A look of concern came over the demon's face as Genghis approached and took it.

"Yes, Gary?"

"Listen 'ere," Gary whispered. "If that turdsicle screws up, then you take over right away. Fix his screw up and let me know when I return. Got it?"

"Yes, not a problem. Will do."

Genghis played his poker-face so that Adolph wouldn't know what was said.

190

Click!

Genghis handed the phone back to Adolph.

"Well?"

"Just as you said, mate. You're in charge. End of."

Genghis turned and walked back to the door, with a secret smile forming.

Outside the throne room, the flames that flanked the stone pavements were no longer as fierce or as hot as they should have been. Two demons in Procurement were sweating, but not because of the heat, but for the lack of it, and what their boss would do if the flames went out altogether.

The rest of the demons were starting to crowd around the portcullis and were watching the angry mob on the opposite side of the gates at the far end of the 'Walk of Shame' path. The angry mob, apart from being angry, had formed the idea that maybe they were not going to enter Hell after all. They figured that whilst they would wait for Death to return and apologise for the inconvenience, they would make the gates of Hell look prettier with a touch of graffiti. One of the waiting souls thought it would be funny to give another, much meeker, but psychotic looking soul, a wedgie and hoist him onto one of the spikes that topped the iron gates.

"D'you figure we ought to say something?" asked Oswald to Wilkes-Booth, having both returned after the constant bell ringing by Steve.

"Mmm. Yes, I think now's the time. Come on, let's go," replied his friend, and off they went in search of the demons in charge.

191

"Boss. I really don't think the fuel's going to last. The guys are spreading it as thinly as possible, but it doesn't look good," Berkowitz said, looking worried at Gacy.

Gacy knew that what his subordinate had said was true and was scouring his brain to figure out how to get around this. Suddenly Gacy had a 'lightbulb' moment.

"Who's covering the teetotallers?"

"Holmes and Fish, why?" queried Berkowitz.

"Run down there and get them to stop pouring the booze down the throats of the inmates and get 'em to pour it into the gutters. It doesn't burn as hot, but it's better than nothing."

Berkowitz jumped up from his desk, liking the idea greatly, and shot out of the office towards the teetotal wing.

***

Gary had resumed his reading of the magazine and was trying to be interested in an article about a gym instructor, a traffic warden, and a pogo-stick, when a chill came over him. A small cloud of concern formed, shadowing his face, and looking up from the magazine, the thought of Godjustgod mocking him entered his head, so picking up his phone, Gary brought it to life and again dialled a number.

"Hello, this is Karma. I'm sorry I cannot take your call right now as I'm in the process of kicking someone's ass. If you'd like to leave your name and number and a brief message, I'll get back to you as soon as I can. If this is you, Gary, then don't bother. I'm sure I'll be seeing you soon enough... Please record your message and press hash or just hang up."

"Karma, baby! How's my beautiful best friend? Just thought I'd give you a quick call and see how you're doing. Noticed you've changed your voicemail. Nice touch to think about me. Tell you what. We must get together sometime and have a glass of wine and a meal. Promise I won't leave you to pay the bill this time, I just had to rush off as I had some urgent business to tend to. Call me. Mwah!"

Karma was sitting in her favourite hairdresser's chair when her phone rang. The name on her screen made every fibre in her body bristle. She decided not to answer it and let it go to voicemail. Daveed had finished taking out the foils from her hair when he noticed Karma's resting bitch face had changed to not-so-resting.

"Ooh! I sense someone's going to get it in the neck. You alright, darling?"

Karma's face broke into a smile and looked at her hairdresser through the mirror.

"I'm better than what someone's going to be," she replied.

"Do tell. You know I love a bit of gossip. Promise not to tell, cross my heart."

Karma simply shook her head and went on reading her magazine.

"Karma's a bitch Daveed. Karma's a bitch."

Chapter 20

Afternoon had settled in for the rest of the day. The sun had had its fill of a sun's version of coffee and was buzzing more than a Geiger counter at Chernobyl. With its rays shining down on the village of Ashburn, the sun, along with a certain deity, was looking on at the village with an expectation that something good was about to happen.

There was no sign that anything extraordinary was about to explode onto the streets of the village, in fact, quite the contrary. Ashburn would have been well known for nothing really happening if it weren't for the fact that because nothing ever happened, no one knew of the place and therefore it wasn't well known for anything.

In fact, Ashburn-on-Sinkhole wasn't known at all. The recent events with an elderly looking smart gentleman who had attacked Jensen Moonchild and had managed to impale himself on Charles St.John-Fox's garden dibber appeared to go unnoticed too. For all intents and purposes, Ashburn was more sedate than a lab rat on ketamine.

If you were to gaze at Ashburn as close as a certain deity was, then you may find a few chinks in the sedate façade. The Devil was sitting in the village pub reading a stolen pornographic magazine, whilst the village mechanic was fitting an ultra-fast transportation system to a vintage automobile.

The alien spacecraft which the mechanic had been working on was waiting for parts to be delivered through the post, whilst the aliens of the said craft were sitting around playing cards and drinking pots of tea.

Along with the fact that two ghosts, who were high on cannabis, given to them by the lady come white witch, who owned the village café, who were now in the process of enlisting other spirits for the evening's clairvoyant event, it all made for a very interesting village indeed.

***

"SNAP!" shouted Forsta, as he slammed his hand down on a pile of playing cards in the middle of the three aliens.

Dissel and Pitrol looked at each other in dismay.

"We stopped playing that game twenty crits ago. We're on to Go Fish now, you dunderbleek!" said Dissel calmly with an undertone of anger.

Slowly the alien's hand raised from the pile of cards and a nervous smile formed on Forsta's face.

"Ah! My bad."

"Federschit," muttered Pitrol.

"Steady on! I just forgot! No need to call me that," protested the alien.

Pitrol stood up from the small makeshift table, made from a pile of old tyres and a metal sign, advertising oil, and threw his cards in the air.

196

"I'm getting fed up with this. We give this earthling our knowledge about microwave power, and now he's more keen on fitting it to a clapped-out vehicle than fixing our craft! Is it just me who is getting tired with being here? I really want to get back home, or at least back on the 'making money' track!"

Pitrol stomped off from the table with his hands on his hips.

Dissel stood up and exercised his rank.

"Sit the snark down! This 'earthling' as you call him is fixing our craft better than we could. He's told us he's waiting for a part that should be coming soon, so why don't you just sit and wait. Stomping around like a complete scragfeld will not make the part arrive any faster."

Kenneth, who was hard at it, fitting the microwave power source to Walter's classic Mercedes, had heard the commotion so decided to ease tensions.

"Cuppa anyone?"

All three aliens looked at each other.

"Oh, yes!" said Forsta, finishing his tea and placing the cup on the makeshift table.

Kenneth put his spanner down, wiped his hands on an oily rag that he produced from his pocket, and smiled.

"Coming right up. Think I need one myself. Sugar?"

All three aliens glanced at each other again, and slowly they nodded at each other.

"Please?" replied Forsta, not knowing what sugar was.

Kenneth, who had managed to squeeze the large vintage Mercedes into his garage between the UFO and the garage wall, walked past the aliens, picking up their empty mugs, and made his way towards the kettle. Shaking the last dregs out of the mugs, Kenneth popped a teabag into each vessel and clicked on the kettle.

"Won't be long gents," he said as he wandered over to them.

"As soon as Fergus drops it off, I promise I'll have you back on the road... or in the sky... space, well, you know what I mean. Just while we're waiting for the part, I figured I'd help out my good customer with his car. He just wanted a little more pep in the engine."

"Pep?! It'll be intergalactic!" sniggered Forsta.

"Well, he doesn't have to redline it, does he? I figure less than one percent will be faster than any of us will have gone. Of course, I mean us Earth folk when I say us. You guys will have probably put your clog down in the past."

Not too sure what 'putting the clog down' meant, Dissel agreed.

A sudden click from the kettle and Kenneth hopped back over to it and poured the water into the mugs. Quietly sipping and slurping away, the three aliens quickly finished their drinks and requested another. Kenneth knew he had to finish Walter's car, but also knew he had to make sure that the three extra-terrestrials didn't kill themselves in a fight over being stuck on this planet. How on Earth could he explain three badly beaten or dead aliens in his garage to anyone, was a mystery to him?

198

In the village churchyard, under a Yew tree, closely situated to Clarabelle's grave, stood Bernie and Clarabelle. Although they were standing, they were heavily reliant on the tree for keeping them upright, as the smoke that they had recently inhaled down at Betty's was a much stronger blend than normal and had instantly gone to their ghostly brains.

Bernie was holding court as Clarabelle hugged the tree and did nothing but giggle and pinch Bernie's bottom. He attempted to pitch the idea to the other spirits of the evening's clairvoyant show whilst trying his best to appear sober and not react to the inappropriate pinching.

"So. If we can make this work, then that means we can all chat to our loved ones, or at least distant relatives, and then ooh!"

Clarabelle giggled as she firmly gripped Bernie's left buttock.

"Will you stop it!... As I was saying, then if we can make this work, then who knows? We may be able to do this on a more regular basis. Now wouldn't that be... Oh for goodness' sake, Clarabelle!"

Clarabelle giggled again.

"Will you two just get a coffin!" called out a spirit from Bernie's audience.

As much as a ghost could blush, Bernie did.

"Anyway. It starts at 6 pm tonight. So if you could all make your way down there for that time, then that would be great."

"I, for one, will not be attending this ridiculous event!" thundered a voice from the rear of the audience.

Constantine Harper parted the other spirits like Moses parted the Red Sea and swiftly walked towards Bernie with a glare of disdain and menace on his face. Before he could rain a torrent of abuse in Bernie's direction, a look of fear and pain suddenly appeared on the head teacher's face.

"Before you start, Constantine, I think you should stop. No one is asking you to attend as no one wants you there... No one wants you here either, come to think of it."

Clarabelle's look was as fierce as the grip she had on Constantine's groin.

"So if you'll beg my pardon, can I suggest that you just PISS OFF!"

The last two words of her suggestion that were spat out were accompanied by an extra hard squeeze which resulted in the ghostly head teacher making a sound similar to that of a rutting hamster. Slowly and quietly, there came a ripple of applause from the rear of the crowd that quickly fanned out to where everyone was clapping.

"Well?... Piss off!"

Clarabelle added a little twist to her grip, which weakened her captive at his knees.

"OK, OK!" squealed Constantine.

The grip was released, and a modicum of comfort returned to the indignant ghost. Constantine looked down his nose at his aggressor, as he straightened his cape and with a snappy, soldier-like about-turn, he strode off, brushing aside other spirits who were still applauding the harlot's actions.

"So ladies and gentlefolk, are we on for tonight?" smiled Clarabelle.

***

The afternoon had gone quite smoothly, other than the slight hiccup in the churchyard between Constantine and Clarabelle. Hilda Swindlebrook and Elsie Bagshaw had set out the Women's Institute Hall with all the chairs facing the stage and all in their precise position. Not one being a millimetre out of place, that was Hilda for you.

The tea urn, cups, and saucers were precisely positioned at the back of the hall for the intermission. In the foyer was a lone table and chair with a small tin to collect the admission fees, which would be done by Elsie, whilst Hilda would play M.C. for the show. It appeared that there was a tremendous interest in the evening's prodigious show and the couple of elderly ladies expected to make a killing with the takings, all of which would help in the hall's upkeep.

Charles and Edith St.John-Fox had finished tending to their garden and were even picking out clothing to wear when they attended the clairvoyant 'thingy' that evening. The couple only ever wore clothing when they visited the shops for their groceries, but tonight's event required something a little posher. Both Charles and Edith's clothing had been placed on their bed and laid out flat whilst the couple took turns in having a bath.

Everyone who was anyone was attending the evening's event at the W.I. and pretty much anyone who wasn't anyone was also attending. That is apart from Buttercup Moonchild, who had complained that by summoning spirits to talk to the audience was indicative of oppression, and that was something she was firmly against. Buttercup not attending meant that Jensen was also not attending.

This was of great upset to all the ladies in the village who for some reason had taken a shine to him, ever since he had been bitten in the neck by that strange, smartly dressed man. An issue that irked Buttercup but would say nothing about it as jealousy was a possessive trait and thus against the very essence of her nature. However, that didn't stop Buttercup from controlling Jensen as it simply went under the guise of 'knowing what was best for both of them'.

All of this had been observed under the watchful eye of Godjustgod, who for the last half hour or so had been getting ready for the evening's beach party. Godjustgod had met up with a surf dude who insisted on calling him the 'G-man' of which Godjustgod had started to like.

The secret agent spy man persona was alright and yes, he had a great theme tune to any entry he made, but the sounds of crashing waves and The Beach Boys music in the background had an aura about it which was more akin to his own. But for now, at least, Godjustgod remained Godjustgod.

Chapter 21

Evening time had arrived and the sun, being all tuckered out with shining as much as it did, felt it was time for an early night. This was a bit of a surprise for night who wasn't ready and so dusk had to step in until night had got its glad rags on. Dusk was the 'go-to' guy when the sun played these tricks. To dusk, the sun was like a little child, just a massive little child, playing out all day and then suddenly without warning, feeling exhausted, sloped off without telling anyone.

Hilda and Elsie had opened the W.I. Hall earlier than expected as their usual form of transportation, Walter and his lovely vintage car, had turned into Hilda's Citroen 2CV due to important maintenance work being carried out. This was not only an inconvenience for the two ladies but a nightmare for Walter who had been wooing the love of his life, Hilda, for a number of decades now, and only recently had he managed to get her into his car.

However, his dear friend Kenneth had promised him the car back by the following afternoon with a little more power than it previously had. Unbeknownst to Walter, quite a substantial amount... on an unearthly scale.

The two ladies stood in the quiet hall with all the wooden chairs laid out perfectly. The sunny day had warmed the hall up and, being made of old wood, emitted the musty smell that only old buildings could. Hilda inhaled the woody smell with the faint aroma of room spray, smelling of linen sheets, and the rather pungent odour of Elsie's rose petal perfume.

"I do hope tonight goes well," Hilda quietly said to herself.

"I'm sure Betty will be wonderful," replied Elsie with a smile looking up at her best friend and commander-in-chief for the W.I.

Hilda looked at her smiling friend, with a combined feeling of, 'You know, she's right.' and 'Oh bugger, we're doomed!'

Just then, a little tapping sound on the wooden and glass doors leading to the foyer could be heard and the two ladies turned to see the star of the evening's show, Betty.

"Hello, my lovelies. By you've done splendid with the room. I do hope we get enough people in," she smiled, and thought, "I do hope those two are going to get the rest of the ghosts in otherwise it'll be a right shower of sh..."

"Well, I've spoken to loads today, and they all seem to be up for it," beamed Elsie, interrupting Betty's thoughts.

"The ticket price should be fine too, so if you're alright with this then how about we split the takings 50/50?" added Hilda.

Betty figured for the first show that would suffice, however, if it was a success then a further negotiation on the 50/50 split would be needed.

"That's fine, Hilda. Is there anywhere behind the stage that I can go, so when you introduce me I can be ready?"

The only room behind the stage was Hilda's own private office, of which no one went... to her knowledge.

"I'm afraid we don't, really. What we can do though is close the stage curtains with you already on there and I will get Gavin Lewis to lift them when I say my part. Will that do? Oh, I'm afraid we have no plug sockets on the stage if you're wanting any introduction music to be played. Health and safety, you know."

Betty hadn't thought about music to bring her on with, but not having any power for a CD player put paid to that idea, anyway.

"That's fine. I'll just go get some fresh air and prepare myself, then I'll pop on stage."

Elsie thought with the size of Betty the only popping as she got on stage would either be her hips or knees.

With a brief wave and smile, Betty left the room and went in search of Bernie and Clarabelle to ensure that the special guests were going to turn up.

As Betty left the building, an orderly queue had started to form outside the W.I. hall mainly comprising elderly ladies, eager to speak to anyone willing to chat back and their husbands, who weren't so eager, as they were missing a pint or the football match on TV.

Betty turned down the side of the hall and was getting a little panicky over her two helpers, who hadn't turned up yet. Maybe her supplier of a certain herb gave her a too strong a blend and both Bernie and Clarabelle were still 'out for the count'.

The double oak doors opened and there stood Hilda in her finest tweed two-piece suit and Elsie sat at the table, waiting to take the admission fare.

"Ladies and Gentlemen. If I can have your attention, please!"

Hilda paused to add more drama.

"The doors are open!"

"Bloody see that!" heckled one of the reluctant husbands from the rear of the queue.

A stern gaze from Hilda and a sharp jab to the ribs from the angry and embarrassed wife prevented any other husband from making similar comments. Hearing Hilda announce that the doors were open, and peering around the corner, Betty spied the two spirits entering the square by the side of The Blind Cobbler's Thumb.

"Oh, thank the Lord for that," she breathed a sigh of relief.

Out of the sight of the crowd, Betty waved to the two ghosts to beckon them over to see if they had managed to contact anyone and if they had enough spirits for a good show. Betty strained to see what was behind her two helpers, who had now seen her and had waved back, making their way over to her. Behind the couple appeared to be a faint blur and Betty wasn't sure if she could see other ghostly bodies or if it was just the dimming light of the day that played tricks on her eyes.

Bernie, in a childlike manner, skipped ahead of his friend who promptly burst into fits of giggles.

"Betty! Look who we've brought! Nearly everyone...Everyone but that old Headmaster, Mr Harper," beamed Bernie.

With a sigh of relief and placing her hands to her heavily bosomed chest, Betty smiled at the prancing spirit.

"Oh, thank you so much, Bernard, and you Clarabelle, for all that you've done. I'm sure I can arrange a regular payment if this keeps up."

As the blurry crowd became less blurry, but still too much to figure out who was who, Betty's smile broadened.

"50-50, eh? You, old bat," thought Betty as she glimpsed Hilda welcoming the village folk into her hallowed halls.

Betty ducked back into the side road and was met by her two new friends, followed by a blur of other ghosts.

"Ta-dah!" beamed Bernie as he struck a pose like a magician's assistant. "What d'you think?"

Betty looked in the direction that Bernie was pointing, but could barely see a blur of figures.

"That's great Bernie, but I can barely make out who they are. I think we need one of you on stage with me and another with this group. Whoever comes on stage with me can translate from whichever of these fine people are with us to their respective folk in the audience."

"Me, me, me, me!"

Bernie was jumping on the spot and clapping his hands as he had not set foot on the stage since the little incident when he was alive and his class did a version of

Westside Story. That evening ended up with minor injuries and damaged chairs as his pupils became a tad excited during the battling scenes between the Sharks and the Jets. Over the fits of Clarabelle's giggles, Betty agreed.

"Right, you two. Can you ask our guests if they can have a look at who is entering the hall and if they recognise them? Also, if they want to speak to anyone, to let you know, and then one by one we can bring them in?"

"They heard that," said Clarabelle as she caught her breath whilst the gleeful ex-drama teacher still bounced on the spot.

The blur seemed to disappear as Betty did her best to calm down Bernie.

"Come on, young man. Let's get inside."

Under Betty's direction, Clarabelle had lined up all the spirits and was just waiting for the call. Both helpers were feeling very thirsty and had an attack of the munchies but were ready to make good on their promise to Betty.

The sea of best dresses and matching patent leather handbags flowed into the hall on a wave of violet and rose petal perfume, with Elsie taking the appropriate money from each woman.

**

On the other side of the square where Fergus and Morag Hamilton's post office was, a small red van pulled up with a red and gold logo on the side showing that a postal delivery was arriving. Barry, the delivery driver, was, in his younger days, quite a cheeky catch for all the ladies and was not averse to making a different sort of delivery whilst the same ladies' husbands were either away at work or in prison.

However, time had taken its toll on Barry, so had the several beers a night and Arnold Belcher's pork pies. In his postal uniform, whose shirt buttons were under a significant amount of stress, Barry had passed his 'sell by' date externally, but in his head, he was still a lady killer.

Offloading the bags from the rear of his van, destined for Morag to sort out and Fergus to deliver, Barry merrily threw them over his shoulder and wandered to the post office door. The light was still on in the premises and Morag, seeing the van pull up, had started to bring to the front of the foyer all the mail waiting to be sent out that had been posted by the residents of Ashburn.

"Evening, gorgeous," chirped Barry over the sound of the post office doorbell.

"Say what?" Morag's hearing had never been good, but over the years had steadily declined.

"Got this, you old bag," smiled Barry.

"Oh right, the bags. Thanks, Barry, put 'em over there, will you? Fergus is just in the back."

"I will, you deaf old mare."

"Say what?"

"I said I'll put them over there!" Barry shouted.

"Oh, thanks, deary."

Barry quite enjoyed speaking to Morag, as he could pretty much say anything he wanted to and get away with it. He dropped the two bags in the usual place, picked up the outgoing mail and made his way to the door.

"Right, you deaf old bat, I'm off to shag your dog," Barry called out.

"Say what?"

"I said that's that Morag and I'm off shall I close the door?" Barry shouted.

"Thanks, deary. My hearing's getting worse," Morag laughed. "I thought you said something about having sex with a dog!"

Barry laughed and left the place whistling as he went.

"He's a nice young man," muttered Morag to herself. "Fergus! 'ere y'are! Barry's made a delivery!" Morag shouted to her husband.

"It's a damn sight more than I have lately, you frigid old bat," said Fergus as he entered the shop area.

"Say what?"

"Nothing, darling."

Fergus lifted the bags onto the counter and the couple emptied the contents so they could be sorted into Fergus' delivery routes.

Amongst the letters and parcels were two tubular card containers. One containing parts for a strange craft and the other containing, allegedly, a towel from Italy. With the two tubes in his hands, Fergus turned to his wife,

"Darling, just help me out. The writing on these are quite small. Where they going?"

Fergus's sight was as bad as Morag's hearing, which was not what the villagers wanted in a postman. It would have been easier for the villagers if they were to attend the post office on a daily basis and see Morag for any mail, but Fergus needed to work for his own sanity, so insisted that he deliver the mail.

"Say what?"

Morag stopped her sorting out, turned to her husband, and looking at the two tubes and reading the addresses, she loosely pointed to them,

"That one's for Kenneth up at the garage and that's for that nice man, Jeremiah."

Fergus placed the items in different sacks for the next morning's delivery, figuring he had got the right name for the appropriate tube.

Fergus sucked his teeth as he squinted through the post office window at the blurry queue outside the W. I. hall, which was starting to move.

"What's going on over at the W.I.?"

"Say what?"

Fergus sighed, "What's going on at the, oh never mind."

"Say what? Oh, never mind deary. Have you seen the sign outside the Women's Institute? There's a clairvoyant 'do' on tonight. It's that Betty from the café. How she can speak to the dead, I don't know. Anyway, I thought we could go, but what with my hearing I doubt I'd know what's going on."

Fergus gently nodded as he had given up for the evening trying to converse with his wife. He had found out the long way, the answer to his question, so just carried on with his sorting to the best of his ability.

***

Passing Hilda in the doorway, Betty gave a brief smile to the head of the Women's Institute and bid her greetings to Elsie, who was taking the entrance fees from all the eager patrons. Bernie, who was still excited at returning to the hall, and especially the stage, accidentally brushed past Hilda, who immediately shivered.

"Ooh! I think someone's just walked over my grave," she muttered to herself, as Bernie's eyes widened, fearing that he had been 'caught out'.

Quickly walking through the foyer and into the main hall, the two saw the half-filled room, with all the women chatting to their friends, and all the men sat with their arms folded like scolded children on the naughty step.

"Bloody hell!" exclaimed Betty. "And there's loads more outside too! Y'know what young Bernard? I think we have a sell-out show, my dear friend."

Betty made her way to the side of the stage where Gavin Lewis, the village councillor, was waiting.

"Good evening, Betty. Looks like we're in for a full house," smiled Gavin at his friend.

"Yes, so I see. I was only saying to Ber... I was just thinking to myself, it's going to be a sell-out."

Gavin moved out of the way to let the evening's artiste climb the steps onto the stage.

"Are you OK getting up there? I know it's a bit steep."

"Oh, I'm fine," said Bernie and bounded up onto the stage.

"He meant me, you dafty," replied Betty.

Gavin looked a little perplexed.

"I'm sorry. Were you talking to someone?"

"Oh, it's my spirit guide," replied Betty, trying to double bluff the young councillor, "Y'know like that man on the TV? That haunting programme?"

Gavin gave a tap to the side of his nose, trying to make Betty believe that he knew what she was on about.

"Riiight! Gotcha. So anyway, do you want help getting up?"

Betty accepted an inappropriately placed hand getting onto the stage and thanked the red-faced helper, who was very apologetic for his way of helping. Unceremoniously being helped onto the stage, and behind the thick heavy velvet curtain, Betty noticed a comfy chair and tiny table with a small carafe of water and glass on it. Bernie had just stuck his head, literally through the curtains to see the increasing audience then leaned back in and smiled at Betty.

"The last time I was here was when my class did Westside Story. It was wonderful! ... Then it got a little out of hand."

Bernie's face went from one of joy to resignation.

"Don't worry, my lovely. This time this is going to remain wonderful, right through to the end," reassured Betty.

Chapter 22

The new arrivals waiting at the gates of Hell were getting larger and more impatient, not to mention rowdier and destructive. Several lesser evil souls had been 'wedgied' and were dangling from the spikes on the top of the gates by their underwear and were pleading to be let down as it was 'no longer funny'.

Steve had got fed up with seeing his deliveries still at the gate, so had got to the stage where he would open a tear in the ether and just throw the new arrivals at the gate, closely followed by a fluttering card claiming he was sorry that he had missed the occupier.

Another tear had opened up and another lost soul was thrown through with a fluttering card, but this time Steve noticed something which concerned him. Pausing before he rushed off so he wouldn't be caught by the angry mob, Steve poked his head out from the tear and saw that the flames of Hell had significantly subsided to a level where it could be seen as a bubbling flaming stream of fire.

"What the bloody hell?" Steve knew something was wrong, "Oh well, not my problem," and disappeared back into the tear which closed up before anyone could escape through it.

***

"What d'you bloody mean, you told us?! You told me sod all!" shouted Adolph down the phone to a defensive Gacy.

"I told Genghis that we were running low and that something needed to be done! I'd have told you, but you just slammed the door in my face, so don't start having a go at me!"

"But!" Adolph fired back at Gacy, then swiftly turned to Genghis. "You did this, didn't you?! That's why you let me be boss. You knew, and you didn't do anything about it!"

Genghis smiled.

"I solved the problem that *you* let happen. You slammed the door on Gacy when you should've listened to him."

"Solved it?! How?"

"Gas."

"What?!"

"He's ordered some gas instead of bio-ethanol."

"Gas?! That's no good! Why didn't he order the usual?"

"He would have done if you'd signed his form, but *you* slammed the door in his face and now all the fuel has been bought up and we're left with a poor alternative. I signed the form because you didn't. Like I said, if you screw up I'll take over and I become in charge."

"You bloody planned this all along, didn't you!"

"It's 'you bloody planned this all along, didn't you' *boss*."

"You can sod off..."

"Deals a deal and you agreed to it, so get used to it. Anyway, I'm in charge now, so it's my turn in the chair."

Adolph quickly ran back to Gary's throne and jumped onto it, gripping the arms of the throne with his clawed hands. Genghis dashed over, landing a crushing blow to Adolph's jaw.

"Get out!"

***

"What's happening?" asked Berkowitz to Gacy, who still had the phone to his ear.

"I think they're fighting now. Each blaming the other and something about where they're sitting."

"Well, they'll be both sitting in nothingness when Gary comes back, because that's it. We're out of fuel. What we have left is in the gutters, and that's dwindling now."

Gacy placed the phone back on its base.

"Not our problem, lad."

Both demons looked at each other, turned and continued with their own paperwork.

***

To all the people who have ever said, 'It'll be a cold day in Hell when I'll do that!' should have been panicking right at that moment as it was now coming to fruition. Hell as a whole, being immeasurably large, was always ominous with its flaming appearance but was now becoming rapidly darker and more ominous, perhaps if you felt that something like a disused shopping mall was ominous.

The fiery roar of flames had now turned into a faint glowing ember of Hades. Every soul trapped in Hell had suddenly become quiet as every demon wondered why the flames were dying out and had stopped tormenting the trapped ones. Even the angry mob outside who waited to come in had watched as the gullies down either side of the 'Walk of Shame' path started to die out.

"Oh, bugger!" said one of the angry waiting souls at the back of the mob, "That don't look good."

"It's Hell, you dick. It's not supposed to look good," replied another waiting soul.

"You know what I mean!" said the first voice, which was quickly followed up with a punching sound against a lost soul's cheek.

For the first time in... well, for the first time, Hell was both dark and quiet.

***

God was admiring his latest style in his office mirror and feeling that he could get used to it. There was only one more occasion that he'd willingly be Godjustgod and that would be shortly, however, G-man was in da house!

"Oh, yeah!" smiled God at himself in the mirror, "You is da bomb!"

With a surfboard miraculously appearing from nowhere, God turned and made his way out of his office and down the path.

"By 'eck!" exclaimed one cherub to his domino playing opponent.

"Chuff me!" replied the other.

Both cherubs stared at God, then at each other.

"What the bloody chuff is gooin' on 'ere?"

"Buggered if I know."

"One minute he's suited and booted and next he's ready for his jollies!"

"H'is on'y missing his deckchair and a stick o' rock."

"What the bloody 'other place' is gooin' on?"

"In't it that do that's 'appenin' down near 't beach?"

"Is there a shindig gooin' on?"

"Aye,"

"What the chuff are wi' doin' 'ere then?"

The two cherubs packed up their dominoes and scurried off to replace their halos with a knotted handkerchief and to pick up their bucket and spades.

"Travis, my son. Is everything ready?" asked God, as he noticed his friend by a pile of unlit driftwood.

"G-man! Whoa, dude! Check you out! Drop the tux and look at the result!"

Travis was very impressed with the overall look of his new amigo and admired, not only the physique but the board he was carrying. The look in Travis's eyes over his board made God smile.

"Like what you see?"

"Dude, that board is rad to the extreme!"

"Tell you what. If you look after it for me whilst I do a small job, then when I come back, if you've done a good job looking after it, then it's yours." God replied holding out the board.

Travis's jaw dropped and his eyes started to glaze. Without even making a move for the board, Travis went for God and caught him with an enormous hug.

"Dude. Honestly. You're really too much. If you weren't the G-man, I'd swear that you were, if you know what I mean."

God had never been given a hug before as everyone simply accepted him as the almighty and powerful and that was something you just didn't do. Love and acceptance were emotions he had invented a long time ago, and whilst he had felt love before, this was his first hug, and he was enjoying it, albeit a shade too tight.

"Man. You're welcome bra." God said in Travis's ear in a tone that clearly spelled out that he was struggling to breathe.

Travis took a step back, releasing his hug from God, and eyed the board.

"Right bra. Can you look after it whilst I go do this small errand, if so it's yours when I return. Oh, just to let you know, I've got a band that'll fit perfectly with this party and I've also got the driftwood piped up so we can have flames for as long as we want."

With a click of his fingers, the driftwood bonfire lit up and a wonderful citrus smell emanated from the flames.

"Don't worry, it won't go out, not for a long time anyway," God smiled and handed the board to Travis and bid his farewell.

As God walked back to his office, he heard a 60s beach band startup doing cover versions from all the bands of that time. As he reached his door, two cherubs rushed past him with white cotton handkerchiefs on their heads and buckets and spades in their hands.

"'Ey up, God. You not coming?" called back one of the cherubs.

"I'll be there soon, dude," God replied.

"Dude?" replied the cherub who was so surprised, he looked back whilst running and tripped over his spade, "Ooh ya bugger that smarts."

God entered his office and closed the door behind him.

Chapter 23

Gary had finished reading his stolen adult magazine for the seventh time and had suddenly felt a chill. He looked up at his window and noticed it was dusk, so got off his bed, looked out and up the road towards the village church.

As he reached the window and opened it, he felt a warm breeze brush past his face and wondered why it was warmer out there than it was inside. It was an unusual chill that he'd not felt before and was a little uneasy about it. Never having felt it before, he figured that it might be the heating going off in the pub.

Gary, deciding to take in some fresh air, left his room intending to go for a brief stroll and striding over the recumbent Shadow on the stairs, failed to see the flick of the hound's tail. The stench rapidly reached Gary's nose.

"Mmm, home sweet home," he muttered and continued down the stairs.

Down in the main pub area, Gary noticed that it was almost empty apart from three elderly men, Stephen, Stewart, and Sylas. He saw Terry at the other side of the bar and enquired,

"Is it always this quiet?"

Terry stopped polishing a pint glass with his teatowel.

"No mate. Usually, it's fairly busy but there's a show on at the W.I. It's that Betty Grisslebush, she's doing some sort of clairvoyant show. Our lass has gone with Liam so it's just me, one or two others, and the three stooges tonight."

Gary's response came in the form of a raised eyebrow, and with a shrug of his shoulders and a wink, he left the pub. The village square was fairly quiet as Gary noticed the last couple of people enter the old stone building on the far side of the cobbles.

The warm evening air was polluted with the aroma of cheap rose, talcum powder scented perfume, and the musty smell of jackets that had been stored away in the back of the villager's wardrobes. Gary spied the sign outside the hall, and knowing he had time to kill, wandered over.

"Hello, young man. Are you coming in?"

Elsie noticed Gary loitering outside the premises.

"It's a full house so it may be standing room only, but it'll be worth it, I'm positive," assured the elderly lady.

Gary looked through the open doors at the awaiting audience, who were all sat and chatting whilst facing a heavy velvet curtain.

"Why not," Gary said then made his way in. "Jeremiah is paying. Just see him, as I'm his guest."

Before Elsie could remonstrate, Gary had disappeared inside and had made his way to the front of the audience. Much to Gary's surprise, Jeremiah must have already known that he would be attending as there was a seat with a reserved sign and his name written on it. A skinny old lady who was sitting to the left of the reserved seat, smiled at him as he took his seat.

"Should be a good night. I'm hoping to speak to my husband, Claude. He was in the fencing business you know."

"Sword fencing is a business?" replied Gary.

"No silly, fence fencing. He was clearing out a hole for a fence post to be put in when his mate reversed the van into him and he got his head stuck down the post hole and suffocated."

Gary smiled and held back his laugh.

"Oh, really? Not a nice way to go."

"I should say so," the old lady continued. "His friend, Stanley, reversed into him and caught Claude's bottom with the exhaust pipe, jamming it up there. It blew him up like a cup match football."

Gary tried to hold in his laughter, but by doing so let out a snort, and snot shot out of both nostrils.

225

Chapter 24

Hilda was over the moon that they had filled the hall with paying guests. She looked out, into the square, to see if there were any late-comers who may have been rushing up to the Hall before she closed the door. No one did, so the double doors were shut, and with Elsie, wandered into a buzzing hall full of chattering women and moaning husbands.

"Right. If you go over to the light switches, I'll make my way to the stage. When I nod, you turn off the main lights and put on the stage ones," Hilda instructed Elsie.

"You got it, boss," came the eager smiling reply.

Elegantly, Hilda glided down the side of the hall past every waiting member of the audience and stood in front of the stage. As she looked down to ensure her feet were in a ladylike position and looked up to address the audience, Elsie switched off the lights, leaving her friend in the dark.

Gavin, who was behind the curtain with Betty, was suddenly illuminated and quickly pulled the curtain rope, revealing the star of the show to the waiting audience. Hilda's silhouette could be seen, seething. Hilda's thunder had been stolen, and storming off from the front of the stage, she retreated to the rear of the hall and her friend.

"What on earth was that?!" Hilda demanded.

"What d'you mean? I did as you said. You nodded, and I turned the lights off."

"I did not nod my head!"

"Yes, you did. I know a nod when I see it. Your head went down, then back up again. In my books, that's a nod, Hilda Swindlebrook."

"Ladies and gentlemen. Thank you all for coming to tonight's show. I'm absolutely certain that tonight will be a fantastic and thoroughly entertaining paranormal event," started Gavin, whilst the two ladies at the rear of the hall bickered over what constituted as a nod and what didn't.

"Now, you may all know this lady as Betty Grisslebush, the nice lady from the café, but tonight, ladies and gentlemen, tonight, you will know her as... Mystic Betty!"

Betty looked up from the seat. There had been no mention of a stage name!

"Tonight, Mystic Betty will amaze you with her secret powers of talking to our loved ones..." Gavin paused for dramatic effect. "The Dead!"

"Wish my wife were dead," called out a disgruntled husband, who was swiftly rebuked with a sharp elbow to the ribs.

"So, please join me in giving Mystic Betty a huge round of applause!" Gavin raised his arms and started clapping.

Bernie could not help himself and immediately started to take a bow.

"Oi! You silly sod! Stop it!" hissed Betty.

Gavin stopped clapping immediately and looked sheepishly over at the seated star of the show.

"Sorry. Was it too much?" he whispered.

"Not you Gavin, my lovely... oh never mind," came the whispering reply.

Betty stood up from her chair and waved at the audience who started to applaud her. As she made her way to the centre of the stage, Bernie joined her.

"This is fantastic, Betty! Listen to the applause! Oh, I could get used to this," Bernie said with glee.

Betty waved to the audience and whispered out the side of her mouth,

"Let's see how this goes before we hit Las Vegas, shall we?"

"What a great idea Betty," replied Gavin as he continued to clap, "You never know. If you do hit the big time, then how about some tickets?"

"What?" Betty continued to wave to the applauding audience.

"Vegas. Anyway, I'll let you get on, you megastar."

Gavin drifted off to the side of the stage, still clapping, hoping to stir the crowd into a frenzy, whilst Betty nervously waved and Bernie continually bowed in the most dramatic way he could.

"Thank you, ladies and gentlemen," Betty shouted above the clapping.

"Please... Thank you."

The women in the audience were a little too excitable for Betty, who now just wanted the applauding to stop. Bernie, on the other hand, was relishing the sound and continued to bow to his adoring fans.

After a minute's applause, Betty managed to quell the crowd and took a deep breath as this was where the work started. Gary watched on, with his arms folded, feeling still a little on the cool side and still not knowing why.

"Thank you, ladies and gentlemen, for coming tonight and supporting me..."

"Us," whispered Bernie.

"And I really hope you enjoy the show..."

"We."

"Tonight I... we hope to help some of you with communicating with your loved ones that have passed to the other side. Now I... we cannot guarantee to get in touch with everyone, but we shall try our best."

Betty started to wander around the stage with Bernie in tow.

"Now, when it comes to it, whilst I have spoken to people who have passed, it is they who have come to me and not me calling on specific spirits."

Betty gave a quick glance over to Bernie and flickered a smile.

"Now, just like the man on that television show, I too have a spirit guide. Now you may not be able to see him, but may I introduce my guide, Bernard."

Bernie was over the moon that he had been introduced and puffed up his pride and again bowed to his adoring fans.

Everyone in the audience just looked at each other and either thought that Betty had gone completely loopy or she was simply over-egging the show. Everyone but a certain fallen angel who was sitting in the front row. This certain someone could actually see the ex-drama teacher bowing so low that his head was inches from the floor.

"Right, ladies and gentlemen. For this to work, I will need total silence."

Betty was starting to get into the swing of things and was even beating Bernie for overdramatic actions, looking super spooky whilst uttering the words "total silence".

"Oh, give my strength!" muttered Gary, who was very quickly 'shh-ed'.

"So ladies and gentlemen. I am just going to get into my zone, whilst my guide asks the first spirit to come forward."

This was Bernie's signal to call to Clarabelle and get her to send the first ghost in. Betty sat back in her chair and exhaled deeply, muttering some incoherent words to heighten the situation.

The eyes of the audience were all firmly fixed on the lady from the café and her babbling sounds. Bernie had just reached the doorway, to an awaiting Clarabelle, when something unexpected happened.

Betty's eyes opened wide and with her usually relaxed body becoming rigid, she gripped the arms of the chair, letting out an almighty *'AHH!'* as she stood up like a lumpy drainpipe. Bernie stopped in his tracks and turned to see his friend on stage acting like she had been taken over by a spirit.

"My goodness! She is good," he muttered to Clarabelle.

Clarabelle stared at Betty in awe.

"I have never seen anything like it. She's amazing! Best get someone in there soon, as she can't keep this up for long."

The first ghost behind Clarabelle was Hector Williams, who had seen his granddaughter in the crowd and wanted to tell her to stop giving her husband grief over his fishing tackle being left in the hallway.

Just before Hector set foot into the hall, Betty came to life with a cough, a splutter, and a little fart. Music of a particular super spy theme tune started up from nowhere. Hilda looked at Elsie and both wondered as to how Betty had got a PA system into the hall without them seeing it.

"There's no plug sockets up on stage. How's she?..."

"I know!" interrupted Elsie, "It's coming from everywhere like there's speakers all over the place."

The guitar riff was blasting out the intro for a certain Mr Bondjamesbond, much to the delight of the entire audience, apart from one.

"Oh, you've got to be joking!" Gary sagged in his seat.

Betty started calmly walking across the stage in time to the music nonchalantly then swiftly turning on the spot and pointing a finger at a fed-up member of the audience in the front row. The music faded away, leaving the audience in awe at Betty's opening act.

"Ladies and Gentlemen. Allow me to introduce myself to you," Betty announced in a manlier voice, "I am... this man's father!"

"Well, technically, you're everyone's father, so don't you pick me out from the rest," Gary replied to the star of the show.

"Oh well, maybe that might be true, but I'm here for you, Gary," Betty smiled down at the annoyed fallen angel.

"For the rest of the audience, let me tell you a bit about my son," Betty chuckled, "He's a bit of a devil, that's for sure."

"Aren't they all," shouted a woman's voice from the rear of the hall.

Betty looked and nodded in agreement.

"True Margaret, but this young man here can probably trump every other son."

"How'd he know my name?" Margaret whispered to her husband, who was sitting by her side.

"It's Betty from the café, you silly cow. She's known you for years!"

"Oh, yeah!... Hang on! Don't call me a silly cow!"

"Oh yes. He can be a right handful. Did you know, ladies, that it was my son, Gary, who invented women's dress sizes?"

The atmosphere in the hall changed and all female eyes glared at the smartly dressed male on the front row.

"Hang on one second. I only did that because you couldn't be bothered," fired back Gary.

"In my defence, I was busy at work," Betty replied

"And another thing, before you blame it on me, I didn't invent women's hot flushes."

"No, that's true. That was actually Mother Nature, of which I have had stern words with, and she's promised she would make up for it. As far as I'm aware, she did too by giving women excellent memories when it comes to arguments."

Every male head, in the audience, was nodding in confirmation at that last comment.

"And who was it that made men's dick's shrink with age?" Gary continued.

"You actually," said Betty, smugly.

"Oh, yeah... that's right." Gary started to deflate. "My bad."

"I wouldn't say everything that has made life awkward has been created by my son, but I think I can safely say most things. Wouldn't you agree? Son?"

Gary gave a little mischievous smirk, knowing that more than God knew, was down to him.

"Anyway. What brings you up here? Up to no good, no doubt. Thought you were happy with the home I gave you?"

"Spoilt git!" someone shouted from the middle of the audience.

"Hey! You don't know the home he gave me! It was a right hell hole!"

"Bloody snowflake!" someone else shouted.

"Sod off!" Gary jumped up and looked behind, hoping to see the person who had said that.

"Ladies and gentlemen. The stories I could tell you about my son." Betty laughed, "Always playing with his tail as a child, weren't you?"

"Wanker!" another voice shouted out.

"Oi! It's not that type of tail and anyway, I didn't invent masturbation."

"No. You just came up with the name for it and all the other ridiculous names for intimate parts of the anatomy. Ridiculing the human body."

"Oh, give it a rest! You always bring that up, don't you? You never tell folk of your mistakes, do you?"

Betty looked confused at Gary.

"What mistakes did I make?"

Gary walked to the front of the stage with arms open wide.

"What mistakes? Oh, I'm sorry. Did you intend to make the duckbilled platypus? I mean! A mammal that lays eggs that's semi aquatic with a nose like its tail!"

"I think you'll find out that it was after you'd spiked my sandwich with LSD that I'd created that animal, so is that my fault or yours?"

Murmurings from the audience indicated they were in favour of Betty and not the man in the front.

"And it was you who fell out with your brother Michael, who may I say ladies and gents, it was Gary who got a right towelling off his brother."

"I DID NOT!!" screamed Gary, "He blindsided me!"

"So he won then!"

"You know what, you old fart. I've had enough of you putting me down. What have I ever done to you?"

"Well, LSD in my sandwich for a start. Anyway, why don't you just chill? Oh, is that a touchy subject? Let me put your flames out, otherwise, you're going to burn up and we can't be having that. Look, I'm having a party at my place. I'd invite you but, well, y'know."

"BUGGER OFF!"

Gary stormed out of the crowded hall, muttering something about "one bloody apple" leaving the entire place in silence.

"Kids, eh?" Betty chuckled and suddenly stood bolt upright.

The entire audience looked on, as the lady on the stage suddenly slumped back into the comfy chair. Dazed and shaking her head, Betty looked out into the audience and saw a sea of open mouths and wide eyes. Feeling hot and sweaty, but not knowing what had just happened, Betty feared that she had had a bout of stage fright and had just come around.

"Is everything alright?" she asked anyone who was listening.

Silence.

Gary left the building just as an almighty cheer rattled the windows, followed by a screeching cacophony of women asking to be next.

***

"'Eyup! T'old lad's back," one cherub nudged his friend.

"Wonder where 'es bin?"

"Probably up to no good. See look on 'is face? Someone's 'aving 'ard time reet now," replied the first cherub.

"Travis. See, you started without me. How's it going?" God gave Travis a friendly pat on his back.

"Oh, dude! That St. Peter is a riot! He's chugged six cans of beer, and now he's going for the limbo world record. Well, I suppose a 'Heavenly' record for limbo."

God looked over to see his gatekeeper limboing under a long cane held by a couple of cherubs who were cheering him on at the same time.

"Dude. Maybe wear some underwear next time," shouted out Travis to St. Peter as the saint was halfway under the cane.

"Oh dear me," God shielded his eyes from the view.

"Seriously, G-man! You can throw one hell of a party. Oh, sorry! Can I say that?"

G-man just laughed and sauntered over to the table where a pyramid of unopened beer cans was waiting to be consumed.

"Get me one, will you G-man?" called out Travis, "Got some Tom Jones for later."

Chapter 25

"I must say! I didn't expect this," said Reverend Arbuckle to his neighbour Rabbi Cohen.

"I know what you mean, booshka," replied the Rabbi.

Both men had been waiting at the pearly gates for some time now, along with an ever-growing crowd.

"I mean! The sign clearly states 'back in five minutes' and we must have been here for at least double that."

"We are assuming, of course, that time up here runs parallel to our time on Earth," butted in a mathematician.

"Good point," replied the Reverend looking over his shoulder, "Ernest? Is that you? Well, I'll be! What are you doing here?"

"Would you believe it? One minute I was in my class of students and the next thing I know, there's a knock on the classroom door and in walks someone who looks like the Grim Reaper, but called himself Steve. I thought it was very odd, but I felt compelled to go with him and here I am. Heart attack, I'm afraid. I must admit I thought you'd be the last person I'd see here."

Ernest quickly clarified his last comment, realising the implications of what he was saying,

"I mean, you looked so healthy."

"Well, I also got a visit from Steven. Apparently, church bell ringing can be a little bit more dangerous than I first thought. The thing is, you either let go of the rope or you kind of find yourself here."

"Ah, I see."

"It was a damn sight more than I did. Bit of a headache, I can tell you."

"So, how long have you been here?" asked Ernest.

"Myself and Eugene have been here ten, maybe fifteen minutes," the Reverend said, indicating in the Rabi's direction.

"At the same time?"

"Yes, booshka. I wasn't bell ringing though, just minding my own business in my beth midrash when I heard a polite cough and there was my friend," pointing to the Reverend, "and Steven. The next thing I know I'm standing up leaving my body behind and chatting merrily to Frank whilst Steven opens up some hole and here we are."

"Can someone tell me what's happening up there, please?" called a voice from behind.

"It appears we have to wait five minutes," called out the dead Reverend.

"Won't be long, booshka," added the Rabi

"Oh, I do hope not. My Bill is dying for the toilet and these shoes are killing me."

A ripple of giggles appeared with the last comment.

"It's not a laughing matter," chimed the indignant lady, "They really are killing me."

"Oh, the irony," whispered the Reverend.

***

"Will someone let us in! I'm bloody freezing out here," shouted a lost soul at the less than fiery gates of Hell.

"Oh y'know, what? I've had enough of this waiting. We either storm the place or I'm going home."

"Bugger this, I'm off home. If laddo wants me, then he can come get me himself," said another lost soul and started to leave the gates.

"Well, I'm going to give the bell one more try and if they don't come, then I'm off too," shouted another near the gate.

"Can I just ask? Why the bloody hell are you here? I mean! 'Give the bell one more try'! For crying out loud! What heinous crime did you commit with your stroppy snowflake manner?"

"I actually stood up for my rights when *HE* came for me."

"Death? The Grim Reaper?"

"Steve," shouted out another.

"Yes, him. He instructed me that I was dead, and that I was off to Heaven. Well, I told him straight. I said, 'You are not taking me to Heaven and how dare you take the decision out of my hands'. So here I am."

241

"What a cock!"

"EXCUSE ME!! I'm offended by that!"

***

Genghis had managed to remove Adolph from his temporary throne and was sitting there, gloating at his counterpart. The doorbell suddenly chimed several times in quick succession and paused, followed by a more frantic burst of rings.

"What the?!" Genghis said with a start. "Get the guards to bring that lowlife to me NOW!"

"Do it yourself," replied Adolph.

"I'm boss and I say you do it!" screamed Genghis.

Suddenly there was a knock on the throne room's door. Adolph stomped over and opened the door.

"WHAT?!"

"Adolph, I think we have a problem at the door. You really need to come see this," replied the voice from the other side of the doors.

Genghis' interest was aroused. They had been fighting so much that the fuel had run out and now for the first time in a long time had they heard the gate bell clatter. Something wasn't right, so jumping from the throne, Genghis swiftly marched over to the door and pushed Adolph out of the way.

"What's the problem?"

"Dick!" muttered Adolph.

"Watch it you!" Genghis quickly turned to his colleague, "What's happening?"

"Well, it seems you two have been very busy, and no one has given the order to collect the dead from the gates."

"And?" replied Genghis.

"That was quite some time ago and now we've an angry mob waiting to come in... Quite a sizeable angry mob."

"Oh, crap!" Genghis gulped, "Addy? Come on, fella or we're both gonna get it when Gary gets back."

The two demons darted from the room and into the darkened corridor towards the main gates.

"What the bloody home? Where's the flames?" Adolph shouted.

"Your bad, not mine," replied Genghis.

Several minutes later the two out of breath demons reached the portcullis where a group of demons had congregated and were happily watching a group of lost souls beat the stuffing out of another, who kept shouting something about being very offended and knowing their rights.

Draped on the gate spikes were several other lost souls, who were hanging there by their underwear and shouting to be let down so they could have a go at the snowflake. One of the demons behind the portcullis laughed and remarked about a snowflake's chance in Hell, which set off several other demons laughing.

"Bloody home!" said Genghis, "How many's there?"

"More than us boss," replied one demon closest to the bars.

"Sod it! Let's get 'em in. Pronto. Open the gate," shouted Genghis, "Charge!!"

Chapter 26

Gary pushed past Clarabelle and the eager ghosts, fuming that God had made a fool of him in front of all those little tiny people.

"Excuse me?!" Clarabelle protested, as Gary walked through her left arm and shoulder.

"Sod off!" came the reply.

Clarabelle didn't know if the fact that someone had been so rude or the fact that a 'solid' person had actually heard stunned her! Prior to recent events, the only alive person who she could talk to was the lovely Betty. Who was this man and why could he hear her, and why did she feel a little apprehensive about the underlying anger she felt as he passed by?

Gary had felt a little chill most of the evening and walking into the cool village air, felt it more. Previously writing it off, thinking it was merely 'upstairs' and never going up top before, it was probably the way he should feel. He now vexed with a nagging thought in the back of his mind. Since when did God, that oh so annoying deity, use the word chill? He could obviously see that Gary was uncomfortable with the ambient temperature and seemed to be revelling in the knowledge of... what?

The recent phone call he made to home and the two idiots he had left in charge made Gary puzzle over the matter even more.

Wandering and thinking, Gary eventually found himself over the cobbled square and in front of the village fountain. Over the years, the fountain of an angel blowing a horn had eroded, due to a cost-cutting exercise, when the councillors at the time commissioned the item out of sandstone. The stonemasons at the time were more than happy to do this, as they were aware that the village would be coming back soon with another commission and this time in a more expensive stone.

Gary smiled as he looked up at the monstrosity.

"Yeah. A fading angel. Supposed to be looking over this stupid village and this is what happens. You just fade away."

Gary realised that he himself was an angel and not so much a fading one but a fallen one. One that had had his backside handed to him on a plate by God.

"Dammit!" he muttered.

Gary, returning to the matter in hand, continued to wonder what God was up to with his comments and why he felt a chill on, what should be, a nice evening. He pulled out his phone and dialled 'Home', deciding to speak to one of those idiots he had put in charge.

"Genghis! How is everything down there?" Gary said in a tone that would normally strike fear into his subordinate.

"Doing good thanks. How's it where you are?" replied a distracted Genghis.

In the background, Gary could hear a chaos that was a little more chaotic than usual. The sound of cracking whips and souls being prodded with rusty tridents was definitely more prevalent than normal. Plus, since when did the souls ever protest as much? And why were some demons shouting for others to give them a hand?

"What's happening down there? I trust you have it all in hand,"

"Yep! All in hand, boss, I mean Gary. All in hand,"

There was an urgency in Genghis' voice that did not instil confidence in Gary.

"Look, is Adolph there? Let me speak to him now."

"Sure thing, Gary. Adolph is in charge, so I'm not surprised that you'll want to talk to him rather than me. I'm simply doing what Adolph says as he's in charge. I'll get him for you. ADOLPH! PHONE! IT'S GARY FOR YOU!... He's coming. Two ticks."

The indicator of Gary's 'concern-o-meter' was starting to rise. It had only been a short while since there was friction between the two demons as to who would be in charge, and now Genghis was happy to hand the reins over to his counterpart.

"Look! Just get the little bleeder in! Oh hi, Gary. Everything is going just great down here. How's it going where you are?" Adolph panted.

"It'd be better if I knew for sure that you were running my business and home properly and things were going well," Gary's tone was intended to convey trouble would be coming if things weren't.

"Oh, things are just dandy,"

The background noise suddenly became muffled and Gary could hear Adolph shouting something about getting the idiots off the gate spikes.

"Sorry about that Gary, Yea things are going great. Me and Genghis, who's in charge may I say, we're just having a little more fun with the inmates."

"Genghis is in charge? He said you were."

"No! He's definitely the one in charge. He said he wanted to be, and I agreed to let him, so if anything happens down here then it's his fault. Nothing to do with me."

"If anything were to happen? Like what exactly?" Gary was feeling more than a little worried.

"Oh, nothing. Everything is fine and dandy right now, but if you come home and find a few things wrong, then Genghis has been in charge so any punishment should go his way."

"OK, so right now I'm feeling a little chilly when the weather here is fine. I'm just wondering if there's an issue with my flames down there. They're still going good, aren't they? You'll be needing to order more fuel soon."

Gary heard a gulp over the noise of the background.

"Not a problem, Gary. It's all in hand... Just out of curiosity, though. Hypothetically, if we were to run low, then where would we get more if the usual place is out of stock?"

"Well, hypothetically, I would be looking at contacting Gacy in Procurement as he would know all the places and if he couldn't find a place, then hypothetically someone may have left it too late to place an order, then hypothetically someone would suffer my wrath on a scale never seen before. Hypothetically speaking of course."

"Oh, thanks for that. Don't worry though, we've enough so far, but, to be on the safe side I'll place an order now... I'll just get Genghis' authority first though as he's in charge. Wouldn't want to step on his toes. He loves being in charge. I just leave him to it. He's like a demon in a pit of vipers, doing this job. Anyway, Gary, no doubt you're enjoying yourself wherever you are so I'll not bother you and let you crack on. Right, see you when you get back. Adios...GET HIM DOWN FROM THERE FOR F..."

Click!

Gary had an underlying seething that could be seen quite clearly by even the most naïve of people. If his head wasn't like a pressure cooker, he would have boiled over to such a degree that it would have made nuclear fallout seem like a mild pollen count.

Shoving his phone back into his pocket, Gary did not need any further harassment of any kind. This, however, was not the path he was on and Ms Karma knew this.

Leant against the decaying fountain, the fallen angel sat with his hands on his hips and defiantly looked up.

"I swear to G... I swear, if anything has gone tits up down there, I'll lose my shit all together!" Gary called out.

"Utter filth. Who gave you authority to use such foul language?"

Constantine Harper's thunderous voice rattled in Gary's ears.

"What the f..."

"AGAIN, I say! Who gave you authority to use foul language like that? Even the Devil himself does not use such language, and I, for one, am repulsed by your infantile usage of the English language," interrupted Constantine.

"Well, actually I know for a fact that the Devil does use language like that bec..."

"DON'T YOU DISRESPECT ME, BOY!" thundered Constantine.

Constantine raised himself to his full height and got so close to Gary that he could feel the headmaster's nasal breath warming his forehead. Gary didn't know if he should match Constantine's height but double his width, of which he was able to do, or simply pummel the insubordinate worm into the ground. Before he could make a choice, Constantine continued with his rebuking.

"I have been the Head of this area for more years than you have been on this planet. Do you understand? I will not tolerate behaviour like this!" he thundered.

"OK, I'll give you that old lad. You probably *have* been a Head longer than I've been on this planet, as I have only been here a couple of days. And let's just clarify something if I may. What sort of head are you? A dick maybe?" anger and venom spat out with Gary's words.

"WHAT?!"

Constantine's eyes turned a fiery red and would have worried any solidly built rugby player, let alone any normal person. However, Gary was no ordinary person. Neither was he a rugby player, solidly built or otherwise,

250

he was Gary. Gary's eyes darkened to a blackness that was blacker than black with a background of fire that would have turned lava into a steaming pool of nothing.

"DICK...HEAD!" Gary's thunderous voice made Constantine's attempt at thunder sound more like a sneezing hamster.

Big Frank had just served Enzo his drink in The Hammer and Tong when hearing the words looked up.

"'ere! Who's a dickhead?"

Terry, had recently served Sylas with his order in The Blind Cobbler's Thumb, heard the windows rattle and the insult.

"Eyup. Seems like someone's a dickhead out there."

Dissel, Pitrol, and Forsta were sitting in Kenneth's garage whilst the mechanic had all but finished Walter's Mercedes upgrades.

"What's a dickhead?" enquired Forsta.

Rushing out of the W.I. hall, Bernie met up with Clarabelle, who had poked her head through the hall's oak doors.

"What's going on?"

Bernie's head joined Clarabelle's

"Seem's like your old Headmaster has met his match with that man who Betty spoke to," Clarabelle smiled at Bernie whilst biting her lip.

A huge grin appeared on Bernie's face.

"Oh, yes. Have that! Constantine," whispered Bernie, just in case his adversary overheard him.

Constantine's entire ghostly body appeared to back down whilst not moving an inch. The rage on the old headmaster's face disappeared, leaving an uncertain 'what to do next' expression.

"Right!" he eventually said with a wobbly voice, losing the ability to maintain an authoritative tone, "Take this as a warning."

Constantine stormed off before Gary could inhale to start the next onslaught.

The old headmaster left Gary at the village fountain. He was seething and was ready for the next unwilling idiot to pass his way. Heavily breathing like a rabid dog who didn't want to let go of its toy so you could take it to the vets, Gary walked out of the square and down the side of The Blind Cobbler's Thumb. He wanted to clear his mind and ease the troubling thoughts of the potential state his home would be in, leaving it in the incapable hands of either Adolph or Genghis?

Gary's eyes pierced the evening's darkness as he cleared the pub's gable-ended wall. The dim street lighting did nothing to illuminate the road leading up to the village church and Gary was fine with that, even to a point whereby his anger was ever so slightly subsiding.

"Bugger off ya wazzock!"

Grandpa Cyril was sitting outside in the beer garden and enjoying the evening air.

The subsidence of Gary's anger turned into not so much a reduction, but more akin to the sea receding prior to a tsunami hitting the shores of an unsuspecting beach town.

"What?!"

Gary's head snapped to the right to see the stubbled aging face of Cyril looking right at him.

"What did you say?" Gary demanded.

"Bugger off... ya wazzock!" Grandpa Cyril replied.

This was not what Gary needed right now. The flames in his eyes were fanned with a good breeze and fed with kerosene. Like a stalking brick wall, and his eyes firmly fixed on the old man, Gary walked over to Cyril's table at the rear of the pub. Not being fazed by the anger presented in the stranger's eyes, the old drinker lifted his beer glass to take a sip.

"What... did... you... call... me?" demanded Gary.

Cyril took a sip from his glass and nonchalantly, wiping his mouth with the back of his hand, looked up at his aggressor.

"Wazzock!"

Cyril raised his glass again when the entire beer garden was illuminated by Gary's eyes. Gary's whole presence glowed with anger at this old man whose only task in life, it seemed, was to die by the hands of Gary himself and be dragged off to Hell where he would be Gary's personal whipping boy.

"Bugger off!" Cyril continued.

This had Gary more furious, as unlike his previous opponent, this one just did not care as to who he was. No fight, no aggression, just straight up 'couldn't give a crap'. Gary slammed his hand down on the wooden bench table hard enough to send the glass ashtray flying.

The anger in Gary was such that his hand singed the table as he glared at the totally carefree man. Huge devil-like talons appeared from his fingertips and caused five gouge marks in the wooden planked top as his fingers drew together, clenching his fist. Cyril looked calmly into Gary's eyes and whispered,

"Ya wazzock!"

Chapter 27

It was television and social time at HMP Soddem, a high-security prison situated in the middle of a very inhospitable moor on the outskirts of nowhere. Prison Officer Charlie 'Muddy' Waters was on guard in the hall where the inmates sat and watched TV.

This evening's viewing was the latest episode of 'Dan Brantley's SAS Escape from Anywhere'. The entire prison, including the guards, was engrossed in the show for the last four episodes as Dan had been trying to escape from HMP Soddem.

Usually, the supposed ex SAS soldier would escape from a jungle or elsewhere within the hour-long show, but this time it had taken considerably longer with a zero-success rate so far.

Dan Brantley's real name had been Richard Head, but having been beaten up so many times as a child, he'd changed it by deed-pole to something a little more pleasant. Dan had never joined the SAS, but felt that merely thinking of joining allowed him to use the prestigious connection within his show.

It was silent in the prison as the show was airing. The prison officers watching from a gloating point of view, as they had repeatedly thwarted the celebrity's escape, and the prison inmates, to see about any tips on how to take a vacation from their current lodgings.

Dan was currently in the 'Visitors Room' with his producer, pleading to be released or allowed to escape. Sophie, Dan's producer and ex-wife, had other plans though, and thought it best if he continued with his task and genuinely broke out, thus making it realistic.

Prison Officer "Muddy" Waters had left the inmates to watch the programme on their own, as he knew they'd be glued to the television and had disappeared for a cup of tea and a cigarette break.

"Welcome back viewers to Dan Brantley's SAS Escape from Anywhere, with me Dan Brantley. Today I'm still in HMP Soddem and planning my most daring escape yet. For the last few episodes, I've been scanning for weak points and getting to know the prisoners here, seeing where the guards go, and the routes they take. The guards are very clever and always change their routes, making it difficult to escape. Difficult but *not* impossible."

A loud cheer came from the communal TV room.

"Excuse me, gents. I'm looking for..."

Steve suddenly appeared and stood in his most intimidating pose, with his black hooded cloak on with the added effect of having his scythe by his side. Steve hummed whilst thumbing the pages of his 'collection book', and the entire room turned to see the new visitor.

"Bear with me gents, I've just lost my page. I'll be with you in a second."

Steve had not lost his page but had decided to have a little fun with the inmates.

256

"Sorry, gents. It's kinda difficult thumbing pages with just bone. I tell you, you've no idea how lucky you have it, with skin I mean. One of you... mmm, maybe not so lucky. Just give me a second."

"Jeeezus Christ!" shouted out one of the inmates.

"Now that's just silly. I mean, do I look like Christ? I know the chap and let me tell you, I do not... I'm so much better looking than him," Steve let out a little laugh.

"Bloody hell!" called out another inmate.

"Well, at least you've guessed where you're going. Just one more second and I'll have the name."

The whole of the room tried to make a bolt for the door, but in a flash, Steve clicked his fingers and the door slammed shut and wouldn't budge. In the room's corner, under the television set that had been placed high on the wall so people at the back of the room could see, the inmates cowered.

Steve was enjoying the panic that had firmly instilled itself in every living soul in the room, and he was smiling as much as his skull would allow him. Suddenly the air in the room changed and so did Steve's aura. Something wasn't right, and Steve knew there was a disturbance. He looked up from his book, with a much more concerned appearance on his skull, Steve saw the eighty men huddle under the TV.

"I'm really sorry about this, gents, but I'm going to have to leave you for a second. Don't worry though, in the famous words of old what's-his-name 'I'll be back'."

Steve knew where he had to go, and hated the fact that he had to return to the one place he hated with a passion, Ashburn-on-Sinkhole.

"Sodding place. What's up now," he muttered as he disappeared through a tear in the fabric of space, close to the tea-urn on the table next to the chocolate digestives.

***

Close to the lychgate of Reverend Edwin's Church, striding out from the tear, Steve looked down the lane and saw two very familiar figures standing toe to toe. Steve's body sagged.

"What the bloody hell is going on?" he muttered to himself, slapping his forehead in disbelief.

Steve didn't really want to get involved, unless absolutely necessary, so hid in the lychgate and phoned Gary.

Gary's fist was clenched so tight that the blood in his hand had drained out of his knuckles, leaving a scary white demonic fist. Just then his phone rang. The recognisable ring tone was music to Gary's ears, so he relaxed and glared at Cyril as he went for his phone.

"Now you're in for it, you silly old duffer. You'll be seeing someone you really don't want to," Gary raised the phone to his ear, "Steve, my old mate, so glad to hear from you. I need you to come here now and remove this slack old git. It's about time he went with you and you can drop him off at my place. I've a special room just for folk like him."

"I don't think you do, Gary," whispered Steve

Steve was only a hundred yards away from Gary and under no circumstances did he want him to know where he was.

"What?! I bloody do, and why are you whispering?"

"Look, just leave the old git there and move on."

"Hang on a second! How d'you know I'm talking to an old git. I could be anywhere talking to anyone. Where are you?"

Gary looked into the square and up the dark lane towards the church.

As he knew he was safe, hiding in the church's porched gateway, Steve whispered,

"I know everything, Gary. This book of mine doesn't just tell me who to collect but where folk are and I know where you are... exactly, and who're you're with, and believe me, I'm not taking Cyril anywhere."

Gary had just about had enough of rejection and mockery.

"Listen 'ere, you bony old sod. Get your skinny arse here now and do your job or else,"

"Or else what?" came the reply from Gary's side, in a tone that not even the Devil himself wanted to hear.

Steve stood there leaning into Gary to a point where if he had lungs Gary would have felt the warm breath on his forehead.

"Right, now you're here, do your sodding job, you slack bag 'o bones. I'm fed up with you telling me what you're gonna do and what you're not. Just take this old fu..."

"I DO NOT ANSWER TO YOU!" bellowed Steve, "I NEVER HAVE OR WILL DO!"

Normally, Gary would have realised that he might have pushed Steve a little too far, but on this occasion, with the red mist rising and Gary seeing nothing but insolence, he continued with his demands.

"You best start realising who you're talking to and what I can do to you. Now! Take him to my place, now!!"

"And *YOU* best start realising who *YOU* are talking to. I've been around long before you were even a tilt in your old man's kilt. Hell! I've been around before Hell was created, let alone you being placed there for being a petulant little shit. So don't start telling me what to do. I also know *your* name is in my book, and I know when it's coming up, so if I was you, I'd reconsider your current stance and maybe just *BACKOFF!*"

Steve's face was so close to Gary when he shouted the last words that his teeth brushed against Gary's nose.

In a warped sort of way, reality came back to Gary and curiosity took over, wondering why his name was in Steve's 'Collection' book. He was immortal! He was an angel! OK, fallen, but still an angel. Was Steve bluffing, or was his name actually in THE book? Surely God wouldn't have let this happen? A lifespan for angels? Who'd have heard of anything as absurd as that? OK, so back to the Platypus, but still! Gary's thoughts of his current position were interrupted.

"So if you don't mind, I'll get on with my job, and you will..."

"Bugger off ya wazzock!" interrupted Grandpa Cyril.

"Couldn't have said it better myself," replied Steve, and disappeared into a waiting tear.

Watching his formidable opponent disappear, Gary turned to the old man, and was met with two fingers waving in his face and a stubbled, grinning Cyril behind them. The clenched fist quickly resumed its force, but before Gary could swing back and land a crushing blow on the old man's jaw, he felt a searing pain in the arse-end of his trousers, which quickly shot to his brain, courtesy of Shadow.

"Bleeding hell!" was all that Gary could say, as the wolf's teeth sank into the buttocks of the fallen angel.

Failure was the only option as Gary tried to turn and shake off the enormous beast.

"Get this bleeding thing off me!" screamed Gary as the pain increased.

Grandpa Cyril burst out laughing and picked up his beer glass to take a drink.

As the danger to his old human friend was passing, Shadow released his grip and allowed the pain to subside.

Swiftly turning to see the creature who had inflicted pain on the Devil himself, Gary came face to face with the snarling Shadow, who was ready to take another bite out of anything that came his way. Wolf breath and snarling snot from such a beast is not something anyone wants to experience, and having such a bad time over the last half hour, Gary decided to back down. Pirouetting around, Gary glared at Cyril.

"You are *so* lucky, old man. And you!" Gary looked back at Shadow, whose snarling had become more menacing,

"Go lick your balls!" was all that Gary could think of.

Gary stormed off towards the square, leaving Cyril to reward Shadow with a pat on the head and an ear rub.

***

The cowering group of inmates at HMP Soddem were starting to wonder if the Grim Reaper was going to return. Or did he have the wrong address? The group of hardened criminals gradually began to relax the tight group, much to Gerald "Bunny" Jackson's disappointment, who had kind of liked being up close and personal under such terrifying circumstances.

The tougher criminals, who had forced their way to the very corner of the communal room, started to push out, claiming they were all a bunch of pansies for being so scared over something or nothing.

Several of the tougher ones exclaimed that if they had been able to, they would have taken the Grim Reaper out altogether, or shivved him with a lettuce leaf from Bunny's salad.

That was right up to the point when a tear appeared in the centre of the room and out popped Steve with his scythe, but this time, looking not so relaxed. Steve was, in fact, the complete opposite of relaxed, having just had a row with 'that jumped up little toe-rag'. As the group of criminals compacted, Steve thundered out without the use of his book.

"Jeffrey Edwards! Get your arse out here, now!"

From the centre of the crowd, a small ripple started, which resulted in an elderly grey-haired male being ejected from the huddle, trying to fight his way back into the fortress of bodies with no success. Steve thundered out again.

"Here! NOW! I'm in no mood for this. I've just had to give the Devil a right bollocking for his actions, so get yourself here now, or I'll rain down a terror on you and your mates so bad..."

Steve didn't have to end his threat as four burly inmates assisted Jeffrey in coming forward by selecting a limb apiece and hurling him across the floor, scattering all the chairs like a bowling ball down an alley. It seemed that there was no honour amongst criminals when Steve turned up with his cloak, scythe, and bad mood.

Jeffrey came skidding to a halt, just a few feet away from Steve, and looked up at his soon-to-be guide, with a fear that smelled like a baby's nappy.

"I'm sorry, I'm sorry!" whimpered the convict.

"For what?" Steve said menacingly, as he leant down closer to the man.

"Anything, everything, whatever you want me to be sorry for. *I'M SORRY!*" cried Jeffrey.

Steve's mood lifted marginally, and his taunting ways started to trickle back.

"Are you sorry for filling your pants with that stench, when I have to take you to your selected destination?"

"YES! YES! I'M SORRY FOR THAT!" pleaded Jeffrey, "Why me? Why now? How d'it happen?" he continued.

Steve straightened up and thought for a second.

"Yep! I can tell you that."

The entire group of criminals relaxed again and started to approach Jeffrey, interested to know why.

Like a teacher in kindergarten who was just about to tell a story, Steve took a breath into his non-existent lungs.

"Well Jeffrey, why you? Why d'you think you're here?"

"One of the great unanswered questions of the universe," someone called out from the crowd who had by now all settled down to listen, totally ignoring Dan Brantley's show.

"Shut up, you cock!... I mean *here,* in prison."

A sheepish Jeffrey looked down.

"Ah! About that."

"Too late, young fella-mi-lad. You ever been not allowed into a club before? Y'know? 'Your names not down, you're not coming in'? Well, this is the opposite. Your name's written down, you're not going on...Why now? Well?... Look, I don't write the book, I just read it and collect. I mean, I can alter things but only for very exceptional circumstances, but I digress. I know the next in line, time and date, exact location and where they're going, oh, and how."

Jeffrey looked up with a fearful, quizzical tremble.

"And... How do I go?"

"Your ticker. Too many parties and lavish living and not enough exercise. Tick tock tick tock. Arrrgh! Heart attack brought on by extreme stress."

"Oh, bugger!" muttered Jeffrey.

"Excuse me," called out a shrill, annoying nasally voice from the audience.

Steve looked up,

"Yes?"

From the seated audience stood a weaselly, pencil-necked, middle-aged man with small silver-rimmed glasses.

"I just wish to clarify something if I may. My name is Walker Delaney..."

"You don't need to clarify that. I think everyone here knows that," interrupted Steve.

"I'm a defence lawyer, and I must request clarification on the time and reason for my client's demise."

Steve looked a little surprised and pulled out his book to the correct page.

"Jeffrey Edwards. Today. Right here where he's lying. Heart attack brought on by extreme stress... annd... Now!"

"Arrrgh!" was the last thing Jeffrey said.

"See? I don't make the rules, I just follow 'em."

Walker started to make his way through the seated inmates and held up an index finger.

"So, you're telling me, that this morning, Jeffrey was alright and now my client is... dead?"

"Yep. As a dodo. Dead as a dead thing in Deadville on Deadsday, after a small bout of dead."

Walker snaked over to the cloaked skeleton.

"So, is it possible that it was *You* who caused my client's death, by your merest presence, and not his previous actions, that may or may not have landed him in this correction facility? So, knowing when he was going to die and how his demise was to come about would suggest to me that his murder was premeditated and committed by *YOU!*"

Walker pointed a spindly finger in Steve's direction, with the conviction of an idiot who wasn't aware as to who he was accusing, or a prat who thought his knowledge of the law would protect him. A pregnant pause preceded a shrug of a pair of cloak- covered shoulders, and a 'Meh!'. Steve thumbed his opened book and stopped on another page.

"Ah! This is interesting... Walker Delaney... Hmmm."

Steve reached into his cloak, pulled out a pencil, inverted it, and rubbed out the details. He then flicked back to the current day's date and started to scribble on the page, only to stop and gaze at the room's clock. He continued to scribble, pausing a second time, tapping the side of his skull with the pencil, thinking of what to write next.

"I must insist you cease writing and inform me what you are doing. I'd like to think you are going to rectify *your* own criminal act, which has been seen by numerous witnesses," demanded Walker.

Every head in the audience suddenly looked down or in the other direction, and began whistling, not wanting to play any part in the proceedings against the Grim Reaper.

Steve stopped writing and returned both book and pencil to the inside of his cloak, and looked as calm as a skull can look at his aggressor. Walker's face took on an air of smugness, thinking he had controlled the Grim Reaper and was about to win the case of a lifetime.

As Walker turned to show the on-looking inmates his smug grin, an anvil came crashing through the ceiling and landed squarely on Walker's head, burying it deep into the man's shoulders before levelling the rest of the convicted defence lawyer to the ground.

"Now! I don't usually do this but as they say... Needs must... so to speak. I've only seen that sort of stuff in cartoons so to see it in real life?... Bit messier than I expected if I'm honest," Steve announced to the blood-covered crowd, "Anyway, I must be on my way. People to see, places to go."

Steve bent down and recovered the two souls from the floor.

"Come on you two, time to go."

"Can I inquire as to where you're taking us?" enquired Walker.

"Well, I was going to say that you'll not need a warm coat where you're going, but maybe you do," came the reply.

"Heaven bound then," smiled Walker's spirit.

Steve promptly burst out laughing.

"Think again. Downstairs is just experiencing minor difficulties at the moment, but I'm sure normal service will be resumed shortly."

A tear opened up, and Steve threw his two new companions into it. As he was about to leave, Steve turned around and looked at the shocked inmates.

"Don't worry. I'll not be gone for long. I'll see you soon."

Steve stepped into the tear, which closed up just as Prison Officer 'Muddy' Waters walked back into the room after his break.

"What the bloody hell?!"

Seventy plus blood-covered inmates, with faces like startled rabbits, slowly turned to see the officer.

Chapter 28

Adolph, Genghis, and the rest of the demons had managed to cage all the newcomers. Due to a minor oversight in listening to what each newbie had claimed they had done, they had placed them in the areas which turned out to be quite agreeable to the 'freshers'.

Feeling a little puzzled as to the lack of moaning and wailing, the two in charge didn't have time to question this before there was a ring of the bell and a large truck outside the gates.

"Oh, thank G... Gary it's here."

The two demons raced up the 'Walk of Shame' to the gate, to greet the delivery driver. When the demons reached the gates, they noticed the name badge of the delivery driver.

"Oh, you've gotta be kidding me!" Adolph said, "Steve? Really?"

"Yes, mate. I was just about to leave you a card, but as you're here, you can sign for this. One truckload of canisters including two valves and rubber piping measuring...err, a long way. Just sign 'ere mate."

A ragged old clipboard was thrust in front of Adolph with a three-ply self-carbonating receipt clipped to it. The demon took the item from the delivery man, Steve, and looked at him.

"Pen?"

Producing a well-chewed clear plastic ballpoint pen from the top of his left ear and holding it out for Adolph, Steve suddenly looked like he was in mild discomfort. He suddenly pulled the pen back and started to scratch the nape of his rather chubby neck before handing it back over to Adolph.

"Sorry 'bout that. 'ere, it's a bit dark 'ere in'it. Always thought this place was full of hellfire."

Adolph had finished scribbling on the receipt and handed the pen back.

"Health and safety gone mad, I'm afraid. Someone wrote in the 'near miss' register that they had almost singed themselves on the flames as they passed by, so now we've turned the flames off."

"Bloody hell!" muttered Steve, the delivery man, "Was anyone hurt?"

"This is Hell, dingbat. D'you honestly think we have health and safety down here? And, if anyone would have burnt themselves, d'you think we'd have given a tinker's cuss over it? Here, have your greasy pen back, offload the stuff, and just bugger off!" replied Adolph.

"Charming! Right, you want it offloading? OK, I can do that," replied the indignant driver.

Steve collected his pen from the rude demon and replaced it over his left ear.

"Have a *nice* day," he said in the most sarcastic way he could think of.

"Piss off!" replied Adolph.

Steve climbed back into his truck's cabin, winding down his window and firing up his vehicle, revved the truck's engine, crunched it into gear, slipping the clutch, and shot off.

All items, waiting to be carefully removed from the rear of the trailer unit, swiftly tumbled off, bouncing along the cobbled area like something out of The Dambusters film.

Ducking out of the way of a rapidly approaching gas canister, Adolph turned to see the truck disappearing into the distance. With a middle finger raised, Adolph shouted out 'arsehole!' as loud as he could.

The metallic clattering and rubber tube bouncing had ceased, and Adolph looked at Genghis as if to say 'C'mon, give me a hand lifting all this', but before anything was said, Genghis walked back inside the gates.

"You wound him up, therefore, it's your mess... Crack on fella."

"Genghis! Don't be such a dick! Remember, you got us into this mess in the first place!" shouted back Adolph to his colleague.

"Me?!" Genghis swiftly turned around, "You're the one who didn't order the fuel when you should've, not me!"

"Look! Just help me bring it all in. If we don't get the flames going again, d'you honestly think Gary will just have a go at me?"

Genghis thought for a second, then scurried back to help recover the gas canisters and tubing, realising that his counterpart was right.

"Right, we need to get this all in..."

"I know what needs to be done, halfwit!" interrupted Genghis, as Adolph attempted to take charge.

"Want a hand?" called out Gacy, who was wandering up the 'Walk of Shame', his feet honking with every step.

Genghis and Adolph looked at each other and wondered how the demon knew that the delivery had landed.

"Been watching Steve's position on a GPS app on my computer. Saw him from four drops away, so figured by the time I got to the gate he'd just arrive."

Ping!

Gacy took his phone out and looked at the screen.

"It appears the delivery has been dropped off, it says. Its bloody good is this delivery system!" Gacy said with a smile, "There's a quick survey asking about the delivery and how the courier was. Shall I give him five stars?"

"Oh, bleeding hell!"

"Best not make it five," Genghis interrupted Adolph's minor rant.

"I'll give him four then, as it arrived before we expected it," said Gacy, tapping the screen and shoving the phone back into his trouser pocket. "If you two bring in the canisters and get them to Berkowitz, I'll get the piping laid and the gullies will be aflame again before you know it."

"Who's in bloody charge here?!" fired back Adolph.

"Listen, numbnuts. Don't you think you've caused trouble for one day? Let Gacy do his bit and we'll do ours," Genghis said in his most patronising voice.

"Oh, for Christ's sake!" muttered Adolph.

"Oi! There's no need for language like that!" protested Genghis, "Let's just get on with this. In fact, as this was your cock-up, you start on this, and I'll go get help from the others. We should have it all done and up and running by the time Gary gets back." Genghis started to walk off, then turned. "And you can explain to Gary how you royally screwed the pooch."

"It wasn't my fault!" shouted Adolph.

Genghis continued on his walk along the path.

"Yeees it was," he replied.

With the help of all available demons and the road workers, who had found themselves down in Hell (but under no circumstances were they allowed to lean on their shovels and drink cups of tea), the flames were about to be fired up.

Adolph and Genghis made their way to Gacy's office with smiles on their faces, knowing that it had been completed. Not many road workers had got away without any punishment over moaning about the lack of tea and where were their shovels to lean on. The office door burst open, surprising Gacy and his underling, with Adolph announcing,

273

"Right, turn it on!"

Gacy looked up from his paperwork, at Adolph, and replied,

"Do we look like the bloody engine room?"

Before Adolph could reply, Gacy picked up his phone and speed dialled a number.

"Aileen? How are we, sunshine?... Not bad, thanks. Be better if I didn't have Addy and Gengi on my back about this bloody hellfire fiasco... I know right... I know... Oh hell yes."

Adolph and Genghis looked at each other and wondered what the full conversation was between Gacy and Aileen.

"I know, but having said that, Gary's back tomorrow, I believe, so it'll be all back to normal," Gacy chuckled. "Me neither. Anyway, any chance you can get one of your bods to turn on the gas and fire it up for me?... Ah, you're a love. Oh, how's it going with the new chap?... Shouldn't be surprised really should I, you've form for that, haven't you? Oh well, never mind... That's great. Thanks a lot, see ya later."

Gacy put the phone down and turned to the two waiting demons.

"Two ticks and we'll be up and running again."

Before either demon could reply, there was a *WOOF!* outside the office door and the smell of caravan gas started to seep into the office. Gacy smiled.

"She's bloody good is that lass."

Huge weights had been lifted off two pairs of shoulders, relief that their world had been brought back to some form of normality. Both high ranking demons thanked Gacy and left the office, but not before Genghis threw a stapler at Berkowitz just for the fun of it.

Adolph and Genghis left the office and turned to walk down the corridor from Gacy's office to the Throne Room. Suddenly the demons stopped in their tracks as two pairs of eyes lay wide open, with two jaws almost hitting the floor in total dread.

"It's blue!" whispered Genghis.

"It's blue!" replied Adolph.

"Oh, crap!" they both said in unison.

Gacy's door burst open and the two demons charged back into the office.

"They're blue! The bloody flames are blue!" exclaimed Adolph to Gacy, who was picking himself off the floor, as the shock of the door being burst open had made him topple over the back of his reclining seat.

"Err, yes! What did you expect? It's gas used in all caravans. Of course, it's blue. It is also better than nothing! Which is what we had because the order form hadn't been signed?" Gacy looked sternly at the two demons.

"Oh, that's just great," protested Genghis, "Blue flames and stinks like a sodding caravan!"

***

Arthur and Bernice were sat cowering with the rest of the caravan owners, who had also found themselves in Hell, because of their belligerent driving manner and deliberate slowing down of other road users, by driving in the middle of the road and doing 25mph.

They were cowering away from all the 4X4 SUV drivers, who had been stuck behind caravans, who were not only hurling abuse at them but also plastic cups and saucers, commonly found in all caravans.

Suddenly, a nostalgic aroma permeated the air, which choked the SUV drivers, but brought light and happiness to the likes of Arthur and his wife.

"Bernie? Is that what I think it is?" Arthur smiled.

"It is, darling. Oh, heavens above there is a God after all. Shall I put the kettle on? We definitely have enough cups and saucers."

"Why not, honey. I'll get the rickety metal tubed deck chairs out and ensure that when I sit down this lot can see at least one of my testicles from the legs of my shorts."

Arthur and the rest of the male caravanners got up and started to either locate the seating or adjust their scrotums in their shorts for maximum effect. The SUV drivers started to bang loudly on the cell door, protesting that they had not signed up for this and they wanted out.

***

"What the bloody home are we going to do? He'll spot this a mile off!" said the worried Adolph.

276

"Well, there's sod all we can do right now. This is as good as it gets, and may I say this is all because *YOU* didn't initially sign the order form that Gacy tried to give you. Noo, you just slammed the door in his face and tried to explain to me how you were the better person to run Hell whilst Gary was away. Hmm, I think not," replied Genghis with an air of victory.

"Bastard!"

"That's right, bitch."

The two demons made their way down the corridor towards the Throne Room, being lit by a relaxing cool blue hue from the flame-filled gutters.

Chapter 29

Gary stormed out of the side street at the rear of the pub, with Grandpa Cyril laughing as he left. The pain he had sustained from Shadow, who had decided to assist his old human friend, was still smarting, and Gary could feel several small tears in the seat of his trousers where the wolf's teeth had sunk.

The Women's Institute hall was still full of villagers, who were amazed at Betty Grisslebush's clairvoyance act, but at the intermission many of the men had rushed out of the hall to grab a quick smoke before their wives dragged them back in.

The ladies remained inside, wittering on about how Betty was fantastic and that they couldn't wait until it was their turn. Several ghosts were still milling around outside, with some of the male spirits deliberately walking through the plumes of cigarette smoke simply to get one more nicotine hit.

Gary glared at the hall, damning the place and his dad-forsaken father, who had made a mockery of him in there, in front of all those halfwits. Then, to top it all off, Steve had sided with that daft old man and threatened him. *Then* that bloody dog! Gary looked up into the evening's sky.

"Sod ya!" Gary muttered, "Well, it's going to get better. Just wait for tomorrow. Just wait, it's all good from now on."

"Don't count on it, mac," declared a raspy, deep voice from Gary's side.

"What the?!"

Gary turned to see the top of a trilby hat that was balanced on top of a shabby old raincoat. Slowly the right arm of the raincoat raised, a small hand protruding from the end of it and holding a metal lighter, which ignited the end of a cigarette that was barely visible under the trilby.

The end of the cigarette glowed as Dirk Randall inhaled the lit cigarette. He looked up and blew the smoke into the air, away from his new acquaintance. Gary's body sagged, and he too looked up, but for a different reason.

"What the bloody hell now, old man?... OK, I'll go along with this. Right fella, c'mon, what's the game?"

"He took another drag on my cigarette and looked at the young buck through the smoky air," announced Dirk in his gravelly voice.

Dirk Randall was an early to middle-aged man, who was classified as 'care in the community'. He was a small man, who was fanatical about film noir private detectives, to a point where all he would wear was their typical attire, which included the obligatory raincoat and trilby.

He claimed he had been on a twenty-eight-day investigation, looking into a high- profile celebrity and his infidelity, when in reality the investigation made was an assessment in the nearby mental hospital.

Found not fit to be released, the hospital had a sudden financial problem, which resulted in Dirk being released into a 'care in the community' programme, under the care of a social worker called Christian.

Christian had got the job by completing an online course in social care, which should have cost him £2,500, but had a deal that day, so only cost £15.95. The social worker found himself looking after Dirk and other challenged people that were dotted around several villages.

No one really believed Dirk's version of the events, but went along with the ruse out of kindness. P.I. Dirk Randall would wander the village and surrounding areas, solving crimes, or as others would classify it; 'sticking his nose into business that was going to get him a punch on the nose'. Constantly speaking in the third person, Dirk narrated his conversations with anyone who would listen, and to those who wouldn't too. Tonight's conversation was with Gary.

"Looking up at the new guy in town, Dirk examined the unfamiliar face through narrowed, piercing eyes..."

"Oh, give me strength!" butted in Gary.

"So, where you from, kid? Dirk asked, taking another drag on his cigarette, tilting his head in curiosity. A slither of light shone across the detective's face, highlighting the ice-cold blue of his eyes."

"They're brown, you dick! You have brown eyes," corrected Gary.

Dirk remained on his path.

"Looking at the handsome stranger..."

"Nice one, thanks." interrupted Gary.

"I kinda felt this kid was lost, or a gigolo and under the rule of Big Joe. I know how you feel, kid..."

"You're a rent boy?!"

"Dirk's secretary, Valerie, had been sold to Big Joe by her drunk of a husband, Hank, to pay off his debts. She only worked for Dirk to escape from the rat-race hellhole she had been thrown in. He couldn't pay her any wages but then she was happy that he could take her away from those sweaty bodies who just wanted to make whoopee with her..."

"Whoopee?! Oh, this is priceless!"

"He knew she loved him, and he had feelings for her too, but Dirk had had his heart broken too many times and couldn't afford to have it broken again by this doll. She knew that, but still hung on my every word.

Dirk knew when Big Joe had made her do a trick in the morning as she would drift into the office like a dark cloud and light me a cigarette. Usually, I could taste her lipstick on the lit cigarette she passed me but on those mornings, well, I just knew she'd been forced to service some schmuck... Dirk looked at the young man and taking another drag from his cigarette, he asked again. So which one are you, kid? Lost or gigolo? Flicking the half-smoked cigarette away, Dirk waited for an answer."

"You're a nutter!" Gary said whilst locking eyes with his unwanted defective detective.

"Quiet one, eh, kid?"

"Nope, not really. Just my dad told me never to talk to strange men, and they don't come much stranger than you, fella," Gary pondered for a split second. "Why don't you go visit the next village, Lower Shitterton? I hear they've had some strange goings on with Death himself, along with some aliens. I think it needs investigating to a degree that only a gumshoe like you could solve."

Dirk's face lit up with the thought of an actual case. He reached into his raincoat pocket, and pulling out a crumpled packet of menthol cigarettes and lighting one, he passed it to Gary.

"Here kid, thanks for the info."

Gary accepted the lit cigarette, put it to his mouth and inhaled, burning the cigarette down to the filter in one fast drag. Dirk's eyes widened at the sight of someone smoking a cigarette so fast and flicking the butt into the fountain. Gary smiled at Dirk and thanked him as he needed it after his night. Dirk simply gave his new informant a wink, and a relaxed salute.

"Stay safe kid," Dirk said with a smile and wandered off towards to road leading up to Walter Hollybank's place, and onwards to Lower Fitterton.

Chapter 30

Reginald Golightly was the owner of the village newsagents. In his early sixties and standing only 5 feet 4 inches of a stocky build, Reg was like the 'Uncle Sid' everyone had as a child. He was, as all 'Uncle Sids' were, a bit of a drinker and not one your parents would think of first for babysitting their precious children unless they wanted to come back to find them a little drunk and smelling of tobacco. Reg always wore his tan linen warehouse smock coat covering his normal clothing. He had even been seen on occasion taking out the rubbish in the morning with his smock coat over his pyjamas.

Locking the door to his newsagents, Reg turned to go home when he saw Gary standing at the fountain watching Dirk wander off out of the square.

"'ow do fella. Nice night for it," greeted Reg.

Distracted from watching the village nutter make his way off, Gary turned to see who had spoken to him. Gary's eyes rolled on seeing the squat newsagent placing the shop's door keys in his smock pocket and wandering over in his direction.

"Bleeding home!" he thought, "Any chance of some normality?"

Feigning a smile and placing his hands firmly into his pockets to prevent any handshaking, Gary replied,

"Yeah?... Nice night for what?" curiosity got the better of him.

"Owt really," answered Reg, "Standing by the fountain, chatting to Dirk, watching the nutter leave or going t' Betty's show... Was it any good? Didn't want to go, myself. One, I was busy with mi' shop, and two, Mrs Golightly passed away several years ago and it's been blissfully quiet since then. Don't get me wrong, she was the love of my life, but bloody hell could she moan... especially about me having a pint or two. So to go there and have that nagging old bat have a go at me after all this time, I don't think so."

It wasn't that Gary didn't have the heart to let Reg know that his dear departed wife, Millicent, was standing by his side and was clearly fuming, Gary didn't have a heart at all, he just wanted the elderly man to get deeper into trouble with his ghostly wife.

"Well, I'm visiting for a few days and thought I'd go see the show, but when I was there it just wasn't my scene at all... So tell me more about your wife. She seems like a right ball-breaker."

Millie glared at Gary and was about to have a go at him as well, when curiosity butted in and suggested she wait to see what her lazy drunk of a husband had to say.

"Millie? Oh, she was. A real ball-breaker, that's for sure."

Millicent's pale ghostly face glowed a crimson hue.

"But she was my wife, and I loved her. Yeah, she got at me because I liked a pint or two."

"Or twenty!" screamed the unheard ghost.

"But it's a man's right to be able to have a pint, don't you think? Mr?"

"It's Gary. Call me Gary. Yeah, sure. Nothing wrong with a pint at all... Anyway, was it just your drinking she got on at you about?" Gary was going all out to bait Reg into dropping himself deeper into trouble with his present dead wife.

"Oh good God, no. According to her, I never lifted a finger in the house. I never took her anywhere and never bought her nice things."

"Seems like a right moaner," smiled Gary at the newsagent's dead wife.

"Oh, she was. But I tell you what, I'd have her back in a heartbeat."

Millicent Golightly's face change from fury to one of love and softness, which made Gary throw up in his mouth a little.

"Surely not! Look at you now. You're free to do as you please. No moaning, no getting on at you, just total freedom." Gary felt he had a little work on his hands but felt confident that he could cause trouble here.

Millicent's eyes started to well up as she looked at her husband.

"I know what you're saying, but there was a fire in her that would scare the Devil himself,"

"I doubt that," thought Gary.

"She was one passionate woman. OK, I didn't do much in the house, but I did open the shop up at sparrow fart and stayed there until everyone had gone home. I was shagged after all that! The thing is, I'm still shagged now, even more so, and she's not here to come home to, and being nice to all the bloody idiots in the village, well just going home and being able to ignore her moaning is such a relief.

You don't make a million owning a newsagents in a small village, and every penny went into the house... well apart from the pub. Grant you, Terry got a fair chunk of my income, but like I say, there's nothing wrong with a pint, is there?"

Millicent was in two minds as to whether she should be angry with her 'alive' husband or grateful that he put in as many hours in their shop as he did. Then the thought of Terry and his damned pub, and how much he had taken from her husband was a disgrace. Anger welled up in the ghost again.

"Oh well, she's not here now and there's no one to have a go at me so... fancy a pint?... Gary?"

Thinking swiftly about the offer, Gary considered the possibility of getting the silly old widower so drunk that he could change the man's views on his deceased wife and cause even more trouble.

"Go on, why not."

Gary turned towards The Blind Cobbler's Thumb smiling and with a raised arm to show the way, allowed his new drinking buddy to lead on, leaving behind an angry ghostly wife, with her arms crossed and a scowl on her face that would scare the Devil, or maybe not as the case may be. As Reg passed by, Gary winked at Millie and blew her a kiss as a final taunt.

"You're going to regret it!" she shouted out.

"Oh, I'm sure he will," replied Gary.

"I'm talking about you. I know who you are and I know my Reg."

Gary looked a little annoyed at Millie's warning. He was getting fed up with warnings, but his thoughts were broken when a voice from the pub door called out, beckoning him inside. A smile and two fingers were returned to the spirit, and Gary happily made his way to the pub door, confident that a life was going to be ruined this evening.

With an air of devilish confidence Gary entered the pub's lounge, and Reg at the bar, ordering four pints of ale from Terry. He approached his latest victim, rested his hands on the bar top, smiled at Terry, and perused the room to see who was in.

"Now then, sir..." welcomed Terry.

"Gary. Please. Sod the sir bit," interrupted Gary, as he continued to scan the lounge.

"Sorry," came the sarcastic apology, "So. Now then *Gary*. You're not drinking with this fish, are you?"

Gary's blood began to simmer.

"Another bloody warning and I'll lose it completely!" thought Gary.

"Yes. Reg invited me for a drink and I'm fairly sure I can match him pint for pint and maybe a couple more."

The whole pub fell into silence and all eyes were on the stranger who had just thrown down the gauntlet to someone who maybe shouldn't have a gauntlet thrown down at them. Reg looked up at his drinking pal cum opponent.

"Make it eight Tel, would you?" smiled Reg, turning to the landlord.

"And put them on my tab," continued Gary.

The atmosphere in the pub was similar to a western movie where the local gunslinger had been 'offered out' by the young upstart. All that was missing in The Blind Cobbler's Thumb was some rolling tumbleweed and a 'Spaghetti Western' director homing in on the drinkers' eyes.

From the back of the lounge a whistle broke the silence of the theme tune from the classic spaghetti western movies, closely followed by a 'Shhh!' and an elbow in the ribs from the whistler's girlfriend.

Shadow couldn't speak a word of English, or any other human language come to think of it, but knew that something serious was about to happen with the human he had bitten earlier on in the beer garden.

Gary felt a little uneasy as he looked around the lounge as all eyes rested on himself and the squat little shopkeeper, who was about to have his arse handed to him on a platter in what *was* a drinking session and was now a full-on competition. Turning to his opponent, Gary saw a huge smile looking up at him with an air of excitement.

"Well, if they're on a tab, let's have eight each to start off with then," beamed Reg to Terry.

Not knowing the new guy that much, but knowing all too well the local newsagent, Terry began to have two thoughts. One, which was of the amount of money he was going to make this evening, and two, how much vomit would need to be cleaned up before Shadow got to it and helped in cleaning it up the only way dogs knew.

Pretty much all conversation was limited to a murmur as Reg picked up the first pint and emptied the glass within seconds. Gary, seeing how his opponent had drunk his first pint, thought that tonight wasn't going to be a long one.

"Power drinker, I see," commented Gary in a competitive tone.

"Not really. The first few always goes down pretty well, then I steady off," replied Reg.

On hearing the 'steady off' line, Terry let out a snort of a chuckle.

"Steady off, Reg? Do you know how to 'steady off'?"

"Of course I do. Although, I haven't had a good drink in ages," replied Reg.

Terry poured all the requested drinks and called out to the staff area of the pub;

"Liam? Make sure we've a few kegs ready. Reg is in and he's thirsty."

Liam appeared from the rear of the bar.

"Hi, Reg. How's it going?"

"Ey up young fella-mi-lad... nice shirt Liam," replied Reg, with his eyes dropping to the logo on the glass collector's T-shirt.

'I–I've
D–Done
I–It
O–Only
T–Twice'

"So what you done only twice?" enquired Reg.

"Thought," muttered Terry.

"Don't know, really. M'dad got it for me. He thought it suited me. Anyway, I'll get ready just in case you're here all night."

Liam disappeared into the rear of the pub before eye contact was made with the fiend who had stolen his magazine not so long ago.

"Right young Gary, it's bingo time... Eyes down, look in!"

At that, Reg's second pint disappeared just as quickly as the first.

"C'mon lad, keep up," Reg said as he wiped his mouth. "Y'ant even touched yours."

The 'show-off' part of Gary's brain went into overdrive and within seconds two empty beer glasses stood in front of him with a third following closely after.

"Sorry old man, what was that you were saying?"

Gary had not only thrown the gauntlet down but had wiped his nose with it before rubbing it in Reg's face, then threw it down. The entire pub was silent. All that could be heard was the growling of a burp welling up in Gary's throat and the scribbling of a pen on a notebook from the corner of the lounge from the now familiarly placed writer.

"Top lad!" smiled Reg, sensing he now had someone with whom he could have a good drink.

Gary looked at the newsagent and realised that whilst Reg was a good drinker, he wasn't in competition with the man himself as Reg was only here for a drink. It was Gary who was competing with *Gary*. He wanted to prove he was the better boozer, to ruin Reg's night by getting him totally hammered, and get him to say something derogatory about his wife, who happened to be standing next to Reg with her arms folded and a furious look on her face.

Pint after pint was had, and still Reg maintained a friendly chat with his drinking friend, whilst Gary started to feel the effects after his twenty-fifth pint.

"Oi, Tel! Any chance of some peanuts?" asked Reg, "Just to soak up the beer a bit."

"Sure thing. Want some Gary?" Terry looked at the tipsy-looking Devil, who was swaying slightly.

"Go for it. Jush bang 'em on mi tab."

Reg started to laugh.

"Jush? Jush? Have you had enough fella? You sound a little slurred..."

"Nope! I'm fine," interrupted Gary, "Line 'em up. I'm ready for another."

Terry looked at Reg as if to say 'should he pour a couple more?' With a nod from Reg, Terry began to pour the beers.

"Whilst you're doing that Tel, I'll just go shake hands with the unemployed. Back in a tick."

Gary looked at Terry with a curious look, wondering what had just been said.

"He's nipping to the gent's toilets. He'll be back soon. You sure you're OK for another?"

Feeling like he was being treated as a child and warned again, Gary's hackles were up. It was bad enough that God had ridiculed him in front of everyone at the clairvoyant show, but when that silly old sod had a go with him in the beer garden and he had been bitten, then Steve tore a strip off him?! It was all getting too much for the Prince of Darkness. No one told him off! He was Satan! The Devil! He was Gary!

Furiously staring deep into Terry's eyes, so much so that the landlord's very soul felt the anger, Gary calmly slurred.

"I'm bloody fine. Now do your job and pour the beers!"

Normally by now, Terry would have kicked the drunken man out of the pub, but having the Devil himself in your pub was anything but normal. Plus, it would have been his wife, Liz, who would have done the kicking out, but as she was out at the Women's Institute, Terry decided to just pour the beers.

As the pints were being poured and Reg was relieving himself of the numerous pints of beer, Gary looked around the lounge to see that the entire pub seemed to be having an intermission from the competition.

Over in the corner sat the man scribbling in his notebook with a glass of whisky resting by the side of his leather-bound book. As everyone else had been watching, in awe at the drinking match, this man hadn't, so Gary decided to stagger over. It was either to cause trouble or enquire as to what was being written in the book, whichever came first, he wasn't bothered.

Gary flopped down next to the quiet writer, shuffled up next to the man, and looking overtly at what he was writing, he enquired.

"Sho, what you writin'? Crap?"

"Who can tell, matey? Some folks like my writing and for others, it's just not their cup of tea."

A little more scribbling in the notebook was done, and suddenly, Gary felt the urge to buy the man a drink.

"Whisky?"

"Oh, go on then. No ice thanks."

Gary got up and wandered back to the bar.

"I'm sorry for my outburst a second ago. I am a little tipsy so please forgive me,"

Gary's eyes opened wide as to what he had just said to the landlord.

"What the?!" he thought.

"I wonder if I could buy that man over in the corner a whisky... err, with no ice, please."

"What the bloody home is happening?" Gary wondered to himself.

A very puzzled Terry poured the whisky and placed it on the bar.

"On your tab?"

"No, I'll pay for this myself."

Gary reached into his pocket and pulled out a wallet.

"What on earth is happening?! What the home am I doing paying for a drink myself and why when I want to cause trouble, am I buying a drink for the guy who I'm wanting to cause trouble with?" thought Gary.

Just then Gary's phone rang, and retrieving it from his pocket, he noticed it was God's name on the screen. Gary stabbed his finger on the screen and answered the phone.

"Are you doing this?!" he demanded as he heard God laughing on the other end of the call.

"It's not me, I promise." God replied, "I'm just here enjoying my beach party with everyone. The driftwood fire we have is burning quite well. OK, because of health and safety, it's not exactly the wood that's burning but hey, that's another story."

"Who the home is doing this to me then?"

"Oh, I don't know. Why don't you ask your writer friend who you're buying a whisky for?" God continued to laugh.

Gary's brain went into overdrive. How did God know about that man, and that he had just bought him a drink? And why should he ask this chubby bald git about why this was happening? It isn't as though this writer bloke was controlling what he was doing and saying! Surely not?!

"Anyway. Your drinking buddy is coming back now, so I'll leave you be. Don't try to keep up as he'll drink you under the table."

Click!

Gary looked at the blank phone screen just as Reg returned from the toilets.

"Round six, is it? Sorry about that, but my bladder can only hold a certain amount. How in God's good name you can hold so much is beyond me... Ooh, ya cheeky sod! Getting a whisky in without me..."

"No, it's not for me..."

"Terry, my good man! Line 'em up,"

"Oh, Jesus Christ!"

Chapter 31

The beach party was in full swing, with Jesus in charge of the barbeque, serving all the party-goers.

"You feed a few folk with fish sandwiches and you get relegated to catering!" muttered Jesus, "Here you go."

"Thanks, Christ. Do you have any ketchup?" enquired John Paul, a hungry patron.

"Do I look like I have any?! Be thankful you've that. Good dad! you give 'em an inch"

"Well, I'm *so* sorry, Jesus! I only worshipped you all my life and I ask a simple question and you bite my head off! The gratitude of some folk!"

The indignant patron snatched the food from Jesus and stormed off to join the party.

"Don't choke on it!" shouted Jesus.

"Piss off," came the distant reply.

Suddenly Jesus felt a disturbance and deep within his divine DNA he heard a

"Jesus Christ!"

"Dad! Dad! Lucifer is using my name in vain."

God was sitting crossed legged with Swami Magishi playing Derek and The Dominoes' Layla on the sitars in front of the lemon-scented log fire. A group of bikini-clad women and Travis, who was happily passing around an unusually large rolled-up cigarette, were sat listening to the duo. Leaving Magishi to play the main chorus riff, God turned around and shouted back.

"Dude! What is it you're always saying about turning the other cheek? Chill bra!"

"True dat G-man," added Travis whilst he inhaled a large plume of sweet-smelling smoke.

"I know which cheek I'd like to turn and show you," muttered Jesus under his breath.

"Seen it before, son!" called back the G-man.

**

Gary had taken the whisky from the bar and for some reason had delivered it to the writer in the lounge's corner and even placed it on the table with a smile. With an extremely puzzled look, Gary looked at the man who was sat scribbling in his notebook.

"I have not a clue why I've jush bought you a drink when all I wanted to do wash inshult you."

The writer looked up smiling, took the whisky glass, and replied,

"What is it they say? The pen is mightier than the sword? It does seem so on this occasion, doesn't it?"

Gary wandered back to the bar, puzzling over what he had just been told, only to find four more pints and three whiskies waiting for him, and Reg having finished his three shots.

"C'mon young'n. You're slacking a bit."

That was all that Gary needed to hear. Three shots of whisky were downed in seconds, closely followed by two of his four pints.

"Who'sh shlackin' now old lad?" slurred Gary.

Reg looked at his new drinking partner with an air of concern.

"Is tha' back teeth swimming, lad? D'you want to get some fresh air? Might 'elp."

Sensing that the hollow legged shop keeper may be right, Gary scanned the room for the exit.

"It's over there, fella," Reg assisted, pointing at the pub door.

"Thanksh. I'll be back shortly."

***

Buttercup Moonchild had decided to take her beloved dog, Sebastian, for his evening walk. Her partner, Jensen, usually took the dog out, but when he had come back with blood on his hands, claiming that it must have been 'Seb' who had caught a rat, she had taken control. Not wanting this to happen again, she had taken Sebastian out that evening. Buttercup was passing the square when she saw Gary staggering over to the fountain in a very annoyingly drunken way.

"Men! They think they can drink to excess. It's disgusting! I'm so glad you're not a man, Sebastian," she said, looking at her dog who had sought out a crumb that had been left outside Betty's café.

Deliberately making a beeline for the drunken fallen angel, with a view to expressing her disgust with him, Buttercup marched on dragging the hungry Chihuahua.

"Bloody home, that man can drink! Where's he put it?!"

"You make me sick!" interrupted Buttercup.

"Well, drinking with Reg will do that to you too," replied Gary, looking up to see the slender critic and her dog.

"What the bloody home ish that on your lead?!"

Buttercup's eyes widened with fury and the fine downy hairs on the back of her top lip stood up.

"*THAT* happens to be my dog!"

"I wash talking to the dog. Wait! Tha'sh a dog?"

Gary looked at Sebastian and burst out laughing, which infuriated Buttercup even more. Sebastian, on the other hand, was straining to go back to the café frontage and finish finding leftover crumbs.

"HOW DARE YOU?!" glared the furious woman.

"Quite easy. Dare me to do shomething else. Honeshtly! That's a dog? What's it called? Rattington McRodent?" Gary started to giggle.

"His name is Sebastian, and he's a Chi..."

"Rat."

"*Chihuahua!*"

"Called Seb! I've a dog, and he's called Cerberus. Lovely dog. Craps bigger turds than that!" Gary giggled, pointing at the distracted, hungry pooch.

That was all the taunting that Buttercup could stand. Before Gary could register the woman's right foot's rocketing movement towards his groin, a searing pain shot to his brain, indicating that he should fall into a crumpled heap and grab his testicles.

"Stay down asshole, or the next kick you receive you'll find yourself with an extra pair of tonsils!"

Even the amount of alcohol Gary had consumed did not help in deadening the pain, and with a warning of another shot to the same location, the decision to stay down an easy one. Plus, having the wind taken out of his sails, it was highly unlikely that he could stand even if he wanted to.

With a tug on the lead, Buttercup stormed off with Sebastian reluctantly leaving behind some tasty morsels he had sniffed out.

Sid Eccles, the village poacher and drunk, had recently died in the hands, or teeth, of Uriah Tomkins, and left in a drunken ghostly state, staggered into the square having heard there was some sort of 'Do' going on at the Women's Institute.

Sid, being taken to Heaven, but falling back down to Earth whilst looking for a toilet, had not quite grasped the fact that he was, in fact, dead and now a ghost. As a fellow drinker was requiring assistance on the cobbles in what seemed to be a painful situation, Sid decided to stagger over and help out.

"Eyup young'n, you alright? 'ere let me 'elp you up... Ooh bloody 'ell!"

Before Gary could reject the kindly offer from the drunken ghostly poacher, Sid had bent over with a helpful hand, stumbled on the cobbles, and fell headlong into Gary.

From any other ghost, that would have been bad enough, but being a poacher in his mortal past, Sid was not known for his personal hygiene, as it helped with sneaking up to the animals. Plus, being a drunken ghost, the last thing Gary wanted was more alcohol in his system, even if it was by way of ghostly alcohol.

"Bloody 'ell! Sorry about that old lad. D'know what 'appened there."

Sid probably spent a little more time inside Gary than the fallen angel would have liked whilst struggling to get up. The sensation of a ghost inside your body is not a pleasant thing, but a drunken, smelly one was more than Gary's stomach could handle. With a hot flush and a welling up from the stomach, Gary jettisoned the contents of his overly full stomach in Sid's direction.

"Jesus lad! How much have you 'ad to drink?" Sid protested.

Luckily for Sid, being a ghost meant that you had no solid body to which vomit could attach itself. Not so lucky for Gary though, as his legs and trousers were very solid and now quite moist too, reeking of ale and the rest of the acrid odours that come along with being violently sick.

"Best get yourself up old lad an' walk it off," Sid chuckled, "That'll be a hangover from Hell you're going to have. Even the Devil himself wouldn't want that."

Gary was still unable to talk because of searing pain still lingering in his groin and the ghostly alcohol which had now added to his own overfull level. A gentle wave of his hand indicated to Sid that things were alright and simply to leave him alone.

"Right then fella," Sid acknowledged Gary's request, "I'll leave you be. 'ave a good'n."

Sid staggered off into the cool night singing the chorus of the Wild Rover, leaving Gary to tend to his aching testicles and to sober up.

"Eyup young Gary. You alright fella?" Reg poked his head out from the pub door.

From the other side of the fountain, a hand appeared with a 'thumbs up'.

Reg wandered over to ensure things were alright and saw his earlier drinking pal on the floor, covered in vomit and clutching his groin.

"What the bloody hell's happened 'ere mate? 'ere let me help you up."

Used to lugging around large bales of newspapers, Reg very easily lifted Gary back onto his feet.

"Bloody 'ell lad! You seriously hum," Reg said, wafting his hand in front of his nose.

Gary bent over to cradle his injured genitals.

"I'm OK," came a high-pitched rasping voice from Gary.

"Think you need to get a change of clothes, fella. You've two more pints waiting for you on the bar."

That was not what Gary wanted to hear, as another tidal wave of vomit hit the water in the fountain.

"You might have had enough, thinking about it. Oh well, more for me then... err, these still on your tab?" enquired the hopeful Reg.

"Go for it," rasped Gary between wretches.

A big smile came over Reg at the thought of free beer, as Gary's face was still buried in the fountain.

"Cracking! Well get yourself sorted fella and maybe I'll see you tomorrow. I'll just go and have your two p... well, 'y'know what's' before they go flat. Want a hand into the pub?"

From the inside of the fountain bowl came a raspy,

"Na, I'm good,"

A reassuring patting on Gary's on his back, and Reg left the fallen angel to finish off the task of emptying his stomach, and wandered back towards to pub.

"Is he alright?" asked Terry, as Reg entered and made a beeline for the waiting pints.

"He will be," replied Reg, as his hand took hold of one of the pint glasses and half emptied it into his ever-thirsty mouth, only to stop momentarily to inform Terry that the beers were still on Gary's tab.

A few minutes later, the pub door swung open and an acrid smelling, wobbling, Gary entered and made his way up the nearby stairs towards his room. Both Reg and Terry watched as the fallen angel disappeared towards the stairway, closely followed by a loud rumbling sound as if someone had thrown a sack of potatoes down the stairs.

"I'm OK!" came the voice from the bottom of the stairs.

Reg and Terry looked at each other, shrugged, and carried on.

Chapter 32

Morning had started a little later the next day. This was due to night time having to tell morning all about the crowd leaving the Women's Institute, all muttering with some fervour about the events that had just taken place.

In addition, there was also the altercation between a young female and a smartly dressed drunk, then the same drunk had thrown up on a ghost, then to top it all off, some elderly chubby female drug dealer was blowing smoke into the air so two more ghosts could get high. This, of course, was after everyone had left the square, including a slightly tipsy newsagent, who had left the village pub an hour after closing time.

Morning was so engrossed in what had happened, that it had lost all track of time. It was only when the cows in the nearby field had started mooing, wondering if morning had called in sick, that it realised that it was late.

Nighttime had still plenty to tell morning about the other ghosts that had left the Women's Institute. Plus, the angry female spirit who had followed the tipsy newsagent back home, but was kind of happy that he had not succumbed to the smartly dressed drunken man's attempts to insult her.

It was getting late, and this did not give the sun much time to get ready, so morning received a few choice words from the fiery orb. Not being able to properly get ready, the sun decided to hide behind the passing clouds, hopping from one fluffy cloud to another.

Usually, the sun, being quite an inquisitive sort, would always shy away from the clouds, just so it could see what was going on in the villages below, but today was different thanks to morning's lengthy chat with night time.

Way down below, in the village of Ashburn-on-Sinkhole, life had started to awaken and was going on its usual merry way. Reg Golightly was the first to appear and greeted the delivery man as he dropped off the morning's papers.

Betty Grisslebush's bedroom curtains, which were directly above her café, had been thrown open and she was in the process of sipping her cup of tea, whilst Ziggy, her fat ginger cat, continued to slumber on.

Dogweed Moonchild had arrived at his shop a little early, as he too was waiting for a delivery. Jeremiah Brown, aka Eddie, was not usually up at this time but for some reason had decided to enter his fine arts shop with some eagerness. The 'Closed' sign was still visible to all outside, and there he stood, looking out through the glass panel in his shop door.

Morag and Fergus Hamilton were not ready to open the village post office just yet, as Morag insisted that her husband finish his breakfast before he set out on the task of delivering the mail to the village residents.

Walter Hollybank had just been awoken by his beloved dog and faithful friend Bertrand, who had insisted that he get up now or suffer the consequences of finding a little brown island surrounded by a lake of urine by the back door of their home.

Kenneth Turnkey had been working all night on the damaged UFO, whilst the three stranded aliens were huddling up together asleep and snoring. All Kenneth had to do was to fit the awaiting part that should be coming that morning, and the three clients would be able to return home.

Gary had eventually fallen asleep, spread-eagled on the floor with his head resting inside the en-suite toilet and his right hand resting on the toilet handle, ready to flush away another pint of ale. Shadow had taken up his usual place earlier that night, just outside the main guest room of Terry and Liz's pub.

Pretty much a normal morning for any 'out-of-the-way' village, excluding of course having Satan stopping in a guest room in the local pub and having three aliens stranded and awaiting the repairs of their craft. Not to mention two ghosts that were high on strong cannabis who had cuddled up under a Yew tree in the village churchyard and fallen asleep.

A short while later, Betty had opened her café and had her regular three patrons reading their newspapers. Dogweed had bought his regular bacon sandwich and was standing outside his sister's vegan health food shop, taunting her whilst her partner Jensen was trying to cover up the fact that he was salivating over the smell of the sandwich.

"Look, all I'm saying is that the other week, you said that Buddhists followed someone called Sid..." Sylas protested.

"Siddhartha!" interrupted Stephen.

"Even worse! Sid Arthur! Who follows someone called Sid Arthur? Now you say there's a group who follow some bloke called Harry Krisnick?"

"It's Hare Krishna, oh why do I even bother!" Stephen shook his head and took a sip from his teacup.

"You brought up the subject of religion and God." Sylas fired back.

Stewart just buried his head further into his newspaper.

"It was because you didn't believe in the good Lord. You then came out with some ridiculous comment about 'the invention of a water-powered fountain'. When I informed you that everything has a reason you went and said..."

"It's bollocks! Yes, I know. As far as I can see, if there is a God, then what's his game? Honestly! He comes out with some stupid stuff and all you can say is that it's all his big plan! What's that mean?" Sylas said defiantly.

"It's God's ineffable plan," replied Stephen.

"Well, I don't know about ineffable, but I know a woman who is definitely effable," commented Sylas whilst giving a sly nod and a wink towards the Women's Institute hall.

"Dear God, you have just found a new level of depravity! I honestly don't believe you."

Stephen had had enough of trying to educate his friend and followed Stewart's stance and buried his head into his newspaper.

"By! She's a belter!" Sylas smiled luridly. "I wouldn't mind getting religious with her in my bedroom... Oh, God! Oh, God!"

"And there we go again! Your thoughts are lower than a miner's boots!" Stephen exclaimed.

Sylas simply smiled.

"Just like a pit railway line."

Stephen's right eyebrow raised in curiosity, which was unfortunately satisfied by Sylas' following comment,

"One track and dirty."

Chapter 33

Kenneth had completed the work on the UFO, apart from fitting the soon-to-be delivered part, and was now waiting for his other customer, Walter, to attend and collect his now souped-up Mercedes. With all aliens still slumbering and Kenneth taking the last sip of his cuppa, the cogs in his head started to whir.

Usually, Kenneth would like to road test the vehicles he worked on, to ensure that a good job was done, and this UFO was no exception. The only thing was, that by doing it, would he be able to find his way back to the planet, let alone his garage on the outskirts of Ashburn-on-Sinkhole?

Kennet looked at the three aliens fast asleep and with his mind whirring like a gyroscope, he bit his bottom lip in apprehension.

"Bugger it," he whispered.

Quietly putting down his empty cup on a nearby bench, Kenneth opened up the garage doors, crept back inside and entered the UFO. With a slight jog to his walk, Kenneth made his way to the bridge and seeing the captain's chair, slowly lowered himself into it with a childlike, naughty smile on his face.

"Captain Kirk's log, star date,"

//Where would you like to go Captain Kirkslog?// enquired the ship's on-board computer.

315

"Bugger me!"

//As you wish...//

"NO! NO! That's OK. Scratch that."

// Scratching your anus...//

"NO! That's OK. Cancel my last order!"

Kenneth realised that maybe this computer was fully equipped to understand 'earth speak'. Pondering the computer's request to where he would like to go, Kenneth finally opted for a relatively short road test.

"Computer. Take me to the moon and back, as quick as you can. I want to be back before your crew wake up."

//As you wish.//

The craft gently rose and silently left the garage workshop. As soon as it was clear, the craft shot off in a vertical direction. Within a split second, Kenneth had reached the darkness of space when there was a loud double clanking sound.

"Mmm doesn't sound good," thought Kenneth.

He looked through the windscreen, as the large white cratered orb of the moon appeared.

"Computer, slow down so I can see the moon," requested Kenneth.

//As you wish,// replied the computer,

//By the way, my name is Criddick. You can call me that instead of just calling me Computer.//

"Sorry I didn't know you had a name," apologised Kenneth.

//Neither did you bother to ask,// replied the indignant computer.

"Look, I said I was sorry," appealed the mechanic.

//I suppose your apology will suffice.//

"That's OK, anyway, my name is…"

//I know your name, Captain Kirkslog. I am voice-activated and heard you the first time,// interrupted Criddick.

Not wishing to get into a heated argument with a 'snotty' on-board computer, Kenneth decided not to pursue the point.

The craft had reached the moon and was in the process of entering the darker side of the orb. Out of the craft's windscreen, Kenneth peered into the darkness and suddenly his eyes widened.

"Well, I'll be! I'd heard rumours about them being there and setting up shop, but I didn't think it was true," he exclaimed.

//They've been there for many of your Earth years, but not yet set up a shop, as you say. Fuel depots, landing pads, and accommodation but there is no need for a retail outlet,// explained Criddick.

Again, not wanting to get into an argument so far from home, Kenneth decided to let this one lay.

From the fast approaching horizon, light shone from the sun, which meant that Kenneth's road test was almost over. As he looked into space from behind the moon, Kenneth was in awe as to the number of stars that he could see.

"By 'eck! I haven't seen this many stars since I... err... didn't work at the place that doesn't exist in Nevada," said Kenneth, suddenly remembering the warning about mentioning the existence of the place that 'officially' didn't exist.

//I know the place you've avoided to say. As far as I can see they're a bunch of scragfelds who insist on using a propulsion system, that our civilisation had given them to warm up cold pizza. What is it with you lot? Why use a propulsion system that could advance your space exploration and what's wrong with cold pizza?//

Kenneth's eyebrows raised as he felt the on-board computer had made two valid points, to which he could not argue. A shrug of his shoulders in response to the computer's comments went unnoticed.

Light from the sun started to get stronger as the horizon loomed closer. As soon as the nose of the craft was touched by the light, the UFO accelerated and headed back to Earth, again making a double clank as it did.

A split second later, Kenneth had landed the craft and manoeuvred it back into the garage workshop without disturbing the slumbering aliens. Quietly alighting from the UFO and making his way to the rear of his workshop, Kenneth noticed four scratch marks on the front of the craft that hadn't been there prior to him taking it for a joyride.

"Oh bugger!"

Kenneth looked toward the aliens, who were still snoring in an alien fashion, then back at the damaged craft.

"Sod it. A bit of T-Cut will buff those out in no time.

***

Conrad Dipschit raced down the corridor towards Director-General Hank Snide's office, deep within CIA Headquarters. After a very brief knock, he burst into the office to find his boss beavering away on his laptop.

"What the hell is wrong with you?! Caint you see I'm working on something that may very well be not for your goddam eyes!" thundered Hank, having snapped shut the laptop on his Tinder page.

"I'm sorry, sir," panted Conrad, "But we have a major issue. Someone has just taken out one of our spy satellites. We're trying to trace who did this, but so far we're at a loss. One second it was there, the next it just exploded into tiny pieces!"

Hank's face changed to a crimson hue, and he thumped the desk.

"Those goddam Japs are behind this!"

Pressing a button on an ancient intercom that Hank still loved to have, he called his secretary.

"Kelsey? Get me the President!"

"Sure thing. Which would you like?" came the scratchy reply.

Hank's body sagged in desperation.

"We only have one president, goddammit!"

***

Eiichi Wang swiftly marched along the corridor towards General Hansuke Nai's office, deep within the Japanese Naicho Agency. After a thunderous knock on his boss' door, Eiichi waited until he was informed that he was allowed in.

"Hai!" shouted Hansuke just as he closed his laptop on his favourite Pokemon website.

Bursting through the door, Eiichi bowed and informed his boss that one of their spy satellites had just exploded and they were in the process of ascertaining as to how it had happened.

"Those dammed toffee-nosed Brits have done this!"

Hansuke picked up his mobile phone, tapped the screen, and selected his intercom app to contact his secretary.

"Hai?" came the instant response.

"Get the Prime Minister on the phone now!"

"Hai. Which one?"

Hansuke's eyes flared up.

"We only have the one, damn you!"

Howard Longshaft sauntered along the corridor with an air of urgency, towards Chief Euclid Bolschit's office deep within the British MI6. After a gentle knock on the rather large oak doors, Howard wandered in to see his boss straightening his tie as his secretary, by his side, was smoothing down her somewhat tight skirt.

"That will be all Hilary, thank you. What in God's name is the matter, Howard? Can't you see I'm busy?"

"Awfully sorry sir, but I thought you ought to know."

"Know what, man? Come on, spit it out!"

"Well, it appears that one of our spy satellites has just exploded. Goodness knows how. It just went pop!"

Euclid leant back into his deep leather recliner chair and twizzled the tip of his moustache.

"Oh, I think I know. It was those damned Bolshevik Ruskies. Hilary, be a darling, will you and call me the Prime Minister?"

The pony-tailed secretary turned and smiled at her boss.

"OK, Eucky, you're the Prime Minister," she giggled.

"You silly. You know what I mean."

***

Comrade Ivan Oidea marched along the ostentatious corridor towards the huge metal doors of his comrade and director, Khitryy Chushsobachya, deep within the Russian SVR RF. Before Ivan had time to knock on the doors, a thunderous "DA!" was heard. Khitryy had just pulled the cable out of his Sinclair Spectrum computer when he looked up and saw Ivan stood to attention directly in front of the Director's desk.

"Da?"

"Comrade, one of our spy satellites has been made inoperable. It has just exploded with no cause found," announced Ivan, still rigid in his stance with no eye contact with his master.

"Daa! It was those damned Iti's."

Over to the far end of Khitryy's vast office was a small desk with a weaselly faced soldier sat writing in a pad whilst flanked by two burly men wearing 1970s rally jackets.

"Anatoly! Get me the President on the phone!" bellowed Khitryy.

Anatoly jumped to attention and enquired.

"Da! Which president?"

"We only have one pridurok!"

With a slight nod of the Director's head, one of the burly men approached Anatoly from behind and swiftly injected the soldier into the side of his neck, instantly making him fall to the floor.

**

Paulo Cretino sauntered along the corridor towards Admiral Luigi Berlusconi's office, deep within the Italian AISE. Without even knocking, Paulo entered the office to find Luigi in what would have been an embarrassing position with his secretary if it were not for the fact that it was Luigi, who was not embarrassed in the slightest.

"Paulo! Knock dammit! Whaaat?" Luigi said, pulling up his trousers.

"Boss, we gotta problem. Our spy satellite has just exploded. No one knows who or why?!"

Slipping the braces of his trousers over each shoulder, Luigi picked up his smouldering cigar and took a huge drag on it.

"I know who did this!"

Luigi immediately picked up his phone and without dialling a number shouted into the mouthpiece,

"BASTARDO!"

Luigi continued, slamming the phone back down.

"It's a those bludee Americans! Alessandra, get me the boss on the phone."

Whilst fastening up her blouse, Alessandra picked up the phone and asked,

"The President?"

"No. Don Caster."

***

Kenneth had just finished boiling the kettle and made a cup of steaming tea for himself and his three guests when there was a knock on the garage doors. Making his way over to the doors and peering through the grime-covered windows, he saw Fergus Hamilton with a tubular parcel in his hands. The garage door opened, just enough for Kenneth to leave the premises, and meet Fergus outside.

"Morning Fergus old lad. How's it going?"

"Oh, y'know. Here, I got this for you."

"Brilliant! Just what I wanted. Thanks so much, Fergus."

"No problem."

A brief wave of the postman's hand and Fergus was on his way to complete his rounds.

Kenneth hurried back inside with the tube to fix the last bit to the craft.

"Is that the last part for our craft?" enquired Dissel.

"Yep. A pair of wiper blades. Two ticks and I'll have 'em sorted and you can be on your way. Time for another cuppa?" Kenneth smiled at the aliens.

Fergus wandered into Ashburn with the villagers' mail and saw a blurry figure approaching him.

"Fergus my good man!" Fast Eddie called out, "It's me, Jeremiah. Do you have anything for me?"

Fast Eddie came into view with Fergus's poor eyesight, and a look of recognition loomed over the postman's face.

"Ah, Jeremiah. Good morning to you. I think I have something for you. One tick."

Fergus delved into his postal bag, pulled out a cardboard tube, peered at it, and handed it to the eager shopkeeper.

"Thank you so much. Much appreciated."

The tube was taken, and the fine arts shopkeeper, cum conman, raced back to his shop. Eddie entered his shop, locking the door behind him, and breathed a sigh of relief. He held the tube to his chest, knowing that this would be his making.

The amount of money he would make from this was purely mind-boggling. Eddie lovingly looked down at the tube, and in an instant his heart sank faster than an anchor in the sea. Rushing out back into the square, Eddie saw Fergus just about to enter Reg Golightly's shop.

"Fergus! Fergus! A second of your time, please!" called the worried conman.

Fergus looked over his shoulder and squinting, recognised a figure running towards him, a figure that soon became Jeremiah Brown.

"Jeremiah. Is everything alright?"

"Can I just ask? Did you drop a parcel off at Kenneth Turnkey's place this morning or have you still got it? You see, I have his parcel and I'm hoping you still have mine, or have you given Kenneth mine?" panted Eddie.

"Oh, I'm so sorry, I've just come from there. If you give me it back now, I'll go back up after my round and swap them over and drop it back off if you like." Fergus said, squinting at the tube.

"No! No, it's alright. I'll go see him now. It's rather important is my parcel, and I need it as a matter of urgency. Thank you anyway. Toodle-oo!"

Fast Eddie shot off through the square towards Turnkey's Garage.

"Blind Scottish git!" he muttered as he left the square.

Eddie had reached Kenneth's garage and was very much out of breath when he was greeted by Walter Hollybank.

"Jeremiah old boy. Are we on a fitness regime?" smiled Walter, as the sweaty suited man appeared at the garage doors.

Propped against the wooden doors and trying to catch his breath, Eddie looked at his very good client and friend.

"No... It's Fergus... He posted my parcel here... and I have... Kenneth's," Eddie panted.

"Oh, I see. Well, I'm just about to knock and see if my car is ready. I'll knock for both of us if that's alright with you?" replied the kindly old man.

"Please, if you would." Eddie still gulping down as much air as possible.

A small Kenneth Turnkey type of face appeared at the grubby glass in the garage door.

"Kenneth, it's Walter... and Jeremiah. I've come for my car and apparently, Fergus dropped off Jeremiah's parcel here by mistake so he's come to do a swap," informed Walter.

A smile of recognition appeared on the mechanic's face, closely followed by,

"One tick gents, I'll be with you shortly."

Kenneth disappeared from the window and a sudden scuffling sound came from inside the garage, followed by some whispering. Walter looked at Jeremiah with raised eyebrows, curious as to what may be happening in the rickety workshop.

"You three sup up! You're going to have to disappear for a minute or two," whispered Kenneth to the three aliens.

Dissel was the first to look up from his cup.

"What's wrong? Is everything alright?"

"I've got guests here. One to pick his car up and the other has your final part needed for your craft."

Kenneth's whispering was slightly louder and more urgent.

Dissel looked quite at ease upon being told the news, and with a double click of his fingers, the UFO faded as the invisibility cloaking device kicked in. All three aliens followed Kenneth's directions and hid behind a stack of tyres. Kenneth noticed that Walter was trying to peer into the workshop, so quickly grabbed the Mercedes car keys and the recently delivered tube from the nearby workbench and made a beeline for the garage door. As Kenneth quickly found out, whilst the UFO had engaged its invisibility system, that did not mean that you could run through it.

"Wonder what's taking him so long?" queried Walter as he returned from trying to peer through the grimy glass pane.

Clank!

"Oh, bugger!"

"You federchit!"

came from within the garage, which was closely followed by the garage door opening and Kenneth appearing, sporting a red mark the full length of his forehead.

"That bloody smarts!" Kenneth said as he rubbed his brow.

Jeremiah had got his breath back by now and both he and Walter looked at each other with puzzled looks on their faces.

"Just a second Walter, I'll get your car out for you and I believe this is for you Jeremiah."

Kenneth held out a cardboard tube with a small address label, emblazoned it saying something about tubes and towels. Jeremiah's eyes widened with glee and a smile started to form, ending close at each ear. Kenneth thought that Jeremiah was a bit weird, because who would be so happy to have a towel delivered through the post?

"Oh, thank you so much, Kenneth, give us it 'ere!"

Jeremiah snatched the tube from the mechanic, thrusting the right one in his hand instead and running off from the garage forecourt, disappeared down the lane making whooping sounds and the odd maniacal laugh. Such odd behaviour bewildered the two men.

"Must be a very special towel," Walter said, looking at Kenneth.

"These art dealers are a bit weird if you ask me," Kenneth replied, "Oh well, I'll get your car out Walter, excuse me."

Kenneth opened the garage double doors to reveal a beautiful Mercedes Benz... and nothing else but an empty garage workshop.

"I'll just drive your car out and I'll tell you what I've done for you."

Kenneth got into the car and sat on a polythene sheet covered driver seat. The vintage Mercedes roared to life, which was a delight to Walter's ears, and slowly the vehicle was manoeuvred out of the empty workshop with more care than was probably needed, according to Walter.

Exiting the garage and clearing the garage doors, Kenneth jumped out of the parked car and quickly shut the barn-style doors.

"There you go, Walter," Kenneth smiled, holding out the car keys. "It's all done for you, just as you asked... but I've got to warn you, it's probably a little nippier than you expect."

"That's fantastic, Kenneth. The nippier the better," Walter beamed.

"That's fine, but I really do think I need to tell you about it. You see this red button on your dashboard?" Kenneth pointed at the area of the dash just left of the steering wheel.

"If you want the car to accelerate, then all you have to do is press this button while your foot is hard on the accelerator pedal. To stop the system and slow down to a more manageable speed, just lift your foot off the pedal. I've beefed up the brakes to deal with this and even installed a small parachute system under the rear bumper, just in case." Kenneth pointed to a small lever close to the handbrake.

"Absolutely wonderful, Kenneth. I cannot thank you enough. Please let me know how much I owe you and I'm sure I will add a little bonus."

Walter was jumping on the spot like a child in a toy shop at Christmas.

"I'll get the bill to you sometime this afternoon if that's alright Walter?"

"That's absolutely fine. Thank you, thank you!"

Walter jumped in the car and instantly revved the car. The thunderous roar of the engine was music to the millionaire's ears.

"You're welcome, Walter, but as I say, just be careful when you use the booster button. You may want to use your goggles that are on your steampunk hat," warned Kenneth.

"I will, I will, promise," called out Walter as he pulled out of the garage forecourt.

Kenneth waved goodbye to his thrilled client as he disappeared down the lane. As soon as he was out of view, Kenneth breathed a sigh of relief and went back into the workshop.

Clank!

"Oh bugger!"

"You federschit!"

"Turn the bloody invisible thing off! It'll be the death of me!"

Chapter 34

Fast Eddie by name was not fast Eddie by nature. He had only run a hundred yards from Kenneth's garage and had already had to stop to catch his breath. Tightly clutching the cardboard tube, he leant against the dry-stone wall by the side of the road to regain some level of breath.

"I say, Jeremiah? Would you like a lift to your shop? You look like you could do with one," called Walter as he pulled alongside the out of breath man.

"That would be wonderful Walter, thank you so much," smiled Eddie, remembering to put on 'Jeremiah's' posh voice.

"Hop in."

Walter opened the passenger door and watched as the art dealer staggered in front of the car and clambered in.

"I really do appreciate this Walter."

"Oh, don't mention it... So, a very nice towel, eh?" replied Walter, eyeing the tube clutched to his passenger's chest.

Jeremiah looked puzzled for a brief second, then realised what his priceless item was contained in.

"Oh, you wouldn't believe... It's my secret passion, between you and me," Jeremiah tapped the side of his nose with a sly wink.

"Got you! I'll not say a thing Jeremiah, your secret is safe with me," Walter replied with a knowing smile.

The vintage Mercedes then rumbled off towards the village square.

***

Kenneth rubbed his brow where a red welt mark had formed.

"Right gents, you can come out now."

All three aliens emerged from their hiding place and looked at the wounded mechanic.

"Didn't you see our ship?" asked Pitrol.

Kenneth stopped in his tracks and stared at the alien.

"You had your invisibility thingy on, so no, I didn't see your bloody ship!"

Dissel slapped Pitrol round the back of his head.

"So, will it be long before we can go?" enquired Dissel.

Kenneth held up the cardboard tube whilst he continued to rub his brow.

"Just gotta fix these and you're good to go. Be two minutes, max," he replied.

Forsta smiled.

"So have I time to nip to the toilet?"

The other two aliens looked at their friend in disbelief.

"I'm sorry but I have to go!"

Forsta quickly trotted off in the direction of the toilet with his right hand, trying to hold his buttocks together.

"Right! OK!" said the amazed mechanic, "I'll crack on with just putting these on."

The two aliens stared at their colleague and both shook their heads.

Kenneth opened the tube, pulling out a pair of wiper blades for the UFO, and rested them on a nearby workbench. He went to collect his step ladders and bringing them to the front of the craft, opened them up and climbed up to the craft's screen.

With the blades in his hand, he noticed another scuff mark that he had missed when he had returned from his road test.

A quick rub with an oily rag sorted out the minor issue and he was back on with the job in hand. Two minutes later the mechanic had descended the ladders and with a rub of his hands on the oily rag, approached the two aliens.

"All done gents," Kenneth said with a smile.

"Thank you so much for your help and hospitality," replied Dissel, "Come on, Pitrol. We're off."

The two aliens made their way to the UFO.

"What about your mate?" called out Kenneth.

The aliens looked at each other, then at Kenneth, and both smiled deceptively.

"Well, we're just going to take it for a road test to make sure everything is alright. If Forsta comes back whilst we're gone, just tell him we'll only be five minutes," replied Dissel.

"Ohhh, OK," said Kenneth, not knowing if he should believe his alien clients or not.

The two aliens boarded the UFO, which suddenly started to levitate. Part of the main screen started to lower and Dissel's head poked out.

"You couldn't open your garage doors, could you?" he smiled.

"Sure thing... Five minutes, right?" replied the nervy mechanic.

"Yep... Five minutes," grinned the alien, as he leant out of the UFO with his elbow on the screen frame.

The garage doors opened and the UFO silently drifted out. From the open window that had now started to close, Dissel shouted out,

"Thanks again!"

The UFO vanished from sight, not even waiting for Kenneth to wave goodbye. Kenneth was standing quietly in front of his garage, looking up toward the sky, contemplating the technology the aliens had given him, and wondering if they were actually doing a road test or not.

"Where the snark are the guys and the ship?!" screamed Forsta.

Kenneth noticed a panicked looking alien with a lengthy tail of toilet paper trailing behind him, clenched between his buttocks, staring at him.

"Err, they've just gone for a road test. They'll be back in five minutes," smiled Kenneth unconvincingly.

"A road test?! It's a bloody spacecraft, not a car!" screamed Forsta, running to the open garage doors and looking up into the blue sky.

"You pair of Squanchs!" Forsta shouted as he waved his fist at the empty sky.

Forsta looked at Kenneth with an angry alien look.

"This is not the first time these scragfelds have done this, y'know!" he said, glaring up at his mechanic acquaintance.

Not knowing how to respond, Kenneth pursed his lips and with raised puzzled eyebrows wandered back into the workshop, leaving the alien to shout more obscenities at the UFO empty sky.

***

"Thanks so much for the lift, my dear friend. You just don't realise how unfit you are until you try to do a runner, I mean try to run," said Jeremiah, as he exited the car outside the conman's art shop.

"Oh, it was nothing, old boy. Anything for a friend," came the amiable response. "Well, it's time to pick up

Bertrand. I've left him at home as I didn't think I'd be long."

"I haven't kept you, have I?" apologised Jeremiah.

"Not at all old boy, however, I have to go now, so have a good day and I'm sure I'll see you later. Toodle-oo!"

Walter left the village square, Jeremiah waving goodbye with his free hand as the other held a vice-like grip on the tube.

"Morning Jeremiah. Having a lift off Walter, I see?"

Jeremiah turned to see the three old men sat outside Bettys café.

"Good morning Stephen, Stewart, Sylas. Yes. A slight hiccup with the post this morning, so I've just been to Kenneth's to retrieve my parcel and drop off his. Anyway, must dash. Things to see, people to do as they say."

Jeremiah dashed into his shop and locked his door.

"How strange!" commented Stephen.

Neither friend replied as they were busy reading their newspapers.

Inside Jeremiah Brown's Fine Arts shop at the rear of the premises, Fast Eddie stood the cardboard tube upright on his desk and looked at it in awe. With a nearby knife, he delicately cut the taped seal, holding the lid in place, and removed the top.

A faint whiff of Italian aftershave entered the backroom, as Eddie gently pulled out his prized possession. Slowly unrolling the priceless piece of art on his table, he stared at the recently stolen painting, which lay staring back at him.

"Oh my, oh my, oh my! Just look at you, my little beauty. You are going to make uncle Eddie a very rich man!" Eddie smiled and blew a kiss at Botticelli's version of the rings of Hell.

Chapter 35

Gary had been awake for a few seconds when daylight had forced its way through a slit in the curtains and was mounting a full-frontal assault on his eyes.

"Oh, my dad! Now that's a hangover from home!"

As Gary sat up in bed and rested against the headboard, a 'welling up' from his stomach reached the back of his throat before he swallowed and forced it back down.

"Well, that wasn't pleasant," he muttered to himself as the acrid taste lingered in his throat.

"Hello! Mr... err... Gary? Are you up? We have a full English fry-up breakfast if you want it? Fried eggs, sausages, black pudding, fried mushrooms, fried bread, and beans," Liz called from the other side of the room's door. "...Have you spilled the water from the jug on the sideboard? I just heard a loud splashing sound, that's all. Don't worry, I'll mop it up."

The door opened and Gary stood smiling and had just finished wiping his mouth.

"I'll forgo breakfast if you don't mind."

The stench of stale beer and stomach acid was enough to peel a layer of skin off anyone's eyeballs, but Liz had built up an immunity to foul smells, having a flatulent wolf as a pet.

"No problem... Gary. Leave the window open, would you? Just to air the place, if you would. Maybe black coffee and an aspirin?" Liz smiled at her alcohol riddled guest.

"Y'know what? I think I'm good thanks. I've had worse hangovers."

Gary was a good liar but on this occasion, his swaying gave a subtle hint that he may still be suffering from his drinking session with Reg.

"OK, well you know where I am if you change your mind," Liz smiled and left her guest to recover.

With the door ajar, Gary held on to the light switch in an attempt to stop the room from spinning.

"Jeez, that man can drink!" Gary muttered as he walked back to his bed as if he was on a ship in a force ten gale.

Whilst sitting on the edge of the bed, Gary stared at the door and focussed on not being drunk, a trick he had learnt from back when he had invented the concept of the 'hangover'. Like every talented computer programmer, Gary had installed a back door to which only he knew where the escape hatch was.

Within two minutes, the fallen angel had gone from a bilious alcohol-induced wreck to being on the right side of somewhat jaded. Hopping down the stairs, Gary passed Terry, Liz, and Liam in the dining area where all three were enjoying their breakfast whilst being watched with a keen eye from Shadow, just waiting for any scraps.

"You off out for a walk?" Terry asked, having swallowed the last bit of well-chewed sausage.

Gary had opened the rear door leading into the beer garden and turned to see his hosts.

"Yes. My morning constitutional. Clears the lungs and head. Makes me ready for the day ahead. Talking of which, I suspect I'll be leaving today, so if you want to send my bill to Ed... Jeremiah, then I'm sure he'll be happy to settle up."

Before Terry could reply, Gary had disappeared and had closed the door behind him.

"Old Jeremiah is going to have a dickie fit when he sees how much his guest and Reg put away last night," Terry smiled and continued with his breakfast.

Liam, looking as calculating as someone with his intelligence could, waited until the door had fully closed, jumped up and ran out of the room. The thudding of heavy footsteps was heard going up the stairs and the unmistakable sound of the creaking door of the main guest room being opened.

"What's he up to?" asked Terry to Liz as she had sipped her coffee.

"I think it's something to do with a magazine which he had let our guest borrow. Think it was something about pottery. Cups and jugs, that sort of thing," Liz replied.

Terry nearly choked on a mushroom.

***

Gary had made his way out of the rear of the pub and straight away the fresh air had made him light-headed once again. Gary composed himself and shaking it off,

343

smoothed down his shirt, made his way up the lane and away from the village.

The sound of Walter's Mercedes had just entered the square and if Gary had gone the opposite way into the square, he would have seen his supplier of fine art Eddie getting out of the car. As it was, it was a nice sunny day and Gary thought he would take a steady walk past one of his dad's houses and just for a laugh, stick two fingers up at it.

It surprised Gary as to how much effort he needed to walk up the lane and felt himself huffing and puffing on such a slight incline.

"Jeez, that man can really drink," Gary muttered to himself again, thinking of Reg Golightly and his enthusiasm for the pint glass.

The village's church spire poking out above the churchyard Yew trees, and Gary's mischief was clear to see in his eyes. With a full bladder and sensing it was ready for a release, Gary knew exactly where the contents would be jettisoned. As he approached the stone-wall of the churchyard, on the other side of the lane was a very ornate garden hedge and the humming of its elderly owner, who was busy tending to her beloved plants.

Edith and Charles St.John-Fox had finished their breakfasts and were ready for a full day's nudist gardening. Charles had opted for taking the breakfast plates in so he could potter in the garden shed before bringing out the required plants for his wife.

Edith, who was in her usual attire, a big floppy hat and a smile, was busy bending over and pulling out some very brave weeds who had decided to try and grow in the one place they were definitely not welcomed. Gary had just reached the St.John-Fox's garden gate when his attention was caught by the scruff of its neck.

"What the bloody home is that?!" came the loud devilish voice.

Edith stood up and turned to see who had made the comment.

"Oh, good morning! And what a lovely day it is too, don't you think?" Edith smiled with a weed in one hand and a small handheld garden fork in the other.

"Oh, it's you!... A woman! I thought it was a sculpture made of golf balls!" replied Gary with a broad grin on his face.

"I'm sorry?" Edith wasn't too sure as to what she had just heard.

Gary promptly burst into fits of laughter when he saw the gardener from the front,

"Since when do space-hoppers have Bassett Hound ears resting on them and legs below?"

Gary was bent double with laughter.

"I beg your pardon?!"

Edith soon realised that this gentleman was not so much of a gentleman but actually quite a rude man! Charles, who had heard some form of commotion, quickly strode around the side of their home to see what all the fuss was about.

It wasn't long before he had reached the front garden, where he saw Gary at the garden gate and his lovely wife looking somewhat irked, standing in a rather offensive stance. Noticing the gardening tools on the pristine lawn, which included a garden fork and his prized dibber, Charles quickly recovered from a rather vivid memory flashback and darted forward to recover his dibber and fork.

"I say! What's going on here, darling?" Charles demanded, coming to his wife's aid.

"I was just doing the weeding when this, this, this yob started to insult me!" Edith replied.

Not quite hearing what was said, Charles had figured out that this smart man was desperate for a wee and his name was Bob.

"Oh! Well, if he needs a wee, then we should let him use our toilet. Come on in Bob, I'm Charles and this is my lovely wife Edith."

"NO CHARLES! He is a yob, and he has just insulted me!" Edith shouted.

Charles, realising what his wife had announced, looked sternly at Gary, who was still laughing and pointing at the two naturists.

"I think, Bob, that you ought to leave. I don't care if you need the toilet, you don't insult my wife!" Charles said as he stood to attention with a potted Begonia in his hand.

"You two are priceless!" Gary continued to laugh.

346

"And what's that? It looks like an acorn resting on a walnut shell in a nest of dead spiders!" Gary was in fits of laughter as he pointed to Charles' groin.

Charles was close enough to hear the full insult and calmly placed the Begonia on the lawn and approached the gate. As Gary recovered from bending over from his latest belly laugh, he was met with an angry naturist who had his right index finger pointing toward Gary's face.

A quick jab from Charles sent Gary reeling backward when the fleshy part of Charles's finger met with Gary's left eye. Gary stumbled backward enough for Edith to continue her husband's assault.

The garden gate almost flew off its hinges as Edith bolted past her husband and through the gateway, landing a perfect uppercut to Gary's chin, sending the fallen angel a short distance into the air before landing heavily in the middle of the lane. Edith bent over the injured Devil with her face further away than two more noticeable parts of her anatomy and pointed her finger right between Gary's eyes.

"I'll have you know that my Charles is man enough!" she screamed at Gary as her pendulous breasts swung free of her stomach and seemed to taunt the injured man.

"We have plenty of great sex, morning, noon, and night! Even this morning I rode him like a wild magnum!" Edith screamed in Gary's face.

Charles suddenly became aware that his wife was in the lane, naked, screaming at a man she had just punched and announcing to the world of their sexual antics. Quickly grabbing her arm by the elbow, Charles pulled her away from the laid out man and tried to usher her into the garden.

"Darling, it's a wild mustang, not magnum, and do you want to lower your voice a shade?"

"No, I bloody don't! Like a wild mustang you hear!"

Charles dragged his furious wife back into the garden.

"So what do you have in your trousers, eh? Two vacuum-packed raisins and a cashew? You're nothing compared to my Charles, you hear? Nothing!"

"Time to go inside darling and let the man recover. I think you've hurt him enough," Charles calmly said as he dragged his wife towards the front door.

"And he makes me scream with orgasmic pleasure when I climax!"

The cottage door slammed shut and a furious face of the female occupier appeared at the small mottled glass pane in the door and muffled shouting continued.

Jensen Moonchild was walking back down the lane, past the church, when he saw Gary laid on the floor just outside the St.John-Fox's house. He had taken Seb for a walk and was just returning when he witnessed Gary holding his face over his left eye and a small graze on the man's chin.

"Bloody hell! Are you alright, sir? Can I help you? Do you need an ambulance?" Jensen said as he knelt beside the injured Devil.

Buttercup had not told Jensen of the previous night's incident and how Gary had insulted her and her beloved Sebastian, as she felt by informing him would somehow demean her. However, whilst Jensen was not aware,

Sebastian the Chihuahua was most definitely aware. Any enemy of his female owner was an enemy of his.

Seb lunged forward with a snarling growl, and with pincer style teeth, sank both top and bottom set of jaws into Gary's groin. If Gary was dazed before, he was most definitely awake now. The scrotal pain flooded his entire body and in a flash was made even worse when the little dog shook its head like he was ragging a cloth toy.

"Holy shit! Seb! Get off the man!"

Jensen tried to pull Seb off Gary and didn't stop to think that pulling the dog off someone when they've sunk their teeth into a scrotum actually makes it worse. Gary let out an unearthly scream, which even spooked Seb enough to release his grip. Jensen quickly snatched the dog away from Gary and picking up his pet, decided to make a hasty exit in case the man exacted revenge.

"You little devil! What d'you do that for?!" Jensen chastised his dog with a slight tap on the dog's muzzle.

Whilst Gary was in considerable pain, he'd also had the wind taken completely out of his sails by the small dog, so was unable to curl up into a ball and wait until the pain subsided. It was then that Gary's phone chirped into life and recognising the ringtone, he decided not to take the call.

"You can just piss off!"

"Gary! How's it going?" interrupted God cheerfully.

"How the hell did you do that?" Gary muttered, "Answer my phone like that? I didn't press to accept!"

"I'm the G-man! I can pretty much do anything. So! What you up to? Anything good? The beach party is still in full swing here, you should come and join in. Oh! That's right, I banished you, so you can't. Oh well, you're missing one heck of a party. The music, beer, surf, and fire is still going on. It's a pity you can't join us, as I'm sure you'd really enjoy it."

"Sod off!"

"Hey!! That's no way to speak to your father! Even if he's called you up to mock you," God laughed.

Spreadeagled in the middle of the lane with his mobile phone on his chest and loudspeaker on, Gary enquired as to the real reason for the call.

"Well, I just wondered when you'd be going back home?" God replied.

"What's it got to do with you?" croaked Gary.

"OK, OK. Seems someone is in a bit of a foul mood. I'll leave you be, shall I? I just wondered that's all. I'm sure your demons have it all in hand," replied God with an air of incredulity.

"This is the second time you've said that to me in as many days. Look, it's me who's supposed to be the troublemaker. What you up to?"

Gary's curiosity spiked but was stamped back down as pain was still in charge and was quite happy maintaining that status.

"Nothing, son. I just know you never turn your back on a demon, yet here you are, not only turning your back on not one but two demons but also you've left the lunatics to run the asylum. Are you sure that's a wise move?"

Gary hated to be told what to do and would shy away from warnings like a ricocheting bullet off granite.

"What makes you think I'm going to listen to your over cautious warnings? I didn't when I was in Eden with silly bollocks and his Mrs..."

"And look where that got you. Maybe you should listen to your old man sometimes. I'm not the G-man for nothing, you know. Hey ho, listen, don't listen it's all the same to me."

"Well, I've something for you to listen to," replied Gary as he reached up and took his phone from his chest and placed it between his legs.

"... I'm waiting. What am I supposed to be listening to?" said God after a lengthy pause.

"STOP STOPPING ME FROM FARTING DOWN THE PHONE!!" shouted Gary, "It's my arse and I'll do with it what I want!"

"Of course it is, and what makes you think I'm in charge of your backside?"

"You didn't let silly bollocks have free will, did you? No, he had to abide by your rules and not pick from the tree. You were in charge of him and Eve, so you're trying to be in charge of me too, well I'm telling you, I'm my own boss and no one makes my decisions for me."

"Is that so? So last night you very kindly bought that writer in the pub a drink because you wanted to, is that right?"

Gary paused a second.

"Yes. Yes, it is. He looked a decent bloke, so I figured I'd buy him one. What's wrong with that?" lied Gary, not knowing how his father knew about that or what on Earth possessed him to do that.

"Liar, liar bum's on fire," mocked God.

Gary knew too well that God would not believe that story, but thought he'd try it, anyway.

"Anyway. What's your plan? You obviously made me do that and I'm sure you got that rat-dog to bite me, so what you up to?"

"As they say 'God's ineffable plan' dear boy."

"Well, you can 'eff' your plan as I'm not playing any part of it. I'm my own angel and you're not going to change that."

"Of course you are Lucif..."

"GARY!" shouted Gary and suddenly regretted it as the tightening in the groin brought another wave of pain, "Jesus!"

"Oh yes, he's here, would you like to say hello to him?"

Click!

Gary had had enough of his father and his 'know-it-all' ways.

"Who does he think he is anyway?" he muttered to himself.

352

Gary's phone suddenly burst into life again, this time with a text message.

'I'm the G-man, that's all. lol xxx,' it read.

A quick glance at the message and Gary threw his mobile phone over the church wall, into the graveyard.

Chapter 36

Bernie Aberline and Clarabelle Windleson were sleeping off the effects of last night's monumental success at the Women's Institute. Under one of the churchyard Yew trees and fast asleep, Clarabelle had snuggled up to Bernie with her hand gently resting on his crotch when their sleep was interrupted by a mobile phone that had just flown over a nearby wall and landed on the ground, passing through Clarabelle's hand and Bernie's groin.

"What in God'th good name wath that?!" Bernie said with a start.

Bernie looked down and noticed a mobile phone on the grass beneath his groin and Clarabelle's hand. His friend had also awoken at the same time and on seeing the electronic article made a move to retrieve it, only to be stopped by Bernie as he felt a little uncomfortable with her hand being placed where it was, let alone delving deeper. Bernie, retrieving the phone himself, tapped the screen, bringing it to life.

"Who'th do you think it ith?" asked Clarabelle.

"Let'th thee if we can find out who'th by looking at the addreth book."

"Why are we thpeaking with a lithp?" replied Clarabelle.

"I don't know but my tongue feelth like ith fur-lined. Mutht be that thmoke. Wow! I feel tho hungry," said Bernie.

The 'contacts' icon was tapped on the phone's screen, and a list of names, including one for 'Pumper' flashed up for the two spirits. Clarabelle giggled at the name and suggested they try that contact and call them to ask whose phone it was. Tapping the screen on 'Pumper' and selecting 'call', Bernie held the phone close to his and Clarabelle's ears.

Steve had just dropped off a load of spirits at Heaven's pearly gates and was surprised to find that Peter wasn't there, waiting, with his annoying ledger. In the distance Steve could hear music and chattering going on inside, so ventured indoors with the group of people who had been crushed by a blue whale. The poor aquatic mammal had been recently tossed onto a beach after having been scooped up by a rather large hurricane out at sea.

As the beach party in full swing, and invited in by Travis, Steve figured that the Universe wouldn't mind if he had a coffee break for five minutes, so joined in with the frivolities. Whilst enjoying himself with a young lady in a bikini who had recognised from about a month ago, Steve didn't hear his mobile phone go off in his cloak and the name 'snot face' flash onto the screen.

"There'th no anthwer," Bernie said and closed the call.

"Whoever they are they can't be a nithe perthon or Mithter Pumper would have anthwered," replied Clarabelle, "Think we ought to thee Betty and thee if thee hath thomething for our tongueth."

Tossing the mobile phone to one side, the two ghosts helped each other up and made their way into the village.

***

Eddie had been staring at the priceless painting on his desk for some time and was still in awe of it. A genuine piece of work painted by one of the masters, and here it was in a conman's shop, waiting to be sold to a client who was more than happy to pay a king's ransom for it.

Eddie's mind was a whirlwind of thoughts, thinking about his Italian counterpart getting hold of this work of art and sending it to him in a towel tube, the amount of cash that was going to be in his pocket.

Even if he paid everyone who needed paying and doubled their fees and his own, he would no longer be Jeremiah Brown but live as Eddie, in a quiet part of the world without people wanting to kill him.

The ticking of the wall clock in his backroom slowly brought him back from his hypnotised gaze on the painting. Eddie looked up at the clock and noticed the time. By now, his client should be awake and ready to take receipt of the painting in exchange for a large sum of money. Carefully rolling up the art and placing it in his safe, Eddie straightened his jacket lapels, sprayed a little aftershave on his neck, and left the premises to see his client, Gary.

Eddie left the art shop, passing the three patrons of Betty's and was on his way to The Blind Cobber's Thumb when Reg Golightly waved and called out to him.

"'ow do, Jeremiah. Your mate Gary can sup, can't he?!" called Reg.

"Oh, bloody hell!... Just as well I'm not paying the bill if that's the case," thought Eddie, "Oh my! I do hope you were kind to him, Reginald," Eddie replied.

357

"Oh, we weren't in any competition, but last time I saw him he was a little jaded."

Eddie had slowly wandered towards the square's fountain as he chatted to the shopkeeper.

"I'm sure he'll be fine," continued Reg.

"I'm sure he will be. I believe he might be leaving today as I have acquired what he has requested, so I'm afraid you'll be minus one drinking buddy," Eddie chuckled on the last part but was a little concerned as he knew Reg's drinking prowess, "Anyway I'm just off to see him now so I'll pass on your regards. Have a good day."

Eddie waved to the shopkeeper and headed to the pub's main door. The road between the pub and the newsagents, that lead to the church, was in plain sight of the conman, whose sharp eyes noticed a human figure laying in the middle of the lane and who had just thrown his mobile phone over the church's wall.

It took less than a second to recognise who it was that was horizontal in the lane, and a fraction longer for Eddie's body to emit stress-induced sweat down his lower back and into the crack of his backside.

"Oh, bloody hell!" muttered Eddie, who darted up the lane to assist his client.

"Gary, Gary! Are you alright?" Eddie skidded to a halt and knelt down by the fallen angel's side.

Before Gary could answer, the lounge window of the St.John-Fox's house opened and Edith's upper body leant out.

358

"He's a bloody good shag!" she screamed before her husband pulled her back in.

Eddie was shocked as to what he had just heard and from who, then turned to Gary, who had cupped his groin and was wincing.

"Bloody hell, Gary. You're a braver man than me!" Eddie whispered, "Come on, let me help you up."

Eddie, bending down and taking hold of Gary's arm, helped the injured client up. He placed Gary's arm over his shoulder and surprised as to how much he weighed, Eddie muttered.

"Come on, soldier. Let's get you back to my shop. I've got a pleasant surprise for you. Although, I'm sure you were surprised with Edith, I know I am. Edith St.John-Fox, a sexual demon. Who'd a thought!"

Gary looked at his helper with an air of disbelief and shook his head.

Several minutes had gone by before Eddie had got Gary back to his shop. They had been stopped outside Betty's by Stephen, Stewart, and Sylas who had asked what had happened and if they could help.

Eddie thanked them for the offer but declined and mouthed the information that a sexual encounter had been had between his client and Edith, which had left him worn and threadbare. The three men sat there agog until Sylas broke the silence with a belly laugh, leaving him breathless.

Helping Gary over the shop's threshold and into the rear, Eddie guided him to the desk and helped him into his chair, ensuring that he was as comfortable as could be.

Swiftly making his way over to the safe, he punched in the required numbers on the digital code pad on the door when then gave an agreeable 'click'.

Inside the safe, and removing it, was a cardboard tube. Eddie placed it in front of his client, gently removed the lid, revealing the work inside, and carefully unrolled the painting to show it in all its glory.

"As requested. What d'you think?" beamed Eddie.

Gary winced as he leant forward to examine the painting. The wince was quickly replaced with a broad grin.

"Bloody marvellous!" Gary said.

Eddie gently picked up the painting and carefully placed it back in the tube, replacing the lid as he did. Gary reached out to Eddie for the tube, only to see Eddie take a step back from him.

"Can we talk about payment first," said Eddie tentatively.

Gary smiled at Eddie and looked away.

"It always comes down to money. Can I assume you do not have the total amount yet? You obviously need Edoardo's fee, then Terry's, less, of course, his discount and of course your own, then to double it," Gary said in a knowing, confident way.

Eddie was taken aback as to how Gary knew his plan.

"Err, err,"

"Don't worry. All you have to do is write the full amount on my letter and you'll have the amount in your account shortly after. You do still have my letter, don't you? Well,

I say a letter, it's more of a contract, isn't it? Y'know, you do something for me and I pay you," Gary said.

Eddie was worried as to how his client knew about his plan and how on Earth would he know the full price, simply by writing on a letter.

"Yes... yes. I have it in my desk drawer," Eddie replied, "But how?"

"It just works, believe me. All you have to do is scribble the amount down and sign the letter in the appropriate place and you'll get what's coming."

Part of Eddie's brain was telling him to cut his losses and run, whilst another part was saying 'just do it'! Eddie decided to follow the 'just do it' path.

"Oki-doke!"

Eddie handed the tube over to Gary, who accepted the item with glee. Gary gave a little laugh as he stood, which turned into a wince.

"Give me a hand to my car, will you?"

Eddie quickly came to his assistance, helping Gary up and escorting him to the front door of his car where it had been parked for the last few days.

Chapter 37

Walter Hollybank had enjoyed his morning road test of his upgraded Mercedes Benz and was eager to see what the red button did.

"Patience is a virtue old boy," he said to himself, "This is for the young upstart who thinks he can get away with trying to show you up, my beauty." Walter patted the top of the steering wheel as he complimented his beloved car.

Far below the sun, the Mercedes Benz eased its way around the hedge-lined corners with the odd whooping sound coming from the driver. Even though still feeling a little groggy, the sun tried its best to shine down on Walter from behind its cloud. To see man and machine in blissful harmony was a treasure to behold, even though the foolish old duffer wore what the sun considered a ridiculous get-up.

Itching to press the button, Walter restrained himself, and decided it was time to go back home, pick up his faithful friend Bertrand. Once he collected Bertrand, he would then nip over to Hilda's home to pick her up and take her into Ashburn so she and Elsie could clear up the hall after last night's show.

Bertrand was more than happy to see his master as he knew the usual routine was to pick up the old lady who smelled of rose petal scented talcum powder and maybe her friend. Elsie always had a little treat for Bertie as the two sat in the rear of the car, and a good ear rubbing on the way to the village was always welcomed.

To top it all off, the lovely round lady in the food shop with that stupid fat ginger cat would always sneak out a little cake, whilst his master chatted to the three men, one of which would always smell of musty straw.

Bertrand knew his master's routine, so when the car pulled into the gravelled driveway, the little dog's tail wagged furiously. The car's engine stopping, and the steady crunching of the gravel as his master made his way to the front door, meant it was time for Bertrand to sit in the hallway with a wagging tail and greet Walter.

"Hello, Bertrand. Have you missed me? Come on, off we go."

The Jack Russell Terrier didn't need asking twice and racing out of the house, across the gravel, the little dog launched himself at the open car door. Completely missing the driver's seat and landing on the front passenger seat, Bertrand was waiting for a food-filled day.

Walter looked with loving eyes at his dog and a broad smile appeared on his face.

"You are a daft one," said Walter with a hint of a chuckle.

Bertrand yapped with glee as if to say 'come on old man'.

Walter fired up the vintage automobile and drove off to pick up the second love of his life. Everything was just right in the Hollybank world.

364

Hilda Swindlebrook was just putting the finishing touches to herself, whilst her friend and subordinate for the Women's Institute waited patiently downstairs.

"Are you ready, Hilda? Walter will be here any minute," called out Elsie.

"You can't rush perfection," came the reply from upstairs.

Elsie raised her eyebrows and tried to bite her tongue. Just then an old raspy double honk from a vintage Mercedes Benz sounded outside, followed by a slight squeal of brakes and the ratcheting sound of a handbrake.

"He's here!" Elsie shouted.

Hilda was standing in front of her bedroom mirror and was practicing her 'Hollywood' tossing of her chiffon scarf over her shoulder. The grumbling of Walter's car sounded outside, and with Elsie calling to her, Hilda quickly gave one more squirt of her perfume vaporiser around her neck. After a final check in the mirror with her best smouldering expression, Hilda went downstairs to meet her suitor.

"Oh my!" said Elsie as her friend entered the lounge, "Audrey Hepburn and Natalie Wood have some serious competition going on. Walter is a very lucky man."

"He's not there yet, Elsie," replied Hilda graciously accepting the compliment.

"Don't know why. You could have bedded him years ago."

"Elsie Bagshaw! You do know how to bring the tone down, don't you!"

A spritely knocking on the door interrupted the chastisement, and Elsie jumped up and made her way to open it.

"Morning Walter. She's just in here, looking as gorgeous as ever," Elsie smiled to the awaiting suitor.

"Morning Walter," Hilda called out in a firm, headmistress type of tone.

"Ready when you are, ladies," Walter smiled and skipped back to the car and his faithful Bertrand, who was standing up in the car eagerly waiting for his treat.

Moments later, the cottage door was locked and all four occupants drove off towards Ashburn-on-Sinkhole.

**

Jeremiah Brown had just helped his wealthy client out of his shop and towards his car when the low grumbling sound of a coasting Mercedes Benz entered the village square. As the vintage car was pulling up outside the hall, Walter spied the young upstart with the very nice Mr Brown, close to his monstrosity of a car.

The ladies alighted from Walter's car, whilst Walter's laser beam glare stayed on the fallen angel as he cruised around the square, passing the decaying sandstone fountain, and parking directly in front of the hypercar. A revving of the vintage car gave the green light to Gary for one last mock before he left the godforsaken place with his work of art.

366

Elsie, who was just in the vestibule of the W.I. hall, heard Walter rev his engine and peered outside to see what was happening. The colour from her rouge coated cheeks drained away quicker than an underage drinker being found in a pub by his father. Quickly scurrying into the hall, Elsie called out to her friend.

"Hilda! Hilda! Shit's going down over at Jeremiah's!"

"I beg your pardon?!"

Elsie was too worried to think of the correct wording about her concerns and just let her mouth do the thinking as well as the talking.

"It's Walter! I think there's going to be a showdown!"

Hilda's heart suddenly burst into life like a ticker-tape machine on amphetamine.

"Oh, my Lord!" Hilda quickly made her way to the hall doorway.

***

"Jeremiah, how are we today? Taking out the rubbish I see," Walter said with contempt, dripping from every word.

Jeremiah felt his client's body tense every single muscle.

"Oh, crap!" he muttered, as Gary stood upright with a sudden lack of feeling to his injured area.

"Well, you silly old duffer, you'd know all about rubbish, driving around in that hunk-a-junk. Isn't it about time you bought a real car? I mean, with all your money, you'd think you'd be able to buy a decent one and even a dog

367

that looked like a dog and not some poor excuse of a gerbil."

Bertrand didn't understand English, apart from certain words like 'walkies', 'Betty's' and 'cake' but listening to what this weird human-looking thing was saying, it wasn't nice, so decided to give it a growl. Instinctively Gary placed his free hand over his groin and continued with his taunt.

"Dear oh dear. Poor car, poor excuse of a dog..."

"Walter is everything alright?" Hilda interrupted as she approached Walter's car with Elsie following close behind.

"And... well... what can I say," Gary continued as he looked at Hilda.

Walter as wealthy as he was had only a few passions in his life and Gary had insulted every one of them, except steampunk.

"Oh and let's not forget your bizarre get up. I mean! What's that all about?!"

The gauntlet had not been thrown down so much as taken a hundred-yard sprint and slapped across the face of Walter with a force that would dislodge any fillings, then thrown down. Walter had faith in his mechanic friend, so tried to contain himself as he replied to the onslaught of abuse.

"One thing I've learned over my many years of business and other money-making ventures is that the ones who make the most rattle do so because they are so inadequate that they can only bluff their way through life with insults and intimidation. Neither of which have you succeeded in.

Whilst your car may appear modern, it may very well be less than a paper tiger, probably more like a paper kitten. Your attire may be of wealth, but to hide what? A lack of character and intelligence, I rather fancy. Whilst you insult the fairer sex, I sense that this is because of jealousy, and because of your lack of personality, you are unable to attract anyone worthy of being seen out with. And regarding dogs? I can only assume yours has three heads or something."

Gary was taken aback by what had just come out of the daft old bugger's mouth and how he had managed to say such hurtful things in such a pleasant manner! Not wanting to look at the small audience who was transfixed by what had just happened, Gary knew he'd had to fire back.

"Really?!" Gary said.

Gary's brain immediately screamed at him.

"What the bloody home are you doing, y'great pansy?! Are you letting this old git off with just a 'Really!'? Come on! You're the Prince of Darkness, the Devil, Satan, for crying out loud. Burn the old duffer. Make him squeal in agony before dragging him to Hell and placing him in the worst place imaginable. You cannot let this steampunk clad geriatric get away with this!"

"You're right about my dog," Gary continued.

"Chuff me! I give up!" cried Gary's brain. *"You bloody snowflake!"*

"But that is where your accuracy ends," Gary's voice was calm and measured.

"Now we're talking!" added his brain. *"Mean and purposeful. C'mon son!"*

"I know all about business and make deals on a regular basis. Probably more than you ever have. I'm regularly making contracts with all and sundry and when it comes to money, then I probably have enough to buy this world a million times over."

The Fast Eddie part of Jeremiah's persona pricked up its ears and realised that if this was the case, then two more noughts on the end of the bill might not go unnoticed.

"Regarding character, I'd think being thrown out by your father at an early age and being made to take control of part of the overall family business, albeit the lower end, would suggest that I have both character and the intelligence to surpass your aging mind."

"Oh, we're on a roll now. Come on, let him have it!" roared Gary's brain.

"Everything is a commodity, including women, and if you treat them any other way, then it just shows how weak you are," Gary smiled at Hilda as he finished.

Hilda's body tensed and bristled with anger as the smartly dressed stranger not only insulted her, but the entirety of womanhood. Walter's synapses were firing at lightning speed, and he immediately replied.

"You youngsters have no idea about love and devotion, and that's where you will always fail. My Hilda is not an object, and if anything, I am stronger with her by my side than not."

Hilda's eyebrows raised and looked at Walter in amazement, which was closely followed by a sigh and the thought that raced through her mind was 'My Walter!'

"You think that power is everything and love is a weakness, so let's see how powerful your hunk of junk is against my Mercedes, which I happen to love. I'll race you to Kenneth Turnkey's garage and back," Walter continued.

Gary's eyes lit up as he knew he was on for a deal that this old man would never forget. Hilda looked at Walter and let out a little "Oh bugger!"

"Is this a bet old man?" Gary smiled.

"You bet your sweet bibby is it. I've just had my car serviced at Kenneth's and she's ready to go," replied the defiant Walter.

Gary just laughed a demonic laugh which even worried Bertrand, who didn't understand what had just been said but knew an evil laugh when he heard one.

"You'll be laughing on the other side of your face when you pull up here and see me waiting for you, you spoiled little daddy's boy."

"DO NOT MENTION MY FATHER!" Gary roared so powerfully that it was heard from up above.

***

"Hey dad! I think Lucifer is a little cross," called out Jesus to his father, who was in the process of learning to hula dance.

371

"Hey G-man. I think Heysoos is calling you," Travis tugged at God's elbow, "Something about Lucy being cross?"

God stopped dancing and went over to Jesus with Travis following behind, lighting up another thick joint.

"It's OK, son, I heard. I may just have a look-see. I think we're going to enjoy this, I hope."

"You hope?! You. Hope?" replied Jesus. "Dad, if you hope then something is seriously going down!"

"G-man. Is shit getting real?" Travis said through a plume of sweet-smelling smoke.

"Possibly," God smiled, "Shall we have a look?"

With a click of his fingers, a huge flat-screen television slid out from the trunk of a nearby tree and sparked into life. The television's logo appeared, 'Life is God' and faded to show the ongoing incident, from up above, that was taking place in a village square somewhere, way below. God, Jesus, and Travis eyed the screen eagerly, closely followed by a number of party-goers who were nearby.

***

"So I said, if he's just washed it then it's fair game to aim for it," said Wayne, the wood pigeon to his friend George, who were both perched on the chimneypot of Betty's premises.

Expecting a response of sorts from his woodpigeon friend and not getting one, Wayne looked over at his friend who seemed to be in a hypnotic trance and looking down on an incident that was taking place below them.

"You alright, George?" his friend inquired.

"I... feel... a... little... strange," replied his friend in a monotone fashion.

"George, you are a little strange. You've been cooing and bowing to Monica all day, and she's still not interested in you. So what's the difference now?"

"I... don't... know... why... but... I... have... to... watch... this."

***

"Dude. What's going down? How you getting such a good camera angle?" asked Travis to God.

"Well, you've heard of 'spy in the sky'? Well, this is kind of something similar. Not so much a spy but more akin to a bird's-eye view... or to be exact a pigeon's eye view."

***

"Touchy touchy," Walter smiled, as he had wound up his opponent to a frenzy.

"So what is the wager?" Gary asked with a laser beam vision locked onto Walter.

Walter stroked his chin and pondered over the question.

"How... about..."

"How about we talk about it after the race," interrupted Gary.

373

Walter was a little taken aback over the suggestion, but feeling confident in Kenneth's work, agreed.

***

"Dude, is that wise? This guy seems a bit gnarly if you ask me," said Travis, looking on.

"You'd be right there, dude," replied God, "He's the Devil, Gary, and I'm not sure that Walter is up to the bet."

God kept his eyes glued to the TV screen whilst he reached out, took the joint from Travis, and took a drag on it.

***

"Now I do not know you, young man, you could be the Devil for all I know, so all bets will be off if there's any cheating. Understand? It's a straight race to Kenneth's and back. No pushing off the road or anything like that, just straight speed. Mano et mano. Man and machine against..."

"I get it, old man. Right, you. Old hag..." Gary said pointing to Hilda, "You can start the race with your scarf."

Walter's eyes shone fire from deep within his soul at Gary's insult to his beloved. Slowly clanking over to the fallen angel, Walter approached Gary and stood nose to chin with him.

"As God is my witness..."

"I am! I am a witness!" interrupted God as he nodded to all who were watching the incident unfold in Heaven.

374

"...I will make you regret saying that, you rancid poor excuse for a subnormal creature. Get in your piece of foreign muck and let's do this."

Walter stood his ground, staring upwards into Gary's eyes with a venom that even shook Gary a little.

"Go on then, *little boy*. Get in your plastic pig and let's see how much I can embarrass you."

"And you get in your zimmer frame, old man, and I will wipe the floor with you," Gary glared back at Walter.

"Walter dearest," Hilda interrupted, "Kick this boy's arse."

From outside Betty's café, where the three elderly men sat, came the whistling tune from the spaghetti westerns, which was followed by what sounded like a kick to the shin and an 'Ooh ya bugger!'.

The Mexican stand-off lasted only a couple of seconds, but for the onlookers it seemed so much longer. Slowly both men headed to their respective cars, both glaring at each other.

Gary was the first to get into his car and fire up the car with a demonic, thunderous roar. Walter clanked over to his vintage Mercedes Benz in his steampunk spurred boots and opened the door. Hilda hurried over to her man and as he closed his driver's door, she lay her hands on it and leaned into the open-top car and gave Walter a gentle kiss on his cheek.

"Get a room!" called out Gary.

Walter looked into the eyes of Hilda and smiled.

"Oh, I intend to," he whispered to her, which made Hilda blush.

Hilda smiled, giving Walter a little wink as she walked away from his car and stood in front of it.

"You, young rapscallion. Park alongside, if you still feel brave enough." Hilda instructed Gary.

With a roar of the car's engine and a squeal of the tyres on the cobbles, Gary's demon car pulled alongside Walter. The vintage Mercedes Benz fired up, but Gary's sleek hypercar eclipsed the engine's sound.

Exchanging glares, Gary and Walter turned to look at Hilda. Not quite sure what to do, Hilda looked over to Elsie who silently mouthed the word 'scarf'. The prompt was quickly acknowledged and Hilda removed her chiffon scarf. As she started to raise it above her head, Walter pressed the red button.

***

"Dude! This is just like in the film Grease," Travis said with his gaze fixed to the television screen.

God was barely visible through the haze of sweet smoke. A hand appeared from the plume and gave what was left of the joint back to Travis.

"Yep," came the croaky voice from within the smoke.

"Whoa, G-man. You OK?" Travis said, looking at the well-smoked joint.

"I am now, bra," came the reply.

"Well, I never! It appears our dear Lord is a bit squiffy," muttered a well-to-do gent to his wife.

"Squiffy on a spliffy," his wife replied with a chuckle.

"Not funny, Beatrice," chided the man.

"Oh, lighten up, Neville," she replied and pinched her husband's bottom.

"Dude, you're the G-man. Why so worried?" Travis asked.

"Sometimes you just gotta roll the dice, Trav baby, as scary as it may seem," replied God.

More and more residents of Heaven stopped partying and gathered around the television, waiting eagerly for the race to begin.

"By 'eck! I'm busting for a pee," said one cherub, jumping on the spot urgently.

"Fella, thas a nappy on!" replied his friend.

"Oh, aye!... Sooo much better."

**

"OK George, now you're beginning to worry me. Snap out of this NOW!" Wayne insisted.

George's head was pointing down at the humans, two in their cars, one stood in front of them and several other onlookers.

"Can't... stop... Wayne... need... to... watch... feel... little... high... like... been... smoking... something."

Even a peck to the side of the pigeon's head from his friend could not break the trance George was in.

***

Hilda's right arm was aloft with her scarf clutched tight in her wrinkly hand. Gary's hands were tight on his steering wheel whilst the car's rev counter screamed at him as it read twelve thousand revs. Gary's eyes were fixed to Hilda's shoulder, the slightest twitch, and he would be off like a bat out of... home.

Walter's eyes were firmly fixed on Hilda too, but for a totally different reason. The raising of her right arm had emphasised the curvature of her bust in the buttoned tweed jacket. With his left foot placed firmly on the clutch pedal and his hand on the gear lever, waiting to shift from first to second, Walter revved his beloved car to nearly two thousand revs.

Both cars rocked as the accelerator pedals were pumped. Hilda shifted her eyes from one driver to another, ensuring both were ready and hoping that her Walter would be quick off the mark. The grip on the scarf tightened as Hilda's hand imperceptibly raised in readiness to snap down.

378

Chapter 38

All eyes were on Hilda and her scarf, all except Bertrand's whose attention was on a slice of cake on a café table outside Betty's. Everyone in the square had stopped doing whatever they were doing and stood agog. Even in Heaven, the party that had been in full swing had stopped and everyone had crowded around the television.

So many spirits were trying to watch, that God had to make the screen bigger, then found himself on the front row, which if anyone has been to the cinema pretty much knows, is possibly the worst place to be. Quickly thinking, God zapped himself to a more central place where, due to holding onto God's Hawaiian shirt, Travis had also been transported and had passed a lit joint to his compadre. Slowly taking the cigarette from him, God never took his eyes off the screen.

Walter had placed his steampunk goggles over his eyes and for the first time had noticed that they were ever so slightly magnified. He could now see everything in high-definition, which included the tensing of Hilda's grip on the scarf and the slight raising of her hand.

Red button pressed and feet hard on both accelerator and clutch, Walter waited for the minutest drop of his beloved's hand. Gary had his eyes fixed on Hilda's scarf and was just waiting for the slightest of ripples of the material before he let loose the awesome power of his beast of a car.

For a split second, Gary took his eyes off Hilda and quickly glanced over at his loser of a competitor and gave a sneer. Unfortunately for Gary, that was the exact time that Walter noticed Hilda's hand start to drop. Quicker than a squirrel on a triple espresso, Walter lifted his foot off the clutch and released the full force of the microwave thruster.

Gary looked back at Hilda as the ripple of her scarf caught his eye, but before he had a chance to tense the muscles to lift his foot off the pedal, his car rocked violently from the vortex from Walter's car.

***

God knew that a beach party was not for everyone, but a race with the Devil would be something that everyone would want to see, so had placed up television sets throughout Heaven. Everyone and everything had stopped. Hilda could be clearly seen from the pigeon cam-view and as her hand started to move, they all watched as Walter shot off.

"Jesus Christ!" said God as the Mercedes disappeared from camera shot.

"Oh, for goodness' sake, not you as well, Dad!" protested Jesus.

"Give it a rest, son," God replied with his eyes glued to the screen.

***

In the village, none of the onlookers could hear Walter's car over the thunderous roar from Gary's hypercar. However, over the sound of three dozen piston chambers exploding in a cataclysmic orchestral cacophony, the

380

sound of a Jack Russell dog yelp was heard, as Bertrand was thrust deep into the leather padding of the seat he was standing on as he viewed the cake on the table.

Walter had every confidence in his good and dear friend Kenneth Turnkey's ability to 'soup up' his car, but had not expected this level of 'soup uppedness'!

Walter's voice screaming, 'Shiiiiit!!!' lingered longer in the air than the Mercedes did in the village square.

Gary's demon car, as fast as it was and able to beat any earthly car, compared to Walter's alien thruster installed car, was no match, and appeared to limp out of the square like a two-legged tortoise with tight-fitting shoes on. Still, Gary shot past Hilda with such speed that sent her into a spin, wrapping the scarf around her face and making her stagger, trying to keep some form of stability.

***

Colin the squirrel, after his recent jaunt through a tear in space and time and causing mayhem in Hell, had started to recover from his ordeal. Bad as it was being trapped in Hell, with his brain arguing with itself over what they should do or which turn they should take to escape the place, it was made even worse when he was grabbed by the skeleton in the black cloak as he tried to get back home and stared deep into the eyes of death.

All in all, quite a traumatic experience. Time had passed, however, and Colin had stopped wetting himself over the smell of citrus aromas and had even started to like the taste of nuts again.

The time had now come where he felt that he could venture out of the woodland and into the fields, and maybe even cross the road onto the other side with the weird old human would leave nuts out for the birds and himself. He also felt like he could be ready to tease the human's dog again by climbing halfway up a tree, just out of reach, and let the dog bark and try in vain to reach him.

Colin edged out of the woodland into a field of sheep, who were all happily munching on the green grass, all but one who was happily defecating whilst the sheep next to it appeared to storm off in disgust.

Bouncing cautiously out of the wooded area, as squirrels do, Colin edged closer to the dry-stone wall. In the distance, he could hear some form of roaring, as if some idiot was revving a powerful metal thing with round black things on each corner. As it was in the distance, Colin felt safe in the thought that it was nowhere near and therefore couldn't hurt him.

Colin bounded over to the wall, leapt over the small nettle patch and sat perched on top of the stonework. He scoured the area and all he could see was what he wanted to see; beautiful countryside, a tarmacadam road, and in the distance an old tree with a wired container holding dinner for him.

The throbbing roar continued in the distance, and ensuring that the coast was clear, Colin jumped from the wall and aimed for the middle of the road. As the squirrel left the wall and was in the beginnings of mid-flight, a flash shot by with a noise that sounded like a human screaming 'Shiiii' and suddenly Colin found himself caught up in the jet stream of the passing vintage Mercedes and a steampunk clad screaming human, with eyes wide open like a Bushbaby on amphetamine.

Colin rolled through the air, not knowing which way was up or down, let alone how he was to land whichever way the ground was. Praying and hoping that the next thing he was going to smell was anything but citronella, Colin tumbled through the air, laying as flat as possible to try to slow the spinning down.

Rapidly scanning the surrounding scenery, he attempted to locate a landing spot, but found one quicker than he'd imagined, on the windscreen of Gary's car. It was a toss-up between Gary and Colin as to who was more surprised, but the award for most fear went to Gary, as the underside of a squirrel blocked his view of the road ahead.

"Jeeezus!" shouted Gary.

***

"Oh, I give up!" said Jesus, who threw the hotdog he was holding into the air and snatched the joint off God and took a huge drag on it.

***

"Get off my bloody screen, you dumb animal!" demanded Gary.

Colin, not really knowing what was happening or what the man on the inside of the vehicle was saying, decided to do exactly what came naturally and urinated on the screen out of fear.

"Oh, you dirty little..." shouted Gary and flicked on the windscreen wipers.

A huge metal and rubber arm came up from under the bonnet and headed straight for Colin, who was now hoping for a skeletal hand to appear and pluck him from the situation like last time.

Striking the squirrel with some considerable force, the wiper blade sent Colin back into the air, somersaulting back over the dry-stone wall and into the field once again. Expertly landing on all four paws, Colin looked over at his audience of sheep who had seen the aerobatic show and were overjoyed at his perfect landing. With rapturous applause of bleating, Colin slowly came to his senses and after realising that maybe he had ventured out a bit too soon, scurried back into the nearby woodland.

Walter had never seen speed like this before and whilst exhilarated, quickly felt a trickle of sweat flow from his lower back and in the unmentionable area of his body which was covered by the seat of his underwear.

The scenery flew past so quickly that even a blur would have been better than what he was witnessing. For a brief second, he thought he saw something grey/brown fly out from what might have been the dry-stone wall on the outskirts of the village.

Not being able to react fast enough and not hearing a thud, Walter hoped that whatever it was hadn't hit his precious Mercedes. He wasn't too sure if he'd heard a squeaky sound that sounded like something as ridiculous as a squirrel saying 'bloody hell' but even if he had, it had long since passed along with quite a considerable amount of road.

Walter had only been driving what felt like a fraction of a second, but thought it was time to hit the brakes. Bertrand, who was at one point pinned to the leather padding of the seat, suddenly felt himself becoming weightless and then fly forward, only to be pinned to the rear of the front seat. The vintage Mercedes came to a skidless halt outside Kenneth's garage with Walter's headwear sliding forward, covering his goggle-covered eyes.

"I say Bertrand, old boy, that was swift!" exclaimed Walter through panted breath.

"Don't ever do that again you, daft old git!" said Bertrand, but all Walter heard was several yaps.

"I know, old boy. Fast wasn't it! Blimey, Kenneth sure did a good job on you, old girl," continued Walter as he patted the steering wheel.

Removing his hat to see where his rival was, Walter stood up and looked back down the road. Way down the road and leaving the village like a scalded cat, Gary's car screamed along the tarmac, skidding to a halt alongside the Mercedes and a smug-looking Walter. Gary was fuming at being beaten by a mere human.

"Lose, did we?" Walter smiled.

"Piss off!" came the reply.

"Now let's see. The race is only halfway. I don't think we agreed on the terms of our wager, did we? Shall we continue the race?"

Gary knew all about deals and was thinking he was going to regret making this one.

"I know," continued Walter, "How about you never visit Ashburn again. I don't care where you go, you could go to Hell for all I care, but never back here, do you understand?"

"Deal," smiled Gary. "Deal of the century," he thought.

"Good, now be gone with you," demanded Walter.

With a flip of the middle finger, Gary revved his car and screeched off, leaving tyre tracks on the road.

"Cheeky little bastard!" said the indignant Walter, who returned the gesture with one of his own.

Walter adjusted his goggles and, settling into the driver's seat, looked back at his faithful friend.

"If it's all the same to you, dear friend, I think I'll drive back at a more leisurely pace."

Not knowing what his master had just said, but picking up on the more relaxed tone, Bertrand wagged his tail and gave a gleeful yap. Walter turned his trusty steed around in Kenneth's forecourt and drove back to Ashburn-on-Sinkhole, to the awaiting crowd and his beloved Hilda.

Passing the mile marker for Lower Fitterton, Gary's car sped into a tear in space and time and disappeared with the tear closing up as if it was never there.

Just before he entered the village square, Walter gave the raspy horn a couple of toots so that they knew he was coming back. Hilda's entire body relaxed on hearing the horn go, as she knew her man was coming back for her.

A smile formed on her face, cracking the solid layer of 'old lady' foundation powder, as the vintage Mercedes cruised into the cobbled square. All but one of the onlookers cheered. Jeremiah was a little concerned that his *very* wealthy client had just lost a race and felt that this may have some bearing on the settling of his bill.

Pulling up outside Betty's and stopping the engine, Walter was met by Hilda at his car door. With both hands on the door and leaning towards the driver, Hilda whispered something in his ear which made the elderly gent blush up and a huge smile formed on his face.

388

Chapter 39

Heaven had seen lots of happy times, but not one person had seen such happiness as was shown right now. God was jumping around in his board shorts and Hawaiian shirt, kissing everyone, whilst Travis homed in on one young surf lady, who had been giving him the eye for some time now.

"Thank Christ for that!" shouted God, as he jumped around hugging everyone and jumping in circles with other cheerful souls.

"True dat, G-man. Thank me!" said Jesus, whose inexperience in smoking cannabis was starting to show.

The beach party music quickly started back up again as the huge driftwood log fire continued to burn a wonderful citrus smelling flame.

**

On the top of Betty's café roof sat George and Wayne.

"What the bloody hell has just happened?" said George as he suddenly came to from his trance.

Wayne just looked at his friend.

"You dick! You scared the living daylights out of me! Don't ever do that again!"
Wayne said, then flew off, with George following seconds later.

***

Apart from the ice blue hue from the gas-powered flames, Hell had returned to some form of normality. Well, the ice-blue hue and the lack of wailing from the new souls who were supposed to be being tortured but had been placed in the wrong torture chambers.

The fiery tear, created by Steve had just closed, leaving several souls from an East London gang who had been shot during a 'drive-by', at the unattended gates. The obligatory card had been deposited and the pounding of the doorbell had been conducted by Steve, who had now disappeared, leaving D'wayne, Calvin, Tommy, and Russell at the gates, waiting to be picked up by the welcoming committee.

"Da hell is dis place? This ain't no 'eaven! It sho as hell best not be Hell or I'll be seriously pissed!" said Russell in his best 'gang speak'.

Russell was from a middle-class background, but had found friendship in his new acquaintances when he produced his father's no-limit credit card and promised to buy anything the gang wanted.

"Dumbass blood clat," replied D'wayne finishing with a brief sucking of his teeth.

Russell placed his right hand down his trousers and cupped his groin as he wandered over to the gate like he had dislocated his hips whilst walking on a trampoline. In a vain attempt to appear 'gangsta-ish' and trying to pluck the card from the gate bars, he missed, sending it flying through the gate and watched as it fluttered into the blue flames of the piped gutters and promptly burst into flames.

390

"Oh, bugger... Oh, I mean goddammit!" said Russell as he turned and bouncily walked back to the group, clicking his fingers of the hand that wasn't down his trousers.

D'wayne, Calvin, and Tommy were disrespectfully looking at Russell, when a tear suddenly opened up and the roar of a high-powered car was heard. The roar was closely followed by the rapid appearance of Gary's car from the tear who shot out of it and hit Russell full-on, sending him flying over the car and landing on a crumpled heap on the floor several yards behind the vehicle.

Swiftly opening the car door and running to see what damaged had been caused to his car, Gary looked back at the groaning crumpled soul of Russell.

"Whose is this sorry excuse of a damned soul?" he demanded.

"D'na bruv," D'wayne replied.

Gary's eyes glared as he slowly turned to see where his reply had come from.

"Bruv?... Bruv?!... Do I look like I was spat out of the same womb as you?"

"Na bruv. My muvver wouldn't shag anyone as ugly as your dad, then spit out somefin' like you. Tell you what vo, for finking yooz my bruv, I'll let you be all our bruvs for the small price of your car."

Gary wasn't too sure if he had just been insulted, even though it probably was meant to be, so slowly walked towards D'wayne with a menace that would have scared everyone else, but the intended.

"My car... to be *your bruv*?..."

"And this tube," Gary was interrupted by Calvin, who had sneaked around the car and spotted Gary's prized possession on the passenger seat. "What's init bruv?" Calvin continued.

"Look, because you're new here, I'll cut you some slack..."

"It's gonna be us cutting you if you don't give us the keys... bruv!" Tommy interrupted, holding a ghostly knife in his hand.

Click! Click! Click!

Three plumes of pink smoke appeared as the card tube rattled on the floor from falling from the 'no longer' hand of Calvin.

"Kids these days!... No respect for their elders!" tutted Gary as he wandered over to the tube and picked it up.

With his recent acquisition in his hands, Gary noticed a distinct aroma in the air. One that smelled of musty, fibreglass caravans. Turning towards his home, blue flickering flames danced, taunting him from the other side of his gates. Gary calmly stood facing his gates and watched the blue flames as they waved at him.

Russell had come round slightly, and even though several yards away from his new master and torturer, knew that a whole new level of soft brown smelly stuff was about to hit the fan. It was one of those moments when it wasn't so much the calm before the storm, but the calm before total annihilation. Gary walked to the gates with a calm ferocity that would worry Steve and even raise the eyebrows of his father, the G-man himself.

Without touching the gates of Hell, Gary walked towards them and with a flick of his hands, both gates flew off their hinges and disappeared, sailing over Hell itself. Every step, as calm as it was, had a sound that suggested that someone may just have a 'ticking off' that they would never forget if they were to survive it.

As Gary's purposeful gait led him into the grounds with his tube under his arm, Russell seized his opportunity to escape and hobbled over to the car where the exhaust pipes ticked as they cooled down. Unnoticed, he slid into the four wheeled beast and finding that the car key was still there, he pressed to start button, fired up the engine, and floored the accelerator.

The latter had an unexpected effect as the car didn't speed off as Russell would have liked, but shot off like the proverbial bat out of Hell, leaving behind tyre marks on the floor and a faint whiff of a young middle-class wannabe hoodlum, who had just soiled his pants.

***

"Listen! You're in charge and that's it! End of story. Finito benito!" exclaimed Adolph.

"Oh no, you're not leaving me with this screw-up! This was all yours from the get-go! You're in charge and you always have been," replied Genghis as he watched Adolph stomp around the throne room.

"Well, if I'm in charge, then my word is final, right?"

"Right!"

393

"OK then, if I have the final say, then I say that you're in charge and you can't argue that as I'm in charge and I say you are now!"

Genghis paused for a second with a puzzled brow, then fired back.

"Oh no no no! If I'm in charge, then I put you in charge. Sod that for a game of soldiers. I'm not getting blamed for this mess!"

Just then a pounding of the doorbell occurred.

"Bloody Death!" shouted Adolph.

"It's Steve now," corrected Genghis.

"Death! Grim Reaper! The bloody Ferryman! I'm in charge, so don't you dare bloody correct me!... Go get those bloody demons to get 'em in, NOW!"

"HOLD ON ONE SECOND!" shouted Genghis. "Don't you dare talk to me like that! I'm in charge here. You go and do it! And if we changed our names, then so has Steve. So it's Steve and not Death!"

"You did not make any sense on that last bit, you do know that don't you," smiled Adolph.

"Sod off and go see who's there, dammit!"

Whilst the demons continued to argue as to who was or wasn't in charge and who should see who had arrived, they missed the faint distant sound of a thunderous hypercar roar. Continuing to argue, the two demons also missed the helicopter rotor blade sounds as Hell's gates flew overhead, disappearing deeper into Hell itself.

"No, I bloody won't!"

"Look! I'm in charge and therefore I make you in charge!"

"Bugger that for a game of soldiers! You can stay in charge!"

"I'm in charge, so you have to listen to me! I put you in charge with no swapsies!"

"Are you serious?! No swapsies?! Grow up you saddo!"

***

Deep within Hell was the smallest dungeon imaginable. It was even smaller than that. It was the smallest dungeon unimaginable. The usual wailing and screams, begging to be let out were heard. On the door was the sign,

'Claustrophobia,'

"God, I hate it in here, Billy. You know I'm claustrophobic, don't you?" moaned Tony.

"You stupid bastard! We're all claustrophobic! That's why we're here! So yes! Yes, I am aware you're claustrophobic and you're not the only one who hates this, all Christ knows how many, of us here hate the bloody place!" replied his cellmate.

"Yes, but I mean, I really hate this! I'm super claustrophobic. I just need to get out now!"

"Oh well, that makes all the difference! We're just normal claustrophobic but *you* are super eh? You're a dick, that's what you are," replied Billy.

"Look at those bastards over there! With all the space in the world! All that space and they're still moaning! YOU BASTARDS!" Tony shouted.

"They're moaning because they're agoraphobic, you dick!"

"D'you think I care?! God, the lucky sods! I'd give anything to see those gates of Hell one more time," Tony moaned wistfully.

A Whoop! Whoop! Whoop! sound drew closer, which preceded an almighty crashing sound as Hell's gates landed on both the Claustrophobic and Agoraphobic dungeons, shattering the dungeon doors and released all within. All but one. Tony, who had been moaning about wanting to see the gates, was the landing pad for one of the massive gates as it crashed through the ceiling, pinning him underneath it, as the others clambered over him in an attempt to make it to the now open, Agoraphobic dungeon.

"Oh, that's just bloody great!"

Tony's voice was barely heard over the cheering and the clattering of damned souls as everyone either ran to the open space or the more enclosed one.

**

As Gary stormed towards his throne room in a deeper and darker menacing way than ever before, a cheery voice suddenly caught his attention.

"Hello! Fancy a cuppa? My wife Bernie... Bernice has just brewed up and we now have another flask of tea." Arthur beamed from his rickety seat.

Gary stopped in his tracks and looked over to where the obscenely cheery voice came from. Gary, at first, didn't see the brown leather strap sandals or the beige calf-high socks, nor did he see the safari shorts, which are only available in magazines that are only found in doctor's surgeries. Gary's eyes homed in solely on one object.

One slightly fuzzy orb, which had the appearance of a year-old chicken nugget, had made itself more than noticeable, as it squeezed itself out from between Arthur's inner thigh and the turned-up material of his shorts.

"Honestly, it's no bother. In fact, just one second... Bernie?... Do we have any Swiss roll?"

Gary's eyes could become quite fiery at a drop of a hat, and even more so with recent events taking place. However, to be invited for a cup of tea and a slice of Swiss roll by an elderly left testicle was probably, in Gary's words, 'taking the piss'. Gary responded, but because of a sudden moan from an SUV driver complaining about the smell of caravan gas, Arthur heard 'duck off'. Thinking it was a strange reply and watching Gary storm off, Arthur figured the passing visitor must have been 'one of those foreign chappies'.

"Mmm, maybe I should have shouted louder and ended every word with an 'O'," muttered Arthur.

"Any-O, time-O, you're-O, passing-O, just-O, pop-O... in-O!" he shouted after Gary.

***

Adolph and Genghis were stomping around the throne room, insisting that the other be in charge, when there

397

was a tapping on the throne room door. As Adolph was nearer to the door, at that time, he interrupted Genghis' demands not to be in charge.

"I'll answer the door as you're in charge."

Adolph opened the door and before looking bellowed out,

"What the bloody home do you want you snivelling little..."

Click!

POOF!

A pink cloud appeared where the abrupt demon once stood.

"Oh bugger me!" muttered Genghis.

"Gladly. Where's the nearest barbed wire pole?" said Gary, as he stormed into the room.

"I can explain!" pleaded the lone demon, "Y'see it wasn't me who was in charge but Adolph."

Gary walked towards Genghis like a tiger stalking an unsuspecting rabbit.

"Do you really think that I give a toss as to who was in charge?!"

Gary's nose was millimetres away from Genghis' left cheek, his eyes glowing fiercer than ever seen before.

"What, with everything that is unholy, have you done to my home?" Gary demanded.

Genghis timidly looked across into Gary's flaming eyes and with a trembling lip replied.

"Oh, shit!"

Click!

POOF!

Chapter 40

"Hello?" Adolph called out into the blackness, "Anyone here?... Surely someone must be here as Gary is always sending folk here."

Adolph tried to look around, but all he saw was black everywhere. There was nothing else to see. No light coming from up above or from below. No shadows cast in the distance in any way or in any direction. There wasn't even a floor to walk on, which the head demon felt quite unnerving. Everything was still, so he didn't even know if he was in a constant state of freefall.

Nothing but black, no noise, unless black made a sound, but was so quiet he couldn't hear it. It appeared that Adolph was there on his own. Maybe Gary had blamed him for the mess in Hell and had forgiven that arse kissing rat, Genghis, even though it was him who had made the mess and tricking Adolph into making these mistakes.

"That'll never happen again. I'll have that bastard when I see him next... Assuming I'll see anyone again," he muttered to himself.

That last thought made Adolph's bottom lip tremble. Would he ever see anyone again? Ever? The thought of being alone and not being able to see, hear or feel anything again was bad enough, but never torturing damned souls and visiting 'up-top' with his second job of secret advisor to the most powerful leader on the Earth, was just a little too much.

It was then a fear he'd never known before, suddenly entered his body forcefully via the genital area and headed straight to where his heart should have been. If he was in here and not allowed to carry on his second job, then would Gary realise that the so-called real Gary, the secret advisor, was actually Gary's second in command, Adolph?

Adolph had seen Gary furious, plus several levels above that, but knowing he had been tricked by his second in command and had called himself after his alter-ego? That may be a can of 'whoop-ass' that should never be opened.

Feeling the sweat trickle down his back and nestle nicely in the little valley between the top of his buttocks, Adolph came to his senses. Whilst standing still and panicking felt a natural thing to do, he had to at least try to find a way out of this nothing and make it back so he could continue with a ruse that maybe he shouldn't have started.

Moving his feet as if he was walking felt a little weird for Adolph. He didn't know if he was moving or not. He couldn't feel any sort of ground below, which would indicate that he was in some form of motion. Adolph figured that it would be better than staying put and waiting for his boss to find out who the real Gary was. The demon's gait was similar to treading water, just there was no water, in fact there was nothing but... nothing. His mind began to replace fear with anger. It was purely Genghis' doing was all this and that snivelling little rat had no idea as to what trouble he had got his best friend into.

Genghis wasn't really Adolph's best friend, as being a demon, neither did they have friends or trust anyone to even be called a work colleague or acquaintance. Still, in Adolph's mind, that seemed to make things better for him.

"After all, I've done for you throughout the aeons and this I show you treat me," muttered Adolph to himself.

"The amount of crap I've helped you get out of and this is what you do... Leave me in here, convincing Gary I was to blame and not you... I cannot believe this!"

Adolph was becoming angrier by the second until he blew.

"Genghis, you bastard!" he bellowed.

***

"Hello?" called out Genghis, "Anyone here?"

Blackness was all around him, no light anywhere, just black. Even the sound was black, if black had a sound.

"Always wondered what this place was like," he muttered to himself, "Never thought I'd end up here though."

Genghis looked in every direction possible and saw nothing but black.

"Oookay, let's have a wander and see if there's anything else round here... Jeeezus! Where's the bloody floor?!"

Genghis discovered that even the floor was black, and that black felt like nothing. Was he on something but just couldn't feel it, or was he falling? Well, there was no wind whistling around his lower region, so unless black was also windless, he wasn't falling. Genghis wasn't too sure if his efforts were working, placing his feet one in front of another as if to walk, or was he just stationary.

"Oh well, let's keep walking and see if I can find anyone in here and if there's a way out."

Genghis was always more positive and Adolph.

It hadn't taken long before Genghis started to think about his predicament and how that so-called friend of his had got him into so much trouble.

"I cannot believe that little toe-rag would do this to me, after all I've done for him!... Well, maybe I can. He never appreciated my efforts and always felt jealous of my leadership skills. Of course, he was going to drop me in it, whatever 'it' was. I should've known he'd do this," he said to himself as he walked, or at least thought he walked.

"How many times have I got that weaselly toad out of trouble, and this is how he repays me? Just wait till I see him, I'll happily tell him I never want to see him again!"

Feeling better with the plan in mind of finding his so-called best friend so he could tell him he never wanted to see him, and give him a good slapping to prove it, Genghis continued to walk.

As he continued to walk and become angrier over what his friend had done to him, he had become even more so with the song that was playing in his head and how his mind had changed the lyrics. A small choir boy was singing.

"We're walking in the *black!* We're floating on crap knows what."

Genghis scolded himself and started slapping the side of his head to rid the annoying song from his brain. However, he couldn't help imagining flying with a green bush hat on and matching scarf.

"Oh, for crying out loud! Genghis get a grip!" he said whilst slapping himself again.

"Genghis, you bastard!"

Genghis' ears pricked up. He knew that voice.

"Adolph you little snivelling shit!" he called out, "Where are you?"

"I'm here!" came the reply.

"Well that's not going to help now is it! How the hell am I supposed to find you, if all you say is *'I'm here'*. Where the bloody hell is *here*?" he shouted back.

"How should I know where *'here'* is?! It's all black!"

"So what's the point in shouting *'I'm here'* when you don't know where you are?!"

Frustration was rising in Genghis.

"You bloody asked, so I replied... OK, where are you then?" shouted back Adolph.

Without even thinking, Genghis replied,

"I'm here!"

"What a cock!" a resigned response came from Adolph.

"Just wait until I find you! I'll bloody have you for that!" said Genghis, his anger exceeding his frustration.

"Go on then, numbnuts, find me! 'cause if you *can* find me that'll be more than I can."

There was a logic to Adolph's sarcastic reply, which Genghis picked up on. The conversation stopped for a moment as both demons thought.

"I know!" chirped Genghis, "Why don't you shout out and I'll follow your voice."

"What an awesome idea. Did you think of that yourself or did you get a pallet of house bricks to help you work out that master plan?... Where's my voice right now?"

Genghis thought for a second and realised that Adolph's voice was everywhere and nowhere. He couldn't determine which way it was coming from. He couldn't even be sure if the voice was in his head! Was he going mad and hearing voices, or did he actually hear his friend?

"You are real, aren't you? You're not in my head, are you?" Genghis asked.

Adolph was about to come back with a reply so sarcastic, but then thought of what his friend had said. Was Genghis's voice in *his* head and that he was nowhere near him! Was Genghis even in the same place? The two demons pondered over the quandary for a minute.

"Are you in my head, Genghis?"

"If I am, that'll explain the wide-open blackness."

"Cheeky bleeder! OK, I'll ask you a question and if you know the answer then I'll know you're in my head."

"Eh? How's that work?"

"Well, if I ask you a question that only I know the answer to and if you don't know it, then that'll mean you're real. But, if you do answer it, then that'll prove you're in my head as only I should know the answer," replied Adolph.

"I think I know you're real Adolph."

"How's that?"

"Only you could come up with something so stupid as that!"

"Unless, of course, you thought that and I'm not really here and it's your brain that thought it."

Genghis considered the last reply from Adolph or his own brain, and out of curiosity and for clarification, gave it a go.

"What's my favourite colour?" Genghis piped up.

"Really? I've been working with you as long as I have and you ask me a question like that? Is that the best you can come up with?"

"Ah, but is that my brain saying that to try and put me off or is that really you?" Genghis replied.

"Are you taking this seriously or are you that stupid?!"

Genghis didn't know if he should reply to that as he was a little concerned, that if it was his brain playing tricks on him, then that would prove he was alone and going mad.

"OK, I got one," chirped Genghis, "When you disappear for a couple of hours, tell me where you go."

"What?! You're supposed to ask me a question that *I* don't know the answer to, not what you don't know, stupid arse!" scolded Adolph.

"Aha! Or, if I don't know the answer to a question and you answer it, then that proves you're real. Only a figment of my imagination wouldn't know the answer," replied Genghis smugly.

Adolph was neck-deep in a quandary. If Genghis was in his mind, answering the question would be fine. BUT, if Genghis was real, then by answering would notify his counterpart that *he* was the real 'Gary' and that their boss had named himself after a lesser demon. That would not sit well with Gary when, not *if*, but when he found out. Adolph was certain that Genghis would definitely tell.

"Err, I have a bowel issue and I need to go to the lavvy, often. It's not very pleasant at all, and the amount of paperwork afterwards is beyond belief!" lied Adolph.

"OK, that's made my mind up for sure..."

"Phew!" thought Adolph.

"You're all in my head and I'm alone in here."

"What?!"

"Not answering! You don't exist la la la la la!"

"I am real and that's the truth!" pleaded Adolph.

"No, you're not! You're a pigment of my imagination!"

"Figment, you dip-shit! Pigment is a..."

"La la la la la," Genghis interrupted, blocking out Adolph's pleas.

"Oh, come on!"

"Nope! You're in my head and therefore you know what I did whilst you were gone," said Genghis with an air of pride.

"I'm not in your... hang on!... Yes, you're right, I am in your head. So tell me this Adolph, obviously not the real Adolph, what you did whilst I was, I mean when the real Adolph had disappeared for a brief moment," quizzed the real, Adolph.

Genghis burst into laughter, which made Adolph feel a mixture of concern and rage.

"You know as well as I do, as you're in my brain! However, you'll never know it was me that did that to your collection of demon pornography..."

"What?!"

"And the time you destroyed Shipman's pet to get back at him, for what I did in your lounge pants and slippers when you thought he'd done it!"

Genghis could be heard laughing so hard that it seemed like he was rolling on the floor.

"Yeah! You're right... I know all that... Yeah, very funny!" Adolph was seething.

"Oh, and what about the time when I changed your normal aftershave to rose petal scented holy water? That was hilarious..."

"ARSEHOLE!!"

Epilogue

Evening time had descended on the streets of Italy, and Nicolo, with his friend Lorenzo, were on their nightly walk after having supper, courtesy of the lovely Francesca. The streets at that time of evening were fairly quiet as everyone had left work.

They were either sitting at home with their feet up or had phoned their spouses and lied, stating they had to work late whilst in reality, they were with their mistresses or male equivalents. The street lights had just flickered on as the strays wandered down a familiar street.

"Would you look at that!" said Lorenzo, *"That car looks familiar."*

Nicolo looked over to where his friend had pointed to with his muzzle.

"Which loser would drive in a car like that?" Nicolo mocked.

Something in Lorenzo's head hinted at the possibility that they had walked down this street before, about a month ago. Something about the trouble that they had got into over something that had happened with a similar car.

Lorenzo's head tilted to one side as if to jog his memory. Was there a huge human involved and another with a flowery, silly looking holiday shirt on? Something told the dog that proceeding down this path could end up either having to run away or be subjected to a swift kick to his hindquarters. Raising his brow slightly, Lorenzo figured if he couldn't remember then it couldn't have been that risky, so the two stray dogs steadily meandered over.

Michele D'Ley was sitting in the driver's seat of the black Mercedes limousine. He had parked up on Viale Della Ombreggiato whilst he waited for his boss, Don Caster, who was paying a visit to some lowlife scum art forger and getting goodness knows what. He could never understand as to why, with all his power and money, would he want to deal with a forger when he could get the real thing?

"Hey ho. 'eez monet," muttered Michele, and drummed the steering wheel with his index fingers.

Michele's senses suddenly pricked and his drumming stopped. Across the road appeared two stray dogs who had paused for a moment and started to sidle over in his direction.

One of Michele's many talents was having an excellent memory and seeing the two mutts, reached inside his jacket and removed his pistol from its holster. Deftly he reached over to the glove box, retrieved the gun's silencer and attached it to the muzzle of the firearm.

"Cum on, you sons of beetches. Cum to papa," he muttered with eyes fixed on the two dogs.

The whirring of the electric window was barely audible as the two dogs wandered closer. Michele rested his arm on the car's open windowed door and steadily drew the silenced pistol at the dogs.

"Pees on zis car, will you?" he said in a tone that would scare any human.

412

"A pleasure doing business with you, Don Caster, as always. Have a safe drive home."

Edoardo and Michele's boss had appeared from the forger's front door.

"Next time miei amici,"

Michele placed the pistol on the passenger seat and quickly got out to let his boss into the rear of the limousine. Swiftly getting out of the car, Michele hissed at the dogs, who quickly remembered who the human was and what had happened last time. The two dogs, deciding that it would be a prudent move, trotted off in the opposite direction, leaving the three humans and the piece of junk car.

Don Caster stepped out of the doorway and onto the quiet street. The financial transaction had been conducted in Edoardo's flat above his shop, and now Don Caster was the proud owner of a cardboard tube with a 'Towel in a Tube' emblazoned along its length.

"Grazie, Edoardo. Until next time," grunted the mafia boss and gave a slight nod and wink at the forger.

"I shall look forward to it," smiled Edoardo deferentially.

Don Caster waddled over to the awaiting open limousine and gave another nod to his driver and bodyguard as he flopped into the vehicle, causing it to rock as his heavy carcass landed on the leather seating. With a solid and very expensive thud, the rear car door was closed and Michele got back into the vehicle, fired up the engine, and slowly drove off along the deserted street.

It wasn't long before the Mercedes had pulled into the gravelled driveway of the mobster's mansion and the boss himself had settled himself into his leather high-back with a cigar and brandy.

The recently purchased piece of art had been placed into an awaiting frame and was already hanging on the wall in Don Caster's private office. The overweight mobster, reclining in his chair, blew out a thin stream of cigar smoke which danced around his head like a nicotine halo. He gazed at the stunning copy of Botticelli's Mappa dell'Inferno, believing it to be genuine, and Don Caster's rotund face formed a broad smile.

A sip of Louis XIII de Remy Martin cognac, also recently purchased from a British fine art dealer and provider of hard to get items by the name of Fast Eddie, made Don Caster's evening.

"Welcome to your new home," beamed the mobster boss.

***

On the outskirts of Ashburn-on-Sinkhole, Kenneth Turnkey's garage cast a dilapidated but pleasant silhouette against the ever-darkening skies. The day had decided that it had had enough and was more than happy for the night to take over.

It had been a very amicable exchange between day and night, which ended up with the two having a brief chat about the day's, and previous evening's events. This gave dusk time to play for a while longer, in which gave the local creatures more time to retire or get ready for the evening's adventures.

A rustling of leaves occurred as two sheep emerged from the woodland and back into the field with the rest of the

414

flock. A quick shudder from one sheep resulted in something being jettisoned and steaming as it landed on the cool grass. This, in turn, resulted in the other sheep bleating and what appeared to be stomping off disgustedly.

A nearby squirrel was quite noticeable by its fearful demeanour as it clung to the bark of an old oak tree and shivered with the slightest rustle of leaves as the evening's breeze passed by.

Turnkey's garage windows were still illuminated from the inside with makeshift curtains made from old newspapers blocking any passer-by from looking in. It was the time of evening where there would be no chance of anyone passing by, but if they did, they would have heard the scratchy sounds of a tired transistor radio playing from the back of the garage workshop.

Earlier that day, Kenneth's garage was full to the gunnels with a vintage Mercedes that had the engine modified to an unrecognisable degree and a repaired alien spacecraft, and its three occupants. Now there was just Kenneth, himself, and one of the UFO's occupants who had been deliberately left behind by the other two for reasons Kenneth didn't know.

"It's OK fella. You can stay here for as long as you like, so long as you make yourself scarce when I have customers around. Wouldn't want them seeing you as that'd create a whole lot of trouble for both of us," Kenneth said to his alien guest. "Cuppa?"

"Please," sniffled Forsta, "Can't believe the scragfelds left me behind!" he continued as he sat on a small stack of tyres.

415

"Oh, it'll be right, fella. They obviously thought you were on board. As soon as they realise their mistake, they'll come back for you," said Kenneth unconvincingly.

"The scragfelds," came the reply.

A minute passed by silently, as the feeling was that nothing could be said which would be considered sincere and positive. The awkward silence was broken by the whistling kettle that informed them it was time for tea.

Grateful for a break in the atmosphere, Kenneth smiled and hopped over to the kettle and the two waiting mugs that had already been furnished with tea bags and sugar. The comforting sound of the water hitting the mugs was then interrupted by the workshop's phone ringing.

"I'll get it," sighed Forsta.

Slowly getting up like an old man, labouring as he did, the alien trudged over to the oily greased up phone. Kenneth nodded as he stirred the tea, thinking that giving his guest a little job, like answering the phone, may just take away the thoughts of being abandoned.

Forsta had seen footage of human behaviour and how they answered such primitive communication devices. He lifted the receiver and twirling his finger around the spiralling cable that attached the handset to the base, Forsta answered the phone.

"What's up bitches!"

Kenneth shot over to the alien, like a bullet from a gun.

"I'll get this, it's ok," he whispered to Forsta, "Turnkey's Garage can I help you?"

"I have General Newcumall on the line, please hold," chirped an American female voice.

"What I do wrong?" hissed Forsta.

"Nothing fella. It's just we don't answer calls like that here," Kenneth replied as he held his hand over the mouthpiece.

"Mr Tourniquet, I'm General Newcumall," bellowed a brusque American voice.

"It's Turnkey."

"Turnkey?... That's what I said. Mr Turnkey, I'm General Newcumall from a department of the US government that is top secret. I believe my predecessor knew you and you assisted in solving... an issue with a certain flying machine."

Kenneth's eyes widened with fear and glanced over to his guest. Forsta had his back to Kenneth and was sipping on his mug of tea whilst looking at a calendar pinned to the wall. Kenneth immediately turned his gaze to the phone base and very quickly composed himself.

"Oh hello, General. You mean Area 51 and how is Billy Bob these days?" smiled Kenneth.

"Dead, Mr Turnkey."

"Oh, I'm so sorry about that. He seemed such a healthy chap. May I ask how he died?"

"Cigarettes Mr Turnkey."

"I didn't know he smoked!"

"He didn't. He was run over by a Marlboro cigarette truck, Mr Turnkey."

"Ah! One way or another those things will kill you won't they, General. I'm sorry but can I ask your first name and please call me Kenneth, I sense you'll be wanting my help again."

"It's Truman, Truman Newcumall, but you can call me General, Mr Turnkey. Now, one of our satellites were inexplicably made inoperable only the other day..."

"You mean it stopped working," interrupted Kenneth.

"That's what I said. Anyway, we traced the source of the cause back to a little place just in the middle of somewhere."

"Somewhere?"

"Yes, somewhere, as it doesn't seem to be on any maps, Google or otherwise. The only place that we are aware of is a place with a small shack and a sign on it that says 'Turnkey's Garage'. Do you know of any such place, Mr *Turnkey*?"

"Well, I'm terrible with directions. I could lose my way in my own bathroom!"

"I am aware of your directional challenges, Mr Turnkey."

"Although I must say, I think I know what you're getting at General. You think whatever happened came from here, well I can assure you that..."

"And I can assure *you* we *know* it DID come from your garage, now you can either stop yanking my chain or we can be friends over the matter," interrupted the General.

Kenneth had worked with such people in the past, and knew that friendly or not, he could expect a visit from a couple of stony-faced men wearing sunglasses and dark suits soon.

"General, you're more than welcome to come and see my garage if you want. I can assure you there's nothing here that you haven't seen before," said Kenneth with an air of truth in his voice.

"You know where I work, Mr Turnkey, and I have seen many things as you well know."

"I did mean in a garage. Nothing you haven't seen in a garage workshop before," lied Kenneth, although Area 51 did have a garage workshop so, in effect, he was still not lying.

"I may just take you up on your offer, Mr Turnkey. You have a good day."

Click!

Truman sat back in his leather office chair and drummed his fingers on his desk whilst he considered his next move.

"Clarice! Who do we have in England right now?"

The office door burst open and a uniform-clad middle-aged woman stood erect with a notepad and pen in her hands.

"Agents Smith and Smith, General."

"Goddammit! Why do they all have to be called Smith?!" he muttered, "Get 'em on the line. I need 'em to pay a visit to old man Turnkey."

"Right away, General."

"Oh, and don't slam the door on the way,"

BANG!

"Goddammit, Clarice!"

Post Epilogue

Heaven is an unusual place where tranquillity is a constant atmosphere, and it never strays from that status. Days and nights have the same peacefulness, and everything is just as it should be... Heavenly.

Dawn was breaking over the bay that God, or the G-man, had created for the previous day's beach party. The ocean beyond the beach was gently tickling the damp sand as it lapped the shore.

The sea birds were just stirring from their slumber on the ocean, bobbing up and down on the gentle waves. The bio-fuel log fire had burnt down, leaving embers that were mesmerising to anyone still awake, and the relaxing clean smell of citrus still permeated the air.

The glowing embers were giving off very little heat, which anywhere else would signal the strongest diehards to go home, but in Heaven, the G-man made sure that the ambient temperature was just right. The beach and surrounding paradise landscapes were festooned with sleeping bodies. Everyone had partied the night away to beach sound music bands, cocktails and the odd cannabis joint handed to them by Travis and his cherub helpers.

Jesus, who had initially left the party early, a little fed up with the number of times his name had been used in vain, had called on Mary for solace. Mary had other plans though, which could be clearly seen by the Hawaiian bikini she wore and convinced Jesus not only to stay but don a pair of the most garish board shorts she could find. Twisting to the music all night had given both of them lower back pain, so the decision was made to sidle off and head for a 'crib'.

Heaven was a very tranquil place except for one night only, and the early hours of dawn. Now, after which, it had seemed even more peaceful. All the daytime souls were sleeping off their Mojito, Margherita, and Sex on the Beach cocktails, whilst the night time souls who had joined in with the party were naturally ready for bed.

Under a recently created palm tree, just feet from the shoreline, lay two slumped figures, one of a divine stature and one of a classic surf-dude physique. Both were still awake, barely, and were gazing out to the ocean's door.

"G-man! You rock beach parties, dude. I mean, this was the beezneez!" said Travis through a weary smile.

God, who had his hands clasped on his overfed stomach, smiled.

"It seems I do know how to throw a party," came the reply, moving his hand out for a 'low five'.

Travis accepted the offer, bringing his hand down on his host's open palm with a faint clap.

Travis smiled a contented smile and did a brief scan of his heavenly beach. Over in the distance was a pillar of sand with what looked like a parasol behind it. Travis puzzled over it for a second.

"G-man, what's that over there?" Travis inquired, his eyes fixed on the sandy tower.

God looked over in the same direction and closed his eyes.

"That was Sandro Botticelli's attempt at his classic Venus."

"Right on," replied Travis, not really knowing what God was on about.

"A good friend of mine, who recently helped me out with a small favour, did some paintings back in his day and one was called Birth of Venus. The original was quite good, exquisite to be honest with you. Well, I think he had one too many cocktails last night..."

"Probably a few too many puffs on the weed too, by the looks of it," interrupted Travis.

"Err... I'll go with that."

Travis pondered over the artist's name for a second.

"Botticelli... Name rings a bell. Didn't he do something about Hell? Infernal or something like that."

"Nearly dude. It is called Inferno, but what you said is pretty much right."

God smiled as he recalled his recent commissioned work.

Travis lay with his back against the tree and examined the poor sand sculpture.

"Think he ought to stick with paint as sand just ain't his thing."

"I'll be sure to tell him that, Travis."

423

The final dregs of bio-fuel had been burnt and the embers finally gave up on warming the sandy stretch. The sun, which shared Heaven's skies with its friend the moon, rose over the oceanic horizon and warmed the deity and his friend's face.

"Right bra, Time for a quick wave ride before I hit my crib," said Travis as he heaved himself up from the comfortable sand, "Oh, G-man, where is my crib by the way?"

God looked up at Travis, clicked his fingers and looked beyond Botticelli's sand sculpture.

"Just there, bra."

Travis looked over to where God's gaze was and there stood a log and reed beach hut on stilts with his favourite surfboard resting against its wall. Travis's face lit up with joy.

"G-man, you're one righteous dude! Maan! That's my perfect crib!"

"Fill your boots, dude," replied God.

Not quite sure what God had said, Travis figured it had something to do with simply enjoying it and trotted over to do just that. Travis jogged to the shoreline, picking up his board, placing it under his arm and smiled.

"G-man, if you would?" said the surfer.

"No problemo dude."

Click!

The perfect waves suddenly appeared beyond the shore to which Travis, the surf dude, ran towards like a child towards a sweet shop.

"G-man, you rock!" Travis shouted prior to launching himself onto his board and paddling out to the awaiting waves.

"Oh, yeah!" smiled God as he closed his eyes, "I rock!"

**

Hell could never be classed as a normal place, or tranquil, in any way shape or form, but the previous day's calamities had subsided and now Hell had returned to just being... Hell.

The gates had been retrieved from their landing spots, and the damage caused by the angry mob, who either were impatient to get in or reluctant to do just that, had been fixed and looked as good as new. Well, not exactly good as new, but looked like what the gates of Hell should look like, ominous and foreboding.

The caravanners had been put back into their rightful place and were again suffering like everyone else within the establishment, so had the claustrophobes and agoraphobes. Gary had managed to get the flames back to normal and smelling like they should, plus the reddish hue returned. Blue flames and a musty caravan smell just didn't suit Hell in the slightest.

Gary had more or less got his place back to normal and had hung his latest acquisition on the wall in his throne room, opposite his... throne. As it was a large room, the painting some distance away from where he was sitting and only measuring in inches, Gary couldn't see the tiniest of additions to his original Sandro Botticelli Mappa dell'Inferno.

Gary had wanted the original painting from Botticelli and that is exactly what he got, just not the one that was the original, original Inferno. It was true that Sandro himself had painted it, therefore it was an original, and it was a Mappa dell'Inferno, just not the one Gary had expected.

Not having his two assistants with him to help in answering doors and making things happen on his say-so meant that Gary had to do everything. This was something he wasn't used to or liked.

However, with the two idiots making a complete mess of Hell, they deserved what they got, which was being placed in 'nowhere'. Gary, however, didn't enjoy having to do the work that either Adolph or Genghis did, so was in two minds as to bring them back or leave them there.

Underneath the recently hung piece of art was his table, with his favourite decanted spirit sitting on a silver platter, waiting to be poured and drunk. Not having Genghis to pour him such a drink, Gary muttered something about his father and got out of his seat to get himself one. Everything was pretty much back to normal, but not having his two idiots to do his dirty work was just not right.

Pouring himself a large shot, Gary took a huge drink, drained the glass, and pondered over the quandary.

"Sod it," he muttered, and with a click of his fingers, his two assistants re-appeared.

The two demons looked at each other in surprise, then over to their boss. The thought of praising him and kissing his feet quickly passed through their brains upon looking at his feet. Both decided against it and just act as nothing had happened. Genghis took his rightful place near the doors and Adolph by the throne.

"Don't make me have to get my own drink again, d'y'ear?" Gary leered at Genghis.

"Sure thing, Gary," Genghis thundered out as he stood to attention.

Gary made his way back over to the throne, and sitting back on it, he crossed his legs and smiled at his newly acquired painting. Not knowing that a tiny 'Godjustgod' in a tuxedo with his legs and arms crossed was smiling back at him.

For now, Hell had returned to its very own form of normality. This would continue until Gary noticed tuxedo-clad addition to his painting... if he ever would.

Outside of Gary's private sanctum, Hell continued as normal. Wails were filling the air along with the overpowering stench of citrus from the 'back to normal' flames.

Both Heaven and Hell had relaxed after a very hectic time. So much so that whatever or whoever had decided that even Steve should relax for a short while and have some downtime.

**

Steve had double-checked his notebook and then double-checked it several more times and still couldn't find anyone to pick up. Nothing in this universe was dying! Steve found this very unnerving, as ever since he could remember, his work was just increasing exponentially.

427

Something didn't seem right, and he wondered whether or not he should worry. Would this be the calm before the storm? Or was he going to get redundancy papers served on him?

"Dumbass!" he scolded himself, "My work and taxes will never go."

Steve closed his book and placing it back into his cloak, he wandered along the paths in his favourite location, Peace Valley Cemetery, until he reached the dome-topped temple deep within the grounds.

Steve relaxed and enjoyed the peace and quiet, leaning against the wall, watching all the visitors come into the place and pass by without seeing him. The living folk were walking around with the dead, and not seeing them, whilst the dead were clearly noticing Steve and giving him a wide birth.

He had been there for what seemed only a few minutes when a mobile phone ringtone blasted out from his cloak. This, however, wasn't his normal ringtone, which always came from that pumper, Gary. Plucking his phone from his inside pocket, Steve looked at the singing phone screen and noticed the banner saying,

'Pestilence'

Steve's bony finger tapped the phone's screen and smiled as he placed it next to his ear.

"Pestilence, my old mate, how's it going? Come out with anything serious lately?"

"Death, my old chug bud, I'm doing good thanks. How's yourself?" came the reply.

428

"Well, I'm a little bored at the mo as no one seems to be dying. It's a bit unusual if you ask me. Are you and the guys having a 'time-out'?"

"Well, I did come up with an idea recently in a Chinese lab and left it to them to sort out as I've been kinda busy with other things. They're pretty good at that sort of stuff," replied Pestilence.

Steve's non-existent eyebrows raised, and a smile came over his skull.

"So what you been up to, you little tinker?"

Steve left the wall side and wandered around in between the graves.

"You still seeing Famine? Must admit she's a little skinny for my liking. Nothing but skin and bones..."

"Least she has that mate. You ain't even got skin!" interrupted Pestilence with a smile.

Steve chuckled.

"OK. You got me on that. So you still doing the horizontal tango with her?"

"Well, funny you should say that Death my old mate..."

"Oh, it's Steve now, mate," said Steve, correcting his friend, "I got bored of Death and the Grim Reaper. D'you realise how long I've had that name? So, please call me Steve."

There was a pause on the phone and a sudden burst of laughter from Pestilence.

"You serious?! Steve? What the hell!"

"Long story mate, but anyhow. What were you saying?"

"Well, as I was saying, *Steve*. Funny you should say that, as I've got to tell you something."

"Oh, bloody hell mate no! You guys haven't split up, have you? I'm sorry to hear that. Mind you, I think you're better off without her. She was a right tart. Always flirting around War she was, and if her mother is anything to go by, then she'd have a turnstile on her knickers. She was that easy."

"We're getting married."

The pregnant pause which followed made the gestation period of an African elephant seem like a blink of an eye.

"Shhhhhit!" thought Steve, however, his thoughts developed into a very awkward audible sound.

"What was that about War?" Pestilence broke the silence.

Steve was scouring his skull for an escape route as he scanned the graveyard for the slightest help... and there it was.

'Francine Warringbottom'

Scratched into a scaffolding board and planted at the head of a fresh mound of earth.

"Oh yeah, Francine was a right one for War. Always fluttering her eyebrows at him. Eyelashes! I mean eyelashes," Steve snorted a fake laugh, "You'd be hard pushed fluttering eyebrows."

"Francine?... It's Famine. Who's Francine?" quizzed Pestilence.

"Oh, I thought you were splitting up with Francine! She was the one at that party over at, oh never mind, Famine? Oh, mate, you've a good one there. Always got eyes for you and no one else."

Steve hoped that the confusion he had tried to create was enough for his friend to get off the subject.

"A party?"

"Doesn't matter, mate, congratulations. So when's the big day?" said Steve swiftly moving on.

"Soon," said Pestilence, who had succumbed to Steve's distraction tactic, "but first I need a stag do and I first thought of my old friend Death, now *Steve*. So? How about it? You up for it?"

Steve would have breathed a sigh of relief if he had any lungs.

"You betcha! You just tell me where and when and I'll be there. So who else is coming?"

"Well, I thought just you and War. I don't want to invite anyone from Heaven as they'd be all *'Ooh you can't do that, it's just so wrong!'* and from Hell? All they'd do is want to be the centre of attention, so no, it's just us three. The three amigos."

"What about him in Purgatory? We did promise, old whats-his-name, he could come next time we partied."

"Err... I know we did, but this is my stag do, not just a party. We'll just not tell him. He's a bit of a weirdo anyway. I mean, who is in charge of a place that's neither up nor down and doesn't even have a name! Even you have a name, well several in fact, but at least you've settled on Steve. You know, on my phone, I have him down in my contacts as 'Nobody–Purgatory'," protested Pestilence.

"Fair point well made," said Steve. "So where are we going to raise a little Hell, so to speak?"

"I've given this a fair bit of thought and with us three, being who we are, we want a place that no one knows of. Somewhere in the middle of nowhere, where we can blend in and just party. I was stuck as to where had such credentials, but then Famine helped out and suggested a place."

Steve suddenly felt a little uneasy. First, it had to be 'somewhere in the middle of nowhere', and second, Famine suggested it.

"So I've booked us into a small pub in a village called Ashburn-on-Sinkhole for a few days."

Steve felt the acidic burn as a little sick rose and entered his non-existent throat.

"Mate, we'll stick out like a sore thumb..."

"Funnily enough, that's the pub's name, The Blind Cobbler's Thumb," interrupted Pestilence.

"No, I mean, Pestilence, War, and Death, I mean me. It'll freak out the village folk. How about... err... Chernobyl? It's right up your street. Nuclear fallout, the new pestilence! You'll love it!"

There was an urgency in Steve's voice that went unnoticed.

"Got it covered, mate. I've told 'em it's a fancy dress stag do and we're going as the 'Four Horsemen'... just that there's only three of us. Anyway, we've nothing to worry about as there's a transvestite crew going the same time as us. Guys in women's clothing and three stag doers in 'fancy dress', mate, we'll fit right in!" replied Pestilence in an upbeat voice.

"Transvestite crew?"

"Yeah! Well, the person I spoke to on the phone called 'em a TV crew, but I knew what he meant. Anyway, we were lucky to get in as they'd booked nearly all the rooms, but we've got a room to share, all three of us. Won't that be great? It's all paid for, so all that's needed is for us to turn up and have a wild time."

If Steve had had his wits about him, he may have corrected his excited friend as to the 'TV' abbreviation, however, the thought of having to return to *that* place overpowered every other thought.

"Yeah!... Wow!... Awesome!" was all Steve could say, and not very convincingly.

"Ain't it just!" replied Pestilence. "I was going to say that I'd pick you up, but how about we just meet up, all three of us, just out of the village and walk into the square like three villains in a spaghetti western? There's a woodland on the outskirts, so shall we meet there and *mosey* in *pardner*?... Steve?"

"Sure... Sure thing. Sounds great. Can't wait," lied Steve. "Tell you what though, Chernobyl is amazing this time of year. Sure you don't wanna change your mind?"

433

"Nah, I'm good thanks, mate,"

"Fukushima?... Tunguska?... Wuhan?... Bradford sewers?" pleaded Steve.

"Bloody hell mate, I wish I'd asked you before our lass suggested the place. You've some belting ideas, but I'm good with this Ashburn place. Anyway, it's all bought and paid for now."

Another barely audible 'Shhhhhit!' was heard over the phone.

"You OK, Steve? I just heard something like an arrow whizzing by and hitting a tree."

"Err... yes. That's what it was. I'm having a little game of Dare with William Tell. Oh well, Ashburn, it is then, but if you fancy changing your mind, just let me know and I'll even pay for it... as... err... an early wedding gift. How's that sound?"

"Oh, you're a true mate, D... Steve. Really do appreciate it. Anyway, a week from today at the woodland yes? Awesome! See you then."

Click!

Steve looked at his phone's screen with an air of resignation.

"Oh bleeding 'ell! Not there, of all bloody places!"

***

Fast Eddie was settling down in his lounge and was listening to the smooth melodic warbling of Engelbert

434

Humperdinck when his mobile phone chimed. From his nearby coffee table he picked up his phone, looked at the screen and noticed a text message from an unknown source. An air of uncertainty and worry flashed across his brain. He tapped the screen and reading the message, Eddie was at first elated, then as he read on, sicker than a flat-backed camel.

"Hi, Eddie. I have put your payment into your account. I have also paid your helpers, so what is in your account is all yours. I figured you'd try to con me by adding more than enough noughts to the..."

Eddie's phone chimed again.

"Bloody character limits on texts! I mean! Who has that these days?? Anyway, more noughts than you should. So I have given you a decent cut, but not what your greedy little mind wanted. I'm su..."

Ping!

"Dammit! Bloody text limits! As I was saying. I'm sure you'll be happy with what I've paid you. Obviously not as happy as you could've been. Thnx. Enjoy Gary."

"Thanks, Sandro, for all your hard work. Here, try this."

G-Man

ACKNOWLEDGEMENTS

I cannot express enough thanks to Caro Simpson, my editor and proofreader, for making this book a diamond from the rough. Having an idea in your head and words written down doesn't make for an excellent book. It takes someone to take the raw materials and make them into something worth having. Thanks a million.

Finally, to my loving and supportive wife, Caroline, and my wonderful son, Kris: my deepest gratitude. Your encouragement, ability to keeping me young, and at times totally bewildered are very much appreciated. It has been a great journey made more enjoyable by you two. My heartfelt thanks and eternal love to you both.

Books in The Sinkhole Chronicles series

The Prodigal Vampire
Gary's Inferno

Sinkhole Chronicles Merchandise

Editor and Proofreader

Caro Simpson
Email: csimpsoneditor@gmail.com

Printed in Great Britain
by Amazon

57215920R00261